A RIVER *of* ASH AND BONE

Copyright © 2022 Wren Cartwright
All rights reserved

The characters and events portrayed in this book are fictitious. Any similarity to real persons, living or dead, is coincidental and not intended by the author.

This book contains sexually explicit material and is only intended for adult readers.

No part of this book may be reproduced, or stored in a retrieval system, or transmitted in any form or by any means, electronic, mechanical, photocopying, recording, or otherwise, without express written permission of the publisher.

Cover design by Bianca Bordianu

Editing by Nice Girl Naughty Edits

ISBN: 979-8-9872533-9-7

CONTENT NOTES

Please be aware that the content in this book may not be suitable for all readers.

This book contains graphic violence and sexually explicit content, and shares some characteristics with dark/bully romance. It's a post-apocalyptic new adult novel, so expect discussions of a global pandemic/virus, as well as blood, death, gore, zombies, and profanity.

The warnings are as follows:
- Sexual harassment and attempted sexual assault (referenced multiple times throughout the book)
- Abduction
- Mention of past suicide/depression
- Mention of domestic violence
- Mention of difficult childbirth
- Mention of parental neglect/abuse

This is a why choose romance (MFMMM), meaning there are multiple men to one woman.
Due to the list above, reader discretion is advised.

For everyone seeing this who loves reading about zombies as much as I do... enjoy! Here's hoping it stays fiction.

CAMP

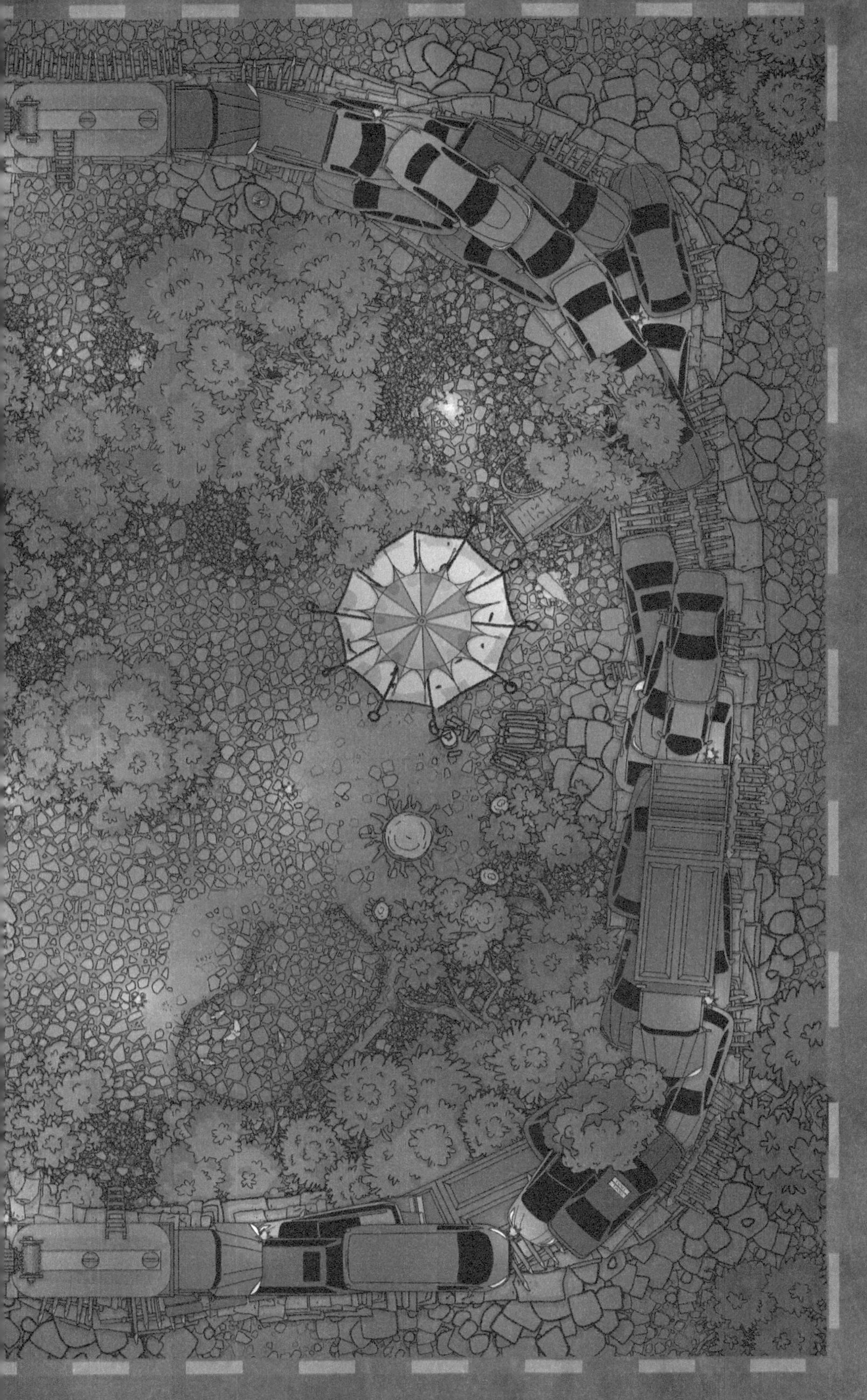

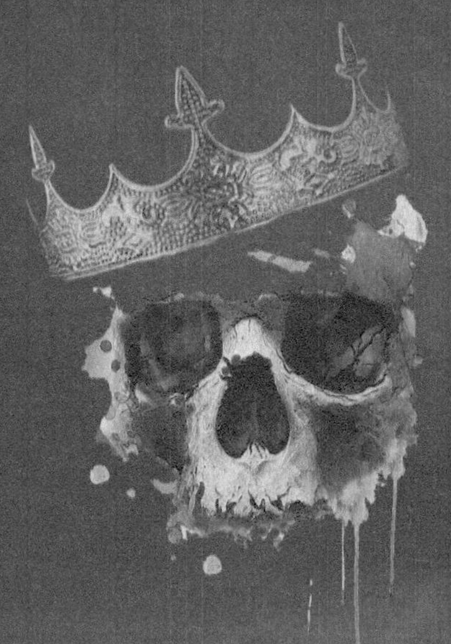

CHAPTER 1

Sometimes I felt as if the blood would stain my hands forever.

I hopped over the halved carcass of the truck and listened for any noises while I wiped my hands off on my pants. I grimaced at the slimy feel, trying not to think about how I was nowhere near a water source. If I cried every time my pants were crusted with blood, I would never get anything done.

As I put some distance between myself and the corpse, I took care to be quiet, avoiding the piles of broken glass that littered the street. The man that I had killed was lying behind me, slack-jawed and pale. Technically, pale might not be the right word. He wasn't pale like me. Instead, he was pale like death, like bleached bones and sickness. Although, he wasn't a man anymore, not really. Once the virus took hold, the infected became something different, something deadly.

My father once told me that people called them zombies even before the outbreak. That they'd been pieces of fiction in a world with vastly different issues that didn't include flesh-eating monsters. I was too young to have first-hand knowledge of the old world; the media, and the electricity that people consumed daily. I was born into the apocalypse one year after the virus mutated. Lucky me. I maintained that I must have been an accident, but my dad insisted that I was planned. That not even zombies were going to stop my parents from their lifelong dream of having a child, even if sometimes when he was feeling particularly sentimental, he would confess the guilt they'd felt over bringing me into a world like this on purpose.

Sometimes I wasn't sure if I appreciated them or resented them, birthing me into a hellscape just to abandon me.

Twenty-four years had passed since the outbreak, and times had changed greatly. My memories of what used to be faded more with every day that passed. Back when my dad and I had a greater chance of finding running water and houses still stocked with food and supplies. When cars still ran and the homes we found were somewhat clean and not falling apart. Now all I had were the stories recounted in dark, crumbling houses, around hasty campfires, and the odd basement bunker. Torn and dusty books, left behind in homes and stores for people who would never have the luxury of spending the day reading, let alone experiencing the things in those stories.

I froze at the sound of a quiet, tortured groan nearby, waiting a few long minutes after it faded to relax my tensed muscles.

It all started with the virus. Some archeologists had gone exploring after a large swath of glaciers melted due to global warming and encountered a prehistoric virus, releasing it into a world that was not ready to receive it. That would never have been ready to receive it. At least that was what the news had told everyone. I'd run into my fair share of conspiracy theorists. They called it the Paleo Virus because it had been dated back to that era. It spread from that location like wildfire, airborne and deadly. It had a 94% mortality rate, and millions died. It was only after the virus evolved in the following year, the new variant allowing itself to be spread only through blood and fluids, that the infected became something twisted and hungry. Something not quite alive but not completely dead either. The only plus side was that the rates of infection decreased. The theorists always had something to say about that as well.

A cure was never found. Scientists estimated that only two percent of the population were immune, and the only other way to find out besides being bitten was to locate a military-controlled testing center, which almost no one did. After people flocked to the centers to try to get help any way they could, desperate to be immune so that they could be granted safety in exchange for testing, horror stories spread like wildfire of the treatments the scientists issued, the procedures they performed, and the mortality rate from their participants. Those testing centers were a death sentence, preaching about sacrifices for the greater good but turning off their empathy and morals to achieve results however they could. Apparently, they'd grown more ethical in recent years, but after hearing story upon story of the horrific treatment people had suffered, they'd burned that bridge. I'd only gone to one of their buildings once, and it was an experience I wasn't keen to repeat.

I kept an ear out for any shuffling noises as I took a can out of my pack and started to pull the tab cautiously. I was fortunate to have found several cans of corn that had rolled under one of the shelves of the last drugstore I visited; I just had to keep them from clanging together in my bag. Pretty much all of the food on the shelves was decayed and rotten, though we sometimes got lucky and found a can or two of old fruits or beans, or a package of beef jerky that had gotten shoved under an aisle. Houses usually yielded better results. I wrapped my hands in the clean scarf I kept in my bag so that I couldn't contaminate the food before I ate it. It was rare that I needed to eat directly after killing a zombie, but I was reaching my breaking point after days of starving and growing dangerously light-headed.

I winced as I tipped the can above my mouth, trying not to gag at the spoiled, oddly sweet taste and desperately trying to avoid comparing it to a bird being fed via regurgitation. It was at times like this that I longed for my parents. To lessen the burden, to keep watch so I could eat a meal in peace, maybe with an actual utensil. As it was, I was starving and didn't have time to find a safe spot to rest, or a spoon to eat with.

Now that the scarf had been dirtied, I used it to wipe the large knife I'd perched on a nearby block of broken stone. I could always find another scarf, but it would ruin the blade if I kept it constantly dirty.

Content that I'd finished all my imminent tasks, I stepped outside of the ruins I was hiding in. Most of the cars surrounding me were tipped over and crumpled, most likely in the owner's haste to escape, and most storefronts had shattered windows and broken doors from the frantic looting.

Now we knew better–to preserve the integrity of the stores and leave them intact for makeshift emergency shelters. Unfortunately, that lesson came a little too late, and most days they had to be cleared of zombies before the back storeroom or walk-in freezer could be used as a sleeping area. A dangerous job for one person, which often led to me sleeping on roofs and in trees, desperate for shut-eye but too tired to face the options below me. The problem was I needed the stores for food, but I was too fatigued without the food to even begin clearing them. Then once I did, I found little to nothing. It was a vicious cycle, and it was beginning to wear on me.

Not for the first time, I felt lost. Purposeless. I hardly ever saw others–that were still alive at least–and spent most of my time trying not to be seen myself. I hadn't left this area in years, the street signs on the ruined roads leading into the city as familiar to me as my own name. The military occupied the area along the coast, and the gangs had commandeered most of the peninsula. I steered clear of those areas.

My dad had explained it to me once while we were eating expired pineapple on the roof of the grocery store. *Women are a commodity to some,* he told me. He smoothed his hand back over his thinning blonde hair and sighed. *You'll need to be diligent out there when I'm gone. You do what you need to, understand?*

I had protested it fiercely, so certain that he'd never leave me, that we could make it through anything. I had been too young to understand what he'd been trying to say, to really weigh his words before responding. Now, I was barely surviving without him, drowning in my grief and loneliness. There's only so much silence a person can take. I was starving, dirty, tired, and my apathy was growing by the day. I tried to avoid inaction, as it gave me too much time to wonder what I was still doing here.

A nearby clatter broke me out of my trance, and I crouched behind the nearest car frame to hide, attempting to stay out of the bright sunlight overhead. I hoped the noise didn't attract more zombies. I could only handle so many at a time and probably wouldn't survive a horde.

The wind rustled softly as I listened for any further noise. Breathing as quietly as possible, I lifted my face to the breeze to try to cool my sweat. I was almost ready to declare it safe when I heard the faint sound of voices.

Survivors?

I frowned. The only survivors left were pockets of people living as best they could. We'd run into several before, sharing our food for a night while the older generations told stories of the past. One time I'd finally found a boy my age and I sure as hell took advantage of it. I could still feel him for days afterwards, and I thanked everything I owned that my dad had been preoccupied with his parents while we snuck off into the forest to fool around. It wasn't remotely enjoyable, besides the minuscule amount of foreplay at the beginning, but at least I could mark it off my checklist.

After minutes passed without hearing any further noise, I ducked out from behind my hiding spot and turned the corner, moving at a quick jog. The voices I heard earlier had disappeared, leaving me in silence with only the wind whistling through the shells of cars. I was already envisioning myself bunking down for the night and the sweet oblivion that sleep would bring when my foot smacked into something, sounding a dull clang and causing me to stumble. I cursed myself for missing the object sitting in my path. I was growing careless. I'd have to leave the city soon to retreat to the forest, maybe find a nice, isolated hunting shack.

My heart stopped as I looked down to see what I'd walked into. A bag. Not just any bag. I could see the dull metal of cans peeking out from the top.

Food.

I bit my lower lip, darting my eyes around to make sure I was alone, then bent over to gently pull it open. My eyes grew damp as I realized what I was looking at. Cans of food, rations of cured meat, a bottle of water. *This could feed me for weeks.*

I needed to leave this area for the forest. It was safer. Fewer zombies, fewer people, but unfortunately, less to eat. I'd have to be here for months just to collect this much unspoiled food to bring with me. Who knows what could happen in that amount of time? This could solve all my problems.

So why couldn't I stop feeling so guilty?

Food was paramount in our society, practically currency. Surely someone wouldn't have left it here if they were coming back for it? Not even someone with a large store of food would be so reckless and wasteful. Scavengers were commonplace. Just because the city *looked* dead, didn't mean we weren't hiding underground like rats, just waiting to snatch up any hint of food we could find. There was only so much scavenging you could do alone before you realized everything had already been picked clean. It wasn't uncommon to eat moldy or rotted food just to be able to continue putting one foot in front of the other.

I hesitated–listening for anyone, dead or alive, then huffed a short breath, shoving down the heaviness in my heart. Decision made. It was every person for themselves, and I couldn't afford to have morals about keeping myself fed. *Surely* there was more where this came from. If someone carried this amount of food around *and* left it unsupervised, they must have an adequate supply somewhere safe.

Snatching the tan threadbare band of the satchel, I hefted it over my shoulder slowly and winced as the cans clanged quietly together. Clearly, the bag had been stuffed with some kind of fabric to keep them silent, but whatever it was only helped so much. My mouth watered at the possibility of getting fresh meat, cured and dried or not. I made it a few blocks away, darting around piles of broken glass and debris and keeping to the shadows when I heard the voices again.

Sometimes I wasn't sure if voices were any better than the groans of the undead.

Another voice rang out, closer to me this time, and I gripped my knife tightly. I was standing around the corner of an alley, halfway concealed behind the crushed remains of a bus, desperately hoping they wouldn't turn it. I'd run into my fair share of desperate survivors. My father and I had stumbled onto a camp with a suspiciously large spit roast one time, and one whiff of the harsh scent of burning hair had us quickly turning tail.

Someone was whistling quietly, most likely walking closer to my location. I tensed, breathing as silently as possible. As the footsteps grew louder, I made a snap decision to back farther into the alley at my back. Sure, it left me at a dead end, but perhaps the darkness would hide me better. What sane person would explore a dark alley? I clutched the worn satchel close to my chest.

Screams, groans, the frantic feeling of being trapped and—

I shook myself out of it, trying not to think too hard about the fact that I generally tended to avoid alleyways.

I cringed as my foot hit a pebble, sending it flying several feet away. My heart was beating wildly in my chest as I waited to see if anyone had heard the slight noise. Just when I thought I was safe, a man turned the corner, wearing a broad grin when he spotted me pressed up against the wall.

"What have we here?" he asked. He watched me with shrewd brown eyes, moving so that his body filled the entrance to the alley, both him and the bus blocking any exit I could have found. His tan skin was dirtied by dust and mud, and his coat was covered in gore. He looked older, his face lined with the weight of years of survival. Maybe in his sixties? I didn't have a good frame of reference for ages, not much to compare them to.

"Just passing through," I said fiercely. I stood taller, trying to project my confidence. The handle of the knife was slippery against my sweaty palm.

"Seems you took my food, darlin'. I only left it but for a moment to go check something out."

Fuck. Fuck!

Of course it was his food. Of-fucking-course. I clutched the bag tighter. "I'm sorry," I said softly, hoping to appeal to any good nature he might have. "I've just been so hungry lately. I'm starving, and it was just sitting out in the open."

It would've been dangerous for me to advertise the fact that I was alone, so I didn't. Though I was worried it was fairly obvious that I wouldn't be crouching in an alley after having stolen someone's food if I was with someone.

"I can see that," he said slowly, raising his hands up like he was harmless. He seemed nice, at first glance, but something about the way he was moving raised my hackles.

I licked my lips nervously. "You left it."

"I did." He nodded.

My eyes darted past him to the end of the alley, hoping he didn't have any friends.

"I'll give it back to you," I said finally. It wasn't worth the trouble, and I felt bad about taking it even *before* I realized the owner had stuck around. It was devastating, the thought of losing so much unspoiled food, but I had a bad feeling about the whole thing.

"That's mighty kind of you, dear, but if you just come with me, I can get you more where that came from," he said, nodding at the bag still clutched to my chest.

Hope bloomed sharply in my chest, more painful than I'd imagined it would be.

"I don't think I'll be doing that," I stated firmly, certain that it was too good to be true. Hunger was slowly driving me mad, making it hard to stick to my convictions. A voice deep in the back of my mind was screaming for me to take it and run, to accept his offer and go with him no matter what the cost. I ignored it.

"You should come with me," he said, as he licked his thin lips. My hope immediately burst into ashes, burning my insides as they danced on the grave of my naivety.

I scowled, unintentionally backing up deeper into the alley just to put some distance between us. "No."

"Oh, sweet girl, no has no meaning here," he said emphatically, raising his arms up and walking in a small circle like he was rousing a crowd. Why the actual fuck was this man talking so loudly? Something seemed... off. His eyes were bulging, and he seemed... feral. The quiet tone he'd adopted upon first spotting me had all but disappeared.

He stalked closer, betraying a slight limp in his right leg. "I'll make it worth your while." He winked. "You don't even have to come back with me, just a few favors for all that food. You're so hungry, ain't ya, darlin'?"

He spoke to me like he was coaxing a wild animal, and I suppose, in some sense, he was. Fear crept through my body, chilling my bones. This was what my dad had warned me about, and yet I'd still foolishly feared the zombies over the men that walked this hellscape, taking what they wanted when they wanted. I felt my dad's absence stronger than ever at that moment. He would've known what to do.

I shifted my weight from foot to foot, getting ready to bolt. The guilt over taking this man's food had all but dried up in the face of his harassment.

He cackled loudly, stumbling slightly as he took a few unsteady steps forward. Once he was closer, I noticed how the whites of his eyes were struck through with red and his mouth was beginning to foam.

Infected.

He'd been infected. Was he with the others I'd heard? How hadn't anyone noticed? My eyes scanned his body, searching for the bite amongst all the gore, for any damage at all. *There.* Hidden just below the ragged sleeve ending at his forearm lay a single bite. How long ago had he been bitten? Just how long did I have before he turned? A typical bite, singular, would take up to five minutes to take effect. Multiple bites caused a much quicker transformation.

By my estimation, it had already been around two minutes, and the infected area was turning into a purple-green mess right before my eyes.

He stumbled toward me, leering at my black jeans and tank top. "Just what I needed," he wheezed. My stomach turned, acid working its way up my throat. I adjusted the bag and brandished the knife. A freshly turned couldn't sense the danger, and they would be too far gone to care. All I could do was keep it in front of me in case he made a sudden move.

"Get away from me," I commanded, hearing the waver in my voice. This was so much worse than a zombie. A living, breathing opponent. Worse, a living, breathing opponent whose designs went beyond theft and was lacking their empathy and morality.

"I don't think I will," he sneered, words slurring wildly. His eyes dropped to my chest, and he staggered forward several more steps, licking his lips again. I jumped back as he coughed, spraying blood all over the pavement between us.

I took a deep breath and then darted to the right, stopped only by his sudden firm grip on my shirt. The newly undead had an abnormal amount of strength. In fact, they were deadliest when they were freshly infected.

I shuddered, still somehow put off by the thought of slaughtering a still-living person. I had some lines I didn't like to cross, and fresh blood on my clothes was one of them. He growled at me, snapping his teeth in my direction and becoming more animalistic by the second. I tried to pull out of his grip, stunned by his other hand lunging at my chest.

Fuck it.

I snarled and jerked back, twisting and slicing my knife across his throat and ducking to avoid the spray.

Most zombies needed to have their heads crushed or damaged to be taken out of commission, but those who were still in the process of turning could still be killed by normal methods. I gagged, disgusted by the hot, infected blood covering my clothes and staining my skin. Thank fuck, I had no open wounds. He made an odd gurgling noise, eyes widening and hands flexing as he took several jerky steps in my direction.

Good. Fucking predator. Didn't make it any easier though.

I lunged around him, avoiding his outstretched hands, and drove the knife into his back. He made a high, keening noise and keeled over. The sound of his body hitting the ground felt like a siren leading right to my location. I swallowed back the bile that rose in my throat, looking away as I stabbed him through the eyeball to hit his brain. It was the only foolproof way to ensure he stayed dead, and it was gruesome. For all I knew, he had gone full zombie in the past five seconds and would rise the second I walked away, so I wasn't taking any chances. I wiped my blade off on his loose pants, glancing toward the opening of the alley and hoping that no one had heard and would come running. My hopes were dashed when I heard the crunch of glass under footsteps. I broke out into a sprint to get out of the alley before I was trapped once more, leaving the man's body where he had fallen. I had just turned the corner when a hand snatched out and grabbed my arm. I withheld a scream, wondering if the zombies had finally caught me, until the man holding me hissed, "Where is he?"

I flinched, knowing that he was obviously referring to the man that I had just sliced open. I did what I had to do, and I was not ashamed. Sickened, saddened, angry, yes. But never ashamed.

"Oh shit," a voice called from behind me as someone rushed over to the body still hidden in the depths of the alley.

"What the fuck did you do?" the man holding me ground out.

I sighed. "He was sick."

"We could have put him down humanely," another voice rang out.

Just how many people were there? I struggled in the man's grip, desperate to protect myself by just seeing how many opponents I was facing, but he held tight.

"How much more humane does it get?" I questioned angrily. "His death was swift."

"You fucked up," a deep voice whispered in my ear.

"I was trapped. He was sick," I murmured, hoping we weren't attracting any unwanted attention. My throat was aching, as I'd talked more already today than I had for weeks.

"He just randomly decided to corner you when you realized he'd been bitten?" I was spun in the man's grip to find myself staring at three men. At first glance, they all looked eerily similar, with unkempt dark hair and blue eyes. The man holding me had a deeper blue than the others, more shadows lurking in their depths. He clenched his jaw tightly as he stared at me, eyebrows furrowed.

I hadn't looked in a mirror for about a year, but I didn't see what was so horrific about my appearance. I had average brown hair and hazel eyes, a combination that I'd gotten from my mother. Yeah, I was pretty dirty, and... okay, so maybe I was so skinny that my ribs showed through my top, and perhaps I maybe hadn't showered in a few weeks... Well, *shit*. Horrible first impression.

"She has his bag," the man said flatly.

"So she's a thief," the one on the left murmured. "Murdering a good man just to keep a few cans of food? Spreading lies to justify it?" His tone was filled with disgust and, oddly... disappointment.

"I–He was infected!" I protested. "He'd left his bag a few blocks away and I found it."

"You deny stealing?" the one holding me pressed, jerking me around. "Deny the fact that he wouldn't have been looking for you if you'd have just left the bag where you found it? That he could've gotten infected *looking for you?*"

I hadn't thought of it that way. *I hope that isn't true.*

I struggled in his grip. "You're foolish if you think a few cans of food aren't rare here. Yes, I 'stole' the food, okay? But I didn't kill him to keep it. I even offered to give it back. He was... he was infected." Why wasn't I telling them what he wanted? Perhaps because I sensed they wouldn't believe me. It would just further offend them, that the man they called "good" would have acted the way he did. They'd accuse me of lying, and I might not get out of this alive. I might not either way if they were of the same ilk, but I didn't get those vibes from this group.

The man jerked me around, pulling me to the side.

Fuck this, I thought vehemently. I didn't deserve this. "Get off me," I hissed, twisting in his grip so I was facing the others once more.

"Oh, she'll be fun," the last man remarked. He had mischief written all over him, and the way he cracked his knuckles suggested he was making a point. Well, point made. He was large, just as tall as the man holding me, but more muscled. Tattoos decorated what I could see of his knuckles and arms. I fought to keep my jaw from dropping. I had never seen someone so young decorated with so many tattoos. Not many people had the fortitude to get that much ink done by hand. I had only seen grisly old men with them, leftovers from the days when electricity was a thing, and tattoo shops were common.

He stared at me thoughtfully, assessing me as I assessed him. "I never liked John," he declared before tugging my free arm.

"I don't give a fuck," the first scoffed. "He's dead now because she murdered him."

"Is it really murder if he was already dying?" I murmured.

The last threw his head back and laughed, until the one holding me smacked his broad shoulder with the back of his hand and hissed, "Shut up or you'll draw them in."

His eyes gleamed, and he began bouncing from foot to foot. Looked like somebody had a lust for violence. "Bring them, brother."

Holy shit, he was nuts. They all were.

"Shut up, Caelan," the first bit out.

While they were talking, I sneakily tried to pull my arm out of the man's hold. His eyes snapped to mine, and he tightened his grip.

"What are we going to do with her?" the other man asked. His eyes were lighter than the other's, but I couldn't quite see the color with the way he was standing in the shade. He seemed much quieter and much less prone to violence.

"She's coming back with us."

"Come on, Merikh. Then what?"

Merikh shook me again. "Make her pay." His smile was wicked, eyes hard as they watched me. How the hell did he propose they do that?

"And if she's not alone?"

I brightened at that. Maybe they'd leave me alone if they thought someone would come after me?

He watched me for a moment. "She's alone. Barely any supplies, dirty and starving. She's like a little rat, scrounging for food and eating mice."

I scowled, feeling my face flush with anger and shame. "I'm not going back with you," I declared. I didn't even know where 'back' *was*. I was happy to be in the middle of this rotting city, free and alone. Foodless and shelterless or not, they had no fucking right to take me away because I did the world a favor and killed a fucking predator.

The quiet man, the only one whose name I did not know, turned to me and cocked his head. "I'm Nix, and I think this is a terrible idea."

It was delivered in such a deadpan manner that I almost laughed. Almost. I managed to hold it in, although it threatened to burst out.

Caelan fixed his deep blue eyes on me, huge arms flexing as he folded them. He shook his dark hair out of his face and grinned wide. Just as he opened his mouth, Nix clapped a hand over it. "Enough of that," he muttered.

I'd heard about men like this, that took women as prisoners for sexual servitude. In the past, when my belly was still full and I wasn't falling asleep standing up, I would've felt that it was better to be starving and vulnerable than at the mercy of a man, traded and used like a broodmare, but the reality of my situation was that I was tired. Exhausted deep down to my bones and aching for a break, no matter how it came to me. Maybe I finally understood what my dad had been trying to tell me. The least I could do was put up a fight, even if it was clear that I was most likely trapped.

I jerked in Merikh's arms, wishing I had a free hand to pull my extra knife from where I'd stashed it in my boot. There was no way I could hide the knife my dad had given me. It would surely be confiscated. I threw my ankle back, trying to make contact with his legs to buckle them, but he held fast.

"I'll find a way out," I said.

Caelan snorted, reaching over to ruffle my dark hair and smiling. "What a cliché, baby. We're doing you a favor. You just can't see it yet."

When Merikh spoke, his voice was ice cold. "If you run, I'll fire three shots. Maybe you'll get lucky and I won't hit your foot, or the noise won't attract any zombies." He hunches down, lowering his face right to mine, his whisper low and threatening. "But lady luck left this hellhole a long time ago, princess, so I wouldn't risk it."

The quiet one, Nix, looked over at me. His mouth opened, but a sharp look from Merikh had him shutting it.

God fucking damnit, he had the upper hand.

Merikh grabbed my arm once more. "You're ours now. Time to pay your penance."

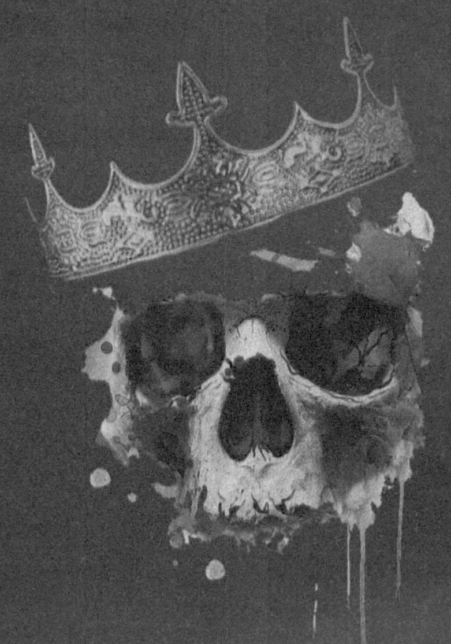

CHAPTER 2

We walked for hours, leaving behind the area I knew like the back of my hand, and venturing into unknown territory.

After years of constant travel, my dad eventually insisted we make this city our home base, and I could understand why. The salty brine of the ocean filled the air in certain areas, along with the fog rolling off the coast. We didn't dare stray too far from the cities except for when we took refuge in the forests, but sometimes the fresh sea air was healing. The cars were thinner in this part of the city since not many people were vacationing at the beach in the middle of winter when the virus mutated.

The roads were empty, long stretches of cracked and crumbling pavement extending as far as the eye could see. The sky had turned gloomy, perfect for my dour mood.

"How much longer?" I complained, clenching my toes tightly in my scuffed boots as if that would take the pain away. Looking around at all the empty land, I was tempted to bolt, but I knew I wouldn't make it far before one of them caught me, and that was if the asshole didn't fire his gun as he'd threatened.

Caelan swung around with a big smile, hefting his bat over his shoulder. "Patience, stranger. All in good time."

I rubbed the back of my neck, wiping off the thin sheen of sweat coating my face, and groaned. "It's River."

Nix gave me a shy smile from where he was walking next to me, whereas Merikh didn't deign to turn around. I could see Nix's eyes clearly now that he wasn't cloaked in shadow. I'd thought they were blue like Caelan or Merikh's, but I was surprised to find that they were a spring green with a ring of hazel around the center. I didn't think I'd ever met anyone with eyes so green.

"River," Caelan purred, like he was rolling my name over his tongue and finding it satisfactory. I blushed, huffing an impatient sigh. The bag of food at Merikh's side clanged every so often, reminding me it was there. Was it fun having a reminder of the fact that I tried to steal someone's food? Much less that the person I tried to steal it from was now dead? No. It was not. As much as I tried to convince myself that it wasn't stealing, after all it had been sitting right in the open, I had heard the voices nearby and had strongly expected that it belonged to one of them. I was fighting back shame, desperately trying to remember that the guy was an asshole, despite the fact that these three thought he walked on water.

Caelan made a noise in the back of his throat, but when I turned to look at him, he was staring off into the distance, eyes narrowed. After a few minutes of squinting, I finally noticed a faint plume of smoke way off in the distance and to the east.

"Friends of yours?" I asked.

"None of your concern," he replied, eyes still warily watching the smoke.

I held my hands out, happy to leave whatever the hell that issue was to them.

After what felt like miles of barren land, I was surprised to see the large car barrier up ahead. More and more cars materialized in the distance, positioned so that they were bumper to bumper, about a hundred feet from the sprawling structure behind them. Only in some areas did a few crumpled, flat cars sit atop an undamaged one, doubling and sometimes tripling the height. I could only see the section facing me, but I assumed it went the entire way around, except for a gap about two car lengths wide at what seemed to be the entrance directly ahead of us.

They marched me toward what looked to be their camp, a camp that I had never seen before, had never even known was right on my doorstep. It was extensive. From what I could see between the gaps in the cars, the camp itself was fenced in by a combination of barbed wire, a combination of chain-link and wooden fencing, and haphazard sheets of metal. Now that we were a short distance away, I could hear the hum of activity from inside. I was blocked from seeing the inside by the layers of security, but I caught glimpses of color and the *smell*–fresh, roasting meat. No one appeared to be cowering or biting their tongues. Why didn't they fear attracting any zombies? Were they really that well-protected? Surely there had to be some kind of catch, like they ate people, or they sacrificed kids or something equally evil. Because... I pinched the skin on the back of my hand, trying to stop my thoughts from running wild, but it was no use. *If dad had known camps like this existed... why had we been barely surviving on our own?* He must have. There was no way he hadn't. He'd been extremely thorough in mapping out the safest areas to travel, and immediately after we decided to settle in Delaware, he'd begun solo scouting missions so that he knew what the surrounding area was like.

Then again, he was pretty distrustful. We'd only gone to one of the nearby military bases once and that was because it was a necessary evil, so I couldn't see him jumping to confine himself with a bunch of strangers. He was always careful to steer around larger cities if he hadn't vetted them first. Once he set up base in a city, we stayed for months. Even so, we could have been so happy in a place like this.

I tried to imagine what it would be like to live unafraid, without the sense that something would creep up behind you if you didn't pay attention or you made too much noise. To sleep soundly and eat well. My heart clenched as I heard the happy scream of a child, followed by laughter. I crossed my arms around my waist, hugging myself tightly.

Merikh tugged my arm, eliciting a grunt from me. I yanked away from his grip just so he knew I hadn't resigned to my fate.

"Feisty," Caelan observed with a smirk. I bared my teeth in his direction.

A lone zombie stumbled across the road ten feet away from us. Straggly blonde hair hung from its head, and it wore a threadbare tank top. Its jaw was decomposing, and its wrist appeared to be broken. Zombies were a distinctive sickly shade, their skin containing a gray pallor that varied in its intensity. Their eyes, if they still had them, were generally wild and rolling, like those of a sick animal. We could have easily bypassed it, entered the camp and avoided it. Yet Caelan left my side with a cackle, striding toward it and bashing its head in with his bat. It was down with one hit. I winced at the brutality, while Merikh laughed.

Merikh jerked at my arm again, commanding my attention once more. I ground my teeth, forcing myself not to react, but sick of the way he kept pulling me around like a ragdoll.

I glanced back toward where we came, toward freedom. *Perhaps I won't even go back*, I mused. I supposed with my dad's death, I could travel anywhere. I had only stayed in this area due to familiarity and sentimentality. I would have to be careful, though, not to stumble upon more groups like these. I could see the darkness in their eyes that peeked out as they watched our surroundings; not with a healthy dose of fear or caution, but with a thirst for violence instead.

We approached the camp at a leisurely pace, with no care as to anyone that might come stumbling upon us. The wide swath of land that encompassed the space between the car barrier and the fencing was oddly clear of zombies and bodies.

The guys walked up to the wide gate, Caelan in the lead. He brushed his dark hair back with a heavily tattooed hand and leveled a wide grin at the petite girl who stood in the guard shack that looked to be incorporated into the fence near the entrance. She near melted under his gaze, causing me to scoff. Sure, maybe he was sin personified. Tall like his brothers with a large, muscled frame to match, but didn't she see hear him laugh when he bashed that zombie's head in? Fucking unnatural.

As she left the shack to manually unfasten the heavy padlock on the chain-link gates, her gaze flicked to me and turned sour. I took a moment to really examine her. She was around my age, pretty, and if they had her watching the gates instead of locked away in some room, that meant they probably weren't the type of camp to enslave women for sexual purposes. That immediately took a huge weight off my chest. She looked well-fed. Healthy. Her hips were filled out, her hair was a long, clean blonde color, and her clothes were nice enough, formed to her shape. Did they really eat that well here? I looked down at my lanky body, never having experienced my curves filling out. Hell, even the jeans had to be secured with a rope I'd found, practically hanging off my frame.

"We bring back strays now?" she asked snottily, a derisive curl to her lip.

I scoffed. "You're telling me this isn't a common occurrence here? Kidnapping people?"

"Consider yourself special," Merikh remarked as he pulled me through the gates. I was vibrating with anger over his constant possessive grip on my arm. I wanted to walk alone, for fuck's sake.

I spun out of his grip, lunging down to pull my knife from my boot and holding it in front of me.

He smirked. "Are you telling me that I need to pat you down daily? Clever girl, hiding a knife in your boot, but it would've done more damage to my unsuspecting body at night than against the three of us right now." His voice ended in a lethal whisper, and I felt a dull pang in my chest. I wanted to make a stand so bad that I wasted my opportunity to use the knife at a more convenient time. My only weapon left since they'd taken my other one and tossed it, and I'd lost it before I even entered the camp. I fought the urge to scream with frustration.

I held the knife steadily in front of me, fighting a grimace. Nix, the only one I had not directly viewed as a threat, jolted me from behind, causing me to lose my balance. As I stumbled, Caelan used his bat to smack the weapon from my hands, the impact reverberating through my skin and stinging my fingers and palm. I watched it fall to the dirt numbly, snatched up the second it fell by Merikh. I tried to ignore the sense of betrayal from Nix. He wasn't my friend; he wasn't anything to me. A few sympathetic looks and just barely disagreeing with his unstable brothers and I had thought him an ally?

"Bastards," I grumbled.

"Saviors," Merikh corrected, a calculating glint in his eye.

I snapped my gaze to his, not liking what I found. For all their depth, his eyes were emotionless. Glacial. I scanned him again, longer this time. Maybe I was looking for a glint of humanity, some sign of a conscience lurking around.

His hair fell just above his ears, dark waves that he kept pushed back so that they didn't fall in his eyes. He stood at around six feet, probably taller because I was shit at guessing heights. My dad and I had measured me a few years ago and found that I was 5'6, which was how I measured everything around me using myself as the basis. His build was lean but corded, and I could see his strength in the definition along his arms and shoulders, thick and powerful. Not like Caelan, who stood at almost the same height but whose build was broad and muscled. Caelan's hair was also longer, curling around his ears and hugging the back of his neck. If Caelan was the brawn, Merikh was the brains. Or perhaps that was Nix.

Nix took my hand, and I allowed my attention to shift to him. He looked eerily similar to Merikh, but his hair was shorter and messier. He was also leaner, and his eyes weren't quite as frigid. Unlike the others, his skin was lacking their healthy tan. *Someone doesn't get out much.*

"You don't own me," I hissed. "I'll escape this place, and when I do, I'll burn it to the ground and come back just to play in the ashes." No the hell I wouldn't, but it felt cathartic to make the threat anyway.

A loud laugh rang out from behind me. I turned to find an older man with dark hair and watery blue eyes watching me. "Bold words, girl. If my sons brought you here, you're here for a reason. We don't take kindly to strangers."

Sons. So it was confirmed, they were all related. There went my shot at any loyalty I could try to scrounge up in Nix.

The older man looked to Merikh for an explanation.

"She killed John, claims he was infected. She had his supplies on her."

"So," he said, as he examined me imperiously. "A thief *and* a murderer, or maybe just an opportunist. You took her as penance?"

Caelan smiled wickedly, though Merikh remained impassive. Nix just pressed his lips together tightly, head tilting forward to gaze at his feet.

"What did I miss?" a different man called out as he approached, and the others filled him in. Long loping steps, he walked as if he had all the time in the world to get where he was going. *Leisurely,* I thought. His blonde hair fell just above his shoulders and his brown eyes watched me warily.

He slung his arm around Caelan's shoulders as he shot me a wide grin. "That's quite a list of charges, huh?"

Oh no, there's more of them?

"He was infected," I protested. "And he… he left the bag out in the open. Alone. Can you blame me?"

"Should've brought him back here. We could've given him a proper burial."

"If you regularly bring infected bodies inside the camp, I'm surprised you have a camp at all. Besides, who wants to carry an infected corpse for several hours?"

"Several hours?" their father asked sharply.

Merikh's grip tightened on my arm before loosening. "John remembered there was a large garden supply store in the city, so we decided to check it out."

Their father narrowed his eyes, demanding a response without opening his mouth.

"Nothing," Caelan spoke up, the corners of his mouth tightening. "They must've gone out of business before the outbreak because it was boarded up and completely empty."

I felt a sudden surge of gratitude toward my own father. What would it be like to have grown up with someone like this man? Cold and controlling?

We were dismissed with a single nod and a casual wave of his hand. He fell in behind us as Merikh walked me past the inner gates, escorting me into my prison.

I grimaced, turning away from Merikh's stern expression to hunt for the source of the delicious food scents filling the air. I inhaled deeply, my mouth watering and stomach growling as they grew stronger. Just ahead, I could see smoke curling into the sky, the source hidden behind what seemed to be their designated food area. My jaw dropped at the large eating area they had established. It was a huge canvas tent, and underneath it were benches, chairs, haphazard tables, and a line where food was being distributed.

I could hardly fathom seeing so many people in one place. Although I knew this was a camp, it hadn't really struck me just how occupied it would be. An entire section dedicated to cooking and eating, buildings, tents, and people *everywhere*. I wasn't even sure I'd seen so many people in my *whole life*.

As they marched me deeper into the camp, a clearing came into view. It looked to be the epicenter of the base, and already people were gathering in small groups. They looked well-fed and happy. Laughter and jokes rang out over the central fire pit that everyone seemed to flock toward. I blinked rapidly as several pregnant women wandered by.

"This is a sanctuary," their father stated as we walked through the camp, his arms crossed behind his back in a military fashion. He spoke as if he were the law here, and for all I knew, he was. There was a distinct proprietary tone to his words.

"Not for me," I grumbled, despite looking around in awe. Teenagers walked by, and children screamed and ran, tugging at skirts. I was surrounded by people of all ages. Nix broke away from our ragtag group, winding his way through the gathering crowd of people and disappearing. I tried not to feel the tiny sting of disappointment that the only sane one had just up and left. The hush of gossiping whispers filled my ears as everyone stopped to stare at our procession.

It seemed our destination lay in the large outcropping of trees to our left. I wanted to say it was a forest... but well, did the car barrier run through there as well? How far did it extend? Or was the camp truly so large that it encompassed the entire 'not' forest as well? I hadn't been able to see all the trees from the entrance to the camp, but I was suddenly grateful they were there. A little taste of what I'd grown up with instead of all this change at once.

A dirt path led us into the trees, and the farther we walked, the more hidden structures appeared. A row of cabins wound their way along the empty areas and numerous tents were scattered in between them. I squinted, looking farther into the distance. *Is that... Holy shit, it is.* I could see the barest glimmer of water behind the tightly packed trees. What looked to be an average-sized lake sat far behind the tents we were passing, hugging the shoreline where the trees stopped.

I kept expecting us to turn into one of the cabins, but we bypassed those, walking down the beaten path silently, away from where everyone else was living and in the direction of the lake. A cold sweat broke out against my neck. Were they going to drown me or something? Surely if they were going to do some freaky public execution, it would've been back at the firepit, right? I rubbed my fingers together, desperately wanting to fidget but not wanting to betray the extent of my nervousness.

Merikh and his father murmured in low tones as we walked, pulling ahead of Caelan, the stranger, and I.

Finally, after several long minutes and the constant low hum of voices had faded, we entered a small clearing. I couldn't have seen it earlier by the way it was artfully tucked into the surrounding trees, but it was much larger than the ones we had passed on the way here.

A wood and glass monstrosity, at least two stories high.

"That's ours," Caelan whispered smugly, winking at me.

I followed Merikh up the steps to the front porch and into the cabin. The inside was just as large as the outside, though instead of two floors like I had thought, there were just really high ceilings. The main room had a couple of cozy-looking brown couches and a large chair crowding a glass coffee table and hearth. Near the wall of windows to my left was a long oak dining table. A hallway branched off from the back of the front room and the kitchen sat tucked away in the corner behind the dining table. It was clean. *Simple.*

"Sit," Merikh commanded. I considered resisting, but decided to save my strength. Maybe I could talk my way out of this. I doubted it, though. These men didn't seem likely to listen to logic.

"Good," he murmured once I sat. His husky approval warmed my insides, much to my dismay. *That's gonna need to be nipped in the bud, and fast.*

The front door cracked open slowly, and I twisted my head around, surprised to find Nix elbowing his way in, a bowl in his hands.

Caelan laughed. "Perfect, I was starving."

Nix rolled his eyes, marching over to me and setting the bowl down gently, along with a silver spoon.

My stomach growled at the steam coming off of it. I didn't care what it was; hot food was a delicacy.

I ignored the spoon, holding the bowl up to my mouth and drinking deeply, gulping until the entire bowl was drained and taking deep breaths in between. The warm stew settled happily in my stomach, effectively raising my mood. I lifted my head to see the five men staring at me. The blonde one had the beginnings of a smirk curling his lips.

The older man took a seat across from me as I dabbed my mouth with a nearby napkin. "You from around here, girl?"

I scowled. "Yes."

"And we've never seen you before?" Merikh asked, accusatory for some reason. It's a big fucking city. Does he run into every single survivor hiding in the ruins or something?

"I keep to myself." I didn't want to tell them about my dad yet. It felt too raw, too vulnerable. I wanted to keep all my memories and stories inside and hoard them where they were safe.

The older man's eyes narrowed. "So, you took John's food, and then when he found you with it, you killed him."

"Because he was infected," Nix added.

I got the feeling he wasn't actually asking. Must be some weird intimidation tactic.

"Yes." I wasn't going to beg for forgiveness, anyway, so maybe honesty would gain me some points.

Merikh spoke from where he stood near the others. Looming over me, staring down at me like I was an insect. "Then you will replace him."

And there was my limit. "Absolutely not! You can't just keep me here."

"We can do whatever we like." Caelan smirked.

I looked to their father, assuming he was the leader, hoping he would say something sensible or lay down the law, but he just shrugged. "Don't break her." He laughed as he exited the cabin.

What kind of fucked up place was this? They brought people in against their will and no one batted an eye?

We were left in silence, watching one another warily. Or rather, I was watching them warily. They were watching me like I was prey.

"You can't just take people off the streets. Do you have a whole collection here? Just how many people are here against their will?"

"None," Nix answered, green eyes searching mine for something.

"And yet here I am."

"And yet here you are," Merikh agreed.

"When can I leave?"

"When we decide," Caelan chimed in.

That wasn't going to work. I refused to be their prisoner, to be dealt with as they pleased. Who knows what the four brutes had planned? Better to escape as soon as possible.

A woman's voice sounded at the door only seconds before she came bounding in. It was the girl from the gate, wide-eyed and breathless. Her top was pulled down lower than before, purposefully I bet, exposing just the tops of her breasts as her chest heaved.

Merikh's voice cut through the air like a whip, deflating her excitement. "What have I told you about coming in here without knocking? This is our space, you weren't welcomed."

The woman pouted. "But she's here," she said defiantly, arm gesturing in a wide arc toward me.

Merikh straightened his back and walked over to her. Damn, she'd really pissed him off. I bit down on the smug satisfaction that came with her dressing down. Maybe if she hadn't looked at me like I was shit on the bottom of her shoe, I wouldn't feel so pleased. "You were just a quick lay on a boring night. Now get the fuck out of our place."

Oh.

Well, that was a bit harsh.

Her eyes widened, and she cast a withering glance in my direction before turning on her heel and leaving like it was her decision. *Holy shit*, if that's how they talked to people who showed up unannounced, then I was screwed. At least I didn't feel bad for her anymore, not with that unnecessary attitude.

"You're terrible," I said, curling my upper lip.

Caelan shrugged, sitting backwards on the chair next to me and crossing his colorful arms over the top. "She knew what she was getting into."

"Cruelty? An asshole with no manners?"

"Precisely," Merikh stated with a hard stare. I didn't shrink under his gaze. I sat tall, mustering my courage. They thought they were so great. They wouldn't break me.

"Why do you care if I killed someone who was infected?"

"That person was a member of our camp. He was personally chosen to scout with us. You took his things and then murdered him when he came searching for them. If he hadn't gone looking for you, *he might not have even been bitten in the first place.* There's nothing I hate more than a person who feels entitled to something they didn't work for."

My stomach rebelled as I flashed back to his foaming mouth, and the dark blood that spilled from his throat after I slashed it. His hands trying to scrabble at my skin–

Stop.

"You're unhinged."

"Careful, River. We hold your fate in our hands. We could just as easily toss you to the infected," Merikh admonished.

He smirked at my shock, and I quickly hid it behind a sneer. "So what's your plan then, big guy?"

Merikh's face darkened while the blonde man laughed. "I like her. What's her name?"

"River," I snapped.

"Careful, River." His voice lowered to a lethal whisper. "Don't test me."

And hell if I didn't believe him.

I licked my lips nervously, gripping the edge of the table so hard my knuckles turned white.

"You're all drunk on power! Just let me go. I promise I'll leave this place and never come back." My heart raced, desperate to hear the answer I was looking for.

"And let you get off easy? Absolutely not." My heart sank at his words. I shut down, locking away my brimming emotions and numbing my anger. I would escape, I would be free, I assured myself. I just needed to bide my time. It couldn't be so bad, fresh food and a safe place to rest until I could go back into the city. Maybe I'd even try a new state, find a nice place in the mountains somewhere.

"You'll stay here," Caelan declared. "With us."

I looked up in horror, all my hard work at soothing my emotions ruined. "I refuse to sleep with you."

Merikh lifted an assessing eyebrow, ignoring the blonde man's smirk and Caelan's laughter. "Good thing I don't desire stray pussy. You need a fucking bath."

I fought a recoil at his words, choosing instead to glare in his direction. *All of this because I killed a friend of theirs and took one measly bag of supplies? Madness.*

"You'll sleep on the couch," Merikh commanded, dead eyes daring me to argue. I knew better. Arguing against the couch would only get me the floor. Truth be told, the couch was a luxury. Before my dad died, we were able to stay in comfier places, the back of a bus, an abandoned house, an old mattress store. But alone, I was always on guard and had to sleep out of sight of not only the infected, but people like John as well. There was no one to keep watch once the darkness fell. Since he'd been gone I'd slept on freezing rooftops, secured into the branches of trees with zombies nearby, in abandoned homes filled with ghostly memories of the people who had once occupied them.

Just to ensure that they didn't read my silence as submission, I rolled my eyes and gave him the finger.

The blonde laughed.

"Enough, Grey," Merikh said. "She won't be a shiny new toy for long. Sans the shiny part."

I glared at him.

"You will obey," Merikh murmured. I looked away then, unable to match the ice in his stare, feeling oddly like I would lose myself to it.

"So," I said flatly. "What will I be doing during my lovely stay?"

"You'll help around camp, assisting wherever your services are needed. You will fetch our meals from the food tent, clean our shared living space, and run any errands we require. You're getting off easy, in my opinion. You will fill the void that your murder created, ensuring that we don't lose any of the help John provided now that someone else will need to take over his shifts."

I clenched my fists tightly, jagged nails biting into the rough skin of my palms.

My dad would tease me often, *I'm not your maid, River.* Every time I was being a stubborn teenager and refused to pick up after myself, since we would be changing locations anyway. He refused to contribute to the debris littering the landscape and would insist that we properly disposed of our trash. We left the homes where we stayed in good condition, always putting away the supplies we used, thinking that maybe someone else would need them.

I stood abruptly, ignoring the screech of the chair against the wooden floor and glancing toward the door like I could see my path to freedom through the wood.

"Sit," Merikh commanded. I ground my teeth, seething.

"Why do I have to stay here, with you?"

"How else will you pick up after us?" He smirked, then sighed. "You're slippery, determined, resourceful. I'm neither ignorant nor egotistical enough to not acknowledge the fact that if we don't keep a firm eye on you, you'll find a way to disappear within a week."

"Why keep me close to do your bidding and replace one man when there's plenty of people already here?"

Nix stared at me incredulously. "You'll have running water–hot water. Hot food, a place to sleep, and safety from the zombies."

"Privileges that you can lose," Merikh chimed in with a wary eye. I didn't blame him; I felt like I was made up entirely of the resentment I was holding in. Could I sacrifice my freedom for luxuries? I didn't want to admit that what they were asking me to do wasn't even all that bad.

I'd heard horror stories of women forced to pay for safety with their bodies, and the conditions they lived in were deplorable. Only a fool would deny sanctuary in a world such as this. I was dizzy from the anger, the indignation, and sick from the small part of me that screamed out for shelter and comfort and *safety*.

"Seems I don't have a choice," I said flatly, crossing my arms.

"That's correct," Merikh agreed.

Did I alert them to the fact that I would escape the second I was given a chance? No, better to take them by surprise. I wouldn't just lie down and submit to them either. I would fight every step of the way and had no interest in holding my tongue. Surely, they knew that.

"Okay, fuckers. What now?" I asked with a yawn as I stood.

Merikh looked suitably confused, as if he was surprised I wasn't crying and screaming at my fate. The others laughed, except Nix, who had a small frown on his face.

Merikh's confusion turned into a glower. "I demand respect."

Ooh, a sore spot already? Perfect for me to exploit. "Yes, supreme leader. Whatever you say, supreme leader." His puzzled brow nearly had me bursting out laughing, but I managed to hold it in. I supposed I should try to find joy wherever I could now that everything had just taken a turn for the worse, and if it came from confusing the hell out of Merikh, so be it.

I looked outside the wide windows to watch the sun setting and was grateful that, no matter the circumstances, I had a safe, comfortable place to rest my head for the night. The more I slept and the better I ate, the easier it would be to travel a greater distance away once I escaped. I would be foolish if I didn't take advantage of the luxuries offered.

"We'll wake you when it's time for you to fetch our meals from the meal tent and start work for the day," Merikh declared.

I ignored him. He strode forward, grabbing my chin with a firm grip and baring his teeth. "You. Will. Listen."

"It'll be a cold day in hell before I ever listen to you," I hissed. He held my gaze for several seconds longer, jaw clenched furiously, before thrusting my chin to the side. He stepped back and murmured to Caelan, who flashed me a flirtatious smile.

"Duties start tomorrow morning," he barked as he headed down the hallway at the back of the living room to what I was assuming was his bedroom. The rest dispersed, leaving me to my thoughts. I could hardly believe that just hours ago I had been on my own, unaware that there was such a large camp to the south. I was also bitter that after only a few months without my dad, I'd managed to end up here. *Fucking fuck,* this was bad.

The worst part... if I had stumbled on this place a day ago, there's a possibility I could've been accepted without any of the stipulations. Sure, I would've had to contribute by working, but I would've been able to come and go as I pleased, and I had nothing against hard work when it wasn't against my will.

I glanced toward the door. *Do I escape?*

The second the thought crossed my mind, Caelan exited the hallway, shirtless with a pair of black sweats on.

"I'm here to keep an eye on you, baby."

I frowned at the pet name, eyeing his freakishly muscled abdomen angrily, and threw myself down on the brown couch, casting a glare in his direction as he sank into one of the large leather chairs to my left. Of course they'd send the strongest looking one to keep me in line.

I thought I would be uncomfortable and unable to sleep, being in a new place with strangers nearby. But I was warm, and the couch was soft and cushioned. I fought to keep my eyes open, reluctant to fall asleep surrounded by people I didn't know, but as the fire roared in the hearth across from us, the crackles lulled me into a deep slumber.

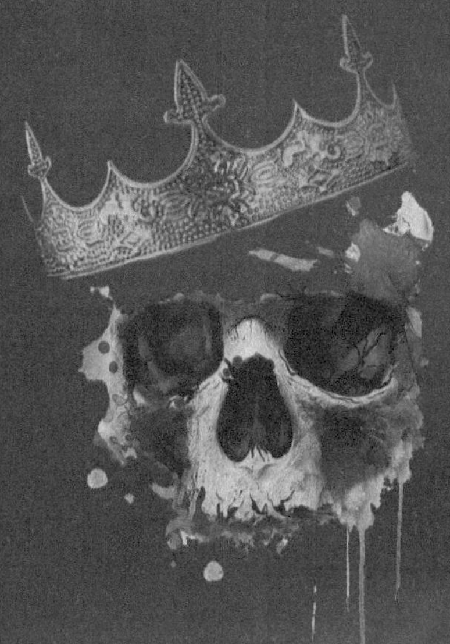

CHAPTER 3

I recoiled in shock the next morning when I opened my eyes to find Caelan staring at me, elbows propped up on his thighs and hands clasped under his chin.

Merikh entered the room, already staring at me with disdain. "Up. Time to fetch breakfast."

I grumbled a few curses under my breath, bristling at being ordered around just seconds after waking. Didn't they know people needed a few seconds to wake up in the morning?

"What was that?" he asked, eyes flashing in warning.

I refused to repeat myself and instead met his gaze defiantly and thrust my chin upwards.

"Cold water today," he declared. He ran a hand through his dark waves and leveled a cool stare onto me, waiting for me to protest. I knew better. I would be getting myself a cold meal too if I kept it up, or maybe even nothing. But that didn't mean I was giving up. I was just waiting for a better time to assert my independence. Like spitting in their food, or fucking up their rooms.

He thought that a cold bath was some kind of punishment? I'd bathed in cold water practically my entire life. Sometimes my dad and I would carry buckets of water to the tub of wherever we were staying if there was no body of water nearby, but that was it. Only a few times had we ever actually tried heating it. As of late, I was lucky if I even got to rinse off after a few weeks. And for that matter, I felt too vulnerable to wait around in the bathroom just to find out whatever method they used to heat the lake water anyway.

"Whatever," I murmured, turning to face Grey as he emerged from the hallway. His wet, dirty blonde hair hung in his face and he was missing a shirt, exposing his golden skin to the morning sun. The light glinted off a scar that snaked from his temple to his jaw. I must've been delirious to not have noticed it yesterday in the low light. And what the hell was up with everyone not wearing shirts around here? Why the fuck were they so well-built? The worst part was that I just *knew* his built physique was carved from years of hard work and labor around the camp, and not just a desire to look good.

I withheld a groan as I watched a droplet of water snake its way down the bumpy path of his abdomen, catching on the waistline of his shorts. Perfect. Not only did they hold me captive, but did they have to look so fucking good while doing it? Hating them would go much smoother if they were a bunch of fat old bastards.

"Morning, sweetheart," he said with a wink. I grimaced, heading toward the bathroom. It was way too early to get into it with him over the pet names.

I twisted the doorknob, jaw dropping at what I found. It was *nothing* like I'd expected.

It was completely done in shades of black and gray. A shower took up the whole back wall, the largest I'd ever seen, and beside it sat a modern-looking clawfoot tub. It was pristine, and I couldn't wait to haul some buckets of water from the lake to the tub. I hadn't had a bath in years, and I didn't think a quick dip in a river counted. It was a shame that the shower had to take up so much space since it wasn't usable, but it was a beautiful sight, nonetheless.

I'd intended to look at my reflection in the mirror to my right, but was sidetracked by the sound of water dripping from the showerhead.

"You have water from the pipes?" I exclaimed.

"What did you think I meant by shower?" Merikh yelled back grumpily.

"I don't know! I just thought you were feeling lazy and didn't feel like saying bath! I wouldn't put it past you to be missing the crucial difference between a bath and shower and using them interchangeably."

Nix popped his head in, a small smirk on his face. "We have a whole underground network that feeds water to the cabins and some of the buildings. We also have a few tradespeople who were able to develop a hot water system with our help."

"Holy shit, I think I'm in love," I murmured, pushing him out and shutting the door behind him. I didn't think I'd ever had a real, working shower before. Maybe back when I was really young, and the water still worked in some of the houses we squatted in, but I couldn't recall for sure. I stripped quickly, uncaring about the men right outside the door. It should've concerned me that I wasn't more nervous about the implications of that.

I squashed the burst of excitement that rose when I looked at the showerhead through the lightly frosted door. It was shaped like a square, with tiny silicone nozzles that the water would come out of. I didn't think I'd ever seen anything like it, but then again, I hadn't paid much attention to showerheads in the past. Surely I could just test the shower and see if they really did have hot water, as they said... *Nah*, I shook my head. There would be other opportunities to test it, probably best to leave it for now. Besides, a cool shower sounded pretty nice after the heat of the fire turned from comforting to oppressive halfway through the night.

I marveled at the cleanliness of the space. Unlike all the other showers and bathrooms I'd seen, there was no debris, dust, dirt, or stains everywhere. The countertops were a fancy black marble, matched by the similarly framed mirror. It was stunning. Even the grout was spotless. It was so fancy I wondered if it was some kind of rich person's vacation home that they just built the camp around, and it said a lot that these four had managed to keep it looking so good over the years.

I opened the shower door using the gold handle and stepped inside, taking a second to admire the long rectangular matte black tiles lining the wall. I'd probably never see anything so luxurious again, so I'd better soak it in while I still could. I spent a minute fiddling with the shower knob, frowning when I thought I'd successfully turned it on, just to hear a strange tapping noise in the wall. A good minute of turning and pulling things later, cold water shot out of the square-shaped thingy and hit my bare back. I shrieked as I cowered on the wall opposite, shivering. The sound of deep laughter rang from the kitchen.

Being pelted with freezing water was a bit different from being submerged in a lake or river. The water coming from the ceiling was gentle, almost soothing. I swiped the water from my eyes, feeling mildly ashamed at the amount of dirt swirling down the drain. There was only one unlabeled bottle on the recessed shower shelf, so I used it to soap up my hair, sighing softly at the feel of my clean scalp.

I slicked my hair back and opened the shower door for a moment to gather my breath, taking a moment to examine myself in the wide mirror above the sink. It had been a while since I'd looked at myself in something other than a dirty car mirror or a shattered gas station bathroom mirror.

My dad had cut my hair for me months ago, and it had grown significantly since then, falling right beneath my chest. My hazel eyes were hollowed with grief, purple smudges spread liberally underneath. I looked exhausted. I'd never worried too much about my appearance, but... I'd also never been surrounded by people that I kinda sorta wanted to make a good impression on, no matter how small.

Merikh flung the door open and strolled in–completely oblivious to my nakedness–causing me to shriek and cover myself with my hands in some kind of warped crouch. My god, it was a horrifying position, all twisted angles trying to cover my bits, and I was still fucking *shivering*.

"What the fuck?!" I screeched.

"Making sure you take a cold shower," he said with a shrug. And I had to hand it to him, he kept his eyes firmly on the wall opposite me. I frowned, ducking back into the shower and shuddering as the cool water hit my face.

I felt exposed with only the thin frosted glass between us, but I wasn't ashamed of my body. I had no energy to waste on petty modesties, even if my appearance was a bit lacking lately. *Zombie chic*, my brain supplied unhelpfully. I laughed softly as I scrubbed my body.

"Are you…" I could see him squinting at the wall incredulously. "Are you *laughing* in there?"

"What of it?" I said lightly, with a shrug he couldn't see.

"She's laughing to herself?" Grey shouted from right outside the door. "Holy shit, did you have to pick the weirdest one? You guys are like a magnet for oddballs."

Merikh sputtered, indignant over the accusation. "You're one of those oddballs!" he shouted back, receiving unrestrained laughter in response. I bit my lip against another outburst of giggles.

That's when I stepped fully under the stream and gasped as the frigid water hit me hard and fast. I heard a low chuckle from Merikh and scowled. Did he have to sound so proud of himself? Suddenly my humor was gone, stripped away by the cold, hard reality of my situation.

"Cold water is all I've ever known," I muttered between chattering teeth, suppressing another shiver. "It will take a lot more than that to break me."

"Excellent, princess. I appreciate a good challenge."

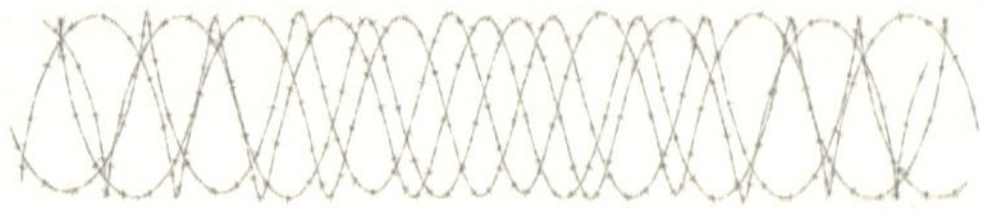

I tugged at the loose clothes covering my body, appreciating the soft feel of the well-worn fabric and the clean scent. I'd been dreading putting my dirty clothes back on when I stepped out of the shower, so I had been pleasantly surprised to find a neat pile of clean clothes on the counter after Merikh left. He'd given me an inscrutable look when I exited the bathroom wearing them, so I assumed he was surprised I didn't make a fuss.

"We passed the meal tent on the way in. That's where you can grab our breakfast," Caelan so kindly informed me. Grey kicked his legs up on the coffee table while Nix sat at the dining table quietly. He fiddled with a bracelet on his wrist, a delicate silver band that looked tarnished by time and life.

Being given an order chafed. I had to keep reminding myself that I'd done worse things to survive. I'd been covered in blood and guts, slicing through decomposing bodies like butter to defend myself. I'd looked into the eyes of the undead and persevered. Surely, I could handle a group of self-entitled men?

I forced a smile and gave a small mocking bow. "Yes, sir. Whatever you say, sir."

Merikh's azure eyes flashed dangerously at that. "Go," he gritted out between clamped teeth.

I hid a smirk, heading down the porch stairs and wringing my hair as I went. The brisk morning air chilled my damp skin, but I shook it off.

Along with being larger than the rest, the boy's cabin was also more isolated. I walked for several long minutes before I started to see evidence of other people. Children played and laughed, dressed in fresh clothes designed for style, and not practicality. The barrier against the outside world was a fair span from my current position, but I could just make it out in the distance.

It was a pretty scene, but being surrounded by so many people had my skin itching. It would take seconds for the virus to spread if an infected were to find a way in. The walls were both a sanctuary and a prison, and I didn't trust my chances of being penned in with a bunch of strangers if such an event were to occur.

"It's thanks to that wall that we're able to live unafraid," a girl murmured from next to me. I looked over to find clean multicolored skirts, light brown skin, and wavy black hair escaping her neat bun.

"Complacency is the kiss of death," I said under my breath as we walked. The words were pulled straight from my memory, a quote my dad used to recite every time I grew reckless. So basically, all the time during our last few months together.

She laughed, a high tinkling sound. "I suppose you're right, although that's an awfully pessimistic way to view things. Some children here have never known differently, the terror of a bony hand reaching for you, the struggle to keep your breaths quiet and paced while you're hiding."

I nodded. I wasn't good at conversation, let alone with someone my age. I made small talk with the tinier survivor groups that we ran into, but my father and I existed in a comfortable silence most of the time. There was only so much you could say to the person who had been at your side since birth.

"Sorry if I'm bothering you," she said kindly, adjusting her hair as she spoke. "You just looked so sad, and I haven't seen you around before."

"I'm... new."

She raised an eyebrow quizzically, but to her credit, she didn't push.

"How long has this camp been around? Have you been here the whole time?"

She glanced at a little boy as he ran by, tripping over nothing and sprawling on his hands and knees with a thud. I smothered a laugh when he got up after a few seconds with a squeal and continued running. "I arrived several years back with my grandmother, who has since passed. I was given accommodations and now I work in the gardens as my contribution. As for when the camp was established, I think it was around fifteen years ago."

Fifteen years...

"I'm happy to hear that she got to pass peacefully behind these walls."

It seemed she was grabbing breakfast too, because she kept my pace all the way to the food tent. The entrance to the camp was just barely visible around the corner, the guard shack larger than it had seemed yesterday.

I winced. "Is that main gate the only way to leave?"

Her eyes darted to me, wary and assessing, and she opened her mouth only to shut it quickly. "I'll find you later," she murmured with a quick glance behind me. "It was nice meeting you!" she exclaimed, louder for some reason. Just then, Caelan approached. No wonder she scampered off. He was huge. His tattoos stretched across his arms and shoulders as he crossed them disapprovingly.

"Making friends, baby?"

I huffed, turning toward the food tent and brushing past him. "Don't call me that."

His arm shot out, grabbing my arm and halting my progress. "Don't fight us," he murmured.

I got right up in his space and pressed a finger to his chest. Then I looked up to meet his light blue eyes. Now that I was standing so close to him, I could see that they were flecked with tiny specks of gray. "I don't think you're in a position to demand anything like that," I snarled.

His eyes flashed. "I think I'll enjoy bringing you to heel."

Whirling on the ball of my foot, I marched into the tent, ignoring the many sets of eyes that fell on me. The girl that burst into their place yesterday shot me an irritated look, ignoring the small group around her as she watched me carefully.

You had got to be *fucking* kidding me. I'd barely been here a day and this bitch already decided that just because I was confined to their cabin that I must be shacking up with one of them? Or maybe that wasn't it at all, maybe she was just mad I had access to an area she'd been denied.

Either way, it was petty, and I had no time for it. Surely the other people living in the camp weren't as superficial?

I stood stock-still as I looked for the tail of the line I was supposed to join, subject to quiet snickering and hushed whispers in the meantime. My ire raised with every single sound, feeling vulnerable and exposed, standing on display in front of so many strangers. I ground my teeth as I helplessly scanned the large crowd of people for some semblance of a line. Just as I was about to spin and walk out, Caelan rested a heavy hand on my shoulder, sending a glare in the direction of the tables and marching me toward the front.

I frowned at him. Surely all these people weren't standing around for no reason? But his motives became clear when the person he cut in front of nodded respectfully and stepped back. I rolled my eyes, entirely unsurprised at his entitlement, but grateful that it brought me off to the side.

After several calming breaths, my frustration began to deflate now that I wasn't on display in the middle of the tent. I'd never seen so many people packed together in one place, and it was quickly overwhelming me. I hated to say it, but I was grateful to Caelan for coming to help.

"It's not usually this busy," he rumbled softly from behind me. "It's just the morning rush, is all."

I nodded, turning my attention to the actual purpose of the tent. As we progressed through the shortened line, my mouth watered at all the delicious scents, foods I had only eaten years ago on special occasions: bacon, eggs, hash browns, and something sweet I couldn't identify. My eyes filled with tears at the abundance of fresh, hot food before me. Caelan took one look at my face and murmured, "Eat. I'll help you carry back their plates when you're finished."

He didn't have to tell me twice. I gathered as much food as my plate could hold, ignoring the curious glances from all around me, and sat at the end of the nearest empty table, observing the way the tent flaps shuddered with the breeze and the sun shone in from several jagged holes above me. I ate my food with fervor, finishing in record time and licking my fingers to get the last of the salt and grease. My stomach was shrunken, but I had been starving for so long that I couldn't resist eating a little extra. I had to be careful not to make myself sick with the amount that I ate. The tastes were just so divine, warm and bursting with flavor on my tongue.

"How did you survive on your own for so long?" Caelan asked from beside me. I hadn't even noticed him taking a seat.

I figured I owed him an answer, since he allowed me to eat before serving them. *Oh, that chafed. Allowed.*

"I wasn't alone," I said stiffly.

Caelan straightened. "You had a man?"

"No."

"A... woman?"

"No."

His muscles lost some of their tension. "Come," he said roughly.

He led me back to the front and together we prepared plates for the others, carrying them back to the cabin in a careful balance.

Damn it all, why did I feel so bad about not answering his question? Had I hurt his feelings somehow? I bumped him with my shoulder, careful not to jostle the plates. "My dad," I said softly, so quiet there was a chance he didn't hear. Even if he did, maybe he would have no idea what I was talking about.

His muscles lost their tension, and he looked at me with a tiny smile on his face. "Thank you," he said.

I heard what he didn't say.

Thank you for trusting me, thank you for answering me, thank you for being honest.

When we reached the cabin, Caelan shouldered the door open to find Merikh, Nix, and Grey sitting at the table and arguing quietly.

I set their plates down one by one, making sure to meet their eyes in challenge. Grey smirked while Merikh remained expressionless. "You'll eat all your meals with us from now on."

I sighed, examining my cracked nails. I would need to explore the camp sooner or later and meet up with that girl at some point. I needed information on potential exits and I had to make a plan for after I escaped. Obviously, I couldn't stay in the area, but maybe I could hike north? I would go back to sleeping on rooftops, bathing with stream water and–

"River," Merikh interrupted my errant thoughts.

I met his stare, refusing to look away.

"You will eat with us," he repeated.

"Why do you care if I eat with you? I'm just your fucking prisoner."

His eyes grew dark, and his jaw clenched as he ground his teeth. "You are our responsibility. You eat with us, or you can eat off the floor."

Well, shit. I didn't know which drugs he'd taken, but I wasn't anyone's damn responsibility, nor did I ask to be one.

"I told her to eat," Caelan rumbled quietly from somewhere behind me.

I couldn't quite place Merikh's expression but he definitely wasn't pleased.

"Our father left last night to go scavenging." Merikh's face was hard, uncompromising, as he changed topics.

"We lead in his stead." Caelan clarified Merikh's vague as fuck statement as he tied his hair back so that only a few tendrils hung in his face.

"What does that entail?"

Nix spoke up then. "Making sure everyone is following the rules, that the children are being looked after, the meals are going smoothly, and the food in storage is adequate, and resolving any issues that arise. Our father is mostly a figurehead at this point, so it's our responsibility to keep the camp running smoothly."

I felt a sudden strong surge of wistfulness for the camp and their easy way of living. They made sure everyone was fed and looked after. No distended bellies, dirty clothes, or violence. Perhaps I would stumble on another camp after I escaped, one that would not be tainted by these four men. One where I could live freely.

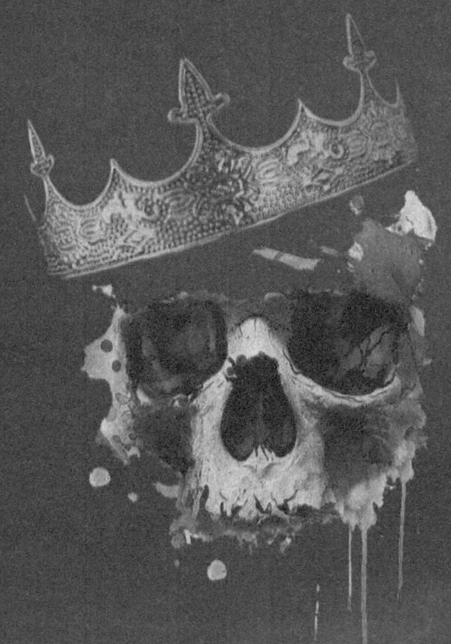

CHAPTER 4

"**Y**ou'll be accompanying me today," Merikh declared once he finished eating his bacon. He dabbed his mouth delicately with his napkin and leaned back in his chair to fix me with an emotionless stare.

"What will we be doing?"

"Settling disputes."

What kind of lawless fucking camp allows a kidnapper to handle arguments? My mood lightened when I realized I could use this opportunity to learn information. Surely I'd be able to learn more about their security measures.

"Do the people of this camp know that you kidnap people?" Sure, they made it seem like a rarity at the gate when I first arrived, but who knew what kind of shady shit was going on behind the scenes?

Grey laughed while Caelan smirked. "You're the only person we've taken, baby. And these people know better than to oppose us. Our word is law here, enforced by immediate banishment."

I bit back a noise of disgust. They would send the people of their camp into zombie-infested territory as a punishment? Sickening.

"They've deserved it," Nix said calmly. Something about the subtle way he implored me to believe him quieted my discomfort. I rolled my shoulders back stiffly, nodding to Merikh. Clearly, the others were prone to exaggeration just to try to scare me.

He pulled a flannel over his white shirt, covering all that golden skin, and stood over by the door to toe his shoes on.

I turned to follow when Nix stopped me with a hand on my arm. I hadn't even seen him approach. "Here," he said quietly, handing me a metal bottle with the telltale slosh of water within. My jaw grew slack once I realized he'd gone through the trouble of finding and cleaning me a bottle, *and* filling it with clean water. I took the bottle from his hand, meeting his eyes in surprise when my hand brushed against his over the smooth metal. The noises around us faded away, and I was immediately captivated by the flecks of amber floating in the sea of green that were his irises. This close to him, I could smell the faint, dizzying scent of vanilla and pine needles coming from his skin. I let my eyes roam his face, consuming his features hungrily. The heavy slash of his eyebrows, the sharp jut of his cheekbones, and the long fan of his dark eyelashes. I didn't think I'd ever seen anyone so effortlessly handsome, and I was overcome by the sudden rush of warmth flooding throughout my chest.

"Let's go," Merikh snapped from the doorway. Nix's eyes shifted away from mine almost guiltily, and a quick glance toward the others revealed them to be deep in conversation. It concerned me that I'd been so deeply enthralled by just his presence, and I was almost grateful to Merikh for jerking me out of my trance.

"Th-thanks. Sorry," I muttered, clearing my throat awkwardly and heading to the door.

Mid-conversation with Grey, Caelan waved at me, winking as I left. I rolled my eyes in response, following Merikh, as we took the path back to civilization. My footsteps made a slight crunching noise as I walked over the layer of frost that was steadily melting from the morning sunlight, and I found myself grateful that they'd had an extra pair of boots lying around that I could borrow. For once I was wearing shoes that weren't too small, covered in filth, or falling apart.

"I do hope you won't misplace your anger when you reach the general populace."

After walking in silence for so long, it was jarring to hear the deep rumble of his voice. It made trying to ignore him impossible, and now I was keenly aware of the heat radiating off his body where he'd just brushed against my arm, and the firm set of his mouth as he waited for my response.

I looked at him incredulously, ignoring the way the sun highlighted various strands of gold and red in his dark hair. How come these jerks were so attractive? And why the hell were they scrambling my brain so often?

"I would never presume to blame someone else for something you did."

I ignored his irritating little humming noise and followed him in renewed silence as we entered the main part of the camp. Upon noticing the woman I'd met yesterday, I gave her a tiny wave, and she offered me a small smile in return.

"You've met Halli?"

"I have," I confirmed cautiously.

"I will arrange for you to spend time with her in the garden one of these days."

My lips twitched. "So gracious of you, sir. Thank you."

The corners of his full mouth turned down. "Don't mistake my kindness for weakness, River."

"Yeah, yeah, whatever." The man nearest us gasped, eyes darting to Merikh for a reaction. Merikh only clasped my shoulder with his large hand, steering me toward a large building. It was several times the size of their cabin and must've been where they gathered for meetings. The outside was a dark red color, the inside a giant hollowed space. Rafters decorated the high ceilings, and a few chairs sat at the front of the room on a dais. It was structured almost like a church. I bit my lip against a crazed laugh. *Well, of course it is. I bet he thinks his word is gospel.*

Already, several people were inside and milling around aimlessly, eyes darting in our direction as we walked past them. Merikh's hand slid down to my arm, pulling me toward the front of the room. I had imagined Merikh's hand being smooth and supple, the hands of someone who had a person for everything. But they weren't, as confirmed by that initial long, torturous walk to get to the camp in the first place, and now, as he pulled me along once more. His hand was rough, scarred, a working man's hand. I shivered against my will under his touch, pulling away from him even as he steered me. Ignoring the burst of heat that arose from where we made contact.

"Let go," I hissed, ashamed of my body's reaction. What was a girl to do? It wasn't like I got touched by handsome men left and right while being hunted by zombies and nomads. There were slim pickings out in the wild; best not to take any chances.

His eyes widened before narrowing in my direction. I could see him weighing the battle in his mind. Did he give me any leeway by respecting my request, and could he afford that? "Fine," he eventually grumbled. I cheered internally, grateful for my small win.

As he took his seat at the chair I'd spotted when we first entered, I walked toward the side of the room.

"Stop," he called out, motioning for me to sit in the chair beside his.

I frowned, reluctantly leaving the dark shadows of the room to take the seat that he'd gestured to. He leaned backward ever so slightly, spreading his legs and resting his arms on the arms of his chair as he watched the growing number of people with a blank face. He looked as if it bothered him none to be facing an entire room of people, like some kind of insouciant king looking down on the masses. I squirmed uncomfortably when an increasing number of eyes gravitated toward me as more people entered. I *hated* being on display.

Although it gave me a good chance to observe the kinds of people who lived here. Some of their clothes were worn, dirt covering their knees and shoes. Others had a freshly washed look about them, skin gleaming and hair tied back. One woman was missing an eye, the empty socket hidden when her hair shifted from where it hung in her face. Another man was missing a leg and used crutches that had been wrapped in swaths of colorful fabric. A little girl sat beside him, most likely the cause of his colorful walking aids, tugging at his arm so she could whisper in his ear.

I didn't see Halli, though I did see the woman from the gate. I supposed it was better that Halli wasn't there, if this was some tyrant's version of court.

Everyone settled as the last few people took their seats near the front, watching me carefully.

After a long moment of uncomfortable silence, Merikh spoke, voice low and authoritative. "This is River. She'll be staying with us for the foreseeable future."

Assent echoed around the room. Several people sneered in my direction, making it clear that the guys were a hot commodity, although there were a few appraising looks as well. The rest seemed blissfully unaffected by my presence, aside from a few kind smiles and nods.

My breathing began to pick up when Merikh didn't immediately start a new topic. Heat flushed from my scalp to my toes, making me feel dizzy and light-headed. The shaft of sunlight from one of the many overhead windows felt like it was zeroing in on me, showcasing my every flaw. I felt as if my heart were beating so loudly that the entire room could hear it. Surely they could if it was already loud enough to drown out my thoughts. I clenched my hands tightly around the arms of the chair, watching in fascination as my knuckles started to turn white under the pressure. Every quiet cough, shifting of fabric and muffled whisper sounded like thunder to my ears. I was seconds away from jumping out of my chair and darting from the room, as humiliating as it would be, when Merikh shifted into a lazy sprawl, taking the arm closest to me and propping it on the back of my chair. His hand just barely brushed my bare shoulder in the process, but it was enough to snap me out of my impending panic attack. All I could focus on was the heat lingering on my skin, the goosebumps rising on my arms. His face was impassive, and there was no sign that he had even noticed that he'd touched me, which made it all the more unfair that I was so acutely aware of it.

"Let's begin. First," he stated finally.

The woman from the gate stood. "We can't afford to feed another mouth." Her eyes were flinty as she watched me.

"I didn't ask, Anna. Besides, we have more than enough food to feed her."

She sneered, brushing her light blonde hair over her shoulder dismissively, and opened her mouth to make what I was sure was another argument.

"Or it can come out of your meals, if you'd like?"

Her face paled and her lower lip trembled. "Why should she get to march in here and accompany you everywhere, not doing her part?"

"Enough." He spoke quietly, but I could hear the underlying threat, and I assumed she could too because she swiftly sat down, arms crossed and eyes stuck on me in a deadly glare.

I felt so incredibly uncomfortable being discussed in front of an entire group of people like I wasn't even there. I pushed back at the anger and the unjustness of my circumstances once more. I knew better than to think of my captors as domesticated and docile just because they liked to wear their polite masks in front of other people. It was obvious just from the barely concealed violence that they hid in dulcet tones, the chiseled cut of their muscles, the tough skin on their knuckles, indicating that the skin there broke often. These were men who backed up their claims with their fists and had the logic and control to match.

Dangerous.

I shifted slightly, tuning her out completely.

Another woman stood. She wore a long linen dress and braided her hair back into something that resembled a crown. Her face was a warm tan, round and welcoming. "The garden is low on vegetables, and we need more seeds to begin planting for the spring season. Since the blight destroyed our crops, we've had to rely on what little seed packets we could find, but the majority aren't taking as they've expired or spoiled."

Merikh's lips thinned. "We'll figure something out," he said consolingly. I'd have had to see it to believe it, his attempt to reassure. "My father left yesterday for a scavenging trip past the bounds of where we've already picked over. He knows to keep an eye out for places that might still have some stored away."

Merikh removed his arm from my chair, this time not making any contact with my body, before crossing his arms and cocking his head to face the man who stood once he'd finished speaking.

"Yes?" he prompted.

The man wrung his hands. "With John dead, we need an extra hand on perimeter duty."

My eyes began to widen before I schooled my reaction. They knew John was dead? Did they know that he was infected? That I killed him? I hadn't realized that I was tapping my foot anxiously until Merikh gently knocked his shoulder into mine. *Of course* they knew he was dead, why else wouldn't he accompany them back after leaving together? If it was this easy for me to get nervous and awkward, I had no chance of not blurting the truth out to someone and that just wouldn't work.

"We'll take care of it."

The man's features relaxed, smoothing out before he sat back down. It was definitely in my best interest that people didn't know. It wasn't like they were accepting newbies with open arms in the first place, but newbies who'd murdered one of their own? I'd get a lot more people upset with me than just Anna.

Several seconds passed before a woman stood slowly, eyes darting around the room, then landing on Merikh and anchoring there. The woman sitting next to her shifted the toddler on her lap to lay a reassuring hand on her arm. The side of her face carried a large bruise, a dark purple and yellow splotch that stretched from her cheekbone to her jaw. She held herself gingerly, like maybe there were more injuries beneath the surface of her clothes that we weren't seeing, but she set her jaw and watched Merikh for several seconds longer before breaking eye contact. He only nodded, his expression inscrutable. She sat back down swiftly, the woman next to her whispering fervently as she placed the toddler into her lap. I tilted my head in confusion but didn't interrupt to ask him what it was about.

My mind drifted as Merikh kept addressing anyone who raised a hand or stood and before I knew it, people filtered out of the room slowly, talking amongst themselves.

He waited until everyone had left before exiting the building, only to find that the sun had lowered in its descent, hovering right above us. "Come with me to collect lunch for everyone."

I followed along dutifully all the way to the tent. I'd only been out for a few hours, and I was already exhausted by the amount of small talk and smiling I'd had to do. Granted, not many people looked past Merikh's perpetual scowl to speak with me, but it was enough.

Already people were jumping from their seats to load up plates for Merikh while I just stood by, watching them make fools of themselves. What did they have to gain? To lose? Just what power did these four men hold?

A child ran up and tugged on Merikh's pant leg, giggling uncontrollably. Merikh's icy exterior cracked, lips curving into a small grin as he bent down to tug gently on her ponytail. He swung her into his arms, offering a nod in greeting to her father when he approached, then grinned wider when he started to spin her, and she broke out laughing. Once she'd had enough, her father granted Merikh his own smile before collecting his daughter and heading to the back of the line with her still laughing in his arms. It was clear that just because he lacked empathy and was a complete dick, didn't mean he wasn't beloved by the camp.

Don't soften your opinions just because he's nice to kids, I scolded myself, taking the plates that were being handed to me by strangers.

We made it back to the cabin within minutes, our walk silent and uncomfortable, mostly focused on balancing the plates. Once we made it to their cabin, Caelan and Grey took the plates from us and set the table. I didn't see Nix anywhere, but assumed he was somewhere nearby.

"I have some clothes for you," Caelan mentioned as he cracked his tattooed knuckles. Merikh winced at the sound.

I cocked my head as he gestured toward the couch. A pile of clothes sat on the middle cushion, what looked to be skirts, shorts, and gauzy tops at first glance.

I raised one eyebrow in his direction.

He smirked. "Donations," he said, adding a quick wink. "You can check them out after lunch."

"They don't look very practical," I admitted. They didn't look practical at *all*, but they resembled the styles I'd seen some women wearing around camp. "Just a small peek?" I begged, adding a pout for good measure.

Caelan bit back a laugh, gesturing toward the pile. "It's your food that'll get cold," he said with a careless shrug.

I picked through the pile, my cheeks heating when I spotted a piece of soft lilac fabric sandwiched in between two ridiculously short skirts, pulling it free to reveal a set of lacy undergarments. I had a somewhat flat chest and had mostly scavenged old sports bras in the past. I was lucky if they weren't completely moth-eaten or full of holes. But to have such new-looking items? Made of fabrics I wouldn't have even considered before? I bit my lip, setting them aside along with a few utilitarian-looking t-shirts, several new pairs of shorts, and one pair of sweatpants that looked like they'd be a little loose, but still comfortable.

"I'm not wearing the rest," I declared. "I don't care how safe you say this place is. I'm not wearing short skirts and tops that don't offer any coverage."

Grey gave me an amused smile. "You won't branch outside your comfort zone?"

I frowned. I was used to sleeping with my shoes on, to having full-length pants and long-sleeved shirts on at all times in case I ran into the undead. It didn't matter if this camp was empty of them; there was always a chance the Paleo virus would break out, and then what? How would I defend myself in a useless skirt? Even the longer ones would tangle in my legs and trip me up if I needed to run. No, I was happy with my old worn-out jeans and the shorts. It would take longer than a couple days for me to let go of the habits and practices that had kept me safe for so long

What could I say that drove home how serious I was about this? I should've taken more care to pick and choose my arguments with them because now it was just going to seem like I was disagreeing to disagree.

It struck me how quiet everyone had gotten. "Thank you for gathering these," I started hesitantly. "But I would feel safer in pants." Caelan opened his mouth, so I rushed to add, "Please." It couldn't hurt to make them feel like they were doing me a favor by agreeing.

To my surprise, Merikh swallowed his bite with a vacant look on his face, then nodded slowly. "That's okay, princess. There are plenty of clothes to choose from. We're not so strict that we'd force you to wear something that makes you uncomfortable."

I stopped my jaw from dropping just in time. "I–okay. Thank you." That was... surprisingly easy. I tried to keep the suspicion off my face. *Too easy.* How could I yell at him for calling me princess when he'd just willingly made a compromise and admitted to caring about my opinion on what I wanted to wear? Aw fuck, was this how brainwashing started?

He patted the chair next to him, his blank eyes landing on me. "Sit."

I stood in place, starving, but reluctant to follow his orders. For fuck's sake, why couldn't he just phrase it like a question so I didn't have to seem like I was giving in if I just sat like both he *and* I wanted me to? It would save us so much damn time.

Grey, who was wearing his hair in a haphazard bun on top of his head, looked at me in both confusion and dawning understanding. At least I really fucking hoped it wasn't pity. "Please come sit," he said. "You must be hungry and you went through the trouble of grabbing yourself a bowl."

Merikh glared at him before taking another bite, thankfully not arguing over it.

I was grateful for the olive branch. If it wasn't an order, then I didn't have to stand my ground, hovering over by the couch when I could be eating. I sat next to Grey, across from Caelan, who sat next to an empty seat. Merikh was next to that empty seat, at the head of the table. His eyes narrowed like he knew I'd avoided sitting next to him on purpose.

I took a bite of the soup, moaning at the burst of savory flavors across my tongue. More spices than I'd had in my entire life and still warm too, it was the best food I'd ever tasted. At the sudden silence, I looked up to find all three pairs of eyes on me. Caelan's lips were parted while Grey's eyes were hooded.

"Well, shit. Don't stop on our account, sweetheart," Grey murmured. I scoffed, finishing my soup quickly as if I would never get a chance to eat warm food again. I had learned to eat every meal like it would be my last, because out in the wild, chances were that it could be. Food was so scarce outside of this haven, never anything savory and never the time to savor it. My father taught me a lot of things, but hunting was not one of them.

Nix walked in then, taking one look at our faces and then slinging his body in the empty chair between Caelan and Merikh. "What did I miss?"

"My hard-on for River," Caelan drawled. I cast a shocked glance in his direction, spoon forgotten inches from my open mouth. Grey started laughing awkwardly, while Nix looked at him with exasperation. Surely he wasn't serious. There was no way he was... for me. That kind of thing only happened in the books I'd read.

"I'm sorry," Nix said softly, green eyes warm and *kind.*

I gave him a small smile, a smile that the others narrowed their eyes at.

When we'd almost finished eating, Merikh spoke. "You will be accompanying Nix tomorrow to check on the children. Make sure you're prepared. The rest of today will be spent cleaning."

I nodded, clenching my spoon in my fist at the demand. An inconspicuous wink from Nix had me loosening my hand and finishing my lunch.

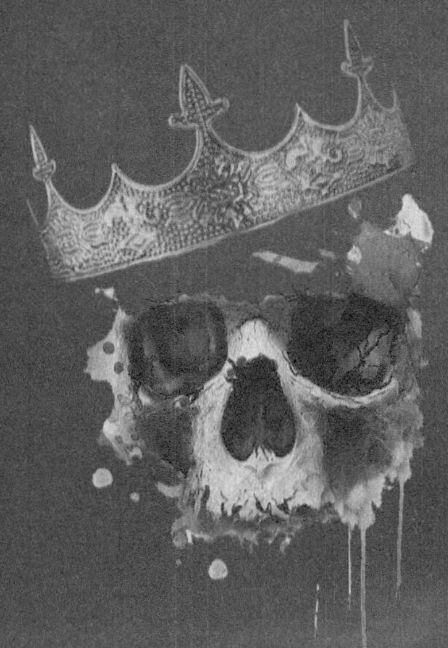

CHAPTER 5

"This way," Nix murmured. I had woken on the couch that morning with Nix sitting across from me, studying my face solemnly. He was so much quieter than his brothers, his eyes carrying secrets that I would probably never learn, nor did I want to. Promise. Even if he did seem so nice and mysterious. He walked beside me quietly, green eyes shadowed under the gray sky. He looked even paler out here, the barest hint of dark smudges beneath his eyes.

I could use the time to appeal to him. Of all his brothers, he seemed the most reasonable, the most likely to let me go, the most conscious of how wrong it was to keep someone against their will. For some reason, I didn't. I would find a way out, but I didn't want to break our unspoken truce and lose my only tentative ally.

"So you check in on the children?" I asked as I struggled to keep up with him. His strides were so long, which checked out because he was like six and a half fucking feet tall.

"I do. We all do. Many are orphans, cared for by the community. Sometimes we stumble on them when we're scavenging, other times the families that care for them found them alone before they came to us. The older ones attend lessons during the day, and the younger ones whose families spend the day working have a care center. That's where we're visiting."

My stomach dropped as I realized... Oh my god, *I'm* an orphan. How did it never occur to me before? Maybe because it felt like we were all orphans these days. But still... what an odd discovery. My breathing sped up as I thought about just how untethered I was now. No family, no friends. Just me.

Nix's hand softly brushing against mine pulled me from my thought spiral, and a bright flash of giddiness and insecurity hit me at the contact. I peeked up at him slyly. *Was that on purpose?* Surely not. I kept a vigilant watch on our hands as we walked, but it didn't happen again.

"That's kind of you all to care for them."

His smile was a sad thing. "Who else, if not us?"

I agreed. We walked into the medium-sized building that sat next to where the meeting was held the other day. I could hear the screams and cries from outside, and my brow furrowed in concern. Nix gave a rare laugh, ushering me inside.

There were at least ten children, all in various states of play. One girl wearing a pink puffy dress scowled at a green-eyed boy for taking her toy. A different young boy pushed another, his head of dark curls swinging with the movement and causing his victim to issue a battle cry. Hovering around them were two women, both red-haired and pale, freckles generously decorating their cheeks.

"Twins," Nix muttered from his place near my side.

"What's in the water around here?" I muttered under my breath. Triplets *and* twins in the same camp?

"Nice to meet you," the girl on the left said with a smile. A young boy sat on her hip, and she slung one arm around his upper body, holding him to her. "I'm Naia."

The other spoke next, with a small nod of acknowledgment. "Nerese."

I was at a loss on how to tell them apart just by their looks when I realized just how different their outfit choices were. Naia wore all pinks and purples, and it looked like she'd mended them herself to the point where they could've almost looked brand new. Whereas Nerese favored darker clothes, choosing to keep the rips, tears, and holes that probably came with the scavenged fabrics.

"I've brought River to see the children, to get an idea of how we run things in case she's needed here. She's new to the camp and will be pitching in so that we have an extra pair of hands."

"We're so happy to have you," Naia said softly. "You're going to love it here. No more going hungry or sleeping with one eye open."

The kind words struck a chord inside me. I wanted to scowl, wanted to rage and yell and pout but I didn't. Not only was it the wrong time or place but because I understood that all hands were needed in a place like this. I just couldn't get past my anger to appreciate all the good that this camp seemed to do. Frustration that I was being held against my will, expected to help in a community I didn't even want to be in. And maybe that made me selfish, but I never claimed to be altruistic.

I once killed a man just for encroaching on the land we had been occupying for a few months and stealing our supplies, for holding a gun to my dad's head when we caught him in the act. It was the first and last time I'd killed a living being, not including John, and I didn't regret it. I could still remember the shock on my dad's face when he bucked against the man, breaking his balance and allowing me to slash his throat with my blade. The stickiness of his blood on my hands, so unlike the turgid fluids of the undead. I dry heaved for several long minutes, slumped over and sweating only several feet away from the man's body. My dad rubbed my back soothingly, getting me a cup of fresh water and taking care of the body while I rested nearby in an abandoned car. Not only could I not allow him to kill my dad, but I couldn't allow him to get a shot off either. Everyone knew that guns were for emergency only since they'd draw more trouble than they were worth.

"River," Nix prompted.

"What? Oh." I noticed the little girl tugging on the ragged hem of my pants, arms outstretched. With a glance at Nerese and Naia, I picked her up, settling her on my hip. She looked to be about four years old, give or take. I was sure half of these kids would never know their ages, their birthdays. It made my heart ache to think about.

"Hello," I murmured, looking into her innocent blue eyes. She had a tiny pout on her mouth, her golden curls tangled and wild.

"'Lo," she said quietly.

I had never held a child before. I realized I liked the heavy weight of her in my arms, the scent of strawberries and apples coming off her hair as she turned her head. I'd never had any desire to become a mother, and I'd backed that up with a trip to the nearest military base, but holding this little girl in my arms gave me the briefest insight into what my mother's thought process might've been as she'd held me. It warmed my heart to think of the possibility of someday taking care of a little one that found themselves without a guardian and who needed a family, much like myself.

Nix's eyes were soft as he watched me, no longer a turbulent emerald but a quiet calm color, like a sea of grass just before the sun rises at dawn.

"Her name is Imogen," Naia told me. "She's currently living with the Akdemir family."

"Im'gen," the little girl in my arms said firmly, squirming so that she could say hello to Nix as well.

Hours passed as we spoke with the twins about how things were going, and played with the occasional child. We stayed for lunch and naptime, until the sun lowered in the sky and the day turned to dusk. By the time we left, I was exhausted, as if I'd done a full day of labor. I had never interacted with so many others for such a long period of time and had never realized just how much of a recluse I was.

Nix's eyes searched mine as we came to a stop on the path to the center of the camp, dark curls falling into his face as he leaned forward. "Are you okay?" he murmured.

Grief held my throat captive, resulting in a choked noise of assent before I turned in the direction of the food tent, ready to grab our meals for the night. His arm brushed mine soothingly, leaving sparks behind. As if he knew I needed the comfort but would never force me to utter the words. I watched his muscles shift as he walked, the way his pale skin gleamed under the light of the moon, enticing and otherworldly. He truly was the most handsome man I'd ever seen. They all were.

How utterly unfair.

As we entered the cabin with dinner, we found Grey and Caelan sitting side by side on the couch and talking in low murmurs as Merikh sat at the head of the table looking bored. I may have been mistaken, but it almost looked as if his face brightened at the sight of us. *Great, he can't wait to dole out more orders.*

He looked sinful in the dim shine of the candlelight all around us. His eyes narrowed as we set down the food bowls like he was anticipating a fight. "We're going out after dinner."

"What the fuck is 'out?'" I asked him incredulously. The sun had set, the camp was settling in for the night, and my limbs were heavy and tired.

"Precisely what I said," he snapped. Fuck, I both loved and hated how he sounded so imperious whenever he got angry. He rounded the table, taking lengthy strides in my direction, then reached out, grabbing my chin with his long fingers and tilting my head to the side. Set his face just inches from my hair and breathed in slowly. "It's a surprise," he whispered into my ear. My face was burning when he pulled away, even Caelan and Grey had stopped messing around to stare at us with confusion. I felt sparks fly in my body, the oddest fluttering heat in my chest. His proximity did things to me, the tan column of his throat in the moonlight, the way his hand felt too calloused and rough for his haughty personality. Thankfully, Nix jostled my side, snapping me out of it.

I'm just deprived of touch, I reassured myself. Of course if someone attractive got all up in my face and breathed on me my stomach was going to feel funny. *Duh.*

He pulled away with an almost angry expression, looking highly annoyed for some reason, and barked something at Caelan and Grey before going to wash up.

Several hours later, we stood in front of the lake I'd noticed when I first arrived, watching as the water lapped at the grass on the shore. The moonlight cut a wide swath through the inky darkness, highlighting the ripples in pearlescent tones. I felt equal parts fear and excitement. I'd been swimming at night, and I had never been undressed around a naked, attractive man before. The very illicit notion of being unclothed around them made my cheeks flush with heat.

Sometimes I felt my inexperience would swallow me whole.

"We usually all visit the lake once a week," Nix said slowly. "I didn't think we'd be going this week." His last words were spoken between clenched teeth.

"But you have access to running water," I stated in confusion. I didn't think people who had such luxuries still bathed in lakes.

"It's tradition," Grey said with a shrug. "We like to swim, and it's good exercise."

"Strip," Merikh commanded. My eyes widened as Caelan laughed, stripping off his clothes in an exaggerated fashion and revealing bounds of skin highlighted by moonlight, his golden color turned silver. My cheeks began to heat as I averted my eyes from his bold nakedness.

Grey followed his lead while Nix stripped slower, less joyfully. His eyes met mine almost in apology.

"No," I stated firmly.

"Then you can go in clothed, or you can sit on the shore," Merikh said slowly.

I cast a glance back toward the body of water, looking past the shiny surface to the dark depths within. Removing my clothes almost felt like taking off armor. My dad once told me a cautionary tale of a girl who'd ventured into the lake one night and never returned. She was enchanted by the lake creature, disguised as a beautiful mermaid. She seduced her with her beauty alone, drawing her deeper and deeper out to the center until she sank under and never came back, drowning in its depths while the mermaid turned back into a creature of nightmares. Maybe I would venture out into the darkness and never return. Sometimes I didn't hate the idea.

Perhaps that wasn't the best story to tell a girl prone to believing in fairy tales who'd only run off into the lake without checking for zombies first *once*, thank you very much, although it certainly cured me of doing it again.

Merikh strode forward, hand outstretched and ready to... I wasn't sure, pull my clothes off? I dodged his hand, smacking it with mine. His lips parted in surprise, and I laughed at his expression, unable to hold it back. Surely he didn't think I would keel over and submit just because he asked? Surely he'd met a single *someone* with a backbone in all his years being a little tyrant?

"I'm just giving you a hair tie," he growled angrily, thrusting the dark elastic band into my hands.

"She's got grit," Caelan remarked wryly. "Good. I like a little bite with my prey," he purred. I winced at his innuendo, looking at Nix for support to find him in nothing but black boxers, watching me solemnly. I fought the urge to check out his deliciously outlined package, but it was goddamn hard. Five minutes shrouded in darkness with them removing their clothes, my heart beating a staccato rhythm, and my cheeks blushing furiously, and I felt drunk with the possibilities.

I sighed, deciding if it was going to happen, I'd better make it a show. I didn't want my clothes to get wet anyway, and I didn't want them to think of me as a shy, blushing virgin. Even if I felt like I was. If I had to follow Merikh's asinine *tradition*, I might as well tease him while I was at it. That would make him think twice the next time he bossed me around. I crossed my arms over my stomach and pulled my shirt off slowly, inch by torturous inch. Then I hooked my fingers under the sides of my pants at my hips, letting them slide from my body slowly and land at my feet in a pile. I left my panties on, and the thin lace bra that they'd scrounged up for me the other day. If they got to stay in their underclothes, so could I.

"Fuck," Caelan moaned, palming his length behind the shorts he wore. Maybe I should have been uncomfortable, but somehow knowing that *me*, perpetually exhausted, socially awkward me, caused that reaction from him? I didn't hate it. The attention made me feel powerful and bold. There was no fear, no shyness, just desire. I looked to Merikh to find his eyes hooded, fists clenched. *Good*, I'd unnerved him. Unfortunately, I seemed to have stunned Grey and Nix as well, who watched me with rapture, their eyes hungry and wanting.

I could fix that.

I took a running leap into the water, anxious to escape their stares, landing with a big splash. Stunned laughter hit my ears when I resurfaced, bodies landing all around me and whoops ringing out in the silence. I was grateful that the lake lay in the safety of the camp because they were noisy as shit, but I was wary about the others hearing us and deciding to join. It would be just my luck that the camp would see me in just these little scraps of fabric.

It felt beyond freeing to be in the water like this, hardly anyone around, no anxious vigilance for the undead, or awkward balancing as I tried to soap my hair up. It was the first time I was doing something just to *enjoy* it and not to survive.

Caelan popped up next to me, warm hands gripping my cold arms under the water. His eyes shone a bright cobalt color from where he was standing in direct contact with the moonlight. Whatever his plan had been, he'd seemed to have frozen once he was touching me. I could see his breath in the brisk night air, intertwining with mine between us. Our lips were wet, and inches apart, when Merikh surfaced, flinging water from his curls onto both of us.

"Baby," Caelan said roughly, shaking off his previous stillness. A mischievous grin formed before he dunked me without warning. I rose with a sputter, knocking his hand off me and spraying him with water. He smirked, splashing me back. Grey came to my rescue and put him in a headlock, trying to dunk him while he fought back, flipping him through the water. Nix laughed as he watched them, no sign of the earlier strain on his face.

Grateful that Grey had distracted him, I sank below the surface, using my hands to keep myself submerged. I liked the quiet of the water and the way it muffled sounds. I could almost pretend that no one existed but me. No zombies, no one keeping me prisoner, no dead father. Just me. The fear of what lay beneath my feet didn't deter me from soaking in the solitude of the depths. I could scream as loud as I wanted when I was submerged like this, no fear that someone would come running, dead or alive.

I was floating absently until a hand wrenched at my arm, pulling me from the water.

"What the fuck," Merikh roared as he shook me. Water flew from my face as I emerged, sputtering and coughing. My lungs burned, a steady ache. I hadn't realized just how long I'd been without air.

"What?" I rasped, gasping for breath.

"You were under for like, an entire minute," Grey informed me with troubled eyes.

They were worried about me.

"I was thinking," I said defensively.

Merikh shook me once more. "We didn't know what happened, you just disappeared. Don't do that again."

I hid a scornful smile, brushing his hands off my arms so that I could tread water on my own.

"It isn't amusing," Grey said with a frown. He exited the lake swiftly, leaving me gaping after him and Caelan patting my shoulder consolingly.

"He'll be fine," Caelan assured me, so different from Merikh's controlled angry panic moments before.

I didn't have the heart to try to insist I didn't care either way.

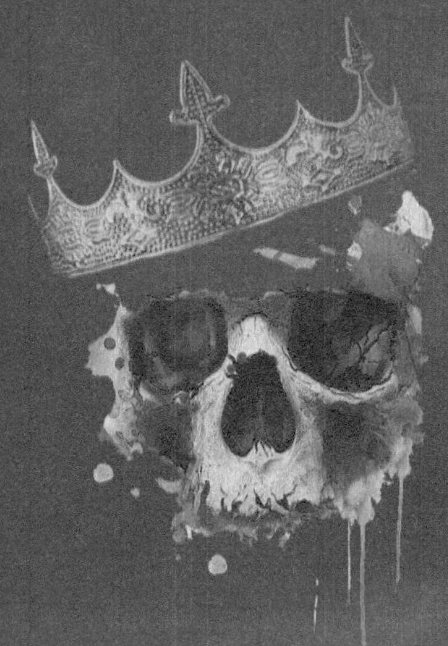

CHAPTER 6

I woke alone the next day, glad that no one was around. Last night was so strange, it felt like a fever dream. I only knew it was real from the scent of the lake water on my skin and the stiffness to my hair. I gathered breakfast without being asked, pocketing my sandwich and carrying the rest on plates. Waving hello to Naia and Nerese when I passed them on one of the pathways, I walked back to the cabin slowly, dreading seeing everyone.

But when I walked through the door, only Merikh sat at the table.

"Sit," he commanded.

Control freak. I huffed, glancing around to see where the others might be. Just then, Nix wandered out from the bathroom, rubbing his eyes and running a hand down his abdomen in an absent scratching motion. My cheeks heated at the sight, my body reacting to his exposed skin.

Merikh smirked like he could sense my attraction, and who knew, he probably could.

"Morning," Nix rasped, joining us at the table. His dark hair was messier than usual, looking as if he'd run his fingers through it repeatedly.

"You will be joining me today, River," Merikh stated plainly. His eyes were shadowed, like he'd barely slept.

"Fine."

His mouth turned down, but he ignored my easy response and made conversation with Nix, eating the food that I had brought him. I ate beside him in silence.

Grey and Caelan never showed up, and I found myself wondering if Grey was alright after last night. I didn't want to be concerned; I wanted to write him off, but something about the pain in his eyes last night was drawing me in. I realized that I didn't know *anything* about these four. Did they grow up around here? Where did they live before? And Grey, how did he come to live here? Was his family here with him? My mind raced with questions that I wanted answers to without having to ask in the first place.

"Come," Merikh ordered as we left the cabin. I gritted my teeth against the command but followed along anyway. Did he have to turn *everything* into a demand? Honestly, I was starting to think he just did it to irritate me.

He took me to an area of the camp I hadn't visited yet, an open clearing beside the meal tent and behind the fire that seemed to be constantly burning in the center of the camp. Already, people were gathered, as if they knew that something important was going to happen.

Violence hung heavy in the air, twisting my stomach.

Merikh came to a stop in front of everyone, tall and foreboding; all crossed arms and disdain, his full mouth turned down into a scowl. He stared down at the group until the voices quieted and finally fell silent.

His voice boomed across the space. "Colby Hartford, step forward."

Several women fixed admiring glances on the way his muscles bulged when he crossed his arms, and how his curls shifted with the breeze. I couldn't blame them. Women were particularly vulnerable and lived with the constant knowledge that we had the option to trade our bodies for protection and safety if we became desperate enough. The days of high, or even mediocre standards had long passed. I was grateful that I had my father for protection. It was disgusting, but the men that stumbled on our territory did no more than look, acknowledging his claim. Paternal or not, I was in his care, his charge, and they seemed to acknowledge that in a way they wouldn't listen to *me* if I'd been the one to tell them no. To have a man, handsome and unattached, in a position of power? It was the ultimate shield against the outside world, and was the only thing giving me sympathy for Anna, despite her constant bitterness.

Voices murmured as someone steadily moved through the crowd, making their way to the front. The man who stepped forward had pasty skin that told me he spent most of his days indoors. His eyes were shifty and dark and his hair was cut short, an unremarkable greasy brown.

"Yes?" he asked, holding eye contact with Merikh. I almost winced at the challenge in the man's eyes. Didn't he realize that getting up in the face of the person offering you shelter was a bad idea?

Pot meet kettle.

A few eyes darted to me curiously as I stood there, side by side with their fearless leader but not contributing a thing. I shifted from foot to foot, determined not to slide an inch to the left and hide behind Merikh, refusing to look like a docile lamb that followed him around camp and shied away from attention.

When Merikh spoke, people gasped and murmurs broke out. "You are exiled from camp. Pack your things and be gone by sundown."

The man sputtered, his face flushing a purplish-red color while I turned disbelieving eyes onto Merikh. "What the fuck?" I hissed. "Is this like some weird, freaky sacrifice thing? You can't just send people out into the wild at random!"

He looked at me vacantly, with a will of steel.

"Oh, now you're not even gonna say anything? Is this some kind of threat? You brought me here to threaten me? That man has barely seen the daylight. He'll never survive out there! He didn't even get a trial. If you're short on food or something, just send me back out!" I exclaimed, my stomach churning oddly at the thought.

"Hey," Colby growled, glaring daggers at me. I took a step back at the animosity on his face, then rolled my shoulders back and met his glare with my own. It would do no good to cower in front of him while I was on display like I was. I wanted to be my own person? Well, this is what that entailed. "I don't need your help, uppity bitch," he grunted as he spat right at my feet.

I took a deep breath in. Grey had just fucking given me these shoes!

He marched toward Merikh, winding up and throwing a punch in his direction. I gasped, taken aback by the sudden display of violence.

A slow smirk spread across Merikh's face.

He dodged the punch fluidly, striking out and catching Colby in the jaw. Colby hissed in pain, clutching his face and stumbling back. Merikh's eyes were no longer heated, they had cooled to glaciers, as though the violence brought out some archaic monster in him. His body was still, yet coiled to strike again. He held himself like some immovable object, like he did this every day. He didn't even shake out his knuckles or wince as I would have.

People were watching me avidly to see what I would do next. Did we not just watch the same fight? Clearly, he wasn't listening to my words, so what did they think I was gonna do next, hit him? I snorted, getting a few odd looks.

"That's all. You're free to go," Merikh commanded, and lo-and-behold, they actually dispersed. Who the hell was this guy?

"Let's go," he murmured to me, tugging my arm and pulling me away from Colby, whose face was now flushed a deep, angry purple.

I pulled us to a stop a little farther down the path, then pressed the back of my hand to his forehead. He reared back, looking at me oddly.

"No temperature," I declared.

"Why... Why would I have a temperature, River?" He was full of exasperation, and I was soaking it up.

"'Cause, you didn't order me to come with you. I mean, sure you grabbed my arm, but no commands involved. You getting sick, big boy?"

"Fuck off," he muttered, rubbing the area between his eyebrows.

"Oh, okay, now that we have that settled, maybe we can talk about *how evil you are*," I hissed. I wasn't gonna lie; his easy capability at disposing of a threat was attractive, but the reason for the whole altercation in the first place? Not cool.

He just rolled his eyes–*rolled his fucking eyes!*–before marching ahead to the cabin. He burst through the door, exposing a grappling Grey and Caelan, while Nix sat nearby and watched, an amused smile on his face.

I was partially standing behind Merikh, my red face hidden from view. My blood boiled at the audacity these men had. How dare they throw people out as if it was no big deal? Like they had no true idea of what a death sentence the outside was? That man would never survive. I itched to smack some sense into them. Though a resonating punch thrown by Grey quelled some of my anger. His blonde hair fell in his eyes as he wrestled with Caelan, his body covered in sweat and muscles flexing as he moved fluidly.

"Close your mouth before you start to drool," Merikh commented with a smug smirk.

I was mortified to find that my jaw had actually dropped, so I quickly snapped it shut and fixed a scowl on my features instead. His low, responding laugh warmed my insides.

"All good?" Nix asked us.

I scowled harder, throwing myself into the nearest chair and refusing to look at them. Merikh walked over to a now distracted Caelan and Grey and began muttering under his breath. Good, I didn't want to know anyway. The less entrenched I was in their business, the easier I could sneak away.

They broke apart after a minute, taking seats on the couches

"Nix, you'll be escorting Colby out."

Nix nodded solemnly. I made sure to shove all my disgust into the look I leveled at him. He frowned when he noticed, something that looked a lot like hurt flashing across his face before a coldness settled over his features. He fiddled with his bracelet, shifting his attention over to Merikh. Grey squinted at me before looking away, which was odd. Caelan just cracked his tattooed knuckles, smiling wickedly at Merikh's wince.

"Are you sure I can't do it?" Caelan asked.

"I'm sure. Now, the matter of River speaking up for Colby in front of everyone and publicly questioning my orders."

I laughed, hiding the frisson of fear that snaked down my spine. What would he do to me?

"Don't worry, princess. No one here wants to sleep with you."

"Speak for yourself," Caelan muttered.

I glared at Merikh, ignoring Caelan's low laugh and Grey's snort. "Good, I wouldn't sleep with you if you were the last man on earth."

"Glad we agree," Merikh said calmly. It irked me how unbothered he was when I was spitting mad. "River, you will be sleeping on the floor in one of our rooms. No more couch for you, princess. I'd put you on the floor in here, but it's not fair to everyone else that they need to keep sacrificing their comfort by spending all night in a chair just to make sure you don't run off."

I wasn't even going to begin picking apart the issues with that statement. The blood drained from my face, and I curled my hands into fists. Being grateful for sleeping on the couch was one thing. For someone who mostly slept on concrete floors and roofs with torn blankets and musty sleeping bags, I could admit that although I was there against my will, I appreciated the couch. But the floor? In their bedrooms? Next to... them? In the quiet darkness, with no crackling fire to break the tension?

"Absolutely not," I declared, crossing my arms.

Caelan's eyes darkened as he leaned forward. "You will, baby. Take your punishment like a good little River," he murmured, the corner of his mouth lifting slightly.

Nix looked uncomfortable, shifting in his seat slightly while avoiding my eyes. Merikh was expressionless in the face of my defiance.

"Every night, you will sleep on my floor, or you will not eat, and you won't leave the cabin at all."

"I refuse."

"Then starve."

Caelan cut in, "I want her too. You don't get her all to yourself."

I jumped to my feet. "No one gets me!"

Merikh ignored me, turning to Caelan with a calculating glint in his eye. "Fine, we'll take turns. She can sleep on each of our floors."

Grey punched Caelan on the shoulder. "Better clean up your tissues and socks," he commented with a leer. Caelan burst out laughing, leaning forward in his chair.

"I'm sold," he murmured, still ignoring me.

I wanted to refuse to eat, to accept the punishment and make a stand somehow, but years of almost starvation kept me silent.

"I'm not a–not some *thing*," I insisted, my voice cracking. It was all too much.

I thought I saw a flash of sympathy in Merikh's eyes, but I knew better. "As you're very aware, you are not an average member of the community," Merikh rumbled, "and that was not a situation open to discourse. You made a scene of questioning my orders, and short of coming up with some elaborate public punishment, this will teach you to keep your mouth closed on matters that don't concern you."

I was seething. My nails left indents on the skin of my palms from clenching my fists so tight, and I had to fight to keep my expression as even as his.

"She'll sleep in my room tonight," Grey said quietly. His eyes narrowed, as though he was expecting to have to fight to back up his declaration.

The others just nodded, somehow knowing what he needed right then, allowing him to stake his claim.

I considered arguing more, making a big deal of it, but remembered Grey's crestfallen face the other night and decided against it. I would sleep quietly on his floor, and hopefully, would be able to sneak out of the camp before completing the rotation. The others I could stomach, but being in Merikh's personal space? Absolutely not.

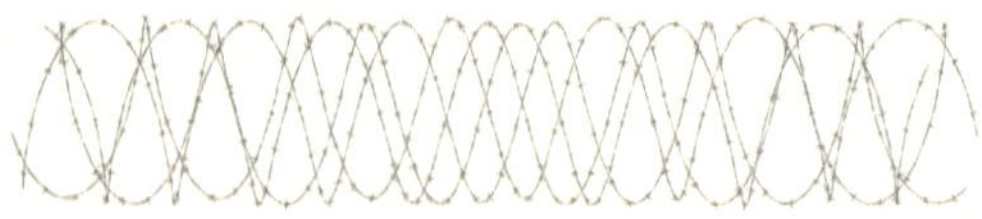

Hours later, I left the others behind to use the bathroom, changing into a pair of pink sleep shorts that Caelan had found and an old t-shirt of theirs, I didn't know whose.

I stared at myself in the mirror, hands clutching the edge of the countertop. My father didn't raise me to be weak. He raised me to fight, to survive, to be independent. I felt ashamed that I had allowed myself to grow complacent in this place, sleeping on their floors like a dog. It disgusted me. I used that anger, compiled it deep in my heart where I could draw from it next time I felt concerned over Grey's quietness, or Nix's brooding. I'd use it to build my walls, to keep these men out. I had to keep telling myself it was only the close proximity making me feel things. Of course I'd be a little starved for company after years spent with only my dad, not to mention the luxuries; punishments aside.

A knock sounded at the door, gentle and hesitant.

"River... I'll be in my room."

I nodded at myself resolutely in the mirror, bowing my head as I clutched the counter and took a deep breath in. I exhaled slowly before opening the bathroom door and marching to Grey's room. It was at the back corner of the cabin, facing the forest behind us. The sun had fallen, allowing the moonlight to shine through the large window against the far-left wall at the end of the hallway. I shook my head. How privileged to be able to have exposed glass windows in the first place. Everywhere on the outside was reinforced with wood and metal sheets, rusty nails scattered all over the place.

I knocked softly before twisting the knob and entering slowly, looking my fill of his private sanctuary.

I hadn't been in any of the guy's rooms besides Caelan's, and that was just to grab a shirt of his. It was sparse and clean. I wasn't sure what I was expecting, but it wasn't this. I saw no clutter, no trinkets, no signs that a man who had the luxury of living in a camp and collecting items lived there. He lived like a nomad. He lived like me.

"I put a pillow on the ground for you," he stated gruffly. He lay flat on his back, staring up at the ceiling. I could only see his silhouette in the darkness, the hint of navy covers and a wooden floor. One dresser stood to my left, a light oak color. I walked silently over to the side of the bed, looking down at the blue pillow with disdain. I lowered myself quickly, swallowing down the disgust and shame I felt by being forced to sleep on the floor when there was a perfectly good couch in the other room.

It was practically pitch-black, and the silence felt anticipatory, like I was holding my breath. I could hear Grey's deep breaths from next to me, and I felt a certain freedom in the darkness. We were so close, almost touching, with only the height of the bed separating us. I laid on my back, chest rising and falling slowly as I tried to keep my breathing slow and even, realizing after a minute that I was subconsciously matching his. I briefly considered trying to seduce my way into his bed, but quickly decided against it, not wanting to fight off his advances if he made any.

"You're quiet," he rumbled, breaking the fragile silence of the room.

"Thought you'd like that," I countered. I fixed my eyes on the shaft of moonlight streaming through the gap in his curtains, the way it carved a path through his empty room.

After several moments of silence, I spoke again, my voice low. "What's it like to be safe and sound, sleeping on a real bed every night?" I was truly asking out of curiosity. I didn't begrudge him for his safety, or his community. If I allowed myself to think about it, I could admit that a large part of me had always ached for the same. When I realized my father never intended to settle somewhere permanently, how could I express my desire to? He would have done anything to make me happy, including living somewhere that, while safe, would have made him miserable.

Grey took his time to answer, and when he did, his voice was hoarse. "It wasn't always like this, River."

Shit, he never called me River. It was always teasing nicknames and endearments.

"What was it like before?" I asked hesitantly, fearing the answer.

"You don't want to know."

"Try me."

Silence. It was quiet for so long that I thought he'd gone to sleep. His slow breaths evened out and there were no movements from the bed. And then... "I had a family once. I'm lucky to count the triplets as my brothers now, but I had a mother and father, a little sister."

I knew it wasn't good; stories of the after were never good. We were born into a generation filled with turmoil. Just young enough that our parents were still acclimating to the apocalypse and trying to keep us safe and alive, all while trying to live themselves.

"Why were you upset last night, Grey?" I knew in my heart of hearts that they were linked somehow.

A sharp inhale, his body shifting on the mattress.

"It's a long story," he warned. "It's sad, and fucked up."

"I think I can handle it," I whispered.

I watched dust motes highlighted by the moonlight float in the air as I waited.

The story spilled out of him like he'd been holding it in for years, his voice low and rough.

"I was sixteen when my mom and dad died. We were sleeping in a warehouse, getting our first decent shut-eye in days. We were tired, drained, and exhausted from trying to find a place safe enough to call our home. We had been searching for months after our last place was overrun, constantly on the move. I never said anything, but I could see the growing shadows under my father's eyes, ashamed that he wasn't able to provide us with enough food and water or a decent night's sleep."

I bit my lip against a sympathetic noise, turning onto my side so I was facing the bed frame.

"My sister cried herself to sleep that night, like so many nights before. She was quiet about it too, discreet, but my mother could still tell. She'd hum lullabies until my sister fell asleep, and I always acted like I didn't care if she sang or not, but I barely slept when she didn't." His voice was ragged, filled with so much pain that it made my heart ache. It never got easier to hear people's tragedies, even though most everyone had one.

I heard a low rhythmic noise and opened my eyes to see the outline of his hand tapping anxiously against the side of the bed in a repetitive motion.

"They came for us that night." He paused for so long that I thought he wasn't going to continue. "It had been raining, the water hitting the corrugated metal roof and drowning out the sounds of everything around us so that we didn't hear them outside."

"Zombies?" I whispered.

"Worse," he choked out. "A few men had apparently spotted us a couple of days earlier, and they waited until they were back with the rest of their group to hunt us down. They'd seen–" His voice trembled.

"It's okay," I murmured soothingly. "You don't have to finish."

"No," he said bitterly. "Better you know the whole story. I'm not some naïve, spoiled asshole, River. I'm not sitting high in my castle without any idea of what it's like out there." I felt a fresh rush of shame that I'd made him feel like he needed to tell me his life story just to clear up my misconceptions, like my opinion actually *mattered* enough to him that he felt like he needed to prove himself to me.

Grey took a deep breath. "They'd seen my mom and sister bathing in the river and decided they wanted a piece." His voice was tight with fury, yet still thickened with sadness. I focused on the rhythmic tapping of his hand against the wooden frame. "They came through the large warehouse doors that we'd tried to secure with rusty chains and bashed my father in the head after he stabbed one of them. They tied his arms behind his back with rope. I had a small hunting knife at the time, and I was swinging wildly at anyone I could reach before I was overwhelmed as well." His next words were so, so bitter. "Taking down the undead is much different from trying to kill real, live grown men. I was only sixteen, outnumbered, and too skinny and malnourished to do shit. My sister was screaming and crying while my mother just stood there. She knew what they came for, even if I did not."

I couldn't take it anymore. He seemed so *desolate*. His voice was ragged and I could hardly stand to hear the pain in it. I reached out slowly, hesitantly, stroking his scarred knuckles with one finger.

He exhaled a shaky breath. "They..." His voice cracked in the middle of his sentence, and suddenly my entire hand was clutching his, knuckles turning white from his desperate grip.

"They discussed the price they would get for my sister, raising their voices so that we could still hear them over my dad's screams. They made sure to say it all in front of him before throwing him outside. I saw a zombie tear into him right before they shut the warehouse doors one last time, my last memory of him being on his knees, his face a mess of tears and blood. He looked so goddamn defeated–" Grey's voice broke. "Like he'd failed us somehow."

I choked on a sob, realizing that I'd been steadily crying throughout his whole story. I thought myself tough, impenetrable after all the tragic stories I'd heard, but his pain brought me to my knees. I loosened my grip, flexing my hand until he allowed me to slide mine from his so I could stand. I rounded the bed slowly, giving him a chance to say something, to put me back in my place, to cut me down for daring to get close to him, but he kept silent.

I knelt on the edge of the bed, the creaking noise echoing through the room as I laid down slowly. I was careful not to touch him, cognizant of the fact that he probably wanted space. We were inches apart now, both on our backs and watching the shadows on the ceiling. I kept my eyes straight ahead, ignoring the hitch in his breath, the scents of salt and sorrow filling the air. My breathing evened out as I lay there silently, rubbing my nose on my sleeve as I sniffled and tears leaking from my eyes and running down the sides of my face. I tentatively stretched one hand out into the center of the bed, letting it rest with my palm facing up.

"Yelling and crying did nothing. No matter how much I thrashed and fought, I couldn't get out of the rope," he continued brokenly, "until they slit my mother's throat in front of me. No loose ends, they told me. She wouldn't fetch a price, was too old and–" His voice stuttered.

His hand made its way into mine, clutching it tightly for support. His skin was warm and calloused, scarred and rough and oh so strong. I risked a glance in his direction and found that the moonlight had highlighted the tears on his face, deepening the long silvery scar that stretched its way across his skin.

"I broke then, dove for the knife they'd tossed aside after using it to kill my mom and cut through my binds. I murdered the man nearest me with one stab to the eye. I took his machete and swung it toward the man holding my sister, knocking him down and slitting his throat, then leaving him to bleed out. My sister, she was just... covered in their blood."

I winced at the graphic details, knowing that to describe it so vividly, it must've been eating him up inside. "What was her name?" I asked quietly, trying to make his sister into a living, breathing person that had died and not a story, trying to honor her in the only way I could. I stroked my thumb across his knuckles.

His hand flexed in mine. "Hailey."

"Pretty," I whispered. "Will you tell me about her?"

"She had brown hair like you–but darker–and no one knew where she got it from as both our parents were blonde like me. She was only a few years younger than me, and she laughed at *everything*. She always stopped to appreciate the small things and she had this weird habit of finding flowers and carrying them around until they wilted, and then she'd just tuck them away in her little notebook."

He tugged me softly, rolling me across the bed and into the shelter of his body. My leg was slung over his, my arm braced on his chest. His arm came around to circle my back slowly, giving me time to pull away if I wanted. I thought about it, but the weight of his heavy arm against me, his warm solid body cushioning mine, was irresistible to me. I felt like I had been alone much longer than I had, and I'd certainly never had anyone hold me in such a way. I sighed, snuggling into his side and burrowing my head into his chest. He smelled like salt and citrus. His arm tightened around me, clutching me closer to him.

"What happened next?" I prompted, my voice shaking. "Is that how you got this?" I traced the scar from his temple to his jaw, noting the bumpy texture under my fingertips.

He cleared his throat, his hand flexing where it lay near my hip. "Yes, that's how I got my scar. I killed the few zombies that were lingering outside and then pulled my mother's body out with Hailey's help. Then I buried my parents–what was left of them–by digging a deep trench in the pouring rain with a shovel that I found in a nearby shed while Hailey watched."

It was somehow worse knowing that it wasn't over yet. Knowing that although they both escaped that situation, somewhere further along his journey, his sister became another one of the many casualties of this hellscape and my heart broke for him. Losing both parents in one night, and in such a brutal manner. My tears soaked his shirt as I wept quietly.

"Don't cry for me, sweetheart," he whispered. His hand stroked the side of my face that he could reach, wiping away the wet trails on my cheek.

"Finish your story," I murmured desperately, eager to get his pain into the moonlight and out from his soul where it festered. My stomach churned as I waited for him to continue.

"Hailey grew despondent. I had to tow her along everywhere we went. I killed the zombies, found us food and water, continued our search for shelter. Eventually, she stopped crying, and hopelessness consumed her. She had been so soft and kind before, and my parents had sheltered her as best they could. I tried my hardest, but I was so bitter and tired. One day, I left to gather food from a nearby grocery store and it took longer than usual due to the number of undead gathered around the storefront. I returned to find Hailey's body, foam spilling out of her mouth and an empty bottle of pills that she must have stolen from the last store we went to. And to think, we'd been so excited to stumble on a pharmacy that hadn't been cleared out. Apparently, we weren't excited for the same reasons."

I clutched him tighter, as if I could somehow hold in all his broken pieces, and he held me closer in turn. He was whispering now. "She left me a note. She had planned it, the pills, the paper, the pen. She'd been waiting. She told me that she was so sorry she couldn't do it anymore. That this life was too much for her, and that she was ready to see our parents and be at peace."

I felt his body shake slightly beneath mine and reached a hand up, searching by touch to wipe at the wetness on his cheeks. "What did you do?"

"We never left the immediate area where my parents died, like we had some kind of tether to their graves, so I buried her next to them. The sun was shining that day and it felt wrong, like an affront to her burial. I felt that the sky should weep like I did, as it did for my parents. Now I'm grateful that at least someone was smiling down on her. She deserved better." He sighed, an exhale I felt to the very core of my being. "I wanted to join her. I laid by their grave for days, killing any zombies that came near, and sleeping near the mounds like a puppy. I thought maybe if I didn't eat, or drink, I would just fade away and join them."

I cried harder, for the boy that wanted nothing more than to be with his family, who had lost everyone close to him. He turned then, enveloping my body with his, allowing me to sink into his chest and resting his head atop mine. We clutched each other tightly, as if the other person would be ripped away if we let go.

"Days later. I got up, stomach growling, vision doubled. I couldn't die. I didn't have it in me. Something was pushing me to live, to survive. So I scavenged and I fought and I persevered. I was a nomad for a long time. An entire year passed before I stumbled on Caelan while he was scavenging. He brought me back to everyone. Practically adopted me into the fold."

He drew his hand back from my hip to trace small circles on my back.

"I blamed myself for a long time. If only I had done something sooner, found the pills earlier, recognized the signs of her depression, made her life even easier. The triplets helped me realize that there was nothing more I could have done to fix things. Maybe, just maybe, if we had found this place, she would have made it, but she didn't, and I'll live with that for the rest of my life. Helping out at this place gave me an outlet for the pain inside me, the violence."

I held him tighter, memories of my dad flashing through my mind and compounding my sadness. God, I missed him so fucking much.

"I always thought I was so lucky that my family had survived when others didn't. I'd dreamed of us making it out of the city and onto a little homestead somewhere, out in the wilds where there were fewer zombies. It was foolish of me," he admitted, squeezing my arm gently. "And I lost them anyway, not even to the zombies we spent so many years defending ourselves against, but to human fucking cruelty."

My body shuddered as I tried to stop myself from crying. I was supposed to be comforting him, how could I do that if I was even more affected than he was?

He kissed the top of my head. "No more tears, sweetheart."

I sniffled, burrowing my face into his warm chest. I mourned for the boy who became a man that day, grieved his losses like they were my own. I knew what it was like to lose your only family. He was so much more than I'd given him credit for; he'd suffered so much pain and loss, but I had treated him like some privileged, pampered boy who'd never suffered a thing in his life. I was ashamed. No wonder he'd panicked when I was under the water for so long the other day. Did he think that

I hated being here so much I would take the same escape as his sister did?

"You don't have to worry about me," I murmured. It hurt. Hearing someone's pain always hurt, but I tucked his story along with all the others I carried with me, nonetheless. A living, breathing tribute to the people who didn't make it.

My eyes were heavy and stinging, so I squeezed them shut to ease the strain.

"Sleep," he whispered, and as my tears continued to drip onto his shirt, he began to hum softly.

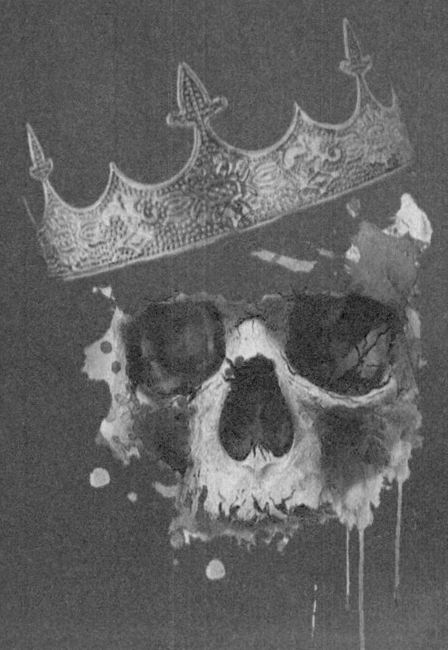

CHAPTER 7

When I woke, Grey was gone. My legs were tangled in his navy sheets and the sun shone directly onto my face, assailing my swollen eyes. I blinked blearily, turning on my side to watch the trees just outside the window bend in the breeze. I'd spent almost my entire life with nature–many nights were spent sleeping in clearings and knolls and the odd tree–but never quite getting to *see* it. I was always on guard, listening for groans and the patter of feet or the chatter of voices. Here I had the luxury of relaxing. Of *enjoying*. Circumstances aside, I supposed I was at least grateful for the break before I had to get back out there.

I stretched languidly, rising from the bed and padding over to the pillow on the floor. I beat it several times, making sure to rid it of any dust before placing it back on the bed. My cheeks were tight from the tears I had shed last night, eyes puffy and irritated. Though I felt much better, like I'd had an emotional reset. Why was crying so goddamn cathartic? Ugh, emotions were going to be the death of me. I hadn't cried like that since my dad died and since that wasn't all that long ago... my track record was suffering.

"River," Grey blurted as he swung the door open to find me standing and not in bed where he'd left me. His face softened as he took in my rumpled sleep clothes, tangled hair, and puffy face. "Breakfast. Nix and I grabbed our food this morning." He winked. "Don't tell Merikh."

I gave him a conspiratorial smile. His blonde hair was half up, half down today, several shorter strands having escaped and worked their way into his face. I decided to test our tentative new relationship, striding toward him until we stood inches apart and tucking the loose hair behind his ear, gently stroking his cheek as I did so. He shivered slightly, eyes shuttering and head tilting into my touch.

I withheld a smile. *Would it be so bad if I didn't hate him?* No, I decided. It wouldn't. I couldn't help viewing him differently after last night. I was still angry with him, but *he* hadn't taken me from the city, instated a rigid set of rules, and prevented me from leaving. He'd even shared his bed with me. Even if he was complicit in keeping me here... It wouldn't be the end of the world if I allowed myself an ally. If I clung too tightly to my hatred and anger, I would become someone I didn't recognize.

I met his deep brown eyes, admiring how they turned amber in the bright sunlight and smiled widely. "Thank you, Grey." I hoped he knew just what I was thanking him for. The warm bed, holding me all night, his confessions.

He smiled back, slightly puzzled, but clearly pleased by my change in attitude. I took a few steps out the door... then hesitated, darting back to slide my arms around his waist. His body jolted from the impact, a low chuckle rumbling through his chest where it was pressed against my head. His arms found their way to my back, holding me just as tight.

"I meant it," I whispered. "Thank you." I impulsively rose onto my tiptoes, pressing a quick kiss to his cheek before making a quick retreat to the bathroom as I'd first intended.

When I finished splashing my face with cold water, because *holy shit* I looked like a mess–I couldn't believe he'd let me anywhere near his face–I walked out to the kitchen and took a seat at the table beside Nix and across from Grey and Caelan.

"Where's Merikh this morning?" I queried between bites of bacon.

"Filling the guard shift at the wall."

I frowned, remembering that since John died, they were a person short. I brushed off the flash of guilt, spearing my eggs angrily and stirring the food on my plate.

"You'll accompany me to the garden," Grey commented. "Then after that, I've been tasked with disposing of a group of zombies that have been hovering too close to the outer barrier."

"I thought you had the gate? And what does it matter if they're out past the car barrier anyway?"

"If they make it through the car barrier, we have further precautions like ditches and spikes and even small explosives. We try to avoid shooting them, even though it would take them out at a distance because we don't want to attract more and waste ammo. The goal is to avoid being overrun or overwhelmed. If we have undead constantly testing the barriers, it could compromise their structural integrity over time. So we usually give groups a few days to wander away on their own, but sometimes they're scarily persistent, attracted to the noises and smells from inside the camp, and we need to take care of them ourselves. The people who leave for scouting missions shouldn't have to deal with it."

"That makes sense. I want to come," I declared. I could use a good outlet for my anger. What better than killing zombies? Sure it was gross and a little morbid, but excellent exercise. Plus, it would ensure that I didn't become complacent.

Caelan smirked. "Our bloodthirsty girl." He laughed. "Pay up."

I frowned, looking from Caelan to Grey and Nix as I tried to figure out what the hell he was talking about.

"Caelan bet Grey that you would ask to go along," Nix explained.

"What did you bet?" I asked curiously.

Caelan's smile was roguish. "I bet our dear darling Grey I could have his next turn for when you sleep in his room."

I rolled my eyes, finishing my breakfast and standing hastily. "So we can go now?" I was practically vibrating with excitement, ready to see Halli again. I wanted to know more about the camp and... I wouldn't hate having a friend.

It was rare, but sometimes when I was younger I would meet someone around my age when their group traveled through, trading secrets and stories during the little time we had, but they always left.

Always.

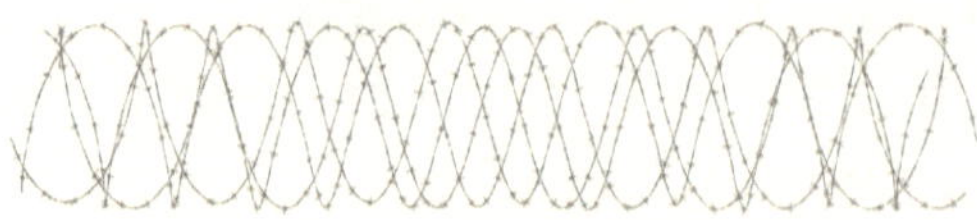

The path to the garden snaked around the building where the older children received their lessons. Apparently, their curriculum was a mixture of old-world information and life skills. They taught them things like gardening, scavenging, prepping food, mending clothes, self-defense, reading, writing, history, and math. I was a little envious. My dad had taught me most of those things; he'd done the best he could, but what would it have been like to receive such a well-rounded education from the safety of a camp? All the survival things I'd learned had been largely from experience and necessity. Not pleasant.

I slipped my shoes off, holding them by their shoelaces as I tiptoed down the path. It was lined with purple, yellow, and red flowers that made the air smell sweet, and the soil felt cool and soothing beneath my bare feet. The sounds of the voices coming from the school building faded as I made my way farther down the path and toward the sprawling gardens.

Grey loped behind me, stopping every so often to speak with someone. He took his role in the camp seriously, addressing issues and solving problems wherever he went. For all that he was bloodthirsty, he was a good mediator. Unlike Caelan, who seemed to have no such patience whatsoever for problem-solving and dealing with people.

Long stretches of the garden were fenced in by a mesh netting, only coming up to about my knees. I ran my finger along the cucumber vines snaking across either side of me, admiring the extensive herb section, along with a few other patches of vegetables that were only just sprouting.

I turned to speak with Grey when I found Halli kneeling in an empty section of dirt near the right side of the space, hands buried in the soil and her long pink skirt trailing behind her.

I walked up shyly, unsure of how to approach. What if I was bothering her?

"River," she greeted me warmly, tucking a stray curl behind her ear.

I grinned, leaving Grey to his conversation with one of the camp cooks and lowering myself down beside to her. "What are you doing?"

"I'm trying to plant this section of squash. We're low on seeds, so I'm really hoping that these take. Usually, with a lot of our vegetables, we can replant the fresh seeds to grow more, but after the blight destroyed our last batch of crops, we only have the few that survived along with what we've scavenged, and what we've dried."

"Well, how many did you dry?"

She winced. "There was a leak in the area where we stored a lot of the dried seeds, and the moisture caused most of them to rot. I'm nervous that anything we find now in stores is going to be old and most likely decayed. Finding them still preserved would take a miracle and a dark, dry storage area."

How would they feed everyone if they weren't producing enough fresh food to supplement meals? Their camp was in the middle of nowhere, and every building nearby was surely picked clean of food and supplies. I absently played with the hem of my shirt. "I remember Anna mentioning that you were low on food, but Merikh said not to worry."

Halli rolled her eyes dramatically. "Don't get me started on Anna." Her eyes flicked to Grey, who stood nearby speaking with the dark-haired man that was usually watching the large fire behind the cooking tent.

"You don't like her?" I asked with a laugh.

"I'm not sure anyone does," she retorted. "Least of all anyone she considers 'competition' for literally any man around her age." Halli glanced once more at Grey, making sure he was occupied, before leaning in to whisper. "You mentioned wanting to know more about how to get out of this place?"

Relief filled me at the fact that I wouldn't have to awkwardly switch topics from gardening to security measures, and a little sadness too. I could so easily see us being friends.

"They forced me to come here," I whispered back fervently, feeling the hot burn of shame in my chest. How would it look to her, someone who's also experienced life outside these walls, wanting to leave the safety of camp voluntarily? "I was just fine on my own, and I liked being independent."

She grimaced, brushing the dirt from her hands before clasping mine. Her deep brown eyes, so dark they were almost black, scanned my face like she was making sure of something before she nodded grimly. "I can't say I understand, and you'd better say goodbye before you leave, but alright. The main entrance has two guards at all times, and the perimeter is monitored daily by a group of ten people that take turns. There's also a person stationed at each of the four lookout points at each corner of the camp."

My face fell. "That's more security than I thought." Great for protection against raiders and outside threats, bad for me and my escape.

Her hesitation was telling. "We've... There's been a few issues. Recently." She worried her bottom lip, clearly debating whether or not to continue.

"Like what?" I urged.

She sighed, her words escaping in a rush. "We dealt with raiders in the past, people thinking that they could come in and take over. They only attacked us once, but we patrol often just in case. Obviously, there are a few weak spots, but for the most part, it's pretty covered. Although more recently... There's been a group hanging nearby, causing trouble. We found a body last month, a few feet away from one of our scavengers that had been missing for over a week," she whispered, checking again to ensure no one was listening and leaning in. "He wasn't too skinny, had a bag full of supplies, and looked like he'd been fairly clean before–well, before. There were no signs they'd been bitten by zombies, just plain old corpses with stab wounds, and they were each holding a bloodied knife. Considering we've had some noise disturbances in the past month that drew more zombies to the area, and a few of the traps had been sprung inside the barrier, Caelan decided to amp up security in case they're casing the place before making a move."

I frowned. "And everyone is just going about their day like there's nothing to be worried about?"

The guilty expression on her face instantly cleared up my confusion. "Only a few people know. Merikh and John didn't want to worry everyone, so they decided to keep it on a need-to-know basis. They only told me because I kept bothering them about sending out scavengers for more supplies and they wanted me to know why we're restricting the number of outside tasks."

"I see."

So I would have to sneak out in the middle of the night between the lookout points and away from the main gate, then bypass any perimeter guards. "There's two at night on the front gate as well? No other exits?"

"No other exits. We had another gate once, but it was compromised before I came and then sealed."

Worth checking out. Maybe I could convince the guys to give me perimeter duty. No, they would definitely know what I was up to. They were infuriating, yes, but not ignorant. I sighed, brushing off my pants and switching from a crouch to just planting myself in the dirt.

I didn't want her to think I was only talking to her for information, so I decided to change the topic. I had all the information I needed for now anyway. "So have you always been interested in gardening?"

She smiled, her entire face brightening. "Yeah, I found a book when I was little, with lots of pictures and instructions. I carried it everywhere with me, and I used to imagine all the things I would grow, but I never thought I would get a chance to try it." She sifted through the dirt, fingernails darkened by her digging. "When we arrived here the man who largely oversaw the garden was ready to pass it on to someone else, but no one was interested enough to take on the mantle, so I studied all the books he gave me and trained under him until he decided was ready to hand over the reins."

"Does he still like to help now and then?"

Her smile was soft, and sad. "He passed in his sleep last year, but he would come at least once a week up until that point just to help in some way. Said that there was something grounding about sticking your hands in soil and he wasn't giving it up anytime soon."

I was seconds away from offering to help when she said the words that sent me panicking.

"I heard you killed John," she commented casually. I stilled, my head flooding with noise. Who had told her? I was under the impression that no one knew I'd been involved.

She must have sensed my inner struggle because she rushed to clarify. "I overheard Merikh talking with Grey about it the other day. I don't think it's common knowledge, and you can trust me to keep my mouth shut. I didn't mean to listen in." She sounded sincerely apologetic, and it immediately soothed any worries I had that she'd brought it up to be malicious.

I nodded, torn between being grateful that she wasn't going to say anything and being frustrated that I wasn't able to move past that horrible man. The last thing I needed was a bunch of angry people harassing me for killing him. That was the way the world worked! People died every single day, so why did having his death on my conscious make me feel so uneasy?

I still felt the need to defend myself for some reason. I didn't want to keep this secret to myself anymore, maybe because telling someone else would absolve me of my misplaced guilt or because I wanted to feel validated that I'd done the right thing. "I might have stolen his food, but it was sitting out in the open, alone. You know what it's like out there, to be so desperate, so hungry, that you'd eat almost anything."

She clucked sympathetically, turning to give me her full attention. "That was all they said. That you were a thief, and you killed him because he was infected, but it was all your fault in the first place."

I took a deep breath in. "He was infected when he found me. I guess he'd gone back for his bag and found it missing, so he went looking, and on the way, he'd run into a zombie." Halli nodded, encouraging me to continue. "He..." A deep pit opened up in my stomach. "You know, the newly infected lose their mental capacities fairly quickly. His inhibitions were just... gone. He kept insisting I come back here with him in trade for... favors. When I refused, he tried to take them anyway. He kept coming at me, trying to touch me, and he was clearly turning by the second. I even offered to give him his things back, but he refused."

Halli's eyes grew wide and flew up over my head. My body froze as a deep voice sounded from behind me. "What did you just say?"

I squeezed my eyes shut, shoving down the rising feeling of dread in my stomach to turn my head slowly to face Grey. His expression was stormy, eyes no longer a warm brown but an icy dark color. I looked to Halli for support, but she just watched us carefully, her face frozen in an awkward grimace.

He clenched his fists tightly by his sides. "Why didn't you say anything?" he seethed.

"What does it matter? He was infected, so I did him a favor. You clearly made your decision on the facts you had at hand."

As Grey's face slowly drained of color, his scar turned a purplish gray. I winced, remembering our discussion last night. Of course this would hit him hard; he'd had firsthand experience with men like that. I suddenly knew with complete conviction that if he had known what John had attempted, he wouldn't have kept him in the camp, let alone punished me for his death, theft or not. The piece of me that deemed myself guilty for taking his supplies felt like I deserved that punishment, no matter the events that followed. My dad had raised me to be good, and kind, but he had also raised me to survive no matter the cost.

I shut my eyes for several beats, then opened them slowly. "Please don't tell them," I begged.

He shook his head, fists rapidly clenching and unclenching. "I can't just not tell them, River. They deserve to know. How could you–I can't–they wouldn't have insisted on bringing you back here!"

"And what if they accused me of lying? Besmirching the name of someone you all had known for years just to get off easy? Do you understand how much more of a target I would've become? I had no *proof*, Grey. Nothing. I stole his supplies, it was *my* fault he diverted from his path, *my* fault he was distracted enough to get bitten–which was a death sentence in and of itself–his actions once he found me aside."

I looked at Halli to find her head bent down as she studied the herbs. Her bright orange beaded earrings swayed with the breeze.

"They need to know," he said firmly, his face smoothing out on a sigh. "They deserve to know."

"Then I will tell them myself, just... give me time."

He hesitated for a long moment, observing my pout with a scowl. "Days," he muttered, rubbing the space between his brows. "Just a few days."

"Fine," I agreed stiffly. I stood shakily, brushing off the remaining dirt on my legs. "I'll see you later, Halli," I said softly, hoping I hadn't managed to alienate my only friend.

She gave me a kind smile. "Come back soon, okay? I mean it."

My returning smile was tremulous as I murmured my thanks, oddly relieved that she didn't hate me or all the drama I dropped into her lap.

Grey strode out of the garden, long legs eating up the distance to the front of the camp. "Wait for me!" I called out as I ran behind him to catch up.

How would this change things? I hadn't even thought it mattered, that it was reason enough that he was infected and a danger to myself and others. I didn't want to be seen as a victim, and as much as I wanted a get out of jail free card, I didn't want to be freed on a technicality. What did that say about me? Perhaps I was enjoying the safety of camp more than I would admit to myself. I couldn't help the thoughts rushing through my head. *If I had told them, would they have let me be? Would I have never found this place, with its hot running water, freshly cooked meals, and* safety?

"I can't believe you didn't tell me what happened," he finally confessed once I caught up to him. He ran a hand through his blonde hair, creating an unfairly handsome, mussed look.

"I didn't mean to. Besides, you know I ultimately did it because he was sick. Either way, I'm sorry." I spoke quietly, remembering his whispered confessions, the feel of his chest under my head.

His sigh was loud. "Don't be." He held my arm softly, pulling me into an awkward embrace. It was stiff at first, and it felt odd to be touching in the daylight, but I gave in, clutching him close. It was nice to hug him, to feel his warmth against me. I felt my pulse speed up as I nuzzled his chest where his shirt dipped low, the scent of his skin making me dizzy. He clutched me tighter, as if he knew where my mind was traveling, before pulling away to look at me. His eyes were no longer frozen, but back to their heated caramel color.

Our eye contact was broken by the sound of a high-pitched voice.

"Grey," Anna called out with a wicked smile creeping over her face. "I came to find you in the garden, but you looked like you were busy. I was just letting you know it's time to take care of the zombies."

Fuck, she didn't hear, did she? I wouldn't have even known if she'd been behind us, too lost in Grey to notice my surroundings. I expected Grey to walk over to her with a polite greeting, but instead, he rolled his eyes, just for me to see, before ignoring her. I stifled a grin, my mood lifting. Somehow he knew exactly what would cheer me up.

We walked past her all the way to the front of the camp, ignoring her petulant scowl as she followed to approach an older man with thick gray hair and light blue eyes. He smiled as he saw us, handing a machete to Grey.

"And you?" he asked me. I was puzzled at first, though as Grey hefted his machete around, I realized he was referring to weapons. A thrill rushed through me at the thought of having a way to protect myself once more.

"I'll take a bat," I said excitedly. I had no go-to weapon besides my dad's knife, and I wanted to see what it was like for Caelan to fight with one.

Anna snorted from her spot, slumped over the little check-in point. Her blonde hair shone under the sunlight, and her skin looked tanner than it had the other day.

I ignored her, accepting the weapon from the man and following Grey outside the gates, where I drew in a deep breath.

Freedom.

The ground was dusty and dry. Nothing like the rich soil of the forest that lay tucked inside the fence on the other side of the camp. It hadn't rained in a few days, which probably wasn't helping their garden.

"Stay close," he murmured.

I frowned at him before remembering that they had placed traps. I traipsed after him, bat slung over my shoulder, admiring the way the light hit his white shirt, illuminating the build underneath.

Grey turned around abruptly, catching my appraising stare with a smirk. He winked–really no one should look that good winking–but he did. "Like what you see, sweetheart?"

I didn't feel like playing coy. In fact, it might feel nice to give him some of his own medicine. "So what if I do?"

He stumbled over his own foot, mouth opening slightly before letting out a deep laugh. My insides warmed at the sound, and I suppressed a smile of my own. It quickly dropped when I noticed the gaggle of zombies standing nearby. They were congregated right outside the car barrier, with one leaning halfway through a car.

We stalked toward the group of five, slowing as we got closer. Zombies couldn't run fast, nor were they capable of complex thought. They were, however, difficult to kill. Damaging their heads was the only surefire way of taking them down, ironic that we needed to destroy the thing they were so rumored to crave. At least they did in the stories my dad told me. These ones just liked flesh in general, at least while it was still living. Several good blows would do the trick, making the undead dead once more.

"I call the three on the right," he yelled gleefully.

I shook my head in reprimand and swung my bat toward the nearest zombie. It wore a frayed pair of jeans and sported scraggly brown hair attached to its graying scalp. The head bashed in upon impact, the concave section making me gag slightly before I drew back and hit it one more time, avoiding its contorted mouth. The next one advanced, teeth clacking as it snapped at me, desperate for a taste. I grimaced, kicking it squarely in the gut—or where its gut would be—before lifting the bat up over my head. It scrambled to its knees, grasping my leg tightly with its gnarled, bony hands. I shook my foot, trying to dislodge it but only succeeding in angering it. I couldn't bring the bat down without possibly hitting myself, but it was only seconds away from digging its teeth into my skin.

"Come on," Grey encouraged from next to me. He hacked through his zombies with ease, severing any limbs in his immediate proximity and finishing them off with blows to the head. He looked positively ecstatic. "Stop teasing and get on with it," he said with a laugh.

I sighed, throwing my leg upwards to dislodge it, and when it leaned backward with the momentum, bringing my bat down over its head.

"Good girl," he murmured appreciatively. I tried to fight my blush, distracting myself from the lick of heat that traveled to my center at his words by toeing away a discarded limb at my feet. Even spattered with gore, he was beautiful. His blonde hair was now free of its tie, falling across his face and framing his chiseled jaw. His muscles flexed as he gripped the machete, raising an eyebrow at me. He knew. He definitely knew where my mind had gone.

"Nice job," I quipped as we trudged back to the gate, all the residual tension from before replaced with endorphins and adrenaline. Anna raised an appraising brow at his disheveled state, but looked away as I glared in her direction. I handed the bloodied bat off to the man, loath to be relinquishing my only weapon.

"See you around, Harry."

Hm. So that was his name. I should have asked him. I should have been trying to learn all I could about the guards and their duties, but something about Grey made me distracted, and unfocused.

"You wanna head to the lake or take showers at the cabin?" he asked, using the clean part of his shirt to wipe the sweat from his forehead. I quickly looked away, flushing as butterflies filled my stomach. It had taken us roughly forty minutes to dispatch the zombies and drag the corpses around a hundred feet beyond the car barrier as a deterrent to the others, and he had worked up quite a sweat. As had I, for that matter.

"Depends, does it have to be a cold shower?"

His eyes flashed as they darted to me, gleaming wickedly as he smiled. "I don't know about you, but I'll need one." I pushed his arm, laughing as he pretended to stagger back.

It was like a barrier had dropped between us after last night and this morning. All the awkwardness and strain had disappeared with our secrets to be replaced with admiring glances and easy smiles.

A sharp, biting voice called my name from behind us. I turned to find Merikh standing several feet away, tapping his foot. He was wearing a black t-shirt, the fabric clinging to his skin as he crossed his arms in disapproval.

His eyes sparked with something fierce. If I didn't know him better, I'd assume it jealousy. But I did, and it just looked like his general assholiness.

"It's fine," Grey soothed, holding his hands up in a calming gesture.

"You let her push you around? Accompany you outside the gates?"

I scowled, taking offense to the fact that he was pretending I wasn't even there. "Yeah, as a matter of fact, I did."

Merikh's eyes widened at his tone, before narrowing and settling on me like I was the one who'd spoken.

"Shower," he snapped. "You look disgusting." I bit my tongue to keep from responding and rolled my eyes, turning in the other direction to march back to the cabin.

Half a day.

Just half a day that things were almost normal and then Merikh had to go and ruin it. It was the perfect reminder that I couldn't allow myself to get too comfortable.

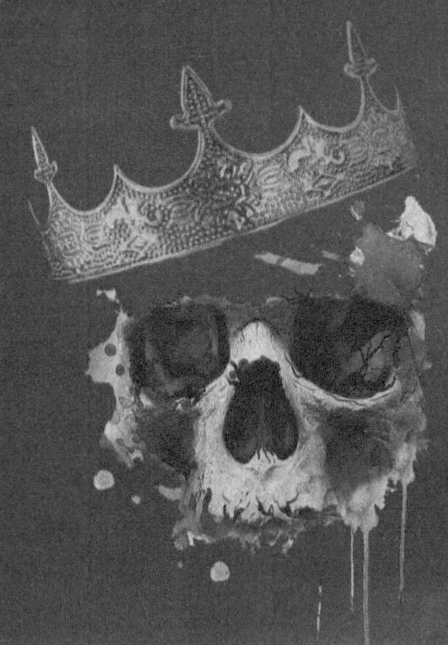

CHAPTER 8

I emerged from the bathroom fully clean, ready for whatever horrors Merikh had concocted for the night, but he was nowhere to be found. In fact, no one was around. The cabin was empty. Silent. I left, wondering if I should use this unsupervised time to scope out the camp, but my exhaustion decided for me.

"I'm gonna fetch their damn food," I mumbled under my breath as I trudged down the path. "And they can go fuck themselves if they complain that it's cold." I marched past their shoddy buildings and into the food tent.

Naia and Nerese waved from their spot at the table closest to the back. The tables were set up in lines, like the school lunchroom my father and I once set up camp in when we took refuge in an elementary school for several weeks.

I wanted to join them, but I knew the guys would pitch a fit if I didn't show up with their food. If I'd really wanted to, I would have marched over and taken a seat, but I was beyond tired and didn't feel like making conversation. Instead, I waved back, joining the end of the line and grabbing a tray to hold all the soup bowls.

I heard the persistent sound of whispers and murmurs as I moved through the line, and felt the weight of numerous eyes on me, but every time I looked around, everyone's heads were bowed in conversation. An uncomfortable sensation crept down my spine like I was being watched, but I shook it off and tried to occupy myself by messing with my nail that had broken earlier that day.

I sighed happily at the spiced scent of the steam coming off the bowls once I reached the front of the line, and headed for the exit while balancing the tray precariously, only to pitch forward as something hooked around my shin. I bounced off the ground, groaning as my knees made contact with a sharp pain. The contents of the bowls splattered all over the dirt, good food wasted. My first thought was that it had been an accident, so when I looked up to see an older man sneering at me, I was stunned. I'd never even seen him before, so what the hell was his problem?

I got to my feet as quickly as possible, wincing at the dull throb in my knee. I could feel my cheeks burning from all attention, and blinked back the faint sting of embarrassed tears in my eyes.

"You girl. Thief. *Murderer*. Clean that up," he spat in my direction.

The blood froze in my veins, moving sluggishly and making me feel light-headed. How did he know…? I scanned the room, bypassing all the stares to find Anna at a nearby table looking slightly uncomfortable. She *did* hear. She'd heard what I confessed to Halli, and she'd told everyone. *Fuck.* I knew it was too good to be true, that there was no way I'd be able to spend my remaining days before I left quietly and without fuss.

I drew back, torn between bolting out of the tent and ignoring him when a warm arm brushed against mine.

"You don't speak to her like that," Nix commanded, his entire body vibrating with hostility. I looked at him, partly in surprise, but also in irritation. I needed to fight my own battles. I *wanted* to. "You don't speak to her at all."

I bristled at his high-handedness, tapping my foot anxiously. The man scowled at Nix but remained silent.

Nix followed my gaze to Anna, eyes narrowing as he immediately put the pieces together and realized she was somehow involved, even if he didn't quite know how yet. "You had no right," he said sternly, angrier than I thought he could get. Clearly, I'd gauged him wrong if I'd thought he liked to avoid conflict.

She just shrugged, looking unrepentant. "I think the people deserve to know, don't you? We wouldn't want to keep secrets. What do you see in her anyway?" she snickered. "Hair the color of dishwater and a face so thin, you'd think she's perpetually sucking on a lemon."

"Caramel," Nix muttered under his breath.

She laughed again. "Excuse me?"

He frowned, his voice growing louder as he dressed her down. "I said her hair is fucking caramel. But if anyone would know dishwater, it's you. Isn't that right, Anna? So why don't you head back to the kitchen and do the only thing you're good for besides spreading your legs?"

Her gasp echoed in the now quiet tent. Several people's faces were visibly red from restraining their laughter or gasps. Anna looked to the people sitting around her for a defense, but not a single person spoke up despite the visible discomfort on their faces. Damn, not even her friends thought she was worth sticking up for? She stomped her foot and leveled a glare in my direction that would've turned me to ash had she the ability.

She spun on her heel, and I had to give it to her, she held her head high throughout her march toward the kitchen. As soon as she was out of sight, voices rose in volume, whispers and laughter filling the tent. I felt a brief flash of sympathy, but it faded the second I remembered that she'd revealed a personal conversation to *everyone.*

It was surreal, like one of those shitty old-world books I'd found that was set in high school. Didn't we have bigger things to worry about? We should've been pulling together for the sake of our survival, not fighting over inconsequential shit like men.

Nix leveled a glare at the room, quieting the murmurs, before walking out of the tent and into the cool night air like he had all the time in the world.

I followed behind him, my body instantly relaxing at the sight of the stars above me, the absence of everyone's glares, and the sudden silence. When he stopped several feet away from the empty center of the camp, I took it upon myself to break the tension. "Caramel, Nix? Really?"

He blushed–*blushed!*–ducking his head and taking a step back. Fuck, it completely destroyed any lingering irritation at him for interfering.

"Wait," I pleaded, suddenly desperate for him to not leave or feel embarrassed. I rounded the wooden bench he had inched behind, catching his sleeve with my hand. I used that grip to stand on my tiptoes, then leaned in to press a soft kiss to his cheek, nose brushing against the evening stubble lining his jaw. "My hero," I whispered in his ear. He shuddered against me, hand snaking out from between us to press against my lower back–

The moment was broken by the intrusive sound of laughter nearby. An answering smile tugged at the corner of Nix's mouth, and I stepped back to let him step away if he still wanted to. Instead, he placed a gentle hand on my arm and tugged me away from the small cluster of people that lingered nearby.

"Are you okay?" he murmured when we were once more out of earshot.

My grin faded as I came back to reality and I shook my head, suddenly weary. I'd had so much constant interaction over the past few days that my head was spinning. All I wanted to do was find a nice, quiet place and think. What was I going to do now that everyone knew the truth about how John had died? At least Naia and Nerese hadn't looked like they hated me. Who knew what Anna had told everyone, though? She could have twisted the story any way she liked.

"River," he said quietly.

"Yes, Nix?"

"What do you want to do?"

I looked at him in surprise. Not one of them had ever asked me what I *wanted* to do. They always commanded, ordered, directed.

I sighed, looking up into the starlit sky and wishing my father had taught me about the constellations. They had always intrigued me. I'd found a tattered storybook once, in which a girl that found herself lost navigated her way back home using the North Star. When I was younger, I thought following the North Star would lead me to my dream home, a safe and cozy sanctuary just for me. After I had pestered my dad for months to follow the North Star with me, he finally explained that it didn't work like that. He hadn't wanted to crush my dreams. It seemed like a cruel joke that I'd find my way to a camp with security and food, and yet be there under these circumstances. Still somehow ostracized, still ready to flee at a moment's notice.

"I'd like to sit by the fire," I said softly. I could pretend none of this was happening, recline on the couch, and have some mockery of normal.

He nodded, leading us back to the cabin. Once we arrived, I changed into a clean pair of clothes, splashing cool water on my face and tying my hair back. *There,* some modicum of control. Given how exhausted I felt—deep down to my bones—I expected to see my hazel eyes lined by dark circles, but when I looked in the mirror, I saw no outward manifestation of my troubles. My hollow cheeks were filling out, and I had the beginnings of a natural blush.

Was I prepared to go back to scavenging? To irregular meals and starvation, sleepless nights, and violence?

I exited the bathroom to see Nix stoking the fire. The flames turned his hair a burnished red, highlighting his pale skin and casting shadows around the high-ceilinged living room.

He was stunning.

I sat on the couch, reclining against the arm and tucking my feet into the middle cushion. I lay on my side, feeling Nix's eyes on me as I watched the fire crackle and pop.

"We used to have a fire every night on the outside," he murmured. He strode over to me, ignoring the empty seats around us and only hesitating a moment before taking a seat at the other end of the couch.

If I was being honest with myself, I would admit that I left my legs tucked close just in case he chose to sit there.

"Isn't that dangerous? You didn't attract zombies or thieves?"

He huffed a rough laugh. "My father didn't care. How dare he lose a comfort due to others? We were targeted often because of it and were expected to defend our territory each and every time. To everyone else, if we were bold enough to burn a fire all night then surely we had enough resources to live comfortably–resources that they could take. He said it was good for us, that it would toughen us up."

His disdain for his father was clear in his voice.

"You don't like to fight as the others do," I guessed.

"I do what needs to be done," he corrected. "But no, I don't enjoy feeling my fist split bone or the blood and gore that follows."

"They don't look down on you for it?"

His face darkened. "My father doesn't appreciate it, as I'm sure you could guess." He cracked a small smile. "My brothers couldn't care less. There's more than enough thirst for violence and control in each of them to make up for any I might be lacking."

"What do you do instead? If they take care of the zombies outside and work camp security and disputes?"

Only after I'd finished asking did I realize how rude it sounded, but he just smiled, and a dimple appeared on his left cheek. It was the first real smile I was seeing from him, and I was enraptured by it. "I swim in my free time, help watch and care for the children, settle disputes in Merikh's stead, and check on the elderly and the livestock. I also manage job assignments and keep records on the food stock."

"Sounds fulfilling."

Clearly, he could hear the envy bleeding through my tone because his expression grew pleading. "Would it be so bad?" he murmured.

I shifted slightly, tucking my legs closer and admiring the sharp cut of his jaw. "What?"

His shadowed green eyes met mine. "Being here? With us?"

"I'm not sure it matters, Nix. Circumstances being what they are and all. Besides, who knows how many other creepy perverts you have hanging around?"

"You don't have to be alone anymore. You could be happy here, we'd just need to give the others time to calm down." His eyes widened slightly as he processed what I said. "What do you mean, creepy pervert?"

I closed my eyes. I'd been trying to make light of it and just... forgot. I made a split second decision to come clean with him. He deserved honesty.

"John. He tried to force himself on me," I said quietly. "I told Halli, and Anna overheard, as did Grey, and Anna ended up telling everyone. Not... *that* part, but the stealing. And the killing. It's the reason for whatever just happened back there." I was worn out and didn't have the patience to go about it tactfully for the second—third—time that day.

"He what?" Nix flew to his feet, looking at me incredulously.

I lifted a shoulder and looked back toward the fire.

"Why didn't you tell us?" he asked between clenched teeth.

"I didn't think it mattered," I said flatly.

He ran a hand over his face, continuing into his dark curls, and crouched next to where I was sitting. "I didn't know," he muttered. His expression was tortured. "You've been fetching our food, cleaning our place, sleeping on our floors, following us around like a dog. Why didn't you say anything?"

"Because I thought it didn't matter!" I exclaimed, sitting up straight.

"Of course it matters," he thundered. Then he blinked, shaking off his anger and sighing. His shoulders slumped. A strong hand lifted to grip my knee, both comforting and heat-provoking. "I'm sorry. Do the others know? Besides Grey?"

"No. I didn't know if you'd accuse me of lying and maybe just kill me on the spot. I thought it would be safer to get a feel for things first, for the kind of people you were and the type of camp you lead. Until then, I thought it would only make things worse."

Nix's face crumpled. He nodded once and stood, exiting the cabin. I couldn't decide if I was happy or upset by his absence. I definitely didn't expect him to just walk out like that.

I spent what felt like forever staring into the flames and wondering where everyone was when Nix walked through the front door, balancing two bowls of soup.

It was a peace offering, him bringing me dinner like I had brought his meals to him.

"Here." He handed me the chipped porcelain bowl filled with the very same spiced soup that I'd dropped earlier. I was ravenous and scarfed it down within seconds. My stomach growled for more, but I knew better than to get used to eating too much food and being unable to meet that standard once I was gone.

I left him by the fire to brush my teeth and was surprised to find him still sitting in the armchair when I returned.

"You're sleeping with me tonight," Nix said as he crouched down to collect my bowl. I turned wide eyes to him, savoring his rough laugh. "I'm not making you sleep on my floor, sunshine. Come on."

His room was shrouded in darkness, with only the light of the candle in the corner. As my eyes adjusted to the change in lighting, I was able to make out a large bed and clothes hamper in the corner, along with a short nightstand.

Nix busied himself by fiddling with something on his dresser, before stripping off his shirt almost shyly. What I could see of his skin was gold draped over muscle. He left his sweats on and slid into his bed on the right side, leaving the left open for me.

What would it be like? To hear his staccato breaths in the darkness and know that his body was so close to mine? Nice, I surmised. It would feel comforting. And... tempting.

I eased my way into the bed awkwardly, laying stiffly several inches away from him. "Where are the others?"

"Probably fighting," he mused. "Some of the camp likes to get together and place bets. There's not much for entertainment here."

"Is the safety worth it? The stagnation?"

"It's immeasurable. Do you think... Would you have ever told us about... you know? I know you said you wanted to get a feel for things first."

A fist squeezed my heart at the pain dripping off his words. I suppose in a way I understood. We'd formed a tentative friendship, he and I, even somehow based on the fundamental belief that they were justified in their actions and I was not, and now it had been upended. He probably felt guilt, and upset. "I'm glad you know, okay? And if I'd have known what kind of man you are... I would have told you right away. I know it doesn't... excuse what I did. There's no way of knowing if he still would have tried if he wasn't infected, but, well, he was. Because of me. So I–um–" I shut my mouth against any more awkward stuttering, grateful it was dark so he couldn't see the pink that I was sure stained my cheeks. It was becoming increasingly difficult to keep my train of thought, knowing that he was so close.

"Thank you for saying that," he whispered, his voice low. "But there's no excuse. None. Maybe we were too surprised, or hypocritical, to acknowledge that in your place we would've likely done the same, or maybe we saw you standing there, hungry and scared, and thought..."

He trailed off and shifted onto his back. As he turned, his arm brushed the thin fabric at my waist, quickening my breaths. It was an accident, but it brought my entire focus down to the distance between our bodies. The touch was so innocent, but inexplicably charged with tension. "Nix," I murmured, rolling onto my back as well, so that my arm was lying between us as well. My heartbeat sped up as his hand brushed against mine and a strange, warm feeling took root in the pit of my stomach.

Nix made a sound low in his throat, and I felt his hand twitch when his fingers briefly touched mine. "You're stunning. Have I told you?"

"No."

"You looked so... beautiful standing among all the wreckage when we first found you. Body at your feet like an avenging angel, and your *eyes*, they were so clear."

"I was covered in scars and filth." I bit my lip against any further protests. I wasn't *ashamed* of my looks per se, but I know they weren't exactly a turn-on.

"Look at how you've survived," he murmured. "Skin kissed by the sun and body finally getting the nutrients it needs. You're *glowing*."

I shifted my hand closer, heart in my throat at my boldness, entangling it with his in one smooth motion. His breath hitched as he clasped mine back. Then he was pulling, rolling me sideways into his body. My head landed on his chest, and my other arm ended up slung across him. He sighed deeply, causing my head to rise just slightly. I flashed back to when I slept in Grey's bed, to how similar the two scenarios were. To think that I'd gone from lonely nights to... *this*. Heart racing, skin flushed, head dizzy.

I clutched him tightly, shuddering in his strong embrace. The arm that encircled my back flexed as he gripped my hip. We were aching for one another, breaths stuttering as more of our skin touched while we settled into a comfortable position. He groaned low and deep as I shifted over him. I turned to check his expression, surprised to find his lips a scant distance from mine. They parted beneath my gaze, and his cool breath caressed my neck.

Oh whatever.

I surged forward, capturing his mouth with mine. I swallowed his moan, unable to suppress a whimper of my own as I savored the feel of his soft lips. Even after reading about experiences like this, I never imagined I'd have one or that it would feel so damn good. He kissed me back just as passionately, not dominating the kiss, but meeting me touch for touch, allowing me to set the pace. I didn't know if I was any good, but I was too drunk on lust to care.

After a couple of minutes of gentle, desperate kisses, I realized I was rocking my hips against his bent leg. I moaned quietly, biting back the sound as he kissed me harder. His hand circled from my hip to my core, gently cupping me over my shorts. I writhed, desperate for more pressure and moaning as he stroked me. It was unlike anything I'd felt before and I had to wonder how I'd lived without it these past few years.

"Fuck," he groaned against my lips. "Just like that."

"Keep touching me," I commanded between kisses. He broke our kiss to trace my lower lip with his tongue before sliding it inside my mouth and twining it with mine. It was warm and wet, sinful and dirty and *delicious.* I sighed into his mouth, using my hand to brace myself against his chest. His hand delved beneath my shorts to circle my clit slowly, and my head fell empty. Fuck, it was so *good.* Leagues more pleasurable than the quick unpracticed movements I'd tried previously with my own hand. It was electric.

My moans grew louder as pleasure radiated through my body at his firm touch. I rocked my body into his ministrations, meeting him stroke for stroke, tiny whimpers falling from my lips.

"You like it?" he murmured. "Want me to stroke you till you come? Slide my fingers into your soaking wet cunt until you squirt all over my hand?"

I shuddered, definitely not expecting sweet, shy, Nix to have such a filthy mouth. His words spurred me on, and I rode his hand faster, hips undulating as he rubbed me. "Yes," I hissed, determined not to be outdone by his sexy as fuck dirty talk. Sure I'd never done it before, but I'd fantasized enough, read enough detailed books, I got the general idea. "Want your fingers deep inside me, want to fuck myself on you until I come all over your hand."

His groan was profane as he eased a finger inside me, quickly escalating to two once he realized how soaked I was. Even with my limited experience, I was determined not to feel shy about declaring what I wanted–*taking* what I wanted. Even if I felt the *slightest* bit embarrassed at the obscene sounds filling the room from how soaking wet I was.

I bit my lip as he thrust his fingers faster, using my hand to explore the front of his sweats while the other supported my weight above him. I grinned to myself when I felt the hard bulge beneath me and looked up at him through my lashes as I slid my hand underneath the elastic band until I encountered his hardness. I circled his cock tentatively, brushing my thumb over the bead of hot liquid at the head and stroking up and down as he powered his fingers into me.

He moaned loudly, hips bucking upward into my grip. "Fuck yes," he gritted out. "Just like that, sunshine. That's exactly it." His praise warmed me from the inside out and his length throbbed in my hand when I let out a particularly loud moan, hot and desperate. I stroked him faster, the wetness from his tip adding to the slick noises, and grinned wickedly at his short gasps of breath as he sped up in return. His other hand traveled underneath my baggy shirt, sliding across my stomach until he reached my breast and rubbed his thumb over my nipple. Sparks exploded at the extra sensation, and I wanted to shut my eyes from the overload of pleasure but was too invested in watching his expression to keep them closed.

I was close. I could feel sparks of heat rolling down my spine, the weightlessness spreading throughout my limbs and making me dizzy. It was unlike any climax I'd had on my own, a level of pleasure I'd thought a myth.

"Close," I gasped as I paid extra attention to his straining cock, determined to take him over the edge with me. "I don't know if, I–"

"That's it," Nix groaned. His dark hair was damp, hanging in his hooded eyes as he watched me, captivated. "I want you to come with me. Want you to come all over my hand, sunshine. *Fuck.*"

I moaned long and loud as he used his thumb to massage my clit while repeatedly stroking a particularly pleasurable spot inside me. I dropped my forehead to his, recapturing his lips and whimpering into his mouth as he drove me over the edge, working his cock until he groaned, gripping my hip tight as he came all over his flat stomach. I collapsed onto his chest–carefully avoiding the mess–panting with him as we collected ourselves and twitched in unison from the aftershocks.

"We're so doing that again," he declared.

I just laughed in response, my heart suddenly so much lighter than before.

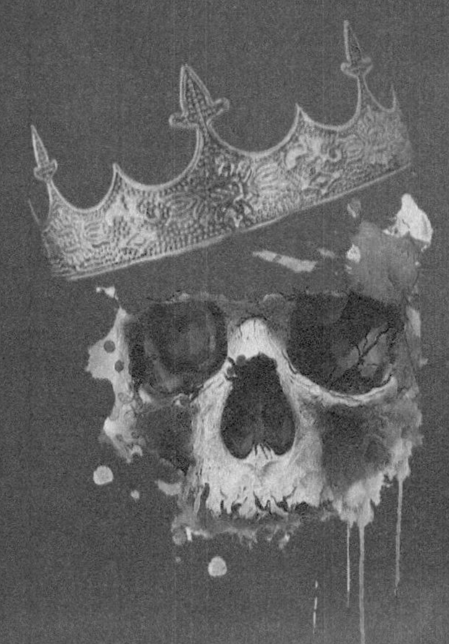

CHAPTER 9

I stretched lazily, tugging at the frayed hem of my shorts and tying my hair back into a loose bun. Nix had woken me twenty minutes prior with slow drugging kisses, tugging my leg over his hip so that I could rock against him. We only rose when we heard the others moving around, getting ready silently.

It was almost as if there was something in the water, stripping away all my inhibitions. Or maybe it was because for the first time in my life I had no father to look after, no zombie to kill, no shelter to find. My stomach didn't ache with its usual hunger, and my eyes weren't drifting shut as I tried to remain hidden from whatever was making noise around the corner. I had no responsibilities, and for once, I *wanted*. Wanted to be touched, kissed, held. I wanted the ecstasy that came with an orgasm and the closeness of a body holding mine, and despite the feeling of shame that kept intruding on my thoughts, I was unapologetic. Last night had unlocked something hungry and bold inside me, and I wasn't sure I would put it back into the box it came from even if I could.

I entered the kitchen, noting that everyone was already gathered around the table.

"You were going to be in my room last night," Merikh stated.

"You weren't here," I said flatly.

"I was busy. Next time, I expect you to be there even if I am not."

Nix's face darkened, as did Grey's. I know Merikh saw. For all that he was irritating, he was extremely observant. His mouth turned down at the corners as he watched them.

"Anything you want to tell me?" he asked.

I begged them with my eyes not to divulge my secret. It was mine and mine alone.

No one answered him.

"You will accompany Caelan today and sleep on his floor tonight."

I grimaced at the order. "And if I don't?"

Nix turned pleading eyes onto me from behind Merikh, while he glowered. "You don't have a choice. If you choose to disobey, there will be consequences."

Grey tapped his foot while he watched, arms crossed disapprovingly.

"Fetch breakfast," Merikh commanded. I clenched my fists and bit the inside of my cheek to keep from snapping at him at the utter disregard in his tone. Let him think I'm going to be docile. I would show him.

Grey followed behind me to help. "Nix told me about what happened last night, in the food tent. It seems that word has spread about the circumstances surrounding John's death, courtesy of Anna. Although not about... the part you told me."

He shot me a meaningful look.

"I don't know what I'm going to do now," I muttered as I picked my way through the dirt path. "Except avoid Anna. Fuck her."

He barked a laugh. "I honestly don't know what Merikh was thinking when he invited her back to the cabin. I think she's more pissed that she couldn't seduce all of us than she is that you've got our undivided attention."

I stumbled over nothing. All of them. I could understand her desires. They were attractive, even Merikh, despite his controlling attitude. I thought back to last night with Nix, his hands on my body, and shivered. Could I still do whatever necessary to escape now that I knew what Nix sounded like when he came? More importantly, if Nix told Grey about what happened with that guy last night... would he tell him what happened between us as well?

"I have your attention, do I?

"Don't play coy with me, River. You should know that all I can see is you."

Something burned bright in my chest, fizzling out to a dim glow long after his words had faded.

"I still think you should tell him," he grunted as we walked.

"In due time."

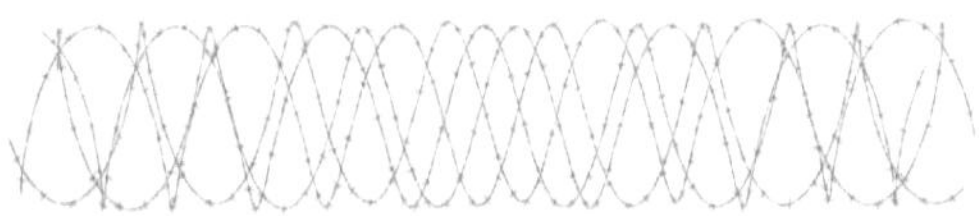

Caelan's hair differed from his brother's in that tiny streaks of gold ran through it. They shone in the sunlight, tangled messily with his dark waves, but on a cloudy day like today, they glowed a dull bronze. His gait was long and loping, and he carried himself with a certain confidence, assurance in who he was. His tattoos were shadowed by the storm clouds overhead and his blue eyes gleamed with mischief.

"I've missed you," he announced as we walked. It was discomfiting how he always seemed to say exactly what was on his mind without mincing his words or crafting untruths.

I didn't know how to feel about that. Part of me had missed him as well, and that scared me. Either way, I wasn't yet brave enough to reciprocate his sentiment.

He was like a dose of sunshine when things got too tense or too real, always cracking jokes and teasing, lightening the room with his laughter.

"What do we have to do today?" I asked, resigned to an entire day of following him around like a puppy.

"Hey, no need for that tone. Who says it has to be boring?" He grinned as his stride grew faster. "Let's go for a swim."

"It's gonna rain!" I laughed, trying to catch up.

"We should be fine until the storm hits. Come on, you scared?"

I laughed, trekking through the forest with him until we reached the lake. "You don't have any responsibilities today? Why did Merikh assign me to you?"

He grimaced. "I don't think there will ever be an end to them, but they don't have to rule my life. Unlike the others, I like to think I have a pretty nice balance going."

"That's so like you, the only one of your brothers that knows how to prioritize relaxation as well as work." My heart sank as I remembered my predicament. "And when your father comes back?"

Caelan's eyes darkened. "Things will continue on as they are. You won't have to see him."

It was strange, our relationship.

Caelan was brash and observant, violent and compassionate. I'd written him off as the "muscle": strong, tall, and argumentative, but I'd done him a disservice by overlooking all of the traits that made him so wily and personable. He was oddly kind, annoyingly persistent, and irritatingly blunt. I hadn't spent much time with him, but we already seemed to have a kind of unsteady connection, and if I could just ignore the steady thrum of desire burning tirelessly for him, I would be fine.

Or not.

He stripped off his ripped and stained gray shirt without warning, revealing a muscular torso completely covered with tattoos. I gaped at the amount of ink covering him, realizing that from his sleeve and hand tattoos that I should have guessed this part of him would be covered as well. I hadn't been able to see nearly as much in the darkness the last time we were here. A large patch of geometric flowers and various swirls covered his side, a lifelike rendering of skeletal ribs poking through, all done in black ink. Over his abdomen was a large skull. It was striking, and how the hell he hadn't gotten an infection from whatever third-rate substance was used for ink was beyond me. I fought the urge to reach out and touch the designs, instead opting to devour them with my eyes.

He noticed my fixation and beckoned me closer with a tiny smirk, taking my hand in his and setting it against his warm skin. His chest rose and fell unsteadily under my hand.

I swallowed my frustration, conveniently placing all the residual blame and resentment on Merikh, and all that was left was desire. Sharp, intense, aching desire.

His throat convulsed as I stroked one of the swirls softly, little bumps raising in the wake of my touch. His eyes fluttered shut, and his hand came up to envelop mine.

The crack of thunder in the distance jolted me into realizing what a bad idea this would be. I pulled away abruptly, breaking the spell, and tugged my shirt over my head, leaving just my worn black bra. I couldn't give in. Besides, how could I when I had already gotten... *involved* with Nix? It wasn't uncommon for one person to entertain multiple people at a time–at least from what I'd seen in my limited exposure to other groups–especially when it was uncommon to find someone worth settling for in your lifetime, but would these fo–*three*–even be open to it?

I immediately shoved that idea to the back of my mind, resolving to never revisit it. It was bad enough that I was growing soft, but entertaining anything other than escaping was dangerous.

Caelan's eyes heated as he watched me, and I could see his chest rising and falling rapidly as his breaths came faster. I hid a smirk, tugging off my shorts in one smooth motion and taking a running leap into the water. His laugh was loud, and he quickly followed, body crashing into the lake beside me. The water from his jump soaked my upper body as

I resurfaced, so I brought my hands down hard onto the surface, the resulting splash dousing us both.

He surged forward, grabbing me by the hips and tossing me several feet away. I hit the water with a loud slap and was already laughing as I swam to the surface. His grin was genuine and so, so mischievous. I couldn't resist splashing him in retaliation. He jerked back, using his arm to sweep an arc of water over my head. I spluttered, treading the water and watching as a droplet trailed down his jaw.

I shrieked as he tilted his head down and shook his hair wildly, sending water flying my way. "Truce!"

It was absurd just how quickly he was able to put me at ease. The friction from moments earlier had completely disappeared.

"I'm no quitter, baby, but I'll agree to a cease-fire just this once." His playful smile revealed a dimple on either side of his face that I hadn't managed to notice prior.

We spent several long minutes treading water as the waves from our antics settled, and watching the storm clouds gather overhead.

"You're really happy here?" I blurted.

"Yeah," he replied, cocking his head to the side in question. "Shelter, food, *safety*. What more could I want?"

I could think of a few things, but I didn't say that. Look at me, a little taste of the good life and already I was moving past basic needs?

"I don't think you'd be asking if you weren't considering abandoning your crusade," he said slowly.

"I–" I shook my head. It was so easy to cling to my righteous indignation. I'd spent days stoking the embers of my anger so that I wouldn't lose sight of my goals, of the magnitude of their misdeeds. It was even harder to admit that maybe in a world like this, they might've had every right to react as they did. I hadn't been mistreated or abused or tortured like any of the horror stories I'd been prepared for. In fact, the most I'd suffered at their hand was a few threats, demands, and minor discomforts. Although I knew the second I finished that thought process all the way to a conclusion, I would lose the motivation to escape, and right now that was all I had going for me. Escape, hide, survive. I couldn't change the plan, not now.

"I don't want to talk about it. Not right now, at least. Right now, I need to tell you something. Something that Nix and Grey already know." My head was spinning. I had no idea how he would respond. Would he be upset? Indignant? I didn't want to tell him, but I knew that Grey wouldn't hesitate to do it if I kept it a secret any longer.

He nodded, his tattooed hands trailing slowly through the water as he waited. He clearly had no idea what I was going to say because he didn't look concerned in the least.

I took a deep breath and let it out slowly. "John tried to... attack me."

Caelan's head tilted, and he looked at me like he questioned my intelligence. "Yeah," he said, drawing the words out slowly. "He was infected, That's what infected people do. What kind of zombies have you been running into?"

Oh, for fuck's sake. "No, Caelan. He, ah..." I felt like throwing my hands up in defeat and trying again another day. I'd actually managed to get the words out in one piece, and he still didn't get it? "I offered to give him back his supplies, and he proposed a trade. He didn't want to take no for an answer, and so he, well, went for it." Caelan's face was turning an unhealthy-looking shade of red. "I killed him before he did anything," I rushed to add, hoping it would calm him a bit.

He stilled. His feet were able to touch the bottom of the lake, and he stood frozen like a statue carved from marble. Face as stormy as the sky above him, his next words were a flat command. "Come again?"

"He was going to force himself on me. He really was infected, but he also... put his hands on me. As in, before he even showed signs of being bitten."

Caelan's eyes were dark, and so very, very angry. "And we stole you away for defending yourself."

I didn't respond. We both knew the answer.

"Fuck," he shouted, slamming a fist into the water. I jumped in surprise, stunned at his reaction.

"I *did* take his food," I said softly. "He might not have been infected if he hadn't come looking for me. We might not have even crossed paths at all," I conceded.

"I don't give a *fuck* why he was near you. If he could do that shit to *anyone*, I would've killed him my goddamn self, infected or not!" he shouted.

Seeing his fury over the situation forced me to face all the thoughts I'd been steadfastly locking away. Was this all my fault? I made myself out to be a martyr, keeping the real events from them, why... because I didn't trust them? Didn't feel like they'd believe me? At the very least, I should've told them I offered to give him his things back. It didn't erase that he was infected in the first place, but it would've at least made them stop and think. I'd thought myself so morally superior to them for manipulating what I thought was a situation that required it by keeping silent when in reality it just made me dense, and them ignorant. I *put them* into a position where this was their only recourse. Ours was a world of swift judgment and punishment, so what had I been expecting? Was it possible that a small part of me had *wanted* to be whisked away?

I swam forward hesitantly, laying a steadying hand on his wet arm while he fumed. I couldn't believe how much he *cared*.

He inhaled sharply at my touch, turbulent eyes meeting mine. His mouth opened and shut with a click. The water lapped at our chests where we stood, gentle and cold.

"I should've told you," I conceded.

There was no response. I maintained our eye contact, swallowing any more nervous statements that wanted to fill the silence. Sparks flew from the growing, heavy tension filling the atmosphere, and the hairs on the back of my neck rose with anticipation. There was one storm brewing above us, and another one between us. His eyes dropped to my lips, and the air grew thick with an intense heat. I felt every single movement of the bead of water that rolled down my spine.

He nodded to himself, as if making a decision, before moving his face toward mine with purpose. With the way he telegraphed his intent,

I had a split second to make my decision. So when he grabbed the back of my neck and pulled me in for a hard kiss, I melted under his touch, bringing my legs up and around his hips. He groaned into my mouth, setting his hands on my ass and grinding me against him in slow, rolling movements. I used one arm to support myself using his shoulder and slid the other into his dark waves, admiring the scattered bronze strands before tracing the column of his neck.

"You don't know what it's like," he rasped, his large hand sliding to the small of my back to keep me close. "Watching you walk in a room wet from the shower, the scent of soap and jasmine on your skin, your little shorts–" He broke off with a low groan, and when he continued, it was a low mutter under his breath, almost to himself. "Never touch you again, no fucking way. Never out of my sight."

I broke away, peppering kisses along his sharp cheekbones and even sharper jawline, then along the column of his throat. His groan trailed off into a needy growl as I twirled my tongue in the hollow of his throat, sucking on his neck.

"Little vampire," he hissed, tilting his head back for a long moment to receive more attention on his throat. "Get back up here, baby." He wrapped his fist around the length of my hair and used it to tug me back, bringing his mouth to mine once more. The sensation sent a shiver rolling throughout my body. His grip was just this side of painful, and I'd never felt anything more tantalizing.

I used my tongue to trace his lips, and when they parted, dipped inside and stroked his. "Wanted this," he murmured, resting his forehead against mine and breathing heavily. "I've wanted this since I saw you standing in the rubble, so fucking fierce and strong and badass."

I stroked his tattoos, tracing his abs and leaning forward so that my still covered breasts were pressed tightly against his chest. "Then take me," I whispered into his ear. This was probably a terrible idea. What would Nix think? Or Grey? I shook those thoughts away. I didn't owe them anything, not when I was finally living for *myself.*

He kissed me so hard, so passionately, that I couldn't even think about wanting anything other than his hands on my skin, his taste in my mouth.

Caelan broke away just far enough to slide my panties down and leave me bare. Good thing those fuckers were down to their last thread because they belonged to the lady of the lake now.

I was apprehensive about getting it on in the lake, so I pulled him to the shore, reclining on the section of grass and dirt just barely dipping into the water. He crawled over me, a dripping wet god. He was carved in all the right places, a deep V leading down to his straining cock. Tattooed knuckles gripped his length, shuttling over the angry head as he clenched his teeth and hissed in pleasure.

Hell yeah, I could get used to having a front-row seat to this.

I whimpered, tired of waiting, and pulled him closer to me. I just wanted to *feel*, not think. Caelan let go of himself to stroke me gently, dipping his fingers inside me the barest amount to gather my wetness and then using it to slowly rub my clit in small circles. I hissed at the intense pleasure of it, reaching down to shift his hand a quarter of an inch above to where the sensation was less visceral. He complied easily, keeping his eyes on my face to gauge my reaction. I bucked against his lower half impatiently, my eyes sliding closed as he finally–*finally*–dipped one finger inside me. I gave a full-body shudder, bringing my arms up to grip his shoulders and occupying myself by nibbling on his neck. His finger hit the perfect angle, and my deep, loud moan had him chuckling softly in response.

I reached between us to grasp his hardness, biting my lip when he stopped everything for a moment to groan, "Tighter." I adjusted my grip, feeling an odd sense of exhilaration and satisfaction when he closed his eyes to snarl in pleasure.

After a few seconds, he brought his attention back to the task he'd momentarily abandoned, alternating between thrusting and rubbing and it was goddamn euphoric. I ground up against his touch, gripping his jaw with my free hand and pulling his lips to mine. It was a sloppy kiss, full of heat and want. Desire pooled lazily in my core, and the light breeze caressed my bare skin, cooling the water that clung to us and sending shivers down my spine.

My pussy clenched down around nothing once he removed his fingers, and I sobbed desperately at the loss. I felt only a little sore from Nix's ministrations last night, and given that I was soaking wet and deliriously ready for Caelan, I wasn't going to think myself to death on the non-physical aspects of whether this was a good decision or not. *Spoiler*, it probably wasn't; I just didn't care. I felt like I'd die of disappointment if he didn't get moving.

He looked up, uncharacteristically serious for once. "I don't have anything on me. It'll just take a second if I go grab one. I've always worn a condom in the past and we have wild carrot growing in the garden, just in case."

It took me a good moment to understand what he was saying, and when I got it, I bit my lip, feeling oddly vulnerable. "I actually... a few years ago, I went to the nearest military base for a fairly new sterility procedure they're offering. My dad and I agreed it was worth the risks of going into the facility, just in case... Well, I don't quite think this is quite the worst-case scenario I was envisioning when I went in for it. Luckily, or rather, unluckily, I tested negative for immunity to the virus, which meant there was no risk of an involuntary stay after the procedure for more tests. So if you've always worn protection..." He hissed out a breath between clenched teeth at my next words. "I trust you."

It was strange, but I found that I whole-heartedly meant it. I couldn't believe that I trusted him so implicitly after what felt like both forever and no time at all, but it was freeing. He spent a moment searching my eyes, as if making sure I was completely sure about my choice, then surged forward to give me a hard kiss, rekindling the heated passion from moments ago.

He notched himself at my entrance, looking to me for permission. I made a sharp noise at the view of his body poised above me, all damp sleek lines and carved muscles, and pulled his hips against mine, urging him forward with a gasping noise of assent. He slid inside abruptly, just one powerful thrust before he was fully seated.

"I'm sorry," he murmured against my lips as I winced. He'd spent time working me open with his fingers, but damn, was he still intimidatingly huge. "I'm sorry, I'm sorry, I'm sorry."

"Don't be," I muttered. "Feels so goddamn good. Perfect. Amazing," I babbled.

I used the grip of my legs on his hips to flip him around, catching him by surprise. It's good that he went easily because otherwise I'd have had no hope of moving him. I sat atop him and slid slowly down the thick length of his cock until he filled me completely and I was flush against his hips. Hopefully, that told him more than my words what I thought of his pointless apologies.

"Fuck yes," he groaned. "So wet, baby. Dripping all over my cock, squeezing me so tight. Look at you on top, riding me like I belong to you. Beautiful." His eyes were heavy-lidded, his hands guiding my hips as I rode him. He surged up and in one smooth movement slid his hands around my back to unclasp my bra and brush it off my shoulders, then captured my nipple in his mouth.

The added stimulation was everything. Using his teeth and tongue, he teased each nipple into a firm point, and each time he gave me a playful nip I clenched down on his cock. I moaned loudly, hands landing on his chest for purchase as I rocked back and forth. "You're all talk, Caelan," I teased between breaths, hoping to provoke him.

He groaned, snapping his hips up to pound into me, proving my bluster false without saying a word. I felt like I was made up of lust and wantonness, a foreign but welcome feeling. Our bodies were slick as they moved together. He toyed with my nipples as I bounced, alternating between stroking them and playing with my clit where I was split open by him. I could just barely hear him mumbling about how tight I felt, how beautiful I looked, and how lucky he was. It wasn't very long before his hips stuttered, and he groaned. "Touch yourself, make yourself come on me. Wanna feel you. I can't last long raw in this sweet pussy."

I rubbed at my clit furiously as I slammed myself down harder, shivering as my orgasm hit me with the force of the thunder overhead. I threw my head back and moaned, muscles contracting around his hard length and making him gasp and groan. He lifted me up by my waist then pulled himself out of me, reaching down to stroke his cock and come in stripes over my chest and stomach, then spreading it around with a satisfied grin.

"Mine," he grunted.

"What are you, a fucking caveman? No," I admonished, rising to scrub my body off in the lake.

He laughed, watching me with a knowing expression as he pulled his shirt back over his head. He ran his hand through his wet hair, slicking it back. "This is only the beginning," he warned.

I shrugged, tugging my clothes back on. I was way too blissed out to think about it yet.

"Are you going to tell Merikh about John when we get back?"

"Not yet."

"He might grant you mercy."

"I'm not ready yet. Fuck his mercy."

He chuckled, tossing me my shorts. I squealed as the first strike of lightning hit, grabbing his hand as we ran back, moving slower from the laughter.

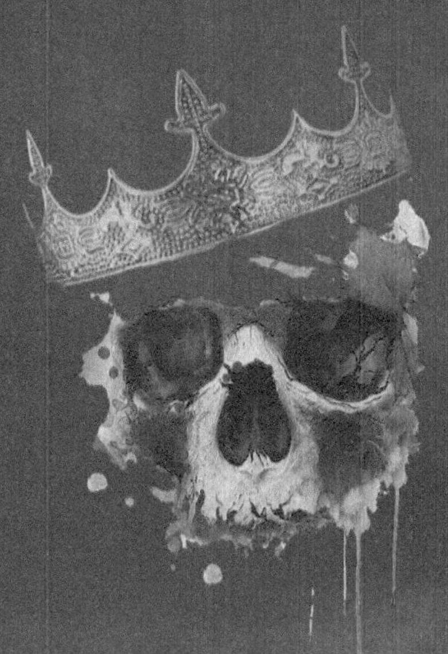

CHAPTER 10

"How was your day?" Merikh asked as I set their food down on the table. Caelan had gone with me, glaring at anyone who'd even looked at me sideways. Now that the news of what I'd done had spread, I heard whispers behind my back constantly. Those stares that had still been wary of my presence in the camp had turned hostile and judgmental.

My cheeks heated as I avoided looking at Caelan. I knew Merikh picked up on my body language because his azure eyes narrowed on me. Why was it that he was always just sitting around when I got back, ready to interrogate me like my dad used to when I disappeared for too long on an errand? Surely he had more important things to do.

"It was fine," I said casually, taking the empty seat beside Nix.

He nodded, looking pensive. "Good. Maybe tomorrow you can help in the kitchen. As for tonight, since you were supposed to sleep on my floor yesterday, you'll sleep there today."

Grey sighed reluctantly, setting his spoon down with a clanking sound. "She shouldn't have to sleep on the floor. There's a perfectly good couch in front of the fire, and she's been doing everything you asked. Besides... Our beds are big enough for at least two people."

Once the shock over his statement ebbed somewhat, I was left with a warm feeling in my chest. I'd earned some serious points with Grey, although I had some desperate need for him to stop talking. If Merikh stopped all the punishments, would it dim my hatred of him? And if I lost my anger with the one person I found myself unable to redeem, would I still be as determined to leave?

Merikh sneered. "I don't know what the hell has gotten into you. Maybe you're forgetting why she's even here in the first place, but I'm all for fairness if you have a different opinion. Let's take a vote."

He had to have been expecting everyone to vote his way. He wouldn't have suggested it if he didn't think he was firmly in control of the outcome.

"Raise your hand if you think the princess should sleep in our beds and not on our floors." Merikh's voice was incredulous, and it was clear he thought the suggestion was absurd.

Grey was first, unapologetic in the way his hand shot up. Nix followed, shooting me a soft smile, and lastly, Caelan. Merikh's eyes rounded imperceptibly as his upper lip curled. "I see," he spat out. "She's got you all wrapped around her little finger? She needs the big bad men to come and save her? Or is it just that you're desperate for some convenient pussy?"

I lunged out of my chair, and without even thinking about it, slapped him across the face. Beyond the sharp sound of my hand hitting his cheek, the room was dead silent. No one spoke a word. I didn't dare turn to see the expressions on their faces–already feeling some semblance of shame and guilt for sinking to his level–instead, I jabbed my finger into his chest and bared my teeth. "Don't take it out on them that they might actually have some compassion, Merikh. I pity you." I scoffed. "All you'll ever be is a cruel, sadistic fucking bastard, using vulgarity to cover up your loneliness because no one other than family can stand to be around you."

He laughed derisively, running a hand through his dark waves. He hid it well, but his expression cracked for a moment, proving to me that my words held power over him. Good. I wanted him to *hurt* like his words hurt me. "Fuck you," he hissed, standing from his chair so fast that it hit the floor. He stormed out of the cabin, leaving the door to slam shut behind him.

"That could've gone worse!" Caelan said jovially.

"How?" I asked in disbelief.

"He could have broken your hand for slapping him in the face," Nix stated plainly, pushing his chair back from the table to cross his arms.

"First of all, what the fuck? And second, *what the fuck*?" I rubbed my eyes, suddenly feeling small and out of my depth. I didn't know how to handle these four larger-than-life men. I was angry that I even cared about the flash of anguish I'd seen in response to my words.

Caelan rounded the table, a mischievous grin in place. He walked up behind me, his body a wall of heat against my back, and tugged me so that I was leaning back on him. He then proceeded to rub my shoulders soothingly, and I let myself surrender to the feeling, my body turning to liquid in his hands. I closed my eyes, studiously avoiding looking at Nix and Grey, but they flew open at the feel of a kiss against my neck. God, what would Nix think? Would I look easy? Did this prove Merikh right, was I just convenient to them?

"Caelan," I admonished as I wriggled out of his grip. He tilted my head farther to the side, allowing him more access to press closed-mouth kisses.

"I know what you need," he whispered. It was hard to keep my thoughts straight with the feel of Caelan's lips on my skin, his breath skating across my neck. Lust was burning me up from the inside out, and I was losing myself to it.

The sound of a low murmur brought me back to reality just enough to be consumed by doubt once more. I was scared to look at Nix and Grey, scared of what I would find. If they saw that my affections had been claimed by someone else, would they refuse to help me? I didn't want to alienate them so soon into us discovering another dimension to our friendship, but it seemed the confrontation was happening now. Trust Caelan to forge that new territory for us, dragging me kicking and screaming into making a choice.

I shuddered as Caelan's tongue darted out to trace the soft skin of my throat.

"Fuck, that's hot," Nix muttered.

I snapped my head in his direction. My heart both sank and rose at his words. Did he like me so little that he didn't care if I was involved with someone else? He was just fine to pass me around? Or did this mean he wasn't going to hate me for getting involved with Caelan?

Caelan laid a hand over my stomach, holding me tight to his front so that I could feel the outline of his hard cock against the small of my back. "What are you so afraid of, baby? Do they know I already fucked you good and hard today?"

I wrenched out of his grip, breathing heavily and spinning around to face him. "Don't," I declared, shoving him back. "Don't make it sound crass, like I prefer you over them."

"You're saying you don't?" Grey asked. Nix watched me with hooded eyes, waiting for my response.

I softened. "No. No, I couldn't choose even if you asked me to."

Nix's grin was wicked. "Who says you have to?"

Then it was my turn for my eyes to widen. I glanced from Caelan's lopsided grin to Grey's carefully shuttered face. "No," I breathed, heart pounding a mad rhythm in my chest. I shouldn't have been thinking this, shouldn't have been entertaining the idea that they all wanted me. That

I could have... *all* of them. But after what happened with Caelan and the other night with Nix... and how could I deny my attraction to Grey?

More importantly, could I still leave them after we started whatever *this* was? Could it truly be so easy?

"That doesn't bother you, Grey?" Clearly, it didn't bother Nix or Caelan.

"I'll take you any way I can get you," he said gently, after a brief period of silence. "I know we haven't... yet, although I wanted to. More than anything, I wanted to. I don't mind the thought of you with them; it would be selfish of me to demand you all to myself when it's clear that your feelings go both ways."

Feelings. I didn't want to pick that apart.

I tried to process my racing thoughts, but they were a maelstrom of opinions and emotions and doubts, and I was getting nowhere. Though I was grateful that I wasn't being subtly influenced by Caelan's hands on my skin. He'd thankfully backed off to give me time to think over their proposition.

"Fine," I started. "But no more fetching your food, no more punishments."

Caelan hesitated. "We can't speak for Merikh, River. He's determined to make you pay for John."

"Why won't you just tell him?" Nix prodded.

How could I admit that I wasn't ready to let go of my anger? Maybe he wouldn't care, maybe it would change nothing. *Don't insult him by pretending you don't know that he'll be angry you kept it from him.* Besides, even if he did loosen up, I was still a pariah around camp.

I spoke between gritted teeth. "I just can't."

"We can't promise anything," Caelan rumbled, moving in to hold me again, his body vibrating at my back. "We're brothers, and our loyalty is to Merikh first."

Could I accept that?

I had to. I expected nothing less.

Caelan took my silence as agreement and began kissing my neck once more, eliciting a soft moan from me while the others watched. It was unbelievably erotic to have multiple eyes watching as Caelan touched me. Movement caught my eye, and I tilted my head to see Grey rubbing himself through his pants. *Fuck.* I shivered. I'd never felt so desired, so on display. It was a heady feeling. I wound my arm up and around Caelan's neck, the other covering the hand he had splayed across my abdomen under my shirt. The movement arched my back, making the sensations that much more intense.

Caelan tugged the lobe of my ear with his teeth, his free hand sliding up to cup my breast over my shirt. Nix grunted, canting his hips ever so slightly as I watched. I closed my eyes when Caelan started moving his hips in a slow grind, his breaths coming faster and stirring the hair at the back of my neck, goosebumps scattering over my skin.

While one large hand held my breast in a proprietary grip, he slid the other down my stomach, the tips of his fingers teasing the strip of skin above my shorts and just barely dipping under the fabric. I moaned, the anticipation driving me wild. Who knew Caelan had so much patience?

I smirked to myself, deciding to try to get him to speed up. I ground my ass back onto him subtly and bit my lip at the sound of his deep groan, interrupting the slow, steady movements of his hips. When he didn't stop his teasing, my hips bucked upwards, trying to get his hand lower to right where I was aching. It was surreal watching his scarred, tattooed hand span across the majority of my pale, unblemished skin.

"Look at how badly she wants it," Grey said with a smirk. He stalked forward, pressing his body against my front. Two hard bodies surrounded me now, all anticipatory heat and delicious warmth. I dropped my head back on Caelan's shoulder with a shudder as Grey took over and kissed my neck. My breath hitched once Caelan's hand finally dipped down into my shorts, dragging through my wetness and circling my clit softly. Grey tugged my shirt and bra over my head and bent to lay kisses over my breasts, teasing my nipples with his teeth and tongue. I whimpered, thrusting my chest upwards into his mouth. "More, please,"

I begged anyone who would listen. I was too impatient for this slow seduction. I wanted it all and I wanted it right then. I was burning up, all my senses sharpened to the brush of bare skin on skin, the scents of citrus.

I cracked my eyes open to look around Grey, finding Nix leaning lazily against the counter, cock out and in his hand. His eyes were hooded as he watched us and when our eyes met, he bit his lower lip, running it through his teeth slowly. The heat in his gaze left me breathless and *wanting*.

"Come here," I mouthed to him. He winked, looking more self-assured than I'd ever seen him, and strode forward until he reached me. I pulled him to my side, grabbing his chin and kissing him soundly on the lips. Three hot bodies surrounded me now, and it was intoxicating to know that I was the sole subject of their attention.

I knocked his hand aside so that I could stroke his cock instead, still keeping up my steady grind against Caelan. He was so fucking large that I could hardly fit my hand all the way around him. He kissed me harder in response, teeth nipping at my lower lip and groaning into my mouth. I took my arm from where it was slung around Caelan and ran it through Nix's hair, grabbing his dark waves and pulling his mouth firmer against mine.

"I like it when she takes what she wants," Grey murmured, heated eyes looking up from where he was lavishing attention on my nipples.

"He doesn't get it all," Caelan muttered grumpily. He wrapped his hand around my hair and tugged my head backward, meeting my lips in a passionate kiss over my shoulder.

I laughed against his mouth, my laughter turning into a loud moan as he thrust two fingers inside me. "Jealous much?" I breathed as he withdrew his fingers slowly, then pushed them in once more.

"I think if anyone's jealous, it's me," Grey murmured. "Apparently, these two have been off corrupting you while I've held back, trying to make a good impression."

"I think you've done an admirable job," I praised as I continued to stroke Nix. I used my free hand to rub Grey through his pants, drawing a deep groan that I felt throughout my entire body.

"Just like that, sweetheart," he growled, hips thrusting forward to seek my touch. His warm brown eyes met mine, searching and needy, growing darker when they dropped to watch Caelan's fingers plunge inside me.

"Fuck this," Caelan said roughly from behind me. He extracted me from the others, pulling me after him to the couch, then tugged my shorts and panties off in one smooth movement and sat down, drawing me onto his lap so that I was once again facing away from him. He spread his knees, hooking my legs around the outside of his so that mine spread wider the more he moved, and then I was completely bared. I felt my face flush, but one look at the dark desire on Grey and Nix's faces, and I immediately felt soothed.

Caelan slid one muscular tattooed arm down and started to spread me open, exposing me to the room and playing with me but not exactly touching me where I needed to be touched. His chin rested on my shoulder, watching his movements with hooded eyes.

"Look at this pretty pink pussy," he groaned. "All fucking ours."

One of them groaned, and the other one muttered a curse, but I was too busy willing Caelan's hand to move to notice who it was.

I threw my head back, clutching his arm as it played with my folds, dragging my wetness up like he'd circle my clit and then avoiding it.

"Grey," he called out. "I've already had her, so get the fuck over here."

Grey's eyes narrowed, most likely in irritation at the way he was summoned, but he still walked over. He sat next to Caelan, their knees touching, and patted his lap. I huffed as I was transferred like a fucking ragdoll. I decided to make the most of it, writhing on his lap and grinding against his hardness. He placed two firm hands on my hips, staying my movements. "Fuck, River. You're gonna make me come before the fun part," he grumbled. I burst out laughing, but stopped when he reached into his pants and pulled his throbbing cock out.

"Yes," I breathed. I was a little sore from earlier, but definitely didn't need any more foreplay to take Grey. My mind was spinning at how deliciously naughty this all was. Not only was I completely laid bare for three mostly clothed men, but we were also surrounded by floor-to-ceiling windows. *Anyone* could walk by, and damn if that didn't get my pulse racing.

He helped me spin around so that I could watch Nix while I rode him. I raised myself slowly, using my knees where they lay planted on the couch on either side of him, hovering over his tip so that it just barely ran over my entrance. Despite my lack of experience, it all felt oddly natural, as though my body knew exactly what to do before anyone had showed it. Going from being practically a virgin to having sex with multiple men should be scary, shouldn't it? But I felt no such fear or shame. I felt comfortable, safe, reassured. I still felt resentful, but it was overshadowed by something larger.

"My sweetheart is a tease, hm?" he spoke between harsh breaths, using his hands on my hips to pull me down roughly onto his length. I cried out at the impact, our moans mingling as he slid inside, filling me so fucking full. He thrust his hips upward, slamming in and out of me in smooth movements. His fingers gripped my hips so tightly I knew he'd leave bruises behind, and I moaned as I thought about how they'd look in the mirror the next day. He was a little larger than Caelan, and I could feel every thick inch of him as he withdrew.

Caelan reached over from his spot next to us, one hand stroking himself and the other playing with my clit. Sparks flew through my body as I shivered from the onslaught of pleasure.

"Fucking take him," Caelan groaned. "You like everyone watching you? Watching you get fucked right in front of us? Don't you just love our view of your wet pussy taking all that cock?" I groaned, shuddering at the rough sound of his voice, the dirty words that were filling our space. All my earlier frustration and stress had been consumed by a feverish desire, leaving my mind blank and my body pliable.

But we weren't complete yet.

I motioned Nix forward, positioning him right in front of me, then took over Caelan's stroking with my left hand, smirking at his choked moan. If I'd had any worries that I wouldn't be able to handle all of them at once, they were completely erased by their responses to me. Then I used my other hand to grab Nix's hip and pull him forward until he reached my lips. If I was going to do this, I might as well go all the fucking way. No inhibitions, no shame. I wanted it, so I was going to take it.

I just... didn't quite know how. I'd never blown anyone in my life. I had all the ambition and none of the experience. Nix must've sensed my hesitance, because he used his thumb to trace my lips, dipping into my mouth for me to suck. He hissed between clenched teeth, taking out his thumb and pulling my head forward until I was just kissing the tip of his cock. It was messy, precome covering my lips as I was jostled by Grey's movements. I grew bolder, licking his length with my tongue and hesitantly drawing the head into my mouth. He groaned, so I was obviously doing something right. His hand fell onto my head soothingly, not applying any pressure, but just comforting me.

I peeked up through my eyelashes, clenching down on Grey when I noticed Nix's half-lidded eyes, his mouth parted in pleasure. My confidence grew as the sounds of their pleasure echoed around me, grunts, pants, and groans filling the room. I took Nix's hardness fully into my mouth, sliding down until I hit about halfway and drawing back when I began to choke.

Grey moaned as he watched. "Oh shit, that's a good girl. Take him in your mouth again, you can do it." I did, surging back for another taste and swallowing a more manageable amount. I used my hand to stroke the part I couldn't reach. He was salty and slightly acidic, but the larger, more dominant taste was musky and unique to him.

Nix was already close, I could see it in how his pale skin flushed pink, the tendons in his neck straining as he threw his head back and groaned. His hand grasped the back of my head harder, fingers tangling in my hair. Grey's hands gripped my hips tighter, pulling me down onto his cock harder and faster as I stroked Caelan and sucked Nix. Caelan's hand remained firm on my clit where I was split open, and I was sweating from the overload of pleasure. Every single nerve was singing in ecstasy, it was otherworldly.

Then the door opened.

Merikh stomped in, jaw-dropping in shock as he watched us. Sure it was one thing to suspect, but to see us all... together, in *his* living room?

He was livid. His stare was hard–glacial–and his eyes grew darker as they ran the length of my body and paused on where Caelan was still massaging me in miniscule circles.

He curled his lip, then marched to his bedroom, slamming the door with a resounding bang.

I swallowed down the instinctual flash of shame, reassuring myself that I'd done nothing wrong. Unrestrained laughter bubbled up in me at the completely inappropriate timing of Merikh finding one brother's cock inside me and the other down my throat. My fucking god, there were so many dicks out.

Caelan laughed, stopping only when he was shushed by Grey. We all stopped for a moment, put back into motion by Grey thrusting into me impatiently. I sucked in an unsteady breath, leaning back slightly.

"Do we... I mean..." I trailed off as Nix shook his head. The glide of Grey's hard cock sent shivers down my spine. I arched my back, taking Nix back into my mouth once again and working him harder than before. I shook off the awkwardness of knowing Merikh was down the hall, a weird, excited sensation filling me at the thought that he could hear us.

"No damn way are we stopping now, baby. I wanna see you come for us, sweaty and hot and squeezing my dick so fucking hard," Grey rumbled. I moaned, wriggling my hips.

My eyes darted to Caelan as I stroked him, his lips puffy from our kisses and his eyes hooded from pleasure. He winked, mouth parting as I gripped him tighter.

The pleasant ache built, compounded by Caelan's hand on my clit, rubbing and stroking softly, and Grey's hand doing the same to my breasts. I rolled my hips, chasing after my climax and letting the ecstasy consume me. It was hovering just within reach, so close I could taste it.

Nix started murmuring about how he was close, his hips stuttering as he came with a groan, filling my mouth with his salty release. He'd attempted to pull back, murmuring about how I didn't need to, but I grabbed onto his hips and held him in my mouth. No way was I spitting it out like I had no idea what I was doing. I swallowed every drop, licking my lips for him once I finally pulled off with a pop, meeting his heavy-lidded green eyes. He grunted, hips propelling forward several more times before he collapsed backward into one of the armchairs with a tired groan.

Caelan laughed, only stopping when he started to tremble under my hand. He came with a loud groan, taking over my movements and stroking himself roughly, almost angrily. The sight of his tattooed hand gripping his twitching length was almost too much to handle.

I turned my attention to Grey as he took over for Caelan, rubbing my clit in a rhythmic motion. At the euphoric feel of his hard body beneath me, the sight of the prominent veins on his hand at my clit, and the salty taste of Nix in my mouth, I shattered.

Caelan leaned forward, nipping at my ear, and murmuring just for me to hear as I shook. "That's it, baby. Milk his cock. I bet you're clenching him so fucking tight." I shuddered as his hot breath hit my skin, eyes shuttering from the overload of my senses. My muscles spasmed as my pleasure crested, sending violent tremors throughout my body. My moans were louder than they probably should have been, for two reasons. One, I'd never been able to express my pleasure so vocally before when I'd masturbated; either I was scared to attract zombies or there were people in a camp nearby that could hear, not to mention my dad. And two, I knew Merikh could hear me, and I felt an acute tingling in my chest knowing that he was listening to the sound of me coming right outside his door at the hands of his brothers.

Grey thrust several more times before pushing me up gently and pulling out. He grunted, and wetness hit my back as he came with a low groan.

"Well, shit." Caelan snickered as he looked at everyone. I withheld a smile of my own. From no sex to twice in one day, if they kept it up, I'd be craving them all the time. Grey pressed a soft kiss to my forehead before depositing me on the couch next to Caelan.

I was exhausted.

Caelan pulled me against his sweaty body where he was reclined against the cushions and used his discarded shirt to clean my back off. I murmured my thanks, burrowing into his warmth. Nix settled more comfortably on the chair adjacent to the fire, legs spread and zipper down, meeting my eyes with a secretive smile while Grey settled at the end of the couch, pulling my feet into his lap and stroking them softly. To stave off the impending post-sex discussion, I reiterated what I had told Caelan earlier when he'd asked me about protection.

I sighed, turning so that my back was against Caelan, and I could watch the rest of the room. My eyelids drooped as the fire crackled beside us. "Merikh?" I asked.

"Sleep out here tonight," Nix commented. "With us."

I gave a sleepy smile at that. I didn't think I'd ever felt so complete, so satiated.

Caelan stroked my hair soothingly before chiming in. "Sleep, baby."

I let my eyes close all the way, succumbing to my tiredness and feeling oddly safe surrounded by them all.

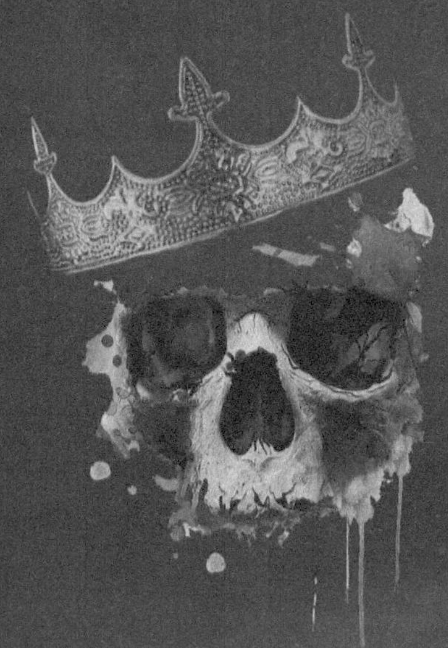

CHAPTER 11

Someone was whispering.

"Shut up! You're gonna wake her up."

"I don't fucking care if I wake her up. Why do *you* care? You slept with her all of the sudden and now you care if she sticks around? If she *likes* you?"

Silence ensued.

I stretched, cracking my eyes open and looking around the living room. I felt something moving underneath me and realized that I must have fallen asleep against Caelan, who was still sleeping soundly.

Nix, Grey, and Merikh were in the kitchen, watching me cautiously.

I felt my face flush, and I wanted to squeeze my eyes shut and pretend they weren't there. Everything was different in the darkness, in the nighttime. Facing the light of day after what we'd done... Did they regret it? Did I?

Relief flooded through me as Nix gave me a wink, and Grey smiled behind Merikh's back. Merikh just watched me. He was expressionless, aside from the muscle that was jumping in his jaw every other second. At this rate, he was going to ruin his teeth.

"We're grabbing breakfast," he said flatly before leaving. The others leveled hopeless looks on me before following.

Caelan and I were alone in the silence left in his angry wake.

"He's jealous," Caelan rumbled from underneath me, causing me to jolt. I laughed, smacking his arm and arching against his front as he kissed my neck. "He is," he mumbled against my skin, sleepy and soft. Sometime over the night, they must have draped a blanket over me because it covered me from just below my collarbones to my ankles. "Look at you, baby. Delicious," he drawled as he stroked my sides teasingly.

He laughed when my stomach growled, ceasing his lazy kisses. He sat up, cradling me to his body as he perched at the edge of the couch.

"No matter what he says, don't shut down on us. Okay?"

I doubted I would, but then again, I couldn't know for sure. There was something about Merikh. I saw the way his eyes traveled my body when I was spread out before him, both hate and desire in equal measure. Would he command the others to leave me alone? Could he force me out of the arrangement I'd stumbled into with these three?

"Don't overthink it," Caelan muttered. He stood with a yawn, all tired blue eyes and ruffled dark hair. He looked so innocent if you ignored his intimidatingly large stature and extensive tattoos. And his scars. And his muscles. Okay... maybe he didn't look so innocent after all.

He was so much taller than me, I had to tilt my head backward to meet his eyes.

"I'll try not to," I replied, while also trying not to gape at his shirtless upper body.

"Stop tempting me," he growled playfully, grabbing my chin and holding me still for a heated kiss. I groaned into his mouth, smacking his arm and pulling back.

"Come on," I insisted. "I'm starving."

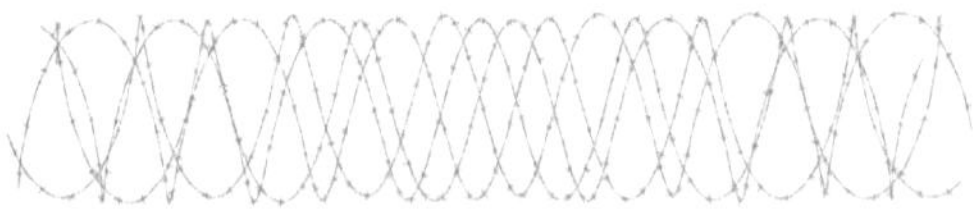

They didn't usually stick around to eat with the camp, but it seemed they did that morning. My attention was drawn to them from the second I entered the food tent, and I spent our entire time in line watching them out of the corner of my eye.

"Pretty girl," Caelan murmured from behind me. "How I want a repeat of last night." He sounded so put out that I just had to laugh.

"Insatiable, that's what you are."

"I never claimed to be easily satisfied," he said in a low growl. He picked me up, spinning me around and smacking my ass before setting me back down.

I hit his chest playfully, but with a very real fear behind it. "Not in public!" What would people think if they saw the girl who murdered their friend cozying up to the leader's sons? The same girl who so adamantly protested her presence in the camp to anyone that would listen? I was constantly attempting to suppress both mortification and anxiety over the fact that I had switched sides so easily. I just had to keep reminding myself that I'd be leaving as soon as the opportunity presented itself.

He rolled his eyes with a flirtatious grin. Obviously, he didn't care what people thought of him. He did what he wanted, when he wanted, and he was surprisingly unapologetic about it. I admired that about him, even if it didn't bode well for any future public appearances.

We got our food quickly, heading over to where Merikh, Nix, and Grey were occupying a table near the center. The immediate space surrounding them was empty, and others watched them cautiously. It seemed I wasn't the only one wary of what they were capable of. I supposed I would steer clear of anyone who had the power to kick me out of camp too, mercurial bastards.

I winced as I sat down, and I should've known Merikh wouldn't miss it, as observant as he was. He shot me a venomous sneer. "Sore?" he asked innocently, eyes flickering dangerously and betraying his anger.

Fuck this guy. "As a matter of fact, yes."

Caelan laughed between bites. "Oh, I like her," he purred.

A girl glared at us as she passed by where we sat, her many braids lit by the sunlight streaming through the holes in the tarp. She was stunning. "Another conquest?" I remarked sharply. For fuck's sake, I just couldn't help myself.

Grey grinned, slowly at first, then it spread wider and wider until it was lighting up his whole face. "You're jealous."

I crossed my arms. "Absolutely not."

Nix winked while Caelan snorted, pulling me into his side. "Nothing to be jealous about, baby," he commented as he nuzzled my hair. I huffed a reluctant laugh.

Merikh watched quietly, jaw set firmly. I loathed him. I hated that he took me, I hated that he kept me, I hated that he sent some random man into isolation all because his *rule* was threatened. I hated how much I *needed* to hate him for everything to make sense.

I must have been broadcasting my thoughts or something because the emotion on his face shuttered. "We'll be visiting the children today."

"What about Nix?"

He glanced at his brother. "He has something else to do."

I was silent, which he took as assent.

"I'll meet you there," he said shortly, getting up from the table with a pensive frown on his face. Those around him steered clear, sensing his darkening mood. Was it ever not dark? I gave a mental shrug.

"What the hell," I muttered as I picked at my potatoes with my plastic fork.

"It's been just us for a long time," Nix said softly, looking after his brother with a crease in his brow.

I sighed, feeling a tightness in my chest. I knew what change was like. A woman a few years younger than my dad had breezed through our temporary camp once, flirting with him every chance she got. It made me wildly uncomfortable. He could no longer accompany me when I went scavenging or to gather water because she always pressured him to stay back with her, telling him that I would be fine and what would she do without him? *Cue the teary eyes.* I hadn't wanted to begrudge him his happiness; he'd had nobody around except me since my mother passed. Eventually, she slipped up by asking him to move on with her and to leave me behind, saying that I was plenty old enough to survive by myself. He kicked her out then, firmly declining her offer and apologizing to me that he let it get so bad. I just laughed it off and told him that I wished him better luck next time. I'd caught the weird bitch eating her own toenails one morning, and that was *before* I'd written her off. It made my heart ache when I remembered no one else had ever come along, and now he'd never get the chance.

I hoped he and my mom were happy wherever they were.

Grey flashed me a reassuring smile. "Go easy on him, River. It's hard work trying to keep the camp in order, all while making sure everyone is safe."

"I guess I'll go join him, then, before he gets impatient and takes it out on me." I shoveled my last bite in my mouth and groaned happily at the flavor as I slid off the bench. I turned when Grey called my name and tugged me right into his waiting arms. He gripped my chin, kissing my lips passionately before pulling away with a smirk as I melted in his arms. I kissed him once more, his lips firm against mine, sending shivers down my spine until I realized all eyes were on us. *Of course, he's just making a statement.* Hopefully, the whispers would lessen and stay behind my back instead of right in front of my face.

"Stop it," I hissed. "We're in public!"

Nix covered his mouth, coughing out a laugh while Caelan didn't bother to hide his. Grey smacked my ass affectionately before sending me on my way. I swatted at his arm, frowning as I left and hoping that my cheeks weren't as red as they felt.

Halli approached me as I exited the tent, a secretive smile on her face. "Soooo... it seems congratulations are in order?"

She wore a bright orange skirt today with golden bangles that jingled as she moved. I eyed them wistfully. I could never wear jewelry before; I was always too concerned it would make noise while we were hiding, attracting unwanted attention. Or that a zombie would get too close and rip it off me, slowing me down somehow. I supposed... *maybe* that could change now.

"I like your bracelets," I said with a smile that quickly turned into something contemplative. "And... I don't know. I just know that things are different."

"But you're happy?" she pressed.

"I'm not unhappy." I toed a wayward clump of grass by my foot, swinging my head up to gaze at the bright sun overhead. "I don't know, Halli. I still plan on getting out of here." I whispered the last part, confused at the anxious twisting I felt in my gut. If I could tell anyone about my second thoughts, well, it would be Halli.

"Don't let your resentment ruin a perfectly good thing," she said softly, lips curving. Her lids were painted a burnt orange color to match her skirt. It was so hard to find makeup that hadn't grown mold or decayed over time. Maybe she'd made it herself; it seemed like something she'd be good at, and I'd heard it was possible.

"Shouldn't I though? Shouldn't I be resisting as much as possible?"

"It's not weak to make the best of your situation, River. Just like it's not the end of the world if you change your mind. Circumstances are always shifting." She squinted as she followed my eyes to the wispy clouds overhead. "Give it time." With that, she patted my shoulder affectionately. I felt tears rise unbidden at her advice. It was odd having someone who cared, who knew me enough even, to offer advice.

She clucked at my watery eyes, pulling me in for a tight hug. She was stronger than she seemed, all long limbs and lithe arms. Gardening had given her a secret strength.

"Thanks, Halli," I muttered as I pulled away, swiping at my face. She patted my shoulder again, turning in a swish of fabric to enter the food tent while I continued along my path to the building where the children were. I could hear screaming coming from inside, and quickened my pace with concern, only slowing when I heard the accompanying laughter.

I opened the door to find Nerese comforting a crying child, red hair falling in her face while she soothed him. Merikh spoke with Naia in hushed tones, a girl that came up to about his knee hanging onto his hand and swinging. He smiled at her absentmindedly, ruffling her golden girls. I tried not to grin, but it was hard. He seemed so... approachable. So sweet.

Then he saw me.

His face shuttered, and he ended his conversation with Naia. I immediately wanted to bolt back out the door and meet Halli, Grey, or literally anyone else. Maybe I could beg Caelan to take me to the wall for guard duty. I just couldn't be in this tight space with him looking at me like he was.

"River!" Naia exclaimed. She pulled me in for a hug, guiding me aside so we could talk. "The kids missed you," she informed me as she watched them play. There was an abundance of toys and worn books scattered across the floor. "It's not often they see fresh faces."

Then she glanced at Merikh, who was crouching to speak with the golden-haired girl. "What's going on there?" she whispered conspiratorially.

I sighed. "You know I'm not here because I chose to be, right?"

Her face dropped. "I don't understand."

"I killed John, and... maybe tried to take his supplies first, and was brought back as penance."

"I heard that you killed John and about the whole theft part, but for some reason, I guess I thought they took pity on you and invited you here. They've done that with most of the orphans and strays here over the years."

"No. I found his bag of supplies and took it. When he found me, he was infected and he... tried to force himself on me. I was just protecting myself."

A tiny furrow creased her brow, and her translucent skin was flushed, hiding her freckles from view and practically matching her hair. "I find it hard to believe that they would fault you for that."

"They didn't know," I mumbled. She cocked her head, and I rushed to clarify in a hushed whisper. "I mean, they could see from the body that he was infected, but I didn't tell them he was going to force himself on me. It just looked like he finally hunted me down to get his stuff and was bitten in the process, and that I killed him for that with the added benefit of still making off with his supplies. The others only found out recently and Merikh still doesn't know."

"Wouldn't you want him to?"

"I... No. At least I think I don't. So it's fine for him to bring me back here against my will for killing an infected man, but release me out of pity once he finds out the circumstances surrounding it? I wasn't weak or defenseless, and I don't want a free pass because I definitely would have killed him anyway, just because he was infected. Yeah, maybe he wouldn't have gotten bitten in the first place if he didn't go off course to find me, but I can't say I feel too bad since he was a fucking pervert anyway. If anything, I'm embarrassed that I resorted to taking someone else's stuff, but there was no one around and I was starving."

She sighed, resting her head against her thin hand. "I can't say I agree with you because he was the one foolish enough to leave his stuff somewhere, but I understand. You must feel so conflicted about everything, especially now that everyone knows what you did, just not the how or why."

Well, that answered that question; clearly, Anna hadn't told anyone about the other aspect of our encounter.

We watched Merikh split his attention between the two kids hanging off his arms as we stood in comfortable silence. My cheeks turned crimson with embarrassment when I realized I had been talking about myself for so long without asking her a single thing.

"How long have you been here?"

"Our mom found this place ten years ago and we've been here ever since."

I didn't ask about their father, since it was probably a guaranteed tragedy, and I wanted to spare her the pain I would feel if someone asked me. I felt my dad's loss like a limb sometimes, an aching phantom pain. He had been with me always: laughing, teaching, guiding. Sometimes I felt so adrift. Purposeless.

"It must've been nice growing up here," I said wistfully.

"Would you stay? If you had a choice?"

I looked at Naia, laughing with one of the older girls as she braided her hair. I thought of Halli, of the kids, and the garden, and the lake. The showers and the beds. The *safety*. If I was free... where would I go? I'd be a nomad once more, sleeping with one eye open on dirty floors and even dirtier roofs, scavenging for scraps. But there was something disconcerting about the number of people here. The noise, the bustle. Sometimes I felt as if there were a target on this place, and I needed to distance myself in order to minimize the threat.

"Maybe," I finally replied.

Merikh looked up, and when his hardened eyes met mine, I felt the sudden urge to fan myself. He had no *right* to be so damn alluring. He was all cool glares and disdain and, for some reason, it was pushing all my buttons.

"He does it for you, huh?" Nerese joked as she sidled up next to us.

My cheeks flushed at being caught blatantly ogling him. I was fortunate that he was once more occupied with the kids. "I mean... look at him. I've only ever known dirty old men. Not... whatever he is."

Nerese threw her head back and laughed, drawing the attention of every person in the room. Everyone except Merikh, who was once again eyeing me, this time with suspicion. I rolled my eyes, scratching an itch near my collarbone with my middle finger. Discreetly, of course. Just because the world had gone to shit didn't mean I needed to be a bad influence on the kids.

He looked… adorably confused. Hadn't *anyone* ever humbled this man? Damn, I had my work cut out for me.

Naia broke my concentration by dropping a little girl into my lap.

"Oh, hello," I said, swallowing my surprise.

Her eyes were huge, dark brown pools. "Hello."

"What's your name?"

She played with the hole over the knee of her pants, squirming slightly. She looked to be about… five? I wasn't sure. She was taller than the others but skinner too. "Mama calls me Khira, but my whole name is Sakhira."

"I haven't heard that before, I like it. My name is River."

"I swam in a river once!" she exclaimed. "Daddy killed somebody there."

My jaw dropped, and I looked to Nerese to find her hiding a smile behind her hand. "Oh?"

"Yeah." Her face screwed up. "Some nasty zombie lady. He said he'd show me how to do it one day too."

I widened my eyes at Naia, begging for assistance. My god, were all kids like this? "Do… show you how to… kill zombies?"

"Yah." She nodded. "We just got here, and we had to kill them all the time before. He promised he'd teach me when I get older. I'm gonna be the best at it."

The girl I'd met last time I visited walked over and plopped in front of my lap. She didn't say anything though, just stared at me.

"Uh… hi!" I said hesitantly, internally freaking out that I was going about this all wrong. How do I switch us off from zombie talk?

"That's Layla," Sakhira declared loudly.

Suddenly Merikh was there. "Come on, Khira, I've got a surprise to show you and the others."

"I love surprises!" she shouted, jumping off my lap and grabbing his hand. He led her over to the rest of the little crowd he'd gathered, and I took a deep breath.

Holy shit, she was going to be a force of nature when she grew up. "Are they all like that?" I asked Naia and Nerese.

"Not all," Nerese said with a snicker. "It's so different for them. When we were growing up, the virus had only just mutated, and the world was still adjusting. Our parents tried to cling to what they knew, shielding us from the violence, keeping us hidden away, distracting us from the fact that people were dying left and right. These kids' parents have had more time to adjust, so they're less strict about what the kids are allowed to see and learn. We make sure they know how dangerous the zombies are, how fast it takes someone to turn once bitten, how to scavenge and judge the quality of any foods they find. They're growing up so much faster than the generations before them."

Naia chimed in, "At least when they make it to the camp, they're able to take it easy for a while and just be kids. It's easier to... pretend. To forget."

"Don't I know it," I sighed. Layla shifted, big blue eyes finally done examining me as she handed me a tattered children's book. I gestured her over, my heart twisting as I read the cover.

The North Star.

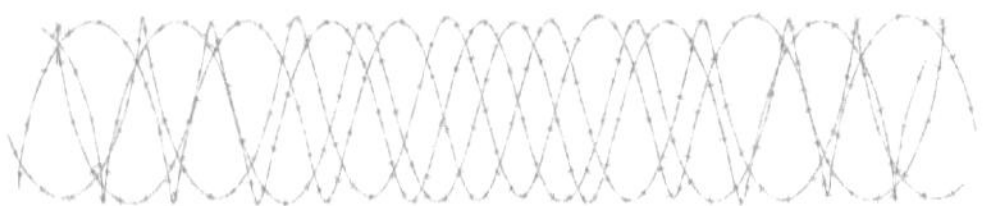

L unch came faster than I'd anticipated. Time had flown by.

"Do you guys bring something to eat? Or..." I whispered as I rolled a toy car across the floor, passing it back and forth between my hands.

"Nah." Nerese shrugged. "We're so close to the food tent, usually someone pops in so we can take a break."

"Go ahead, then. Merikh and I will stay behind and watch them. We can take turns."

Naia smiled kindly. "Thanks, River. We'll be back soon."

And with that, they left, closing the door quietly behind them, leaving us sitting in silence. Most of the children were napping, as they'd eaten their lunches a little earlier. Apparently, they only slept for an hour or two and then they had some outside playtime. Naia said that just last week they'd taken a field trip to the garden.

Merikh sat across the room monitoring the few children that were tossing and turning. I watched him for several long moments before he noticed, lips pressing into a firm line.

"When will it be enough, Merikh?"

He blinked, cocking his head to the side.

I clarified. "When will my penance be paid? You can't keep me here forever."

His long legs were outstretched in front of him, crossed at the ankle. He always looked so... *composed.* When he spoke, his voice was low and thick. "When I say so. Besides, are you so desperate to leave your new adoring fans?"

I felt a burst of anger for him then and fought the impulse to launch myself at him and... I wasn't sure.

"Something's got you riled up, princess. Do I have the pleasure?"

I huffed, turning my head to the side and ignoring him. It wasn't enough. I could still see his clasped hands out of the corner of my eye. For a man so obsessed with control, I liked to see that his fingernails were bitten.

He scowled when he caught me looking, turning his hands so that his nails faced inwards. "I'm not just going to let you go, River. You killed someone. You stole from him. It was all your fault he was infected."

"If it was anyone else, you would turn them out to the wilds, yet you do the opposite for me."

He shrugged, a half-hearted lift of his broad shoulder. "That's the worst punishment for them. For you, who was already free..."

Yeah, yeah, I get it.

"I hate you."

Another lift of his shoulder. He huffed a breath and reclined his head so that the column of his throat was exposed, pale and smooth. I looked away, unwilling to submit to the desire that stirred for him.

"They like you," he murmured finally, throat moving with the words.

"Naia and Nerese?"

"The others."

I tilted my head contemplatively. Did they like me? Or was I just a convenient lay for them?

"And that bothers you."

He was silent, but he brought his head back up to face me. I decided to test my theory. I stretched where I sat up against the wall, arching my back so that my chest rose. My breasts strained against the cheap, threadbare bra, exposed by the black shirt I was wearing as it went sheer in some places. I leaned my head back to stretch my neck and pretended to close my eyes, cracking them open just a sliver to watch his reaction.

Ha. Heat, need, want, all swirled together in his deep blue eyes. His fists clenched and his eyelids grew heavy as he watched me. I finished my stretch, cracking my neck before facing him. His expression was once more shuttered, tucked away behind that stony facade. The only sign that he was still bothered was the way his jaw was working as he ground his teeth.

He wanted me. He wanted me and he *hated* it. Fuck. Holy shit. I could *use* this.

He eyed me suspiciously. I immediately pushed down my eagerness, storing it away for later. Distraction time.

"You're protective over your brothers," I commented as I watched him.

"Who else?"

"Themselves."

He waved a dismissive hand, and his face hardened. "Caelan used to get into fights nightly. If we hadn't redirected his energy to killing the zombies outside the wall, it only would have escalated. Nix wouldn't speak. My father... he would be silent for days afterward. Only sending that manipulative bastard on frequent scavenging missions and making him think they were his idea broke Nix out of his shell. Grey was so shattered after the deaths of his family that he was acting recklessly and taking risks, no matter how many times he insisted he wanted to live. He needed a purpose."

My eyes widened as he talked, more than I'd ever heard him say all at once. He was impassioned, eyes blazing with conviction and the hurt of past wrongs. He stopped short, somehow looking angry at himself for revealing so much.

"I'm sorry. Truly. For all that you've been through," I said softly. I hadn't realized just how much he'd done for his brothers, how much he *saw* them, just like I hadn't understood how much they'd been through. Or maybe I just didn't want to see it. It was easy to see them as privileged, they lived in the equivalent of a castle. They were well-fed and powerful, safe and secure, and I'd forgotten that they didn't start out that way. It was a selfish point of view that was proven wrong more and more each day.

He nodded stiffly, giving me his profile.

"And you?"

"Me?"

"What about the boy that had to grow up too fast to take care of the others? Who's protective over you?"

He opened his mouth. Closed it.

"That boy died a long time ago."

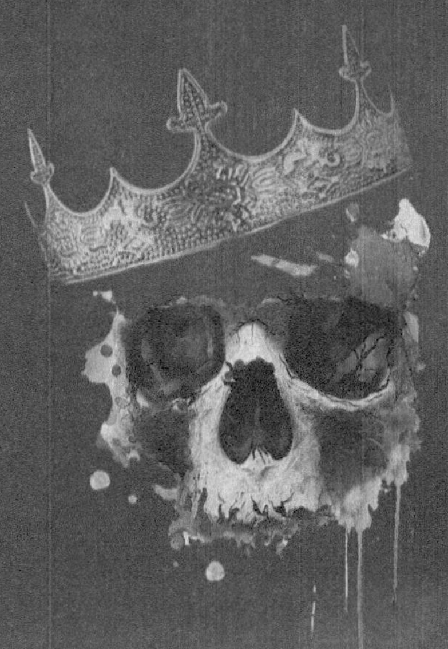

CHAPTER 12

"Do you want to come to a gathering with us tonight?" Naia asked. She took a seat beside me in one of the colorful kid-sized stools and began to organize the array of toys before us.

I almost laughed. It was so distinctly reminiscent of the conversations I'd find within the pages of the novels I'd scavenged over the years.

She took my silence as hesitation and rushed to reassure me. "We have a good stock of unspoiled liquor–"

Nerese interrupted, scrunching her nose. "Not that junk that Lincoln makes in his tent."

Naia cut back in. "And sometimes a group of us like to gather in the meadow and drink after sundown. Sometimes someone will play music and we can dance, other times we all just trade stories and talk amongst ourselves."

I peeked outside to gauge the time and found the sun just setting, streaks of pinks and purples running through the reddened sky and turning it bloody.

I looked to Merikh for some reason, gauging his reaction. Was this the kind of thing he would ban me from attending? A muscle in his jaw jumped, but he inclined his head slowly.

I pretended not to see it.

I wasn't sure if anyone noticed, or even cared.

"I'd love to," I said with a growing smile. Friends. Normality. Fun. I could get used to this. I'd had alcohol before, sips of vodka or whiskey here and there. I was fortunate my dad wasn't a drunk. We'd met more than a few people that spent their days looking at the bottom of the bottle and letting whoever was with them do all the work to keep them alive.

Merikh gave me one last censuring look, then left.

Naia laughed. "Freedom must feel nice, huh? Glad your warden isn't coming."

A rush of relief and something that felt a little too much like disappointment hit me. "He doesn't usually attend?"

"Nope," she said with a smile, exaggerating the p with a loud pop. "Merikh? Have a good time? I don't think he knows the meaning."

I sighed, already feeling the stress of the last few days melt away in the anticipation of doing something fun. "I'm so ready to let loose."

My mood instantly soured when I remembered my predicament. "You don't think... Will people want me there?" The tremor in my voice betrayed my nervousness, no matter how hard I tried to suppress it.

Naia patted my knee gently. "I promise people aren't as upset as you think, despite all the whispers. A lot of us remember what it was like to be starving and desperate, and don't begrudge you for doing what you needed to survive. Besides, the majority of us don't even see a connection between a bag of supplies left unattended and the events that followed."

That was a relief. Hopefully, I could find a spot near the back and blend in so I didn't draw any attention.

Once the children were all picked up by their assigned caregivers, we left. The moonlight was out in full force, and it streamed down on the buildings, reflecting a pearlescent sheen off the metal sheets they were reinforced with. I rubbed my bare arms, shivering slightly at the chill in the brisk night air.

"This way," Nerese called from up ahead. We skirted around the food tent, walking behind it until we hit the first stretch of trees.

For a long few minutes, we followed the trail in silence, stumbling slightly over rocks and dips that were impossible to see just by the moonlight and dodging shadowy branches that jutted into the path.

Eventually, we were spat out into a clearing where a bonfire sat in the center. Several people were already there, various glasses, bottles, and mugs in hand.

I didn't see anyone I recognized, except for Anna. Anna was there, and she looked *pissed*.

"Ignore her," Nerese insisted. "Here, this will definitely give you a boost of courage." She pulled a short bottle out of her satchel and passed it to me. I tried to stall by attempting to read the label on the side, but it was too faded and dirtied to see. Realizing it was now or never, I took a deep breath in, hoping I wasn't about to make a fool of myself and took a sip of the foul-smelling liquid. The minute it hit the back of my throat, I had to work on suppressing my gag and the urge to wipe my watering eyes. The liquid settled unhappily in my stomach, and I was grateful that Naia had given me some homemade crackers earlier.

She laughed when she saw my reaction. "It's strong, yeah? I can't imagine you had many chances to drink out in the wilds."

I snorted, passing her back the bottle. "No, definitely not."

More and more people began to show up as we found seats around the fire. One guy had brought a guitar and was strumming along, while others danced freely to the music. It was unlike anything I'd ever seen. No censure or whispers or fear. Just freedom.

Naia leaned into me, red hair spilling over her shoulders. This close I could see a trio of freckles near her right eye that Nerese was missing. "Most of us have had to grow up too fast and many of us have no parents or family here. The others respect that we want time to relax and need a safe space to do so."

"So you're saying no old man is going to come barreling down the path with a bottle?"

She threw her head back and laughed, a high tinkling sound. "Exactly that. There's no hard and fast rule, more that they probably wouldn't have a good time. We have different events for all ages to try to accommodate everyone. Storytime by the fire for the kids, knitting and tea, or a mini jazz concert."

That sounded magical. I took the bottle back from her, taking an adventurous gulp this time and hoping to drown the wistfulness that rose up to choke me in response to the picture she'd painted with her words. The drink went straight to my head, compounding off of what I'd had earlier with my smaller sips, and I swayed slightly where I was sprawled out. A slow warmth rolled through my body, causing a content giggle to escape me.

The hair on the back of my neck stood up, and I felt warm for a whole different reason. The others quieted in a way I found familiar at this point. My head snapped up to find Merikh standing at the center of the bonfire, surrounded by a few guys I'd never met before.

His gaze was solely on me.

My eyes flew open, and I leaned heavily on Naia to hiss in her ear. "I thought you said he wasn't gonna be here!"

She just gave me an apologetic shrug, looking just as mystified as I was.

"I could eat him up," Nerese murmured from my other side. I laughed, too loud and too enthusiastic for her declaration. I pushed down the irrational jealousy that reared its head. *He's not mine and I don't want him to be. It's just the alcohol.*

His dark blue eyes were glowing in the moonlight, tousled curls looking positively sinful. The shadows crisscrossed his face, emphasizing the sharpness of his jaw and the hollows under his cheekbones. He was beautiful, but it was a cruel beauty.

"What's so funny?" he called from across the fire.

"Wouldn't you like to know," I replied boldly.

I flushed the moment I realized I'd spoken the words aloud. His eyes sparked in response.

He rounded the fire slowly, bottle dangling from his fingertips, black shirt tight across his chest. Anna intercepted him, laying a hand on his shoulder and leaning to whisper in his ear. I quickly looked away, the tips of my ears heating as I studiously ignored them.

"Must be nice living with him," Naia said as she raised her eyebrows suggestively.

"You know I can't stand the man, right?" I complained with a shred of desperation, reminding her for what felt like the fiftieth time.

"Doesn't mean you can't have fun!" she retorted, laughing.

"It does! It does mean that I can't!"

"What does?" a deep voice asked.

I resisted the urge to flinch from the realization that he was now within spitting distance, instead leaning back on my elbows so that I was sprawled across the ground, then tilting my head back and back and back until his face came into view. Anna stood nearby, pouting.

Ah, he turned her down? So sad.

"Nothing," I replied with a raised brow. That was casual, right? I sure hoped so.

"Having fun?" he bit out.

"I am." My smile was a slow thing, liquid and filled with promise. He blinked, before narrowing his eyes like he didn't know what I was up to.

Even I didn't know what I was up to. I just knew it felt good to needle him, to watch the surprise flit across his face. I felt powerful, giddy, weightless. I wanted to see all that cruel, wicked beauty taken down a notch.

Someone plopped down behind me, jostling my back with their knee. "Nice to meet you," a different voice said. I tossed my hair to the side, turning to get a better look. My body turned with me. Brown hair fell to his shoulders, messy and threaded with caramel. His eyes were green, and broadcasting interest. Any other time I would have been wary of the attention, but intrigued. But after my night with the others, I couldn't imagine entertaining an advance from anyone else.

I decided to irritate Merikh even further and let a slow smile surface. "Pleasure," I greeted him. "I'm River."

"River," he repeated, looking victorious. "I'm Thomas."

I rolled his name around in my mouth. "Thomas. I haven't seen you around." A quick glance at my surroundings revealed that Anna was fuming from her spot across the fire, whereas Merikh was still standing before us with a pinched expression, his lips pressed into a flat, unimpressed line.

Thomas grabbed my attention with a disarming smile. "I've been on guard duty. Sometimes I help out in the kitchen."

I hummed, looking for the bottle and smiling gratefully when Nerese pressed it into my hand. I took another large gulp, wincing at the burning sensation in my throat.

"You're beautiful," Thomas said in a low voice. He stroked a loose wave back from my face, caressing my cheek as he went. I didn't hate it... but I didn't like it either. There were no sparks, no tingling in my chest, not like there was for Grey, Nix, and Caelan.

I leaned back out of his reach, letting out a nervous giggle. My head spun with the movement, and I took a second to wonder when I'd drank so much. The flames intensified, and my toes grew uncomfortably warm. I stared into the fire, watching the embers fall onto the grass and remembering all the times I'd lectured my dad during our own campfires, insistent that the grass would catch fire from the little flurries of burning ash.

My mood turned heavy the moment I thought of my dad, and I realized how alone I was, even though I was surrounded by people. Thomas reached a hand out to grab my attention once more, moving way too close. I squirmed, opening my mouth to make an excuse to leave, when an arm grabbed mine.

I was pulled upwards and straight into Merikh's firm embrace. "Enough," he growled, glaring at Thomas.

I blinked until my vision cleared, focusing on where my hands rested on his warm skin, how his muscles twitched where I touched him. His hair was tousled and messy, cheeks flushed, though he didn't seem to be drinking as I had. He smelt strongly of smoke and jasmine, but none of the acrid scents of liquor.

Thomas stammered out an apology, and everyone politely ignored Naia's uncomfortable giggles. The guitar playing continued across the fire, along with murmured voices and laughter, but the area surrounding us was largely silent except for the crackling of the fire.

"I'll be fine," I whispered to a concerned Nerese. She nodded, giving me a halfhearted wave.

"Come on, princess," Merikh said gruffly, letting me out of his hold and pulling me along. I followed him, stumbling as we walked and grabbing onto the hem of his shirt so that I didn't fall.

I didn't know where he was taking me, and I didn't particularly care. We left the clearing, taking the trail through the forest back to the center of the camp when he tugged my hand roughly, pulling me to the side and shoving me up against a tree so that my back hit with an *oomph*. The fresh scents of soil and evergreen almost drowned out the jasmine on his skin, and the bark was abrasive against my back. The tiny shock of pain helped clear my head a little, allowing me to focus on him better.

"What the fuck were you thinking?" he rasped. His breath was hot on my neck, eyes angrier than I'd ever seen them.

"I don't understand," I told him honestly, slurring my words only a little.

"Thomas would chew you up and spit you out, parade you around for a week until he's ready for a fresh flavor. Don't go to these things and speak to random men. You're not theirs."

"Then whose am I?" I asked, searching his eyes for an answer. *What am I even asking him? What do I want to hear?*

His hands flexed where they grasped my arms, and his chest was heaving as he breathed unsteadily. He leaned in, lips lingering near my jaw as he paused. Desire replaced any lingering uncertainty I might have felt, lighting me up from the inside out.

His hand left my arm to cradle my face, thumb swiping over my lower lip. *How many more times do I have to tell myself I don't want him before I actually believe it?*

A piece of my hair tumbled over my shoulder to settle against my chest, and his gaze followed its journey.

"River," he said hoarsely, resting his forehead against mine. I could feel myself growing damp and squeezed my thighs together for some kind of relief, desperate to be touched. I couldn't help the way my body responded to his nearness, his magnetism. I was too inebriated to care about our circumstances, to care about anything but the feel of his hand as it moved to settle on my waist, the pressing need to explore his lean body as it crowded mine. I tilted my head back to gaze into his deep blue eyes and everything else fell away. The desire was clouding my head, making everything grow fuzzy and unfocused. His weight as he leaned into me was firm and warm, and his lips hovered just inches away from mine.

"Do it," I whispered, licking my lips and closing my eyes when he groaned. I was panting now, aching for him to close the distance.

Voices echoed from up the path, startling us out of our position and breaking the moment.

"Fuck!" he roared, slamming his fist into the tree trunk above my shoulder. I held my breath, watching as he shook his head in recrimination and backed off, leaving me with a low string of muttered curses.

I took a few minutes to compose myself, reining in my emotions. I lingered in that spot, the effects of the alcohol quickly wearing off as I realized how close we'd come to giving in.

Whoever must have been coming up the path had to have turned back, because they never came into view.

Do I run? Do I use this unsupervised time to make a break for it? No. I'm in no state to look after myself right now. I'd become too soft; I'd probably die within minutes.

I trudged back to the cabin, thankful that I didn't run into Merikh along the way and that the fuzziness in my head had all but receded. I figured he must have already returned, yet when I opened the door, I saw only Grey and Nix sprawled out on the couch and chair.

"Sunshine!" Nix called out. His dark hair was tousled and wild. "We had no idea where you were."

"Merikh didn't tell you?" At the shake of his head, I explained. Grey watched on with inquisitive brown eyes made amber by the flames of the fire.

"Sorry, I thought he came back here and told you." I collapsed next to Grey on the couch.

"Haven't seen him. Caelan either." Grey sniffed me, throwing his head back with a laugh. "I take it you had fun?"

Nix looked over, eyes glinting with heat at the way my top was falling off my shoulder. I leaned against the armrest, throwing my feet in Grey's lap and meeting Nix's stare.

I guess I wasn't over the tension with Merikh, because with the way Nix was looking at me, it was like I'd never even cooled down.

Grey talked while he rubbed my feet absentmindedly, and I squirmed at the feel. His thumb caressed the arch of my foot, leading me to draw in a sharp breath.

"Are you even listening, sweetheart?" Grey asked with a smug smile. He knew what he was doing.

I was still wet from my encounter with Merikh, my body wound tight. Nix smirked, swiping a thumb across his lower lip and shooting me a knowing wink.

Fuck, was I that obvious? I squirmed again, feeling the roughness of my shirt rubbing against my over-sensitized breasts, the rise and fall of my chest excruciating as my breaths came faster. I arched my back as Grey lifted my foot and placed a soft kiss to the inside of my ankle.

Nix groaned in unison with me, hand placed in front of his pants like he was either hiding or stroking his desire.

Logically, I knew I could use this, use *them*. I could endear them to me with sex and promises, right up until the moment I left.

But I wouldn't.

"You really don't mind sharing?" I asked with a lifted brow.

Grey glanced at Nix, a smirk fixed on his wicked mouth. "I don't know, how badly do you want it?"

"You know I want her," he said, voice gravelly.

"It would seem that you get both, sweetheart. The real question is, can you handle both?"

I answered his question with an eager moan. Grey began sweeping his large palm in wide strokes across my leg, up to my thigh, then back down to my ankle. Every pass got higher and higher to my aching desire, and his hands were warm and rough on my skin.

The two friends exchanged a look, and Nix beckoned me over to his chair with a hand. I rose slowly, kissing Grey firmly on the lips before sauntering over to where Nix sat by the fire.

A knock on the door interrupted us. It couldn't be Caelan or Merikh, as they'd just walk right in. Who else would knock this late?

Grey and Nix exchanged glances, and Grey stood up to get the door. A high-pitched voice grated on my nerves. Anna stood on the threshold, cheeks flushed, and lips pursed in a pout.

"I just wanted to check on River, she left awfully soon," Anna said with fake concern, peeking past Grey to peer inside. Her eyes lit up when they landed on me. "There you are! Everyone was worried when you left, but I told them you were just overwhelmed, and that it had nothing to do with Thomas."

I gritted my teeth. What was she getting at? I didn't have enough experience with manipulation to guess what her game was.

She continued. "Of course, we all know that you don't *really* want to be here, so it only makes sense that you wouldn't want to stay longer to get to know everyone."

Grey took a heavy step forward, but I held up a halting hand and approached Anna. I was seething with anger. I couldn't tell if it was because she had just reminded me of everything I had been trying so hard to forget or because she had the guts to come to their cabin and run her mouth just to upset me.

I stopped a few feet away from her and looked her up and down with disdain. Her cheeks grew flushed with indignation as she waited for a response, but she kept up her innocent facade.

"It's a pity you left the gathering just for me, Anna. I'm sure there are just as many people cursing the fact that they're not getting any tonight now that you're not there to service them as there are gossiping about me. I hope I'm not overstepping; that's just what *I* heard about *you.*"

Sure, there was no issue with sleeping around. Hell, I was contemplating fucking four guys at once. *Three* guys, damn it. But I knew she would take it as an insult, incensed that I dared bring up her other conquests in front of the few unattainable men in camp that she just wouldn't stop pursuing.

Her lip curled as I walked up to Grey where he stood with a firm mask in place and arms crossed, and kissed him gently on the lips. He unfolded his rigid body, gripping my waist with one scarred hand, and reciprocated. I pulled away after a few seconds, feeling flushed and disheveled, my point having been made.

"I think it's time you leave now," I said cheerfully, giving her a little wave and withholding a smirk. Her face was a dull red, and she was practically vibrating with words unsaid. When she didn't make a move to walk away, I swung the door shut in her face with a small thud.

It was only then that I allowed myself to take a deep breath. Nix's eyes were wide where he sat watching me on the couch, and Grey looked stunned.

"Marking your territory, sweetheart?" Grey rumbled approvingly.

I wanted to laugh, but I was so damn tired. Just exhausted. I wanted to laugh it off, and rejoin them both. At the very least, I wanted to sit in front of the fire and relax, but it all felt wrong somehow. She'd achieved her goal of tainting my night. The thoughts came rushing back in full force.

"I'm heading to bed," I said flatly. I pretended not to notice their concerned looks. "I'll be sleeping in Merikh's room. I don't feel like watching him throw a fit because I avoided it again."

Nix opened his mouth to respond, but I walked out, heading down the hall to use the bathroom and brush my teeth. Once I was finished, I re-entered the hallway, listening to the fervent whispering coming from the direction of the kitchen, and headed to Merikh's room. I eased the door open, allowing my eyes to adjust to the darkness.

A king-sized bed filled the room, dark blankets covering its surface. One solitary black dresser sat up against the far wall underneath a window that had steel bars running across it. At least someone hadn't grown complacent sitting in this settlement.

Nothing good ever lasts.

I peeked through his drawers, seeing if I could find anything to hold against him or at the very least, anything that told me more about him, but there was nothing.

I shifted my eyes to the large bed.

Did I take a pillow and blanket and open myself up to getting humiliated when Merikh came home and decided I didn't deserve those luxuries? Or did I sleep without them and stew all night over the fact that I was forgoing comfort just because some self-obsessed man on an ego trip said so?

Ugh.

Fuck it. I settled on the empty stretch of floor on the right side of the bed–opposite the side with the window and dresser–and stretched out, pillowing my head on my arms. The sound of a home in use met my ears. Dishes clanking from the kitchen, the water running through their system somewhere. It was soothing.

I didn't let myself get used to it.

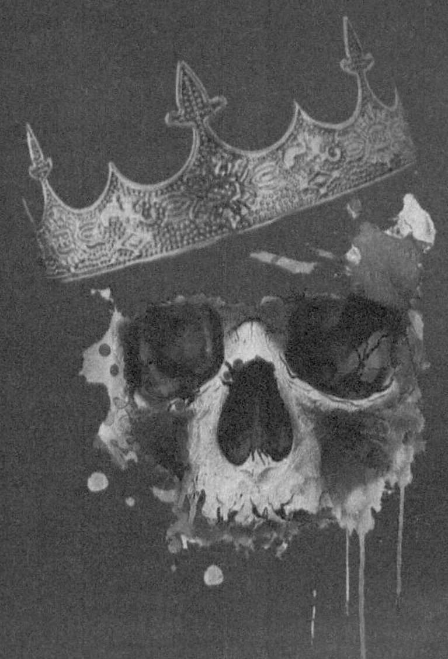

CHAPTER 13

A muffled sound woke me. I listened closely, relaxing when I heard the creak of the bed as someone turned over. Then, a deep sigh sounded.

Merikh.

It was only after a few seconds passed that I realized there was something soft under my head, that I was no longer freezing, but warm and toasty. I opened my eyes to find that there was a pillow beneath my head, and the blanket that had occupied the end of Merikh's bed was draped over my body.

I squeezed my eyes shut when he got out of bed, pretending to be asleep so we didn't have to make awkward conversation. He walked over to my side of the bed, standing still for a long moment before I heard the rustling of clothes. I could only cross my fingers and hope my cheeks weren't turning pink.

It wasn't too long before he left the room. I gave it a few minutes, making sure he wasn't going to come back in before stretching languidly and sitting up. My head spun, and I grimaced as I unstuck my tongue from the roof of my dry mouth. I was a little surprised that he didn't wake me up just to be spiteful. I hated to admit it but maybe there was a nice bone somewhere in his body.

I took my time getting ready, feeling somewhat subdued. For once, there was no big urgency pressing down on me to *do* anything. I threw on an oversized shirt and a pair of shorts–fuck it still felt so nice to feel the wind on my bare legs as opposed to stiff and tight jeans to protect myself from scrapes and bites–and used the bathroom that was right next to Merikh's room.

Once I was finished and headed out to the kitchen, I was surprised to hear the low murmur of whispers. Not just any whispers either, there were no *careful not to wake her up* whispers here. No, these were fervent and angry. Secretive. I stopped just out of sight, the hallway hiding me from the kitchen and living room around the corner, and listened carefully.

"Whoring herself out," someone hissed quietly. "You don't care that she'll fuck anything that makes eyes at her?" they said bitterly. Who the hell... *Merikh.*

"She wouldn't do that, man. Are you so fucking jealous that she won't choose you that you'll just make shit up now?" Nix whispered loudly.

"I am *not* making shit up," Merikh growled. "Did you know I've heard whispers about *your girl* making plans to run away still?"

A sharp breath, and then silence. Fuck, fuck, *fuck*! Why did I feel weirdly guilty that he'd just told Nix that? Surely, he knew, right? He wasn't naïve enough to think that just because we'd started doing... whatever we were doing, I'd stick around.

I adjusted my stance, switching my weight from one foot to another, when the floorboard creaked underneath me. I squeezed my eyes shut in consternation, hoping that maybe they wouldn't have heard it.

Several seconds passed before I heard, "Why don't you come on out, princess. Not sure if you learned this from your many books, but eavesdropping is bad," Merikh said drolly.

I frowned, rounding the corner and pretending like I wasn't mortified to have been caught.

Nix was staring at me, eyes wide with hurt and *something*. "You're still planning to leave," he said flatly. He absentmindedly fiddled with the bracelet on his wrist while he waited for a response.

I didn't... What could I say? I bit my bottom lip, searching desperately for the blasé attitude that had come so easily days before.

I ended up going with a shrug, neither confirming nor denying, but that was enough for Nix. He frowned, his mouth twisting into a sneer. It looked wrong on his face, out of place and unwelcome. "Were you just playing us for fools so that you could sneak away easier?"

"That's not–I would never–" It dawned on me with increasing horror that that exact thought had crossed my mind the other day. When had I become someone I disliked so much? "I never said I'd stay!" I argued helplessly. "It was never even an option." I crossed my arms, feeling uncomfortably defensive.

"So you *were* using us," he said with disgust, curling his lip.

Anger flooded through my veins, replacing the hurt and the shame as Merikh just stood by, expressionless. "What did you expect?" I hissed. "That I'd get some dick and suddenly want to stay here forever? I'm not welcome here and I don't even have a skill to offer! I don't *belong* here. Especially not as your fucking maid. I don't have to be using you just because I still want to leave."

Nix flinched and took several steps back from me, coldness filling his eyes and turning them glacial. A shaft of sunlight fell across his face, highlighting his strong jaw and full lips. He looked like some kind of dark angel, just missing the wings.

"Then go," he said thickly.

"Excuse me?"

"Go!"

I looked at him incredulously and backed away slowly, easing the door open behind me and pretending I didn't see the hurt flashing across his face as I walked out. Merikh didn't say a word, ignoring my exit and looking at Nix with concern. Nix, who never moved, never spoke, aside from the stiffening of his body.

I turned and ran. It must have been only several minutes of freedom, breathing the cool, brisk air and admiring my surroundings before I thought of the look on Nix's face when I ran. Betrayal, hurt, pain. Only glimpses, but enough. I was finally getting what I wanted, what I spent every day obsessing over, so why didn't it feel good? Why did I care if he was upset? A sudden tightness gripped my chest, and I fought the urge to double over. My vision blurred, and when I tried to swallow, I realized there was a lump in my throat.

It was just when I started to slow that I collided with a body, no longer looking forward as I should have been but lost in my thoughts.

"River," Caelan exclaimed. My eyes darted to the rest of the camp behind him, and I huffed in frustration, holding back a pitiful laugh.

My freedom gone, just like that.

"I'm going to grab lunch, come with?"

"Do I have a choice?" I snarked.

Hurt flashed across his face. I took a moment to force my roiling emotions into something less volatile and nodded. He fell in step beside me, seeming to sense I was in a weird mood.

"Why are you running way out here?"

"I needed to clear my thoughts and the forest air helps. Apparently, Mom used to preach about the benefits of woodland air compared to all the other types. My dad used to say that she had no idea what she was talking about, clearly the sea breeze is the best."

"Apparently?"

I laughed bitterly. "She died when I was four. Too young to really remember, too old to forget random little details that I've half convinced myself I made up. Most of what I know is from my dad. The worst part is that she didn't even get infected with Paleo, just some other terrible disease that no one had treatment for. Maybe she would've lived if we'd been here. At least you have herbs and people trained in first aid."

Caelan frowned. "I'm sorry, baby. I... had no idea."

"How would you have?" I said with a shrug. My insides were twisting, winding, *churning* at what I'd just done back in the cabin. I could barely think about anything other than the sound of Nix's voice.

Caelan made small talk with me the whole way to the food tent and the entire time my mind kept flashing back to Nix, the look on his face. He'd fully expected me to leave, and why wouldn't he? I was here against my will... right?

When we got to the tent, we joined the back of the line instead of jumping ahead. It was almost as if Caelan knew I needed the extra time. I dreaded the awkwardness of going back to the cabin, and it was obvious in the way I dragged my feet. I was filled with more emotions than I knew how to handle. I was familiar with disappointment, with grief and fear and confusion, but not this festering emotion laced with a heavy guilt twisting up my insides at the thought of facing them again.

I was only just starting to calm down when I realized how foolish my plan had been. To leave in the middle of the day with nothing but the clothes on my back and no supplies or weapons? Experiencing a taste of true domesticity for the first time in my life had made me reckless.

"You alright?" Caelan asked gently before we entered the cabin.

I spared him a smile and nodded. After all, he had no idea what he'd interrupted. I sucked in a breath as we walked through the door, eyes immediately landing on Nix where he sat at the table, quiet and withdrawn. He played with his bracelet, Merikh watching him warily, while Grey was speaking with exaggerated hand motions, trying to cheer him up.

His gaze zeroed in on me as I entered, full of confusion and hurt. He stood in one fluid motion, slender body stretching to his full height as he walked out of the room. He left Grey mid-sentence, shutting the door to his room so loudly that we all heard it.

"What's his problem?" Caelan asked as he set the plates on the table. Grey started offering him an explanation in a low murmur while I met Merikh's stare. He looked at me as though he knew that I was secretly relieved I hadn't made it out of the camp. I wondered if he knew as well as I did that even if I had made it to the gates, there was every chance I wouldn't have walked out. I shook off my apprehension and joined them at the table. When Grey finished speaking, Caelan stood to bring Nix his plate, sparing me a disappointed glance.

"You'll be on the couch tonight," Merikh declared once we finished eating in relative silence.

Regret built in my chest the longer I pictured Nix's crestfallen face as I walked away. I felt *shame* of all things, like I had to have been seriously unworthy to make the most steadfast man here get so upset. Odd that sleeping on their floors was supposed to be a punishment and yet I felt like being relegated to the couch was even worse, a silent chastisement, an acknowledgment of their collective disappointment in me. It was all communicated in undertones: the assumption that things had changed throughout the week, that feelings had formed, and loyalties had shifted. No one spoke up and said it, but it was clear we'd somehow gotten comfortable and let the lines blur, and now it was time to face the consequences.

I just nodded.

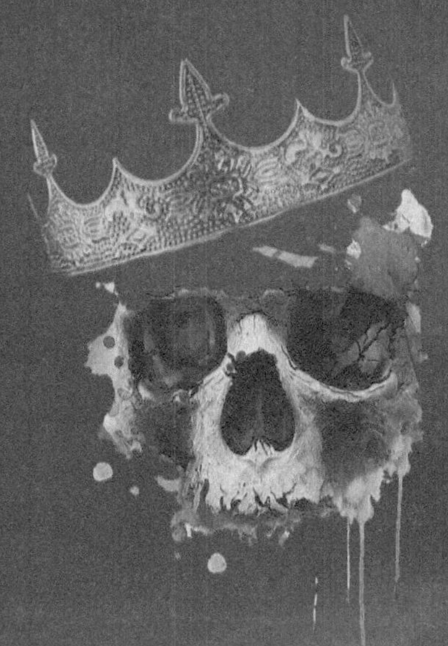

CHAPTER 14

I spent the day doing nothing. No following the guys around, no one watching me like I would steal their supplies and bolt any second. I had wanted to feel like I wasn't being scrutinized every second, so why instead did I feel like nobody cared? Wasn't that what I'd been hoping for?

I sighed, brushing my hands off onto my pants and adding to their general grimy appearance. What was one more stain?

Halli laughed from somewhere off to my right, having left me alone for a bit to get my thoughts gathered. She insisted that gardening was a great tool for mindfulness, but I was just sweaty and bored to tears.

I looked up when I heard the faint sound of clanging and yelling in the near distance. I turned to face Halli, who waved her hand, dismissing my concerns. She ended her conversation and took a second to wipe the sweat from her forehead before heading in my direction.

Correctly interpreting my confusion, she launched into an explanation. "It's the anniversary soon, so we're gathering supplies to have a big bonfire in the center of camp."

I rubbed the spot between my eyebrows, realizing all too late that just because I wiped my hands off on my pants, didn't mean they were completely free of dirt. Halli laughed, pouring some water from her canteen onto the rag that was looped through the belt on her skirt and wiping the mark from my forehead. The breeze felt cool against my wet skin, and when I sighed contentedly, she brushed the rag along my cheeks as well.

"Thank you," I sighed, feeling much better now that I wasn't boiling alive in the sun. It wasn't even all that hot, the last remnants of winter clinging with a passion as we transitioned into spring. Though the sun had been shining earlier before it hid behind the angry storm clouds, the physical labor had me sweating profusely. "I have no idea what you're talking about. Do you mean the anniversary of when the camp was established?"

Halli's jaw dropped. "No one told you?"

I tossed the old spade to the side and planted myself backwards. "Told me what, Halli? It's not like I was–*am*–planning on sticking around. I don't know half the shit that goes on here."

She shot me a look of reproach, ticking off her fingers as she listed each item. "You know that's not true. Naia and Nerese brought you to the meadow, you met all the kids, cleared the perimeter, accompanied Merikh to a camp meeting, and helped out in the garden, need I go on?"

I huffed, brushing my hair over my shoulder. "Fine," I said grouchily.

"I don't know what's crawled up your ass and died, but you need to snap out of it!"

That got a small laugh out of me. I'd never heard her be so direct. "Sorry, it's... I don't know. Things are weird right now."

"I'm not sure they ever stopped being weird," she said sympathetically. "But I'm willing to listen if you want to talk."

"I appreciate that. It's–I–" I sighed, realizing there was no way around it. "I had a fight with Nix, and he... told me to leave."

Her eyes grew round and wide. "Obviously you didn't because you're still here, but... why?"

Why was I ashamed to tell her this part? It almost felt like... a betrayal. "I... tried. I mean, I left the cabin. Then I ran into Caelan, and it was a whole thing. The moment was gone."

She tsked, playing with a curl that had fallen loose from her bun. Clearly, she wasn't satisfied with that answer.

"Andddd..." I said slowly, drawing the word out. "Maybe I didn't want to after all."

Her grin was radiant. "See! I knew you'd like it here."

"This doesn't mean I know what my plans are or what they have to say about it; I'm just admitting that maybe I'm not wanting to run anymore," I admitted. It felt good to say aloud. *Real.* I wasn't the same person as the one who'd been dragged into camp a week ago, and the circumstances had changed. It was unfair to pretend they hadn't. Perhaps that was why Nix was so hurt by my reaction to his telling me to leave.

"I'm proud of you." Her smile was soft and kind. I felt a rush of warm affection for her, so grateful to have someone I could talk with that was around my age.

"It won't always be like this, you know. Me dumping my problems on you."

She scoffed. "As if I have much else to do. My biggest issues as of late are the seed shortage and garden troubles, plus the fact that we haven't had chicken pot pie in weeks. You're the most excitement I've had in years."

I laughed, hanging my head. "Well, I'll be ready to listen once you do. So, the anniversary?"

She grew somber, rearranging her skirt as she shifted to sit more comfortably. "I told you about how we had issues with raiders in the past, right?"

I nodded.

"We've hosted nomads before with larger numbers that were just passing through. This was when we still opened our gates to just about anyone, but this group in particular…" She shuddered. "About five years ago, we had a few men pass through. They told us they were traveling into the city to scavenge, but needed a safe place to stay the night. They looked a little rough, but we didn't think much of it. After all, everyone did. We welcomed them in, shared our resources and food. I was only nineteen at the time, and even I could feel something was off."

My heart dropped once I realized where this was going.

"They were looking at the girls oddly, taking huge portions of food at mealtimes and squirreling them away when we would have just packed them a bag if they'd asked. They gave Grey the creeps, and he was constantly following them everywhere, watching everything they did. Still, Mark let them stay. They'd only been here for a few nights before they decided they were going to leave without telling anyone." Her face darkened.

I tried to reassure myself, even though I knew something bad was coming from the tone of her voice. It was just a few men, right? Unfortunately, a few men could do a lot of damage. I knew the camp hadn't always looked this way, so reinforced. It seemed for a long time, that their only threats had been the zombies that plagued the area, and this event was the turning point. "Spit it out already! I can't handle the suspense."

She chuckled, her face brightening just a tad. "They decided to leave… but they tried to take half our weapons cache with them. Not only were they taking food and supplies, but they packed a bunch of weapons from our storehouse into these duffel bags they brought. If no one had caught them…" She shook her head. "Luckily Grey was watching, because most of us were asleep, and he sounded the alarm when he noticed what they were trying to do. They didn't stick around, though. They knocked Grey unconscious before reinforcements showed up, murdered the guard who was on duty at the gate, and left."

I bit my lip, picking absently at my thumbnail. "Somehow, I don't think that's the end of it."

She sighed, tipping her head back to enjoy the breeze. The sky was even darker now, so drastically different from the sunlight I'd woken with. "You're right. That wasn't the end. They came back a few weeks later, just when we thought we were in the clear. They thought we were 'being selfish', whatever the fuck that means. Apparently, they were just casing the place, and they were always going to come back. Attempting to take the weapons was just another surety that no one would be able to fight back. There were around fifteen of them, and the camp was maybe forty people at that point, except half were elderly or kids. They came in through the back gate since it wasn't as guarded and was used less frequently and killed anyone they ran into. Of the few that were too injured to retreat, the one we left alive said they were just going to take as many supplies as they could and run, that it wasn't worth trying to gain control of the camp." Her voice was filled with disgust.

"I'm guessing the supplies included the women they'd had their eyes on?"

She nodded, and my stomach sunk. "They killed seven men and one older woman before we drove them out, killing enough of their group that they decided to cut their losses and leave."

"So that's the anniversary," I said flatly, finally understanding. It wasn't a cause for joy, but for remembrance.

"Yeah. There hasn't been an incident yet, but we've heard stirrings in the past month or so. Scouts finding homes that have been occupied recently, tracks that don't belong to zombies around the perimeter of camp, loud noises nearby."

I decided to breeze right on past that concerning statement. "So you do a bonfire to remember the victims?"

She nodded. "Not just that, but everyone who lost their lives to the virus and the mutation. It's a pretty somber day. We have a big meal, tell stories, and just spend time together."

I leaned back on my hands, thinking it all over. It was easy to forget all the other dangers that lurked while I was safe and protected here. I'd never realized how far removed my dad and I had been from all these groups and their politics. *And maybe you don't want to leave them in case something were to happen,* my brain admonished. I guess even my mind was getting pretty sick of my denial.

"Well," I said on a deep breath out. "Enough of that." I looked over the garden, at their decimated harvest and frowned.

"Try not to think about it," she insisted. "We'll figure it out. Always do." She stood, brushing herself off and offering me a hand. "Now, how about you help me with the carrots?"

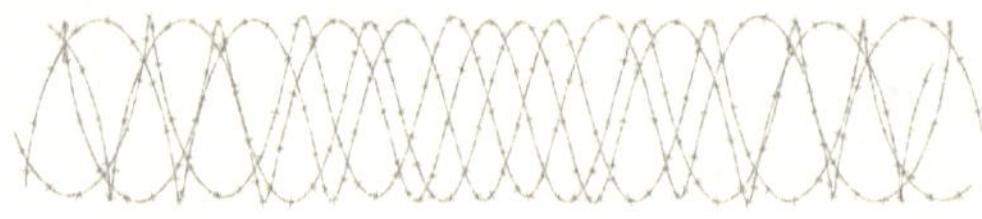

I was so deep in thought with my hands buried in the cool soil that I almost didn't hear the first scream. I jerked my head up, hoping that it was something small, like a fire getting out of control or a small injury. My hopes were dashed the second I heard the pain and terror in the second scream. That wasn't a sound made over something inconsequential, that was a scream born of bone-deep panic and fear.

I whipped my head around, searching for Halli, but she was nowhere to be found. More shouts rang out as I sprinted out of the garden, almost tripping over a little boy as he ran into my legs, tears blocking his vision. I stopped for a second, setting my hands on his shoulders and steering him toward the closest building. My heart raced in my chest as I tried to find the source of the sounds.

People were darting past me as they moved toward the front of the camp. The survivor in me begged to follow them, but I knew I didn't have that luxury. If the threat was what my brain was cautioning me it was, these people would need all the help they could get.

My insides contorted sharply when I passed the center of camp and noticed the first zombie. It was lying face-first on the ground, obviously already having been dispatched by someone. Its hand twitched despite the caved-in skull, and perhaps that was the scariest part of all. They were so deadly, like wolves in a henhouse, that it would take one infected person reaching the others for the virus to spread like wildfire, decimating our numbers. In an instant, these people that I'd worked, eaten, and slept alongside would be undead, a sliver of their previous selves.

Fuck, it was jarring to have to switch back into the person that dealt with these things daily. The intense focus, the concentration, the violence. I'd spent days fearing this exact situation, the intense, cloying fear that came with being penned into a busy enclosed area with a predator. If I was going to face the problem, I'd need to shove my panic back where it came from.

Many of the people here were young and elderly, and just as many were disabled or incapacitated. Some of them haven't left the safety of camp for years, so how could they be expected to suddenly take up arms to defend themselves and others? The few with combat experience and those who left the camp semi-regularly were running to grab weapons, and part of me wanted to curse them for not already being armed, but the sensible part whispered that it would be excessive for them to carry their weapons all day if they weren't guarding the gate or the perimeter.

My lungs grew tired as I sprinted, a sharp pain made itself known behind my ribs, and I kicked myself for getting too comfortable. Some actual rest and good food, and I'd somehow forgotten the severity of the threat outside these walls and how easily everything could change. Pitiful.

I shuddered once Caelan came into view up ahead, bashing the head of a persistent zombie until it finally keeled over with an odd keening sound, its teeth gnashing. I didn't see Nix or Merikh, but I did see Grey further along, ushering people in the direction from which I'd just come.

"River!" Caelan roared, as he jogged my way. He grabbed my upper arm roughly once he reached me, looking me over frantically and then relaxing once he saw I didn't appear to have been bitten. "Nix is back at the front of camp, administering first aid and keeping watch. Those with training are combing the area for the zombies that have slipped through." His eyes were wild as they searched mine. "We have no idea how they got in. They'd already made it a quarter of the way through camp before anyone noticed, and we're too busy making sure they're all taken care of to investigate," he said briskly. He handed me his bat, wrapping my hand around the handle.

My brows pulled together as I realized he would be left weaponless. "What about you?"

"Don't worry about me," he bit out. "I'll grab something in a minute. You take this and you stay safe, understand?"

I nodded silently, my mind reeling as I tried to process everything.

"That's my girl," he rasped, pulling my forehead to his lips for a kiss. He hesitated before turning to look back in the direction of the shouts, and I stopped him with a quick grasp of his arm. I spun him around to face me, grabbing the fabric of his shirt at his chest and bunching it up in my fist so that I could pull him down to my level, then kissed him fiercely.

He groaned into my mouth, lips moving enthusiastically over mine. I pulled back, panting softly as I stared him down. "You stay safe too," I commanded, refusing to even contemplate him getting hurt.

His grin was both sinful and soft. Once I left him behind, splitting off in a different direction, I prepared myself for what I was about to face. Would I see anyone lying on the ground, injured and dying? Would I find anyone I knew freshly turned and still wearing their clothes and skin, like undead imposters? My stomach twisted at the thought.

I was stunned when I turned the corner and ran directly into Naia. Her eyes were watery with tears, and she grabbed my arm in surprise, frantically trying to get my attention.

"Sakhira is missing," she said between gasps. "Nerese is with the others back at our building. We were on a field trip to the meadow when everyone started yelling and we realized we didn't have Sakhira when we were halfway back and I can't find her anywhere–" she broke her rambling to suck a deep breath in, doubling over to rest her hands on her knees as her frantic breaths sawed in and out of her chest.

"I can find her," I declared. "Go help Nerese with the others; it's not safe for you to be out here."

Her eyes filled once more. "But she's my responsibility! How could I have fucked up so badly? I can't just go back without her."

As much as I wanted to reassure her, we didn't have time for this. Every second that ticked by was another where she could be injured, or worse. "Listen," I said urgently. "It's not your fault. It could've happened to anyone, but you haven't been outside in some time and while that's okay, I was still killing them just a few weeks ago. It's not weak or cowardly or irresponsible to play to your strengths. Now, I'm gonna find her and bring her back to you, okay? Where have you searched so far?"

Her words tripped over each other as she told me she'd searched the entire section where Grey and Caelan were, near the meadow, and the whole food tent and center of camp area in case she found her own way back.

I nodded as she spoke, mentally racking my brain for where she would have gone. It was a gamble, but since Naia had already scoured most of the front and east sections of the camp, I decided to go farther past where she was now, closer to the forest and the fence. Maybe she'd run into the trees to hide and twisted her ankle or something.

"Go," I said forcefully, giving her a little push. "I've got this."

Naia nodded, taking off at a dead sprint just as I heard a groaning noise nearby. I saw a glimpse of something moving a few yards behind me, heard Caelan's triumphant shout as it hit the ground.

Okay, where could she have gone?

I took off at a run toward the trees, my mind racing over the different possibilities. I kept my eye out for any dark curls or bright fabric. *Fuck it,*

I decided, calling out her name. All the better if I attracted any zombies, at least then I'd be drawing them away from anyone else.

Even after a full minute of yelling, I saw nothing, heard nothing. No small voice answered my calls.

I'd gone so far that I could see the perimeter fence in the distance and was already calculating my next move when my body froze. No... she wouldn't, would she? Surely there was no way. I took off at a sprint near the general area where Halli mentioned the old gate was, nestled in between the trees near the end of the woods. It would seem I had the answer to my question when I first arrived. The fence cut through the woods, swallowing up almost the entire forest with only a few odd trees cropping up on the other side. Where the other chain link sections were reinforced with a second panel of wooden posts, boards, and barbed wire, the old gate remained just rusted metal with what looked like some rotted, torn away boards lying on the ground before it.

My stomach lurched when I saw the handful of zombies right outside the gate, and my blood froze once my eyes landed on the wide gap where the wire had been cut away from the pole. My thoughts were chaotic as I tried to process everything at once. Three things were incontrovertible. One, the fence had been deliberately sabotaged. Two, this was where the undead had entered the camp. Three, somehow this group of zombies had made it past the car barrier without being noticed by any of the patrols.

I gagged when I stumbled over the ravaged raccoon and rabbit carcasses lying right in front of the gate, realizing what had grabbed and kept their attention once they were corralled to this point. I had no idea if the zombies could hear and smell the camp activity from this distance, and someone must have been unsure of that lure as well because they clearly set bait out to draw them farther inside until they could. I ground my teeth at the pure waste of all the little creatures lying about as I bludgeoned the skull of the zombie that was currently halfway through the gap.

I squinted at the spot of color among the carnage, the blood rushing to my head as I realized I was looking at a bright blue strip of fabric hanging from one sheered-off section of the fence. I sucked a deep breath in and ran through my options. There was no time to run and get someone, and I had no idea how far she'd run or if she was injured.

I raised the bat in front of me, holding it outwards and jabbing it through the hole in the fence several times until it shoved the body back enough for me to swing through. The whole time, I silently thanked Caelan for giving me a bat that had several nails sticking out of the end. I winced as I ducked through, my side catching on one of the rough pieces of metal and scraping my skin through my shirt. I tried to move as fast as possible, aware that it was an extremely vulnerable position for me to be in.

Once I was finally through, I quickly rose to my full height, hefting the bat over my shoulder and swinging it toward the nearest body with a resounding *crack*. Having smelt the blood on my side, the undead before me gave me their full attention, trading their indifference for a frenzied gnashing of teeth as they tried to reach me. There were only three left, which wasn't the end of the world. Unfortunately, I had no idea how many had actually made it inside the camp at this point. I just had to hope that everyone was safe and okay.

Don't think of them, don't think of how you have no idea if your friends are okay, I coached myself, taking another wild swing at the nearest body. It was older than the others, taller too. Its hoodie hung off of its skeletal form in rags, and its eyes were a milky white shot through with red. I muttered a curse as it jerkily ducked to the side to miss my swing and switched my focus to tackle the other two, grimacing at the sickening noise that came from the impacts of wood on bone.

I dry-heaved at some of the odd-colored bodily fluids landing on my shirt, bitching at myself for becoming so spoiled. It was a constant battle to retrain my mind not to frown upon taking it easy or actually enjoying being safe, and this wasn't helping. I was panting wildly now as I faced the last zombie, the only one who had been smart enough to dodge my attempts to kill it. The others had succumbed to their ravenous hunger, becoming wild and impulsive, and it was just my luck that this one was craftier than its peers.

It lunged forward, too close for me to use the bat, and its boney fingers scraped their way down my arm as I jerked back at the last minute. I sucked in a breath, throwing myself back so that I had enough space to raise my weapon, then swung the bat up and toward its head, twisting to the side to get out of the range of its gnashing teeth as it hit the ground. The momentum sent me sprawling onto the dirt beside it and I scrambled back as it moved at a slow crawl toward me, then hurried to get to my feet and put it out of its misery.

I didn't dare wipe the sweat from my face, not wanting to transfer any of the gore staining my arms and hands. A few calming breaths and I was moving once more. Away from the safety of camp, away from the walls that were supposed to keep us sheltered.

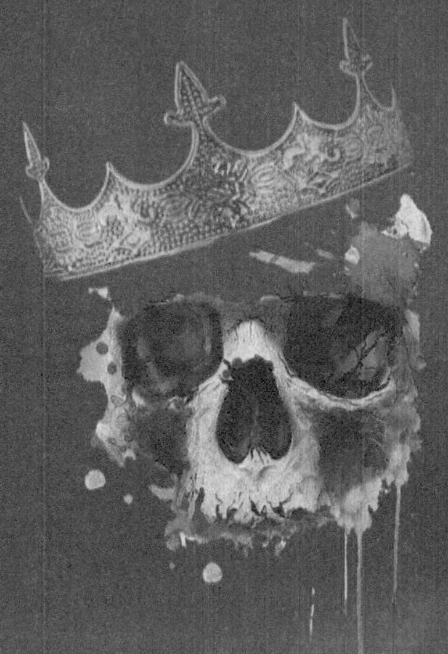

CHAPTER 15

Now that there was nothing else that needed my attention, I took my time scanning the landscape and noticed a few stray trees nestled up against the car barrier in the distance and a couple of zombies lingering near them. One of the trees was larger than the rest, its trunk extending well into the sky and branches covered liberally with leaves unlike the stripped clean appearance of its neighbors. I squinted, taking off at a run, when the faint sound of a sob grabbed my attention.

"Sakhira!" I shouted, trying to grab her attention.

She came into view as I got closer, her skinny body trembling where she clung to the large branch near the lower part of the tree, and I realized that the few zombies that hadn't been queued up at the broken gate to go through one by one like they were in a fucking lunch line were snapping their jaws at the base of the tree, waiting her out. Not just lingering as I'd first thought. Fortunately, there were only three.

"I've got you, Khira," I murmured as I inched closer, noting small details like the fact that she was clutching a dead branch close to her chest like a weapon, and that she didn't appear to be injured although she was clearly distressed.

"I'm sorry," she sobbed. "I saw a bunny and we never see bunnies so I followed it thinking I could bring it home to show my mom, but it ran outside the fence so I climbed the gate and I heard people talking so I had to hide–"

"Hold on a sec," I grunted, trying not to get distracted. "It's gonna be okay." I was curious to hear more of her story, but was more concerned about the fetid undead as they approached me at a loping run.

I circled the one closest to me, kicking it squarely in the chest once it lunged and wincing when its ribs caved in. Khira made a gagging noise in the tree above me. "Don't you throw up on me," I groused, dodging the second one as it ran straight for me. She hiccupped a laugh through her tears, going silent once more and allowing me to focus.

I slammed my bat into the first one, praising myself when it went down with just one hit and then rounding on the second. It made a horrific screeching noise as I slammed into it and jerked aside at the last second so that I caught its arm and not anything vital. I cursed as it drew closer, wishing I still had my knife. This was a great bat and all, but my arms were tiring, my shoulders sore from the repeated impacts and the swinging. I was totally going to feel it tomorrow.

"River!" Khira screamed from the tree, her leg slipping for a second before she yanked it back up. The third one didn't even care about me, it was utterly fixated on her. I finally managed to hit the second straight across the face, then once more for good measure before I took care of the one staring up at Khira.

"Shit, kid, what the hell are you doing way out here?" I asked as I leaned heavily against the tree, panting heavily and too tired to watch my language.

She sniffled, brushing a bunch of leaves aside to peek at me. "I was following the bunny out here when I heard voices, and I didn't have time to crawl back over the fence so I ranned over here and I crawled up into the tree and saw some men come by and cut the fence. I wanted to 'vestigate, then I was gonna go back and tell everybody, but they brought zombies."

"And you got stuck out here," I said softly. "Good thinking on getting somewhere off the ground, okay? Your parents are gonna be so glad you're okay."

Her eyes widened and grew unfocused, and she sucked in a deep lungful of air before it left her mouth in a scream.

The air left my body as something bony gripped my ankle and squeezed tightly. I immediately tried to muffle my pained cry, not wanting to draw any more attention or scare Sakhira even further. I'd almost forgotten just how oddly strong they could be. I spun as best I could to find that the first zombie I had hit had crawled the short distance to me. The delicate bones in my ankle screamed as it clutched tighter, using me as leverage to pull its mouth closer to my leg. I used the last of my energy to raise the bat over its head and bring it down with all my strength, hitting it a few extra times for good measure.

I was furious with myself for being so sloppy. Everyone knew you had to hit them more than once and make sure they were down for good before you turned your back on them.

It made a soft gurgling noise as it went still, and I had to pry its hand from my ankle, the force of its grip not loosening even as it embraced a second-and final-death. My swallow was thick with pain at the deep furrows its fingers left in my skin as I pulled it off.

Distant voices had me swallowing an exhausted groan. I would've given anything to hear someone speaking from the direction of the camp, but these were coming from out past the cars. I wasn't taking any chances, and I knew better than to expose myself and Khira to strangers, especially when I was too tired to fight them off.

I shuddered, burying the sharp pain in my ankle, all my scrapes and bruises catching up with me. I took a hesitant step toward the tree, only to bite my lip against a cry, tears welling up and blurring my vision from the pain. *Shit, that thing did some real damage.*

I tried to block out the pain, realizing that the bodies on the ground next to us would draw their attention quicker than anything else if they were to come back. I whimpered as I reluctantly put weight on my ankle, dragging the bodies one by one for what felt like hours but was probably only minutes into the rusted-out backseat of the nearest car. Whoever was speaking was still too far out for me to catch a glimpse of them through all the tangled cars, so I figured I had enough time.

Tears mixed with the sweat and blood on my face as I finished hauling the last of the trio off, and I took a second to peek through the broken driver's side window at the group of men that had grown steadily louder and stopped a scant distance away.

"Fuck this," I grumbled quietly, walking as quickly as I could back to the tree. "There's no time to get back through the fence," I whispered to Khira. "I think they're coming back to check on how their plan went. I'm coming up there, and we're gonna head to a higher branch, okay? I think the leaves can hide us completely."

Khira worried her bottom lip, dropping the branch she'd been clutching so tightly. "But your ankle," she whispered loudly.

The voices grew louder, and I shook my head. "Doesn't matter. No choice." I grabbed the lowest branch, hauling myself up and using my good foot to try to gain purchase against the trunk. I heaved my body over the thickest part, panting silently with the effort and hoping they wouldn't spot me over the cars before I was safely ensconced in the leaves. Sakhira scrambled upwards to make space for me, grabbing the arm that wasn't scratched and pulling with all her might.

I whimpered quietly between gritted teeth as I worked my way up branch by branch until I was flush against the tree. My various cuts and scrapes were stinging from the rough bark, and every injury I had was throbbing intensely now that I was still. Khira perched beside me, arm clutching mine as the men's voices grew even louder. I grabbed her attention, holding a finger in front of my lips to indicate that she shouldn't make a sound. She nodded resolutely, her tears from earlier gone and in their place, determination.

I held myself deathly still as they crept up against the cars, not making their way through, but just watching.

"Damn plan," someone muttered under their breath. "Too quiet now. Didn't lure enough fuckin' zombies."

I clenched the fist that wasn't gripping the tree, reminding myself that it would be beyond foolish to make a move right now. But still, what the actual fuck? It disgusted me that even now, some people had no regard for human life.

"Someone killed those ones over by the gate," another grunted. "They probably left to grab the others and some supplies to patch the fence."

"Then we better get the hell outta here before they come back," the first one bit out.

There was a long moment of silence where I didn't know if they were just waiting or had already crept away that I didn't dare look. I settled my free hand on Khira's arm, gesturing for her to wait. She nodded with rounded eyes, waiting patiently as we listened for any kind of noise, either of the undead or the alive variety.

I heaved a deep sigh when I finally deemed it safe, easing myself down from my perch using a branch above me. I swallowed a scream when my injured ankle landed abruptly on a branch below and rolled, causing me to lose my grip and tumble out of the tree with a thud.

I groaned from where I lay flat against the ground, my back aching fiercely. "Good motherfucking god," I cursed, shuddering as I tried to lift myself. I so very badly wanted to not get up, to just catch my breath and sleep the pain off, but I needed to get us back to camp. We *had* to keep moving, even though it felt like I'd been run over repeatedly by one of the many cars behind us.

Sakhira's small giggle had me giving a tiny smile in response, though it quickly faded when I realized I didn't know what we were walking back into. The screams and shouts had faded some time ago, but for what reason? Was everyone safe? Or...

I shook my head.

Khira swung her way down the tree like some kind of koala and I held my hands outstretched in the air once she landed beside me. "Help me up, missy."

She giggled, grabbing onto my hands and tugging me with a loud grunt. I laughed, almost delirious with pain now, as I tugged one hand out of her grip and used it to propel myself off the ground.

"Wow, have you always been that strong?"

She flexed her arms, grinning. "I told you my dad was gonna train me to be big and strong like him."

"Damn straight, Sakhira. You're going places."

She frowned at that, tilting her head to the side with a squint. "I'm not going anywhere, though."

I stifled a chuckle. "I know, it's just an expression. I'm not even sure why we say it, I just know my dad used it all the time."

She tapped her chin. "Oh. Hmm. Hmmmmm. Okay, I'll add it to my vocablary."

"Vocabulary," I corrected gently, grateful that the short conversation had allowed me to catch my breath.

"Vocablarary," she said confidently, slipping her hand into mine.

We'd only walked a couple of feet before I gasped, pulling her up short before she could take another step. "Hold on, someone mentioned you guys have traps out here to keep things away." Holy shit, I could've gotten us killed! And for that matter, why would she run out here in the first place knowing there were traps? How did those men make it all the way to the fence?

"Don't worry," she said wisely, patting my arm gently. "Daddy said they don't have any in this spot since nobody ever got around to adding them once they stopped using the gate. Least that's what they told him a while ago."

I heaved a sigh of relief, hoping she was right.

We continued our walk at an achingly slow pace, me stumbling and limping, and her patiently tugging me along until my vision started to turn gray a few feet from the ruined gate. My side felt wet and inflamed, and a tentative touch revealed that I was cut more deeply than I had first realized. Blood soaked my hand where I'd pressed it against my skin.

Sakhira said something, but her voice was fuzzy and far away sounding. I stumbled a few more steps, determined to make it through the gate. I *had* to get us inside where it was safe.

"RIVER," someone roared. I widened my eyes, blinking away the fuzziness to see Merikh shoving through the gate and rushing toward us, reaching me just as I fell to my knees with exhaustion. I was certain if I really pushed myself I could make it before I passed out, but he was *here* and I was *safe*. Merikh was muttering and mumbling as he ran his hands over my body, checking every inch for a bite. Now I *knew* I was out of it, because I could've sworn he sounded worried. As I finally lost consciousness, the soft caress of Merikh's calloused hand on my cheek pulled a reluctant sigh from my lips, and the last thing I heard was someone shouting Khira's name from somewhere close by.

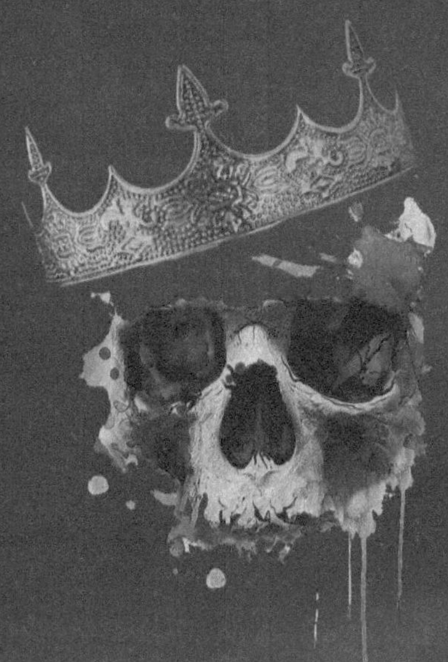

CHAPTER 16

My body practically wept as it was jostled.

"Motherfucker," I mumbled, turning my head into the broad chest of whoever was carrying me. Each step reverberated through my sore muscles, tensing them further.

"Come on, princess," a deep voice rumbled. I sighed happily, flopping around in his arms until I was a bit more comfortable and curling up tighter. I must've been hallucinating because there was no other way the man who was carrying me pressed a soft, barely there kiss against the top of my head.

"Did you just... smell me?" I asked, aghast. I opened my bleary eyes to find Merikh staring down at me with a smirk.

"And if I did?" he taunted.

I groaned loudly, "This is it, this is the moment I realize how weird you are. You never stop being annoying, it's impossible."

His chuckle was deep and low, and it warmed all the cold, aching places threaded through my bones and sinew.

"Let me see her!" someone shouted as they pushed through the group of people flanking us. Caelan's eyes widened when they landed on me.

"I think I left your bat inside a zombie skull," I rasped.

"Fuck the bat," he said roughly, striding forward and kissing me soundly. I whimpered into his mouth, clutching the front of his shirt tightly to keep him close.

A few throats cleared, Merikh's included, before I regained my senses enough to push him away. "Put me down," I sighed, my secret dream of being pampered disappearing as I realized it was time for real life to intrude. I looked around to see a few of the people from around camp staring at me, worry broadcasted all over their faces. No more distrust or dislike, only concern. A short distance away, Sakhira was talking up a storm as the giant of a man who must've been her dad listened.

"No," Merikh said gruffly.

I scrunched my face up, staring into his eyes. Beautiful deep blue, so stormy I could get lost in them. Then the stubborn twist of his lips, broadcasting complete arrogance and ruining his angelic appearance.

"Yes," I grumbled, wiggling around as he curled me upwards so that he could get a better grip on me.

"We're going to see Nix," he continued, like I hadn't said anything. "He'll take a look at you and get you all fixed up. Khira insisted you hadn't been bit and fortunately you would be showing signs by now if you were, so we don't have to worry about that."

"My little champion," I snorted softly. "She was fearless out there. Her dad should be proud. Now let me up!"

"River," Caelan pleaded from his spot beside us. How could I deny him when he used my actual name for once?

"Fine," I said grumpily, too tired to argue anymore.

"Give us some space," Merikh commanded, raising his voice to be heard. Aside from a few quiet protests, everyone who had been clustered around us slowly peeled away, leaving just Caelan.

As Merikh carried me through the forest and down the familiar path to the cabin, I frowned and tilted my head back to meet his eyes, surprised to find him already looking down at me. "I thought we were going to see Nix?"

"He's at the cabin now. There were no serious injuries among the others, and no bites or deaths. He's done all he can do for now."

Caelan chimed in, "He didn't know you were missing, or he would've insisted on looking for you like we were. We needed him to look after the others in our stead, so he's... not going to be happy that we didn't say anything."

I rolled my eyes, throwing my head back over Merikh's arm. Ugh, save me from overprotective, bossy men. A large, calloused hand grabbed my good ankle, the heat soothing, and I twisted my head to find Caelan holding me reassuringly. I held back a smile, the feel of his skin against mine making me hyper-aware of my proximity to Merikh. I was practically plastered against his broad chest, his arms brushing against my skin with each step. It was closer than we'd ever been before.

Fuck, my head was spinning.

Nix must've been looking outside because when we approached, he threw open the front door and jumped down the steps.

"Is she okay?" His hands hovered over my body, checking for injuries. I could barely get a word out to reassure him. "Is she–" His voice broke, and Merikh quickly took over, his voice deep and soothing. I hadn't known he was capable of sounding like he didn't hate everyone all the time.

"She's fine. Khira was missing." His voice was hard now. "River left the camp alone to save her and didn't tell a soul."

I was too tired to argue at present, but that didn't mean I wasn't still anxious to defend myself. I settled on a quiet grumble. "Naia said that Sakhira was missing, so I said I'd help look for her. When I found her, she was surrounded by zombies and there was no time to run back inside before those men came back."

Nix shook his head reprovingly, but at least he was no longer panicking.

"Merikh," I groaned, squirming. "Put me down now. I can walk by myself."

"You damn well cannot," he grumbled. "She hurt her ankle," he explained to Nix. "Passed out from the pain and could hardly walk. There's some bleeding along her side and multiple bruises and scrapes. I'm not sure if she hit her head or not."

I frowned. Was that a dig? *Whatever.*

Nix nodded silently, biting his lip and yanking us all inside. They looked at each other for a long moment in the doorway, then headed to Grey's room. Did they have some kind of weird triplet telepathy? I wasn't sure where Grey was, but I hoped he didn't mind when he came home to find me occupying his bed.

Caelan rushed ahead to arrange the pillows just so, allowing Merikh to place me gently in the center of the bed and prop me up against them. I winced as my bones settled into the soft mattress, my muscles finally losing some of their constant tension. It was almost embarrassing how much care they were taking with me. I didn't want everyone fussing over me.

"Quit your frowning and let us help, baby," Caelan commented.

My laugh was short and pained. Nix was quiet as he got to work, ordering the others to grab supplies for him. He cleaned my side and the other scrapes with a warm, wet cloth, then examined my ankle with cool, soothing fingers. The gouges on my arm were treated with some kind of numbing ointment, as were the burning ones on my side. I cringed as he manipulated my foot and ankle in small back-and-forth motions, his fingers gentle and yet the pain overwhelming.

"I don't have a tetanus shot to give you," he said worriedly. "I think you'll be okay, though. We'll keep an eye on you and make sure nothing worsens. As for your ankle, I'm pretty sure it's just a hairline fracture. It shouldn't take too long to heal and if we wrap it up properly and you take it easy, you could be walking as soon as next week."

My eyes grew wide. His expression was sympathetic but firm. There'd be no convincing him, but I wouldn't be me if I didn't try. "I have things to do," I insisted stubbornly. "I can't just lounge around all day!"

"You wouldn't be lounging," he said sternly. "You need to heal. If you walk on it before it has time to get better, you could worsen the damage and hurt yourself even worse. In fact, the recommended time for you to be off it is much longer, but I know you, and I know you'll force your way out of bed way sooner than you should. At least this way, you'll be extra careful."

I relaxed back against the cushions, not even realizing that I had been sitting ramrod straight as I argued my point. I blinked rapidly so I wouldn't tear up, surprised to find myself oddly emotional. I'd always been able to defend myself, never doing anything risky so that I'd never get hurt and become a burden to my dad. How was I going to handle this? Feeling so... stuck? Useless?

Almost like he'd read my mind, Merikh spoke from where he stood with his arms crossed near the door. "It could just as easily be me lying there, River. I don't have half the patience you do either. It doesn't make you less of a survivor or a badass to give yourself time to recover."

Now his kind words were what was going to make me tear up. What the hell was wrong with me? I'd never felt so looked after in all my life. Even my dad had been the type to usher us along after a tumble, brushing off scrapes and bumps as inconsequential. When did our relationship shift so wildly, that I would be lying here in one of their beds, being looked after like I was? Like I mattered?

"I need to explain," I said tiredly. I told them all about the men Sakhira had seen, the ones that had returned and everything we'd overheard, and was justifiably confused when they exchanged worried glances.

"They most likely belong to the group that's been hanging around," Caelan stated. "It's odd that they'd make a move so close to *that* day, and I'm hoping that it's just a coincidence. If they're actually going on the offensive now..."

Merikh grunted. "Enough of that. We'll discuss it later and let River rest."

"I have some expired pain meds for you," Nix said softly. "You'll take them for the next few days. It'll be fine, you'll see." He handed me a glass of room-temperature water and watched as I forced them down with an audible swallow. *Bleh*, why were they so huge? I coughed a few times, feeling like they were still lodged in my throat. His smile was worth it, though. Messy hair, tired eyes, and still looking so sweet and soft.

Caelan shifted where he leaned against the door frame, his big body blocking the view of the hallway. Great, I had my own personal jailers to make sure I didn't push myself too hard.

"Fine," I said slowly, aiming to ease the somber atmosphere. "You make a handsome doctor, Nix. You can come examine me anytime." I gave him a sloppy wink, my smirk growing as Merikh groaned loudly. Caelan laughed, and Nix blushed, giving me a shy smile. The tension from the other day had all but disappeared, but I knew it was only a matter of time before we needed to address it.

"Troublemaker," he scolded with a laugh, fidgeting with the bracelet around his wrist and shooting me a look. He leaned over and gave my forehead a soft kiss. "We'll let you rest for now, but Grey isn't gonna be happy when he gets back and hears what happened. He'll probably barge in here demanding answers."

"I can handle Grey," I said drowsily, my eyes already fluttering.

"Seems to me you can handle anything you put your mind to, baby," Caelan rumbled approvingly. It gave me a warm feeling in my chest that I didn't care to dissect. My mind overwhelmed by the pain and the adrenaline and the medicine, it was easier to finally admit to myself that I was falling for them, as terrifying as that was.

Caelan's voice was low as he whispered to Merikh and Nix, and just as I trained my ear to try to listen, he left the room with the others and shut the door behind him.

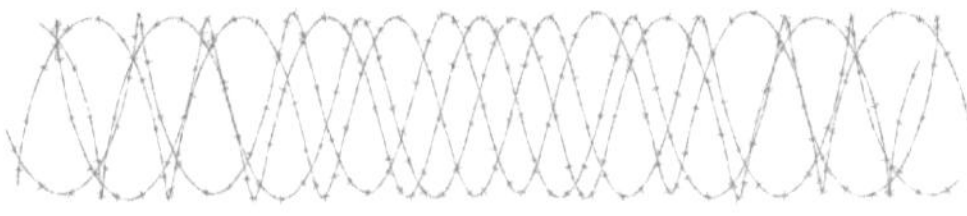

Just as Nix predicted, the sound of a slamming door woke me. I must not have slept for long, because I still felt the blessed numbness from the pain pills Nix had given me. I turned my head on the pillow to face the bedroom door.

Hushed voices came from the front room, escalating into quiet shouts until, finally, footsteps rang out in front of the bedroom. Grey eased the door open quietly, letting himself inside before closing it behind him. He refused to look at me, instead moving to the dresser and standing in front of it, staring down at the plain wood. From this angle, I could see his jaw clenching repeatedly, and the way his hands had formed into tight fists. He didn't dare turn around, instead just silently stewing. I was hesitant to speak, concerned by the reception I'd receive. But I wasn't afraid. Never that. I could see that his anger came from a place of fear and anger. His memories were probably choking him.

His turn was sudden, as was his question.

"Why?"

It was obvious he'd been informed of what went down. I took a second to think about his question. He deserved a real answer, not just some placating statement. "Khira was trapped and scared."

His sigh was heavy. The scar running down his face was contorted by his frown. He looked as if he didn't know what to do with himself.

"Come here," I said softly, gesturing toward the empty space on the bed next to me.

His steps were jerky and hesitant, but he came. He sat gingerly, eyes scanning my body where it lay under the covers.

"You could've been bit," he rasped.

"I know," I whispered. "But I'm okay."

He just shook his head. I shuffled down the bed a little to reach him and laid my hand on his. My body ached from the movement, but it was worth it to be able to touch him. His eyes when they met mine were tortured. "I should've been there."

"None of that," I said firmly. "You were busy saving people, and I'm my own person. I made an executive decision, the same one I'm sure you would have made had you been in my place." His expression told me he couldn't disagree, and that he wasn't happy about it. "Just be here with me." I pulled my hand back, settling into the pillows and blankets once more.

He was still for a long moment, exhaling all his tension in one long sigh. Without saying a word, he shifted me over just an inch, then settled onto the bed next to me. As soon as he was laid out fully, he carefully pulled me into his arms, still wrapped in the blanket and all. Our heads rested next to one another on the pillows, and our eyes met for what felt like an eternity.

"I need you to stay safe," he whispered, his whiskey eyes intense. "I can't lose anyone else."

My smile was small. It felt so good to be so treasured. I leaned forward slowly, giving him a soft kiss, and instantly wishing I wasn't injured. His lips were so damn soft, so pliant under mine. Before I pulled away, I leaned my forehead against his. "Same goes for you." One more gentle kiss and I pulled back, squirming around until I was lying more comfortably in his arms.

His laugh was quiet, his breath stirring my hair where his chin rested on top of my head. "You're a gift, River."

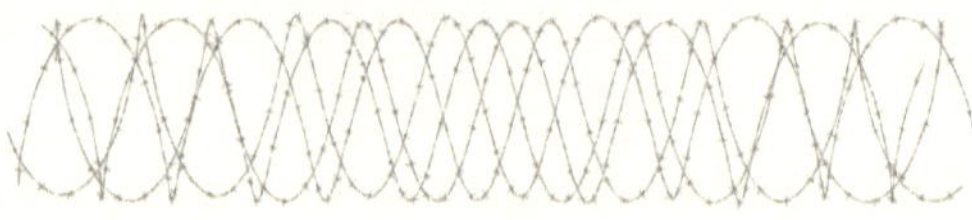

I was woken by tossing and turning. I looked out the window to see the moon shining brightly. Beside me, Grey grunted softly as he tried to get comfortable. *How long has he been struggling to fall asleep?*

"Is every night like this?" I asked quietly, my voice thick with sleep. I hadn't noticed it in the nights previously but maybe I'd just been sleeping too deeply.

He mumbled something incoherent into the pillow.

"Speak up," I pestered.

"No," he said finally. "Not when you're here. The memories are bothering me tonight."

My heart ached for him. I felt terrible that I'd worried him so badly and stirred up things he'd tried to forget.

He turned again, now lying on his back to face the ceiling. His face was blank.

"Come here," I said softly.

He looked at me skeptically. I rolled onto my back, pulling his body closer and positioning him so that his head was resting against my chest. I began to hum softly, carding my fingers through his hair and over his scalp, lightly using my nails to add a little pressure.

If he could purr, I think he'd be doing it now. As it was, he heaved a deep sigh, letting his muscles finally relax and his body lose its tension. He didn't say anything, but he burrowed his head closer against my chest with a soft sound and found my free hand with his, threading our fingers together loosely. His actions spoke louder than words could anyway.

This was dangerous territory. My heart was getting perilously close to bursting with all the feelings it was experiencing. I didn't brush them aside for once, letting myself feel all the affection and softness for the man resting against me as I continued to play with his hair. I hummed lullaby after lullaby, smiling to myself when I finally heard his breathing deepen, allowing my eyes to drift closed as well.

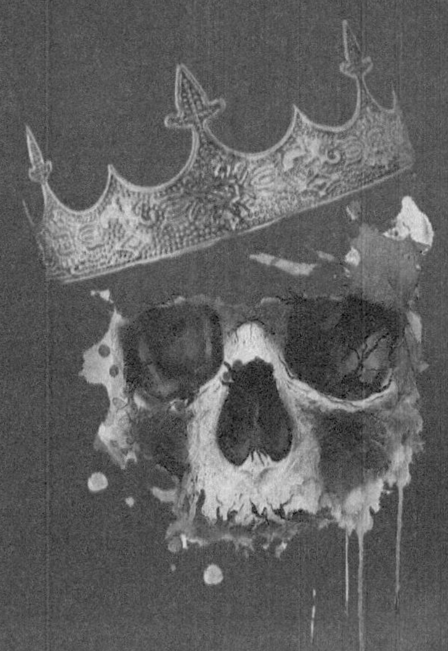

CHAPTER 17

I was dying of boredom.

I'd never been so inactive in my life. It was hard not to feel like a burden, and wasn't *that* just the weirdest feeling. It wasn't like I'd imposed myself on them. In fact, I was certain they wouldn't let me leave if I tried to recover somewhere else.

It was a long few days before I saw anyone but the guys, and I was practically climbing the walls. I sat in the front room and watched the fire, alternated between beds, used the safety rail in the bathroom to shower, but I didn't leave, and I didn't get visitors. Which was why the knock at the door was so surprising.

I cocked my head upon hearing the low murmur of several familiar voices, unable to stop my excitement from spreading. One quick minute later, Naia, Nerese, and Halli walked through the bedroom door, admiring Nix's sparse belongings before turning to me.

"What's that?" I asked nosily, leaning over to peer inside the wicker basket Nerese carried.

Her grin was wicked. "Snacks and games. We figured you'd be bored, so we thought we'd bring some stuff for you to do. Plus, we just missed you."

"I could kiss you! Come sit." I patted the empty side of the bed, watching as Naia hovered silently beside her. She looked... unwell. Paler than usual with jagged nails that she must have been biting. Instead of her signature pinks and purples, she was wearing a tatty brown sweater with jeans.

My questioning glance at Nerese received a small shrug in return. Allllrighty, then. Halli plopped down near my feet, her beaded earrings brushing her shoulders as she got comfortable. Her hair was down today, the curls looking soft and bouncy.

I couldn't just let whatever was bothering Naia go, she looked so unhappy. Unfortunately, I wasn't very experienced in approaching things tactfully. "Naia, is everything... okay?"

She could hardly look at me and her voice trembled as she spoke. "I'm sorry I didn't stay with you when you agreed to help. Maybe if I had..." She gestured toward my body, swamped under all the blankets.

Oh. I'd had no idea she'd been beating herself up over what happened. If only she had come and seen me earlier, I would've set her straight. "It wouldn't have been practical for you to stay with me. You had an obligation to help the others, you couldn't leave Nerese alone with all the children in the middle of an emergency just to go off on your own. It made perfect sense," I said softly. I hated seeing her so upset over me.

She didn't look convinced. "It's what I do, Naia. I'm not hurt very badly, I'll be back to usual in a week or two, promise. Besides"—I threw in a wink—"I'm getting three square meals a day delivered in bed. What else could I ask for?"

That drew a watery chuckle from her. She didn't have to know that it grated on me to be waited on hand and foot. She finally cracked a smile. "If you say so. The Akbaris are overjoyed that Khira is okay. They would have come to see you themselves, but we convinced them to wait until you were up and about."

She was right. It would've been uncomfortable for me to try to greet them from bed. For all I knew, there'd be tears and gratitude. I shuddered at the thought. Send me a flower or two and call it a day. The thought of receiving any praise made me uneasy.

Nerese pushed Naia aside, scooting onto the bed beside Halli. "Enough of that," she said cheerfully. "We're all safe and sound. Now, how about a card game?"

We played for hours, laughing and talking and swapping stories. Naia looked so much lighter since she'd let go of all the guilt she'd been carrying, and in turn, Nerese drew her into conversation frequently. Miraculously, the guys hadn't intruded once. Nerese commented on how well I seemed to be getting along with Grey, Nix, and Caelan, and Naia revealed the crush she had on one of the seamstresses. Halli was content to listen, happy to watch us all trade stories. It was surprisingly cozy and relaxing. Not once did the topic of me getting hurt, or the world outside the camp walls come up.

After several hours had passed, Naia and Nerese left. They'd volunteered their time that evening to help fortify the section of the fence and gate where the incident happened. Halli promised me she had nowhere to be and could hang out for a while longer.

She propped herself up against the pillows next to me and crossed her ankles daintily, smoothing out the wrinkles in her bright orange skirt.

"So... when you get better." It wasn't phrased as a question, yet I knew it was one all the same.

I thought for a good while on how to answer her, and to her credit, she didn't rush me. There was a lot to take into consideration from the last time we'd spoken about it. The way the guys had rushed to my side when I'd been injured, the mind-blowing sex, not to mention the feelings that were taking over my heart more and more with every witty joke, thoughtful kindness, or soft touch. Why did I keep trying to force myself to leave when it was the opposite of what I really wanted? If I could be honest with anyone, it was Halli. She'd make no judgments and wouldn't try to change my mind.

"For now, I'm going to stick around," I said finally, alleviating the weight that had been plaguing me for the past few weeks.

She grinned. "I'm happy to hear that. We'd miss you if you left, good friends are hard to come by."

I smiled, patting her knee softly. It felt nice to be wanted, to feel like I belonged somewhere. I was feeling a sense of community that I'd never experienced anywhere else.

"Oh!" she exclaimed, rooting around in the little satchel she always wore across her chest. "I forgot, I have something for you." She pulled out a beautiful gold bracelet, decorated with green gemstones. "I found it years ago, before we even found this place. It was never really my style, but it was too beautiful to leave behind. I cleaned it with some vinegar and baking soda, and it was as good as new."

My lips parted on a small gasp when she placed it in my hands. It was such a thoughtful gift, I had no idea what to say.

"I noticed you admiring my bracelets the other day," she explained. "I would've given you a stack like I have, but I figured you're too fresh from the outside to be comfortable with jewelry that makes noise when you move."

I had to laugh at that, because she was absolutely correct. I leaned sideways, pulling her into a loose hug and holding back a wince as the cut on my side stretched. "It's perfect," I said softly. "And that was a good call. I've never owned pretty things or felt like I could wear them without ruining them or having them be a hazard to my safety, but this is the perfect gift for the person I am now."

Her smile was incandescent. Then and there, I resolved to help her with the ongoing issue she was having with the garden. I knew that she was getting increasingly nervous and overwhelmed at the prospect of running out of the fresh food on which we relied so heavily. It seemed that every time someone was going to scavenge for more, something came up, not to mention that it would take an extended trip to even find anything, since everything in the area had been picked clean. As Merikh had mentioned days ago, a limited number of people had been performing tasks outside the camp since the first sign that people were lurking around a couple months back. Of course, now that there'd been an actual attack, they'd likely restrict all further outings. I'd mention something to Caelan, see if we could be the exception and take a quick scavenging trip or something. If only my annoying ankle would heal already.

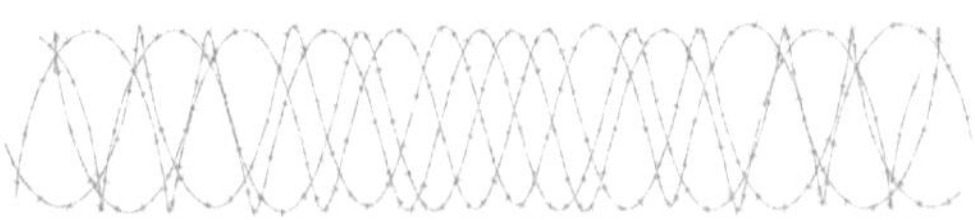

"You're sure she's ready to be up and about?" Caelan pushed, hands on his hips as he frowned at Nix.

"It's been about two weeks; we're lucky we got her to even sit still for that long. Better to wrap her ankle properly and monitor her than have her sneak off because she's so impatient."

"Excuse me! I'm right here!" I said, waving my hands back and forth in the air. "And I'm not *that* impatient, I just haven't been to the lake in forever and I want to swim. That's a good activity for a sore ankle, right?" I crossed my arms, glaring at them both.

Nix stifled a laugh, while Caelan didn't even bother trying to hide his.

"Ugh! Come on already," I groused, ready to pull Nix out by his shirt.

"You kids have fun," Caelan called out as we made it through the front door of the cabin.

"You could come, you know." Nix frowned, watching Caelan as he stood in the doorway.

"Nah." His mood turned serious. "We're scoping out the perimeter today, looking for any more tracks."

I tied my long hair back into a ponytail, wincing as I hit a snarl. It had more waves than usual now that I'd been washing it more frequently.

I saluted Caelan as I hopped down the stairs, ignoring Nix's concerned hiss.

"Careful!"

"It's fine, Nix." It really was. It barely hurt. Between the rest and the medicine, I was starting to wonder if the hairline crack had been more of a... what was smaller than a hair? A needle? Whatever, the point was, it had largely stopped hurting as the days passed.

Part of me was glad that it would just be Nix and me today. He'd been distant with me since the argument a couple weeks ago. Not exactly cold, but just less affectionate. Less free with his words and his emotions. I hated it. I knew I had hurt his feelings by choosing to leave, but was that really my fault? I hadn't yet been in a place where I could weigh his feelings against my own desires over the matter.

In fact, now that he was so emotionally removed from the situation, I had no idea how he was feeling about it whatsoever. We hadn't been intimate since before the argument, and we certainly hadn't done any-thing while I was injured.

He called my name, and I looked up to find him staring at me in confusion.

"Sorry," I mumbled, catching up to him. "Just thinking."

He nodded, picking his way down the path to the lake. The voices in the distance faded, as did all the noises of the camp, until it was just me and him.

The clouds grew heavier overhead, although it didn't seem like it was going to rain just yet. The breeze was cool and soothing against my warm skin, the perfect temperature for dipping my feet into the water. My smile grew as the lake came into view, the water rippling where the wind hit it.

Nix stopped first, unfolding the blanket he'd brought and laying it out on the mixture of packed dirt and sparse grass a few feet away from where the water lapped at the ground. "I brought you water," I said quietly, pulling the metal bottle from my bag and flashing back to when he'd done the same shy gesture weeks ago. I could feel my face flushing pink with nerves, worried about how to approach the awkwardness between us. It would almost be easier if he were angry or upset, but he wasn't. He was placid and kind and easygoing. It felt like there was a chasm between us.

We both sat, far enough apart that we weren't touching, and after a few minutes of breathing the earthy scent of the lake, watching the clouds move, and feeling hyper-aware of his knee resting several inches from mine, the silence grew unbearable.

"I'm sorry," I blurted out, blushing furiously.

"For what?"

"For…" Shit. That's not what I thought he'd counter with. "For trying to leave?"

He snorted, playing with the bracelet on his wrist and refusing to meet my eyes. "No you're not. Nor should you be."

"What do you mean by that?"

"It was unfair of me to expect you to do anything other than run."

I unbent my legs and inhaled a deep breath of fresh air. "I'm not sorry about running, no."

He scoffed, at himself or me, I wasn't sure. I knew we had to get through this if we were going to continue to coexist, but it was so hard. I'd never had discussions like this, never taken other people's feelings into account before.

"I'm sorry that it hurt you," I offered awkwardly, playing with a small patch of clover next to the edge of the blanket.

He was silent for so long that I dared to look in his direction, surprised to find him staring moodily at the ground.

"You tried to leave," he stated plainly, as frustrated as I'd ever seen him. *Now* we were getting somewhere.

"I did," I replied calmly. I didn't owe him anything back then, or at least I didn't feel like I did, but that didn't mean he wasn't allowed to feel hurt over it. He stood abruptly, pacing back and forth with his arms crossed.

I sighed, standing up, so that I wasn't staring up at him awkwardly.

"You tried to leave *me*." His voice broke.

I softened mine. "Nix." I took a step forward, my heart crushed by his step back.

"Don't," he bit out, reproach twisting his handsome features.

"I didn't—*don't*—belong here. At least... I'm not sure I do."

"You belong with me. With us."

The shock rendered me immobile. Thinking it and saying it were two different things. Dreaming of staying with them late at night with only the moon to witness my fanciful thoughts and then feeling ashamed after was not the same as openly introducing the thought into the world. Yes, I'd said as much to Halli, but I had made no such statement about my spot *with* them. Just with the camp as a whole, with my friends. This was... something else entirely.

He must've seen the surprise on my face, because he nodded slowly. "In case you haven't figured it out yet, if for some reason you're confused, or doubtful, or conflicted, maybe this will clear it up. You belong by our side, in our beds, in our space. I want to fall asleep with you beside me and wake up to find you in my arms." He took several steps forward, backing me up against the large tree behind our blanket. His chest was heaving with quick breaths, eyes sparking with lust. "Turn around," he commanded, licking his lips. I could hardly think about the claiming statement he'd just made with the air so thick and filled with desire.

"And if I say no?" I rasped.

He fixed me with a heated stare, the question not extinguishing the ardor in his eyes but fanning it. "Then you say no, and I go douse myself in the lake to cool off."

My body came alive under his words, his want, sparking with desire at the feel of my nipples brushing his shirt through my thin bra with every deep breath I took. I capitulated, turning my body slowly, tauntingly, so that I faced the tree, bracing my hands against the warped trunk.

When he made no move after several long, drawn-out seconds, I turned my head to find a harsh smirk on his lips.

"What do you want?" he asked me. It was unnerving, facing away from him with the intention of being used for his pleasure and then being asked what I wanted.

I refused to answer, breath speeding up as his body crowded mine. I could feel the heat coming off him, closer and closer, until his hard body was pressed firmly against my back.

"Tell me what you want," he murmured, enunciating each word, kissing my neck softly, and breathing across the shell of my ear. I shivered with pleasure, almost shaking in anticipation. A small sound left my throat as he nipped at the skin of my neck, soothing the sting with the flat of his tongue. This was what we needed to fix things, to cap off the honesty. He'd made his declarations, stated his intentions, and now it was time to seal them with our bodies as we did best.

His hands slid at a torturously slow pace around my waist, caressing my hip bones, then moving up to my ribcage and landing on my breasts. He teased my nipples slowly over my clothes, prolonging the excruciating wait before sliding one hand under my tank top to stroke my stomach. I withheld a whimper as he trailed his large, warm hand up my abdomen, careful to avoid the healing wound on my side, then worked his hand under my flimsy bra and cupped my bare breast. He tweaked my nipple then, brushing over it with the flat of his hand when he was done. I moaned quietly, whimpering at the sparks that flew when he touched me. Then he slid his other hand down my torso, slipping his fingers under the hem of my shorts and sliding back and forth at my waistband teasingly. An impatient moan had him finally moving to my soaking wet pussy.

He cupped me like I belonged to him, hand sifting through my curls to find the wetness within.

"Tell me," he snarled, more insistent than before. A backward glance at his face revealed wild eyes. He looked nothing like the quiet, kind man from earlier. This Nix was all desire and demands, no longer leashed by the presence of his brothers and needing to share my attention.

I kept quiet aside from the whimper I couldn't hold back, choking on a cry as he propped his knee up between my legs so that I wouldn't lose my balance.

"Now," he whispered hotly against my ear.

"Fuck me, touch me, make me come," I cried on a sob as he thrust two fingers into me as a reward.

"Good girl," he groaned. He withdrew his fingers from my wetness to toy with my clit, the hand on my breast moving down to grip my waist to stop me from squirming. "You. Left." He punctured each word with a thrust of his fingers.

I almost cried out as both hands left my body, feeling bereft and empty. The only reason I didn't move was because I could hear him working at his pants before he tugged my shorts and panties down. I could feel his jeans against my ass, and it struck me as so deliciously naughty that he'd only pulled his cock out and yet I was standing there half-naked, desperate and wanton for him. His hard length pressed at the small of my back, hot and throbbing, while his hand returned to work me over. I writhed against him, grinding back against him and smiling to myself when he grunted loudly.

He lined himself up against me, thrusting in with one push. I moaned, clutching the sides of the tree for stability and throwing my head back onto his shoulder. He punched his hips once, twice, before holding still.

"Go," I moaned, trying to push back onto his cock. He twitched inside me but refused to move. Rolling my head to the side where it lay against his shoulder, I found him clenching his jaw, eyebrows drawn together in a pained grimace.

"You're mine. Say it."

I thought of Grey, the way his scar twisted when he smiled and the soft way he relaxed in my arms at night. Of Caelan's unrelenting optimism and endless jokes. "I can't," I whispered.

He caught on quickly, thrusting once more and pulling out unhurriedly before modifying his command. "Ours. You're ours. Say it."

"No," I gasped as he withdrew slowly, pumping his hips at a languorous pace. I brought my left hand back to grasp at his hip, urging him forward and huffing when he refused to move.

"Ours," he growled, nipping at my neck with his sharp teeth. One hand grabbed my breast tightly, squeezing, then holding it in a proprietary manner. It wasn't something I ever thought I'd be into but apparently I loved it.

"Please," I begged, rocking back against him.

He splayed one hand across my stomach while the other slid up from my chest to wrap around my neck. I moaned, eyes rolling back as he applied light pressure. "Say it."

"Yesss," I hissed. "Just like that."

"Say it."

"Fine," I groaned, my body on fire from his hand on my throat, holding me like I was his. "I belong to you, all of you. I'm yours."

He moaned triumphantly, powering into me with renewed vigor, snapping his hips and bottoming out.

"God, yes," I shouted, clutching the hand splayed across my stomach with the one I'd been using to hold his hip. Each delicious drag of his cock hit a pleasurable spot inside me, ratcheting my satisfaction higher and higher. The smack of his skin against mine filled the air, along with our mingled grunts and moans.

"Take it," he commanded as I relaxed against him, allowing him to give it to me exactly how I wanted. With my head on his shoulder, his hand on my neck, and our hands joined on my stomach, I was bent backward into his embrace, back arching wildly. My legs were close together, and it created an even tighter grip for him to thrust into. "That's it," he murmured, loosening his hold on my throat but still resting his hand there lightly.

I could feel my orgasm building, knew it was close. He moved the hand on my stomach to my clit, my hand still covering his. We moved in tandem, stroking my bundle of nerves in sloppy, circular motions while he rammed inside me. I moaned loudly, squeezing my eyes shut tightly and climaxing with a shout. He groaned, thrusting several more times before a wet heat flooded inside me and his cock jerked, prolonging my orgasm. I shook in his arms, welcoming his gentle kisses against my neck.

He took the majority of my weight, leading us to the lake where he proceeded to strip off his shirt to wipe his come from my thighs. I sighed at the feel of the cool water lapping at my ankles, leaning on his shoulders as he knelt before me. I was completely fucked out of my mind, so when he stood and his eyes were once more guarded, I wasn't prepared.

"Did you mean it?" he asked.

I hesitated, unsure of what answer to give. Finally, I caved, the fragile hope behind his wary stance making my decision for me. I couldn't keep withholding answers from him just because it made me feel more in control. If he was willing to be vulnerable, then so could I.

"Yes," I said softly. "Just give me time, Nix."

He sprawled in the grass next to the blanket, looking utterly debauched. His eyes were glassy, stray waves sweat-slicked and stuck to his forehead, lightly muscled abdomen glistening. He patted the space in front of him—between his legs—and I sat like it was the most natural thing in the world.

He tugged me into his body, arms coming around to rest against my stomach. I allowed myself to recline in his embrace, luxuriating in the afterglow and appreciating the way the clouds reflected off the water. His scent wrapped around me, a soothing combination of vanilla and something distinctly pine-like.

I played with the bracelet dangling off his wrist, running my fingers over the worn silver.

"Do you know why I'm called Nix?" he murmured from behind me. His chest rumbled against my back when he spoke.

"No... it's a nickname, right?"

I twisted around to watch his face. He smiled sadly, turning my head forward again and placing it so that it rested against his shoulder.

"No. My father named me Nix."

I was unsure of where he was going with this, but decided to stay quiet, letting him get there on his own.

"Caelan and Merikh were born first. Apparently, my mother took one look at Caelan and named him on the spot. Her father's side was Irish, but she was raised here, and she said that Caelan was a variation of her great-grandfather's name, though I can't quite remember what it meant. She thought it suited Caelan's fierceness because he came out screaming. My father chose Merikh's name. He didn't really expand on that beyond wanting something that sounded intimidating."

Damn, his parents were hardcore. I could totally see his dad naming Merikh that though, and a damn good call since all these years later he'd grown into it. I shifted in Nix's arms, worried over what was coming next.

"I came last. My mother was exhausted from pushing for so long. I'm not even sure they knew she was carrying triplets. There were no midwives nearby like we have here. It was only a year after the virus outbreak, just before it mutated, and society was decimated. My mother and father were nomads and unable to find anyone to assist with the birth."

I had a feeling I knew what was coming next. I clutched his arm to my chest, holding him tightly to me. A cool breeze ran over us, creating more ripples in the water and rustling the leaves.

"She began bleeding. Badly." His voice cracked on the last word. "More than was normal. My father was panicking. She told him that it would be okay, but he could tell that something wasn't right. She was bleeding too much, too fast. They were worried something had happened to me and that I wasn't going to make it. She used her last reserves of strength to push me out, and she only got to hold me in her arms for a few minutes before she passed."

I interlaced my fingers with his, squeezing his hand reassuringly. I understood now why he couldn't bear to face me while he told his story. He was feeling exposed. Vulnerable, and ashamed.

"He named me Nix. For nothing. I caused my mother's death. I was the final straw, the reason her body couldn't take anymore, causing whatever went wrong to happen. So he named me Nix, that way he would never forget what I had done. He would look at me and see nothing, nobody."

I wanted to cry for that small boy. I squeezed my eyes shut tightly to stop the tears from overflowing. "You know it's not your fault, right?" I asked quietly when I knew I could speak without my voice trembling.

He exhaled slowly, cool breath stirring the hair at my temple, and avoided the question. "He used to lock me outside. He'd tell me that the zombies would get me and when they did, no one would miss a nobody. Either Caelan or Merikh would sneak out, bringing me cold food they'd hidden in their pockets and keeping watch with me. I don't think he would have cared if I got bit. I fought one off once using my shoe and a stick until Merikh came out with a kitchen knife. Then when fa–Mark–built this place, and he started expending his energy elsewhere."

"Did he ever..."

"Hit me? When I was younger, occasionally. As we grew older and bigger, he knew I would fight back and so would my brothers in my defense, and he just stopped. I know it wasn't me so much as it was his grief and fear and anger, but to a young boy who felt like the cause of everyone's problems, it was devastating. Every time he looks at me, all he can see is my mother's eyes. And... yes. I know now that it's not my fault, but it still hurts now and then. With all the stories he used to tell whenever he'd get too exhausted to filter himself, I think I would've loved her and... I like to think she would've liked me as well."

I nodded in firm agreement, then ran my thumb over the back of his hand in small, soothing circles and inhaled the scent of fresh pine to try to calm down. It didn't work.

"I hate that fucker," I growled.

He barked a laugh. "We all do, but since he set up the camp, he's been preoccupied. He leaves most of the responsibilities to us, no surprise there. He's gone a lot more often now, scavenging and whatnot. We're grateful for it. He's no threat, but it's nice to not have him hanging around."

I sighed, relaxing in his arms. "I'm glad."

"Did your parents tell you why you were named River?"

I smiled, accepting the subject change and turning slightly to press a kiss to his soft lips before facing the lake once more. "I never got to know my mom. Sometimes I think I can remember the scent of her hair, and the sound of her voice when she sang to me, but she died when I was four, so I was never sure if I'd fabricated them or not. My dad didn't talk about her much, but he told me the story of my birth a lot. When she was around eight months along, they finally settled down, finding a small unoccupied cabin to stay in until she gave birth. It was deep in the forest, far away from civilization, and hopefully a good distance from any zombies. There was a river that ran a short distance from the backyard, perfect for bathing or fetching water."

"Sounds perfect," Nix sighed contentedly.

"It was," I whispered back. "She went into labor with no one around to assist, just like your mom. My dad had read plenty of books on birth and delivery to prepare, and he thought he could handle it. They were by the water when she delivered, and she only had to push for an hour before I came out."

I stretched in his embrace, watching the murky water shift and dance under the wind. I felt like purring when he held me tighter, nuzzling the side of my neck. I made a soft noise when his lips brushed my skin, feeling ridiculously happy.

"He was beside himself that she was giving birth on a patch of grass in the forest, but she consoled him and told him that the soundtrack of a rushing river was all she could ever ask for, and after all, woodland air is the best kind."

"So they named you after the river," Nix surmised.

I smiled to myself. "Yeah. Yeah, they did."

"Much better than my story," he remarked, trying to add a note of levity to the somber mood.

I laughed, turning in his arms and tackling him to the ground with a kiss. And if I just so happened to pocket the tarnished bracelet that had fallen off his wrist, the clasp broken, he didn't notice.

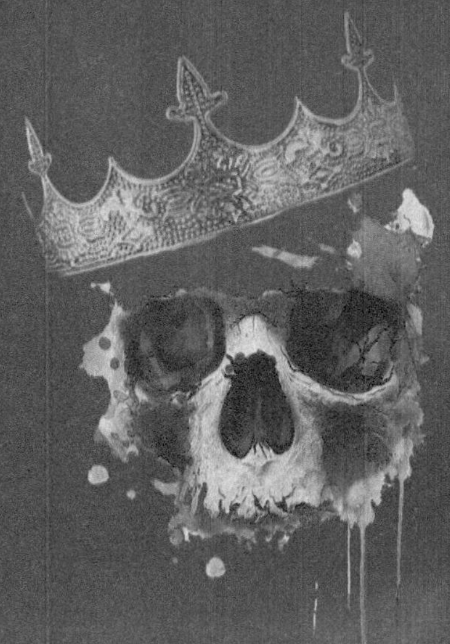

CHAPTER 18

It'd been several weeks since I'd patched things up with Nix and things were going tenuously well. The days were growing longer, and the nights had lost some of their frigid bite. All my injuries were pretty much healed, Grey was sleeping better, and Caelan was his usual happy self.

I usually tried to avoid Merikh. Today, though, I was having no such luck. Things were strained between us, and neither of us was clear on the new rules, or the lack thereof. I was no longer the same captive I'd been a month ago. I went where I liked, ate when I wanted, and didn't perform any chores or tasks for them that I didn't want to, nor did they ask me to. Merikh had seemingly accepted this new development, never going so far as to actually address it but shooting me the odd confused look every so often. It was awkward, and uncomfortable.

I sat on the couch, glancing over at the kitchen table every so often where Merikh was jotting things down into his tiny faux leather notebook. I couldn't stop looking at him, drawn to the whole studious look he had going on with his glasses perched on the edge of his nose. Who knew he could make glasses look so hot? And how the hell did he manage to scavenge an undamaged pair that worked perfectly? He leaned forward, rubbing the end of the pencil over his full bottom lip, and a lock of hair was jostled free with the movement, falling across his high cheekbone.

I was distracted by a dull ache in my hip, and without thinking twice about it, stood and twisted my body just so until I heard the telltale crack of whatever had been bothering me. I was confused by the sudden silence, only to look over and find Merikh staring at me in horror.

"Did you just crack your hip?" he questioned hoarsely.

"Uhh, yeah? You've never cracked your hips before?"

His whole body shuddered as his eyes closed. "Hell no. Fuck, that was horrific. Never do it again."

I burst out laughing. "Wanna hear me crack my knees? How about my wrists?"

"No. Absolutely not. You're gonna dislocate something." He cringed, and I could barely respond, I was laughing so hard. Could it really be that the ornery, grumpy Merikh had an aversion to hearing people crack things?

He purposefully looked away from me and back to his notebook, pretending that I wasn't just across the room laughing my ass off. I fell back onto the couch, collapsing into giggles once more, and propped my feet up against the middle cushion. It felt so good to laugh, as though I were making up for lost time. All the instances where I needed to be quiet, or inconspicuous, I was free to be as loud as I wanted here.

I sighed, my laughter finally dying off, and threw my arm over the back of the couch to watch him once more. For some reason, I loved teasing him. It was so much easier than it was with Nix, who was more serious, and Caelan, who took nothing seriously at all.

What better time to bring up how I was interested in going on a scavenging trip than now, while we were alone? I knew damn well if I went straight to Caelan, he'd check with Merikh first. Then he'd surely say no, and I wouldn't have the chance to make my argument.

I brought it up casually, acting like it was no big deal. "So... I was thinking–"

"No."

I jerked my head up, but he was still staring down at his notes. "No, what?"

"No to whatever you're angling for."

"Why are you assuming I'm angling for anything?"

"Stop changing the subject."

"Ugh!" I threw my hands up. "Fine, I'm interested ingoingscavenging-withcaelan." The words blended together in one long jumble, and I could smack myself on the forehead for messing this up so badly. I didn't like asking permission for things! Clearly, I was no good at it. Although I had to remember that it was a camp wide rule, and not something imposed just on me.

He finally set his pen down, removing his glasses with one hand and rubbing the furrowed wrinkles between his brows and along his forehead with the other. "Absolutely not."

"Why not?"

"It's dangerous, that's why," he muttered.

"You did it just the other month," I argued.

"Okay, well, I don't know if you noticed, but you're not me."

"What are you trying to say?" Seems I couldn't help myself from creeping up on his nerves.

"You heard me!" he shouted, pushing his chair back to stand. "It's not safe. I don't care how long you lived out there, you're here now. Why would you put yourself back in danger?"

"Oh, but it's okay for you to do it?" Just where did he get off trying to tell me what I could and couldn't do? The circumstances had changed. The second I earned whatever freedoms I had in this camp, he lost the right to dictate my actions. Whether I still asked for permission or not. He should know better; I'd find my own way out if I needed to.

He was pacing now. "What if you were to run into the group that sabotaged the gate?"

"We haven't heard anything from them in weeks, surely they're lying low?"

"Just because they're lying low doesn't make them not a threat," he growled from between clenched teeth.

"I've handled threats before!" I shouted. "I handled John, didn't I? You never give me any fucking credit. I know how to take care of myself!"

He stopped still. "John was a different kind of threat," he apprised me. "Killing someone freshly turned is different from killing someone with all their mental faculties in place and who has designs on your person."

I stared at him, struck speechless. How could I have forgotten this one last sword hanging over my head?

"Right?" he hedged, crossing his arms. As the silence grew longer, his mood shifted. His body turned still, eyes dull as he stared at me. "River," he said flatly.

"No, not right."

"Excuse me?"

"Now who's pretending they can't hear?"

I shouldn't have been pushing him like this. He was already not going to take it well, not to mention he was the last to find out. He wouldn't like that either. But I was feeling combative, and all my past hurts were rising up to choke me.

I spoke slowly, so that there was no mistake. "John came up to me, freshly infected, yes. He saw his bag of supplies and realized I took it, also yes. Then he got even closer, and he tried to put his hands on me, even after I offered to give it back."

"Put his hands..." Merikh sounded disgusted. "Like he wanted to bite you? To turn you?"

"No, not just that."

He took a step back. "So you killed him. Because he was—he tried that."

"Yes."

"And the others? Do they know this?"

"They found out in different ways, yes."

He was squinting at me now. "So, let me get this straight. You found John's things unattended and left with them. He went back for them, found them missing and went looking for you, was infected in the process, and then when he found you, he attempted to assault you before trying to bite you. Then I forced you to come here in penance, believing you killed him because he was infected, and so you could keep his things and because he might not have even been bitten if he wasn't running off course to look for you. Then you told Nix, Caelan, and Grey the truth before me. Is that correct?"

His voice was icy, and he was projecting a false calm, but I knew how quickly that could change when I said my next few words. Was it even possible to force myself not to feel the sympathy that was creeping up in response to his cold statement? It was all facts, and it made him look like an asshole, which he was, but for some reason I couldn't help but feel off about it. The words were dragged out of me. "Yes, that's correct."

"And at no point did you think to tell me that?" he roared. "Making yourself into a martyr and making me the villain for no reason other than that you didn't want to tell me what he did? Getting infected and trying to bite you is one thing, but trying to put his hands on you, then you being *punished* for defending yourself." He was seething now, his face flushed redder than I'd ever seen it, hands balled up into fists. I'm not sure who he was angrier with, me or him.

"It's not like you're such a great person anyway," I sneered, going on the defensive. Inside, I was screaming to just talk it out and de-escalate, but I was furious, and I was finally getting the confrontation I wanted so many weeks ago. "You threw that guy out for no reason," I shouted. "What, because he was some kind of threat to your little empire? What do you care what John was gonna do anyway? You're clearly heartless!"

He was stunned into silence on that one. A combination of hurt, disbelief, sadness, and anger flashed across his features almost too fast for me to follow, and immediately after, his face went eerily blank.

"I don't owe you shit," he said flatly. "Clearly, you think so little of me that there's no other possible explanation for banishing Colby. Part of being a leader is making the tough decisions." He glowered. "I didn't ask for your input, or your judgment, or your righteous moral opinion."

"You may not have asked for it, but you sure as hell earned it," I hissed. "You disgust me."

"Fuck you," he muttered, grabbing his jacket from the back of the chair and storming out the front door, slamming it behind him.

The silence left in his wake sucked all the attitude and bitterness out of me until all I was left with was sadness and shame.

Several long minutes later, which I spent standing in the center of the room, lost in my thoughts, Caelan swung the door open, eyes immediately landing on me. "What the hell is up with him?" He gestured back out the door, to where I'm guessing Merikh was currently storming his way down the path back to civilization.

"We fought." My voice was flat and cold.

His brow creased when he realized the situation was probably a bit worse than he first assumed. "He found out, didn't he."

I nodded, playing with the end of the long braid slung over my shoulder.

Caelan's sigh was long. He dropped himself into the armchair next to the couch, throwing his head over the back and staring at the ceiling.

"So dramatic," I tried to tease, the attempt at humor falling flat.

He turned his head to face me, an uncharacteristic frown gracing his face. "So he's angry and hurt that you didn't tell him, and he stormed out?"

"I... Maybe might have brought up Colby in the heat of the moment."

Caelan groaned loudly. "Again with fucking Colby! I'm sorry we never had the time to really sit down and talk about this. I didn't know you had been stewing about it all this time."

"Of course–"

He held up his hand to stop me. "No. My turn. I thought that someone would set you straight, and they didn't and for that, I'm sorry." He sighed loudly, moving to the edge of his chair to watch me, hands clasped over his spread legs. "Did anyone tell you that Colby was innocent, or did you just assume?"

I frowned, turning to gaze at the trees outside the window, the grass swaying in the wind. The eye contact was too much, too personal. "No one told me, but it was obvious. He called him out like some evil overlord, as if Colby were some sort of sacrifice for the undead to keep them busy or something."

Caelan cracked a half-hearted smile before rubbing his thumb over the tattoo on his pointer finger, a skeletal finger replicating the bones within.

"Do you know why I got this tattoo, River?"

I was silent.

"It wasn't all that long ago, maybe a few years, right before the man that did them passed in his sleep. I got it because I wanted to make sure I always understood the gravity of my position here. I knew I would have to point at a person and decide their fate, their future, their continued survival. That I could give it and I could take it away at my discretion to protect the other people in this camp."

"Megalomaniac much? Shit, you're like some twisted Roman emperor. What's next, we build an arena for fights and all scream profanities while we place bets?"

He ignored me. "It's our job to keep the people in this camp safe. Colby? He was abusing his girlfriend, Sarah. It had gone on for way too long. We offered to help for years, but she always declined, allowing it to get steadily worse until he was breaking more than her fingers and leaving bruises where we couldn't see. She finally let Merikh know that she was ready for help, and we took care of it because that's what we do."

My heart sank as I realized what that meant. *The woman from that first meeting that didn't say a word.* I had thought it was strange that she showed up looking exhausted, then stood only to say nothing. It had been a signal, a silent cry for help. And I'd berated Merikh, made him feel less than.

My stomach roiled, and I shook off the gathering tension in my muscles, trying to calm down and stop myself from being sick all over the floor. I had repeatedly brought it up, flaying him with it, and at no point did he set me straight. We had both kept these secrets, too proud and too stubborn to say anything, and look where it got us.

"You didn't know," he murmured as he stood and reached out tentatively to stroke my back.

"I thought you were horrible people," I choked out. I rubbed my forehead soothingly, remembering all the regrettable things that I'd said, and the whole time they had been casting out an abuser. I'd clung to it so hard, as it was the only thing besides them bringing me back here that I could use to defend my opinion of them being bad people. Even when everyone else insisted that they did a good job leading, that they were fair and just, I knew that it was just one example of their tyranny that everyone else ignored, making me feel justified and morally superior. No, not even *them*, just Merikh. I'd taken all my anger and hatred and placed it solely on him, exonerating the rest.

My mind started spiraling, thinking about how different my life would've been if I hadn't come back here with them. If they'd simply asked me, I likely would have said no. I would have walked off on my own again, hungry and tired and purposeless–

"River." Caelan grabbed my attention.

"I'm sorry," I replied hoarsely. He walked me over to the couch, set me down in the center, and tucked me into his side, tattooed arm holding me close.

"Nah." His voice was soft. "This is good, getting everything out in the open. Merikh has been... He just hasn't fit right lately; it's been tearing him up."

My laugh was wet. "You're not trying to say he's jealous? Hurt that I was angry with him?"

Caelan didn't respond, which I supposed was an answer in and of itself.

I bit my lip, curling up against his side and using the silence to think about how I was going to fix things.

Hours passed like that. Caelan couldn't stay long, and the others came and went, but not Merikh. It was well into the night when I gave up waiting for him. I was trying not to be concerned, but I couldn't remember a time he'd ever not come home and opted to stay elsewhere instead.

I walked into Grey's room, leaning against the doorway as I watched him read in bed, using a tall candle on his nightstand.

"You're done sitting in the living room?" he asked as he looked up from his book.

"I didn't peg you for a reader."

His smile was sharp. "Careful, sweetheart. Are you calling me a neanderthal?"

"That's a big word for you," I teased with a smile, walking into the room and perching at the end of his bed. "If the shoe fits..."

He set his book aside, then tackled me without warning. My laughter was swallowed by his mouth as he kissed me deeply once he'd maneuvered me into his lap.

"No deflecting." He pulled away, breath coming slightly faster. "Caelan told me what happened earlier."

I groaned, throwing myself back against the bed. "Is he ever gonna come back?"

Grey's mouth twisted. "He's just... processing his emotions. He'll be okay, and then whenever he comes back, you can talk."

I grumbled, still somehow trying to insist that it wasn't a big deal.

"Enough about Merikh," he growled, pulling my thigh over his legs.

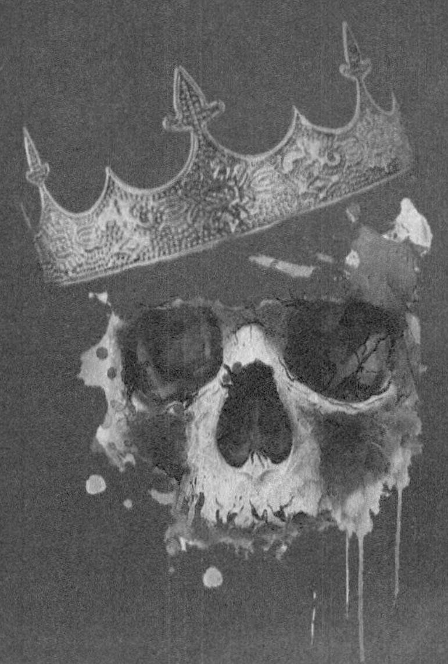

CHAPTER 19

The part of me that was too scared to take chances chanted for me to walk away. Merikh was too difficult, too controlling. It would be impossible for us to coexist without clashing. The honest part acknowledged that this could never work with just the other three. They were a package deal, and damn if I hated that I didn't hate that fact. Truth was, even when I'd fought with Merikh every day, pushed his buttons, and deliberately went against his orders, I still found him intriguing. Fascinating. Now the path was clear, and it was time to make some hard decisions, and face some hidden truths.

I could hear his voice coming from the living room.

Why was I so shy all of the sudden? I should just march out there and... *and what?* I shook my head, waiting until the voices quieted. Several deep calming breaths later and I forced myself to walk out of the bedroom. Maybe he'd left already, and the conversation would get postponed again. That wouldn't be the worst thing, would it?

Except when I turned the corner of the hallway into the main room, he was sitting in the large armchair to the left of the fireplace, expressionless.

A quick glance around revealed that everyone else had left. It seemed I wasn't the only one eager to get rid of this constant tension. I guessed I should make the most of the fact that the cabin was finally empty of people.

My footsteps were silent as I made my way over to where he was sitting. He didn't acknowledge my presence, just kept staring into the flames. I almost winced as I heard my words repeated back to me in my head. *Horrible... Disgusting... Selfish.*

I took a seat at the edge of the couch on the side nearest him, and settled into the cushions, waiting for him to speak, I supposed. After a half hour of stubborn, weighted silence, I dared a glance over in his direction. His eyes were heavy-lidded, his loose waves in disarray. His tongue darted out to lick his lower lip, and I quickly looked away.

I decided to go with a blunt approach. "I'm sorry."

His head turned to face me slowly. When he didn't speak, I continued. "I didn't tell you about John because I didn't know what kind of man you were. I was afraid you would call me a liar, or treat me worse somehow because I'd accused your friend of something terrible. I thought him being infected was enough, and that I shouldn't have to keep throwing out reasons why his death was justified. I was... still struggling with feeling guilty over taking his things in the first place when it was clear whoever had left them was nearby and coming back, and your words calling me a thief and blaming me for his getting infected had struck home. My dad raised me to make choices that I could sleep with at the end of the day, but that was the first time I fell short. I was ashamed, even though I knew I needed the food to survive." I was babbling now, filling the silence with a spill of words and emotions. Now that I'd started explaining myself, I found it hard to stop.

He still didn't say anything. This wasn't even our biggest issue. I'd railed against him for taking me here, for all this shit with Colby, at every turn I'd been spitting in his face, even after he got me out and meeting new people when I'd started to become withdrawn and shy after the whispers and rumors spread. He could have given me tasks like scrubbing toilets or following around strangers when I first arrived, yet he'd gone easy on me instead. Fetch meals, sleep on the couch, clean the cabin. All normal, non-invasive jobs, and he'd only grown harsher when I refused to comply.

I took a deep breath, ready to give him a truth I hadn't told another soul. A fraction of honesty that laid me bare. "I think... that maybe a small piece of me wanted the decision to be taken out of my hands. To come back here with you," I said softly. His eyes widened. "I was too prideful to say yes if you had just invited me. I had to be forced, had to feel like I had no choice. Maybe I didn't tell you about... him because I thought you'd let me go, and I couldn't stomach one more day of scavenging by myself and trying to survive just to wake up and do it all over again." My voice broke. "I didn't know about Colby and his wife. I'm sorry that I assumed."

When he spoke, his voice was deep, almost hypnotizing. "I'm sorry I didn't set you straight," he rasped. "I didn't want to have to justify my actions, and I wasn't ready to have that... obstacle between us gone."

That was exactly how it felt now that he'd put it into words. I hadn't been ready to reconcile the reasons I was angry because I was too scared of what would happen with those buffers removed. He was the last one, and I knew that if I fell for him too, I'd never be able to leave. It was terrifying to someone who'd been on the run since she was born, to find something that made her put down roots. I'd been hiding from it this whole time, but not anymore.

I inhaled deeply, then stood. Merikh looked up at me, the light of the fire playing with the shadows across his face.

"I really am sorry," I whispered. I'd said my piece, but I couldn't force him to accept it. I turned to leave, stopped only by the grip of a hand on my wrist. He was standing now, still saying nothing.

Butterflies filled my stomach as he pulled me closer, using his hand on my wrist. When I was inches away, he used that hand to slide up my forearm to grasp my bicep. My eyelids fluttered shut as he leaned in to press his face against my neck and inhale. To think that I'd been holding on to my hatred so strongly just the day before, and today I was finally letting myself feel everything I'd been shoving down and pretending didn't exist. The smell of smoke and sweat against his skin, the long length of his dark eyelashes resting against his pale cheekbones.

I inhaled sharply as he nuzzled the junction of my neck and my shoulder with his lips, his stubble scraping my skin deliciously.

"I don't know if I want your apologies, princess." His tongue darted out to run delicately along my neck, his breath hot against my skin. "Maybe I want something else," he whispered.

I couldn't hold back my shiver and placed a hand against his shoulder where he was leaning down so I could keep myself steady.

He broke away to stare at me, putting a small amount of distance between us.

My chest heaved as I watched him, and the movement of his fists clenching and unclenching repeatedly by his sides caught and held my attention.

"Be very sure," he bit out.

This was uncharted territory; the desires we'd been suppressing for weeks, the attraction we'd been ignoring in hopes it would go away, it was all coming to a head. Each shouted word and bitter insult some kind of twisted foreplay.

The tension swelled as we stared at each other, the air growing thick and heavy, seconds passing by where we resisted the urge to act without thinking, without speaking, until we both said *fuck it* and met in the middle in a flurry of tongues and teeth. His lips on mine were sinful, parting for me just right.

"Fuck, you taste good," he murmured. A small whimper escaped me when he pulled away. "Not here."

Merikh grabbed my hand, leading me around the corner and to his room. I was breathless with anticipation, all those forbidden feelings of want and need rushing up to consume me.

He pulled my shirt up and over my head, leaving me completely bared, and tossed me onto the bed like I weighed nothing. I landed with a small bounce and a tiny laugh, admiring the way his dimples popped when he smiled in return. He was wickedly handsome when he grinned. He kicked his shoes off, maneuvering so that our bodies were aligned with him hovering over me.

I sighed happily when he took my mouth again, our kisses hot and messy, eyes widening when he took my hands from where they rested on his hips and lifted them up over my head, planting them in the pillows against the headboard. The angle made my back arch and chest thrust upwards against his. I gave an experimental tug, judging just how committed he was to restraining me. He didn't budge an inch, instead smiling lazily at my attempt. Maybe I should've been annoyed or irritated, but I found that I loved the feeling of being at his mercy.

He kissed along my jaw and stopped to tug my lobe with his teeth. His heated words whispered into my ear. "So good for me, princess."

I shivered at the feel of his breath caressing the shell of my ear, hips rocking and seeking friction, only to find empty air. I whimpered out of frustration, writhing under his attentions.

"You want relief, hmm? I'm not sure you deserve it. Teasing me all these weeks, walking around in your tiny little *fucking* shorts, moaning so loudly I can hear you down the hall at night, touching my brothers in front of me. You make me want. You make me *ache*."

"Yes," I groaned, attempting to tug my hands from his grip over my head and get him to fucking *move*.

"Keep your hands above your head. Or do you not want to come?"

I huffed, frustrated beyond belief that he wouldn't just touch me already. I was crawling out of my skin with need.

"I asked you a question, princess." His voice was firm, steadfast, and doing delicious things to my insides.

"Fine. Yes."

"Yes, what?" One hand began playing with my breast, teasing the nipple into a firm point. I could've sobbed at the touch, so close and yet not enough, not enough at all.

I was practically snarling. "Yes, I want to come."

Merikh tugged at my nipple before capturing it in his mouth, teasing it with his tongue, and then working it over with his teeth. I moaned, my eyes shutting against the dueling sensations.

"I like that," I murmured.

I couldn't see his face, but I just knew he was smirking. "Good. So good for me," he murmured, pulling off my nipple with a pop, deft fingers just trailing along my skin now. "Love these tits, soft and small, puffy pink nipples begging to be sucked. Perfect for me."

I bit my lip, unbelievably aroused by his filthy words, his freely offered praise. I groaned in response, hips caressing the air once more. I would've believed him to be unaffected by his need if not for his blown pupils, the tight grip of his hand holding my wrists captive, and his sharp breaths against my skin.

"Gonna fill you up with my cock, with my come," he groaned as his hand drifted down to tease my dripping wet slit. "Just like I should've weeks ago when I walked in on you fucking spread open for them all."

He watched me with hooded eyes, his hair hanging in his face and flushed cheeks working together to form a messy, desperate picture that I loved. His long fingers delved into my wetness, stretching me open. They were rough inside me, calloused and strong and stroking me oh so good. Every few seconds he slid upwards to stroke my clit, just teasing touches, before going back to my entrance.

I groaned, long and loud. "Yessss."

"Yeah? You like that, princess?"

I shuddered, bucking upwards so that our bodies were in contact. He took the hint, draping his body over mine. "Merikh," I gasped.

"That's right," he murmured. "Let me hear it. So fucking wet, just for me. All mine."

I moaned louder, captivated by his possessive, experienced touch. A second long finger dipped inside me, stroking and thrusting at varying speeds. "If I take my hands away, will you be good and keep them above your head?"

I hesitated, wondering when I became someone who would roll over and submit without a fight. But I was so desperate to come, anticipating the rigid length of his cock filling me up, and I knew that if I was obstinate, he would deny me. I nodded slowly in response to his question. I let my thighs fall open under his ministrations, helping him along by lifting up when he pulled my pants off and scooting upwards an inch so that my hands could grip the slats along the headboard.

He immediately went back to teasing me, gathering my wetness and using it to rub my clit in small circular motions. My jaw dropped when he withdrew his fingers and licked them sensually before sucking them into his mouth.

"You taste delicious, River," he groaned. "So fucking sweet."

I rubbed my body against his front by undulating my hips, biting my lip when I felt his hardness behind his shorts. "I want to taste you, too," I murmured.

"Not yet, not this time," he rumbled. His eyes shuttered as he inched his shorts down to his thighs, grabbing his throbbing cock and squeezing it tightly at the base. The veins on his neck corded as he gritted his teeth, eyes just slits as he said, "I don't want our fun to be over too fast, but just fucking look at you. Bared for me, skin flushed, needy and desperate." His moan was tortured.

"Now," I declared, trying not to sound too commanding so that he didn't start all over.

He pulled his shirt over his head in one smooth movement, then *finally*, he notched himself at my core, smirking when I whined impatiently then sliding in inch by torturous inch. It was all too much, the burn and stretch of being filled, his hot skin sliding against mine, the sound he made when he entered me.

"So tight," he gritted out.

"Shit, you're bigger than I thought," I commented with a strained laugh as he pushed in farther.

He gave a rough laugh in response, dropping a kiss on my lips before snapping his hips forward and filling me in small strokes. I could just barely taste a hint of myself on his lips, and I was desperate to touch all that delicious, exposed skin.

He must have seen that in my eyes, as he gestured toward my hands with a small nod. I sighed in relief, bringing my hands down to slide across his abdomen, over his shoulders, and around his neck.

His groans were low and needy, increasing with each thrust of his hips. His forehead met mine, and each heavy exhale fanned across my lips. I slid my hand from his neck to his cheek, stroking my thumb over his cheekbone and jaw. It was too much, too close, too sensual, too *life-changing*.

I kissed him roughly, admiring his swollen lips and moving my hands down to grip his hips, sliding over the small of his back. He caught on, his strokes quick and deep, hitting some gratifying spot inside me perfectly. My pleasure kept building, bringing me higher and higher until I was seconds away from the edge, yet still somehow missing whatever I needed to push me over.

His deep blue eyes, made darker from lust, filled with understanding. His hand trailed from the breast it had been idly caressing to stroke my clit. "Come for me," he commanded as he thrust several more times. "Come *with* me. Give it to me, all mine."

His unapologetic possessiveness and dominance threw me over the edge, and I came with a cry, squeezing his cock as it jerked inside me. He groaned, tucking his head against my neck as his body shook. I gripped his upper arms tightly, nails digging into his skin as I felt myself contract around him. We stayed locked together like that as the sensations worked through us.

Eventually, he lifted his head and shifted his body to my right, no longer resting on me. I lamented the loss of his weight–it had been oddly soothing–but was grateful to finally take a deep breath. We were both covered in sweat, still breathing heavily as we lay side by side, but there was none of the awkwardness or regret I would have expected.

I glanced down at his torso, looking my fill at what I'd been too busy to examine earlier. I looked past his glistening golden skin, the muscles and veins tracing their way across his abdomen, to the deep, ragged scar that lie diagonally across his entire front.

"How?" I asked quietly. I didn't expect an answer, but I would still ask. It had to have been so painful to still be scarred so deep. He could have died from that injury, and I found the thought to be incredibly painful.

An eternity passed as our breathing slowed and my overheated skin started to cool from the air sliding across it.

His laugh was harsh. "You sure you wanna do this now? Might ruin your afterglow."

My shrug was tiny. "If you don't want to tell me, you don't have to, but... I'd like to know about you."

He waited so long, that I thought he'd decided not to tell me after all. Then... "I was outside one night," he said softly. "My dad had kicked Nix out, and he had no weapons on him. He'd..." he trailed off, and I fought my insecurities to lay my hand on his arm where it rested next to mine. Hopefully, it wasn't too familiar, or too awkward, though I wasn't sure how a comforting touch would be after what we had just did. He made a small, grateful sound, then continued. "He's told you?"

I made a noise of assent.

Merikh nodded. "He'd been treating him terribly," he said frankly. "We'd established the camp by then, but my dad liked to lead by example, taking us on scouting and scavenging missions all the time for supplies. Plus, my dad couldn't treat Nix how he wanted around others, not if he wanted to be liked. So on this particular trip that Caelan had stayed behind from, he sent him out for the night and flipped the locks on the little house we were staying in. I snuck out after he'd gone to sleep, and was just about to bring Nix in, because fuck what my dad wanted, when we realized there were a couple of zombies nearby that we hadn't spotted until it was too late. I sent him back inside the house because what could he do without a weapon? He tried to refuse, but he was already banged up from earlier and he would've died in seconds without a way to defend himself."

"Why didn't you just go inside too?" I couldn't understand why he didn't just retreat to where it was safe. There was nothing shameful about hiding if it kept you alive.

He sounded so calm, so unaffected. "Dad put Nix out all the time. We were only eleven when this incident happened, too young to really do anything about it. We'd been at this house for a few weeks, so we had one more to go before we could declare the area picked over and go back to camp. I knew he wouldn't kill the zombies if he saw them. He'd just sneak us all past. He didn't take unnecessary chances, and he certainly didn't put them down to make an area safer."

It dawned on me. "So if he wouldn't kill them, eventually when–or if–Nix got put outside again, he'd run into one. He might not be able to take them on alone."

Merikh's other hand balled into a fist. "I should've done something about it, insisted he stay behind at camp or something, but Dad was relentless. He liked bringing Nix along just because he hated going so much, and if I said anything he'd leave me behind and I wouldn't be able to help."

The nonchalant tone that accompanied his words caused a sharp pain deep in my chest. "So you killed them yourself," I surmised. "And you got that injury."

He nodded, the fingertips of his free hand idly stroking the edge of the scar. "My first solo kill. I threw up for what felt like hours after."

I pulled my hand free from his and shifted onto my side, one hand under my head and the other delicately resting atop his stomach. I traced the length of it, each bumpy, jagged section stoking my anger even higher. "You could've been infected," I whispered.

He made a small noise in the back of his throat, and only then did I realize how tense he held his body. I looked up to find his eyes filled with more conflicting emotions than I could identify. Lust, confusion, desire, shame...

"I think you did the best you could," I said softly, laying my hand flat on his skin. "I think you were brave. I think the scar makes you look even hotter, and that you're a big part of the reason that Nix is still here today."

His mouth twisted awkwardly, like he didn't know what to make of my words. I watched his face closely, delighted to see his cheeks flushing a dull pink color.

Something in my expression must have given away my pleasure, because his uncertainty morphed into disapproval and embarrassment. He frowned, cheeks heating further, and my grin was too strong to suppress. "Come here," I murmured with a laugh, telegraphing my intentions as I leaned over to kiss his lips softly.

Merikh made a sound low in his throat, hand reaching over to grab my hip. I felt his fingers twitch as I pulled away and laid back on my side.

"I'm... sorry for how you came to be here. I would never normally... I–"

It was strangely cute seeing him so flustered. I sighed, the apology smoothing over all the places inside me that were still raw and tender from how we met.

"I almost thought I'd imagined you when I first saw you. You reminded me of a picture in a storybook I found when I was younger about Rapunzel. All long hair and big eyes."

I scoffed, trying to brush off the emotion I felt from his words. "No. Nix said the same thing, so clearly there's something in the water here."

"No," he said forcefully. "It was the way you carried yourself. You were bold. Brave. And yes, even with the dirt or whatever else you think was wrong with you, you were beautiful and strong."

I made a small sound of disbelief. "I seem to remember a certain someone calling me a rat. So is that why you call me princess? Because of the so-called resemblance?"

A grin spread across his sinful mouth. "Smart girl. So what if I had the urge to throw you in the lake to get the smell off before I brought you back with us? You were still–"

I tackled him, laughter filling the air as we grappled.

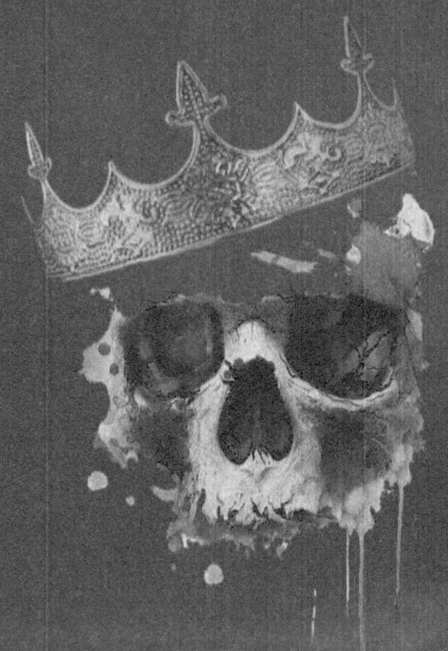

CHAPTER 20

I felt lighter when I woke from my nap, as if a weight had been lifted. Merikh was gone, but I could hear low voices coming from the front room.

I walked out to find all four of them lounging around the fire.

"What's the occasion?" I joked. Though when no one responded, the silence grew tense. Grey darted a look at Nix, who shook his head.

"What the hell is going on?" My mind was racing. Was I getting banished? Just when I'd made up my mind to try to stay? To make it work?

"We need to talk," Merikh said quietly. I tried to tamp down the feelings of betrayal threatening to overwhelm me. Hours ago he'd been kissing me as if I belonged to him and now he was pulling this?

Caelan patted the spot next to him on the couch, making eye contact with Grey, who sat on the other end cushion. My movements were jerky, but I still walked over to the center of the couch and dropped myself down.

Five more seconds of suspenseful silence and my mind was racing. Was it wishful thinking that I could so easily shove aside all my bitterness at our earlier interactions? Because at the first sign of a challenge, it came rising up to choke me again. Yeah, I'd stopped resenting them weeks ago, but did I *forgive* them? I wasn't sure if real forgiveness came with caveats. But how would I know?

"What." My voice was flat, and hard.

That got some alarmed looks. Eventually, Grey was elected to speak. "We want you to stay."

Everything stopped.

Time, the world, my turbulent thoughts, my apprehension.

"Excuse me?"

"We want you to stay," he said again, firmer this time.

What had even given me the idea in the first place that they were going to ask me to leave? And did I want to remain somewhere that made my stomach turn inside out and my insecurities show at the slightest hint of conflict? I was more vulnerable than ever.

"Stop overthinking," Nix said softly.

I took a deep breath and resolved to listen. "Can you elaborate, please?"

"Stay here, with us. Don't go back outside those walls," Caelan declared.

"What's changed?"

Merikh made a rough noise, part disdain, part... I didn't know, irritation? Frustration? I stood up to pace, unable to sit still.

"You were all alone," he said coldly, jumping to his feet. "We had a camp, a whole cabin for you. Food, beds, warmth. You looked so tired, standing over John's body. So vulnerable. How could we not have wanted to take you back and keep you safe? Even as angry as I was, I wanted to bring you back and protect you."

"You can't keep me like a pet!" I exclaimed, whirling around to point at him. "I had freedom, choices, a life. It was shitty, but it was *my* life." I thrust my finger into his chest, holding back a wince once it hit his hard muscles and masking it with bared teeth. "You never explained, never apologized, never–" I spluttered, unable to think of anything else to add.

"I know," he said cautiously. "I know we should have had this discussion weeks ago, and that my apology last night was much too late. I know we were terrible and that you have no obligation to stick around, but I'm asking you to stay anyway. Be with us, be ours."

What would being theirs entail? I would only stay if it was an equal partnership.

He must have seen some of my thought process on my face because he sighed, running a hand through his hair. "As ours, River. Only ours. Not a convenient body to help out around camp"

River.

He'd called me River.

At first, I'd thought their pet names were a targeted way of irritating me, distancing me. If what they'd said was true, about needing me to come back with them, the names had probably made them feel close to me at a time when we were anything but, and now it was safe to strip them away. Though somehow I was sure they were here to stay, and I didn't seem to mind.

"Why did you *really* keep me in your cabin with you?" I asked. The level of honesty in his answer would go a long way to gaining my trust, because even with the excuses they gave in the very beginning, there was no way I needed to stay in their space with them as they'd insisted.

"We saw something in you," he replied softly. "We didn't understand it but we needed you close. What other excuse could get you sleeping here every night where we could keep you safe? If there were no primary reasons, like cleaning or working, you would've been scared. Your mind would have jumped to all the other reasons we'd want an attractive woman sharing our space. We needed to set that boundary, to reassure you that we didn't bring you back for that. And our attraction to you didn't negate our anger either, it only fanned the flames."

Caelan sighed. "Once we... I thought if we just showed you how happy you could be, you would move past it all and forget as time went on. I–we–certainly didn't agree to fall for you as we did, and we should've discussed how this new dynamic would work rather than assuming. It was wrong of me to think you didn't need an apology, so this is me, officially apologizing. I'm so incredibly sorry for what we did and how things went down."

The others echoed his sentiments, and for the second time that afternoon, I felt my world was spinning on its axis. All my anger, my hopes and fears and cautiousness and hesitant dreams were making room for the excitement and relief I felt at finally having this conversation.

"You're an asset to the camp," Nix said. "You fit in well, you help anyone who needs it, and you defended the people here even though you didn't think you were staying. Not only that, but you're bold and bright and kind, and it's selfish of us to want to keep you to ourselves so that you can make our lives warmer with your presence, but I don't care."

I blinked rapidly, refusing to let any tears fall.

"Oh, sweetheart," Grey whispered. He stood, all broad shoulders, muscles, and beautiful blonde hair, and crossed the room to me. He swiped his thumb under my right eye, where one tear had managed to escape, and pulled me into his arms. I sighed, relaxing my body and letting him take my weight. I felt so safe, so cared for. I never thought I'd get to experience this.

"When you mean stay..." I said into his shirt, my voice muffled, "you mean as *all* of yours?" They'd been pretty clear, but I needed to be absolutely sure.

"If you're asking if we mind sharing you, we don't," Merikh said matter-of-factly. "We've always been different. I speak for everyone when I say I can't imagine wanting someone else. How could I be jealous when they care about you just as much as I do?"

The floodgates broke then. I hadn't realized just how much stress and uncertainty I'd been carrying. I broke down, sobbing in Grey's arms, grateful for his embrace.

"You've been so strong," he whispered against the top of my hair. "You survived, persevered, and took everything life threw at you. Now you get to relax, no more fighting tooth and nail to just *live*. You're safe here, you're wanted."

I cried even harder, hiding my face against his chest. I couldn't remember the last time I'd cried so hard. Probably when my dad died. I'd had no time to mourn after all; I was on the run that very night, hiding and searching for shelter, trying to stay alive.

I felt my soul settle, as though I could finally let go of the rigid strength I'd clutched so desperately to keep going.

A body plastered itself against my back, warm and solid. "Please don't cry," Nix said urgently, brushing my hair back with a large hand. He sounded so stressed that it startled a laugh out of me, followed by a hiccup. Grey used his hands on my upper arms to spin me into Nix's arms. I went easily, letting myself be maneuvered so that now I was clinging to his chest.

"You smell good." I sniffled into his shirt, smiling when his deep laugh vibrated against my face.

He used his long sleeve to brush the tears from my cheeks, tsking softly at the new ones that fell at his gentle movements. I tilted my head back, chuckling wetly. "I'm sorry, this is so awkward. I hate crying." My voice was watery and weak.

"Don't apologize," Grey murmured. "I'd be over there too if I wasn't worried I'd be in the way."

That just about broke my heart. Sweet Grey, thinking that he'd take up too much space or be unwanted somehow. I turned, holding my arms out in his direction. His smile was incandescent. He walked into my arms, one hand cradling the back of my head and the other against my lower back.

"I'll stay."

"Really?" Merikh asked. When I pulled away from Grey to look at him, I saw the image he was trying to project. He was sprawled in the armchair, watching me blankly. No emotion, no nothing. But then I looked to his fists, saw the way he was tucking his nails into his palms, at how the corner of his mouth kept turning down. Of course, he had reason to make sure I was being serious; I'd loathed him so fiercely not too long ago, and it had only just transformed into something more. It wasn't his fault he didn't know that it hadn't been hate for some time.

"Yeah," I murmured. "I'm sure."

His smile was shy.

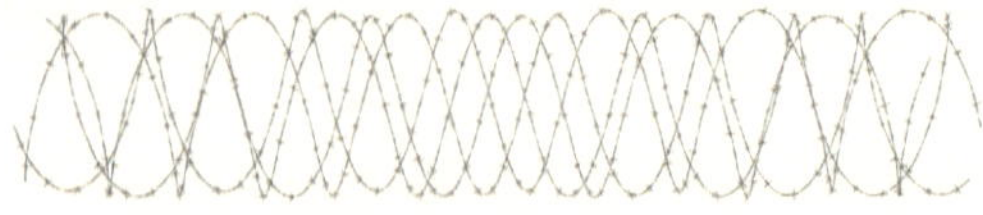

"**S**he's sleeping with me," Caelan yelled across the room.

I rolled my eyes, snuggling deeper into the couch and watching the show. I was full from dinner, cozy and warm.

"No, she's in my room tonight," Merikh seethed behind bared teeth. "I haven't had as much time with her as you."

Nix caught my eye and stifled a smile. His eyes were so green in the light of the fire, they looked otherworldly. "Maybe you should intervene, sunshine."

I sat up and gave a long-suffering sigh. Anything not to give away that I was so happy I could burst. I was staying, no longer hiding any secrets, and they were fighting over spending time with *me*. How could I be upset over that? No, it would take a good few months of those arguments before I tired of them.

"Boys," I drawled, putting my hands on my hips. They stopped arguing to look at me, and having their undivided attention was heady. Caelan licked his lower lip and I just about swooned. "How about you move the couches and chairs back, then bring your mattresses out here and put them on the floor? Then we can all sleep together. Whenever you get sick of it, you just move your mattress back for the night or take the couch."

"That's... not a bad idea," Merikh said slowly.

I rolled my eyes. "Well, let's not be too surprised." I shrieked a laugh when Grey came up behind me and lifted me into his arms, tossing me over his shoulder.

"You know that's not what he meant, sweetheart," he scolded me with a chuckle. Everyone split up to go room by room, grabbing their mattresses and carrying them into the front room while Nix pushed all the furniture into the corners.

"Hold on," I said when the last mattress had been placed on the wood floor. They had decided there wasn't enough space for Grey's mattress and just went with the other three, and they looked plenty big enough to fit all of us. They just about spanned across the entire room. "Won't your dad think this is weird as hell when he gets back?"

Caelan and Nix looked at Merikh, who apparently had been elected to speak on the matter. "I don't give a fuck," he declared. "Besides, I don't know where the hell he is. He was supposed to be back a week ago."

"Good riddance," Caelan muttered, whining when Nix elbowed him in the side. "What? He's an asshole, I can only hope he's been eaten by zombies."

Grey snickered, and Merikh's sigh was long.

We made the beds fairly quickly, looking down in satisfaction at all the soft, blankety goodness.

I beamed, kissing Nix's cheek because he was closest to me. "I call the middle."

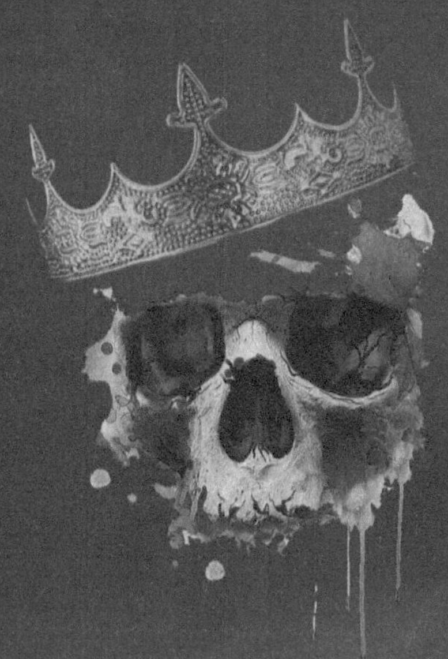

CHAPTER 21

My dad threw his head back and laughed, the crow's feet that framed his hazel eyes crinkling with the motion.

I couldn't help but smile in return. His laugh was infectious, and it had been weeks since I'd last heard it.

I kept on smiling, content to watch him as our surroundings grew darker and darker. Then my smile faded, turning into a confused frown. I ignored the sense of foreboding, instead trying to focus on my father's face, to soak in his attention and his love for the last time before whatever terrible was coming happened. My trepidation grew, the inherent sense that something was wrong.

His grin melted, turning sinister as his face started chipping away, leaving bone in its place. I screamed, reaching out for his arm when the scene changed.

I spun around, suddenly alone. I was standing in the middle of a city street, and it was dark and cold. I shivered, rubbing my bare arms to warm them up and trying hard not to think about my dad's face doing whatever the hell it had just done. "It's not real," I chanted, trying to reassure myself. Where had my dad gone? Was he okay?

A scream caught my attention, and my heart dropped.

No. No no no nononono. I took off running, turning the corner to find a familiar picture.

My dad was hunched over the little boy he'd stumbled upon while we were scavenging. He'd looked so harmless, a little pale, yeah, but mostly scared and sleep-deprived. They were nestled at the end of the alley, surrounded by brick and trash on all sides. A dumpster sat to his left, and it must've been the source of the smell. Trash receptacles had been used until they overflowed, never to be emptied again, and most alleys were swimming in garbage because of it.

I pressed a trembling fist to my mouth to hold back my screams.

Someone that looked remarkably like me stood beside him, yanking on his arm. It was weird to watch myself from outside my body. I could almost believe that it wasn't my story, that it hadn't really happened. I'm taller than I thought, I mused numbly, feeling an odd sense of dissociation.

The boy screamed, an awful ugly sound. Only seconds later, he seized, foaming at the mouth. My dad set him down instantly, face draining of color as he realized his mistake.

"Did he bite you?" other me whispered frantically, pulling her hair up into a high ponytail and palming her knife.

The first zombie turned the corner, and my stomach twisted up into knots as I understood with a dawning horror what I was going to be forced to relive. I belatedly realized that I had broken my silence, yelling and shouting at them. No one noticed me. My cheeks were wet with tears, my voice raw from screaming at them to run, crying harder when I realized I wasn't making a difference.

Other me turned away from my dad as he stopped the little boy from turning any further and took care of the lone zombie that had run our way.

I saw the thoughts play out over her face, mouth twisting as she turned to tell my dad that we'd—they'd—be okay. That maybe it would just be the one, that the others hadn't heard the boy's tortured scream as he turned. I was facing the same direction as he was, unlike other me, so when I saw his eyes widen, I knew the reason, although other me hadn't quite grasped why. Not yet, at least.

She would.

The first screech was deafening, followed by others as an entire horde of zombies trickled around the corner.

They were trapped.

"Go, I'll follow," he yelled, pulling his blade from its sheath.

"I'm not leaving you even for a second!" she shouted. Her hazel eyes were shot through with red, and her face was flushed with exertion and fear. "Come on, if we can make it up the dumpster, we can get to the rooftop, and hopefully they won't create some kind of fucking zombie ladder."

My dad huffed, striking down one that had run too close and nodding. It was the only option; there were too many and no way around them. She killed one more before running over to him and letting him vault her up onto the dumpster. She instantly dropped to her stomach, shoving her hand down and over so that she could help pull him up.

I winced, remembering the wild bruise that maneuver had left. One of the zombies must've grasped their idea, because it screeched loudly and angrily, and put on speed. I wailed quietly as more turned the corner, begging him to hurry up and grab her hand.

Tears were obscuring my vision, making everything blurry. I looked as the one that had screamed caught my dad's dangling leg as he hefted himself onto the dumpster, yanking him off with superior strength.

I watched myself realize that we weren't both going to be making it out.

My dad demanded that I leave him, even surrounded by the undead as he was, making sure that I could get away safe as he stayed behind to take out as many as he could. There was no end to the number. They kept multiplying at the mouth of the alley, each incensed shriek bringing more and adding to their number.

I turned away as the other me made her way up the side of the brick building using whatever footholds she could find, sobs racking her body as the sounds of my dad fighting faded, followed by grunts and growls of satisfaction.

Squeezing my eyes shut tightly to try to block out the sounds, I opened them to find myself in a supermarket and stifled a sob, shifting onto my side.

Fuck, fuck, fuck.

What was I thinking? So desperate for food that I'd ignore the rules my dad set for us? Avoid populated areas, stake out a place first, and don't take risks! I should've never tried this fucking supermarket. I was just so goddamn hungry, and everywhere else was picked clean. Then, while I was in the back, those two reckless teenagers ran by, shooting a zombie instead of just hitting it. I was so angry that I almost didn't care that they'd suffered for their mistake.

I shuddered, my throat working painfully.

Still.

Stay still.

A zombie crept below me where I lay on top of the shelving unit, oblivious to my presence.

All I had to do was wait the horde out. The teens were gone, and the noise had stopped, so surely they'd disperse soon, right?

God, I was so fucking hungry.

Reality came back in stages.

I was being shaken softly, and someone was calling my name. That's right, I had fallen asleep between Merikh and Grey.

I cracked my eyes open slowly, surprised to find my face wet. Grey looked concerned, and Caelan was frowning where he lay on his other side. I was suddenly grateful that we'd left the fire going because the heat was soothing on my face, and the flames were hypnotizing.

"It's okay, princess," Merikh murmured as he wiped my face. "You're awake and you're safe. It was just a nightmare."

Nix had reached across Merikh to hold my hand. I groaned as I remembered my dream. What a disaster. I was covered in sweat, vestiges of my mind screaming out warnings.

Danger, death, unsafe.

At Grey's urging, I took a deep breath in. He looked sympathetic, worried. "You don't have to tell us," he murmured.

I couldn't think of a better place to do so. Tucked away in a cabin, secured behind a fence, in front of a roaring fire, and surrounded by my protectors. They had told me their stories. If I was going to stay here, wasn't it only fair that I shared as well? Not only that, but I *wanted* them to know me as I knew them.

I sighed, my throat growing thick with emotion. "It wasn't a nightmare," I rasped. "Just a memory." I noticed them making furtive eye contact over my head, and laughed quietly. Taking Grey's hand in mine, and bringing Nix's hand up to my lips for a soft kiss, I explained what had happened. How my dad had survived so long just to have his compassion and his huge heart led to his downfall. How we'd gone scavenging a little later than usual before planning to head back to our spot a few blocks away when we heard a noise and investigated to find the small boy. It had been too dark to see the signs that he'd been recently bitten, and when all the noise attracted the undead, how he wasn't able to make it out with me. I explained how my dream morphed to a memory from a few months later, how hungry I'd been, and how I'd been scouting a store when a disturbance nearby attracted zombies. I'd crawled up onto the tallest shelf and held still for hours, starving and having flashbacks to my dad dying.

By the time I was finished, I was drowning in tears, and Merikh had pulled me onto his lap and into his arms. Caelan rubbed my back soothingly and Nix got up to grab me a glass of cold water while Grey just held my hand.

"He must've loved you so much," Nix said quietly when he returned with my water. He rubbed the empty space on his wrist where his bracelet should have been, and I silently reprimanded myself for not cleaning it and getting it back to him sooner.

"Any parent would do that," I assured.

Nix's gaze turned inward. "Not any."

I felt a flash of consternation, embarrassed that I'd confidently stated something so blatantly untrue to someone who had all the examples in the world of why it was false.

"This world can turn humans into terrible people," Merikh said softly, brushing my hair back from my face where it clung to my wet cheeks. "It makes the greedy, greedier. The frightened, more paranoid, and the tired, even more exhausted. A lot of parents might not have made the choice your dad did. Conversely, it's incredible the amount of kindness and hope people exhibit, their capacity to love not impacted at all by all the horrors they've experienced. Your dad must've been an incredible man, to stop and check on what he thought was an abandoned child and to sacrifice himself so selflessly for you to keep surviving."

"He'd be so proud of you," Grey murmured, the corner of his lips turning upwards in a tiny smile.

I groaned, twisting out of Merikh's arms to throw myself onto the mattress and bury my face into the pillow. "Stop making me cry!" I ordered, my voice muffled and teary. Someone laughed, I have no idea who, and a hand reached out to stroke my back.

"It's normal to need to vent those emotions," Caelan said. "It only makes sense that your body is ready to purge them now that it feels safe enough to do so."

"Yeah, well... Normal or not, I don't like it," I grumbled, turning around with a huff. The blankets were tangled around my legs, and I kicked them off, desperate for the cool air.

Caelan snorted a laugh. "She's even more allergic to emotions than you, Merikh."

I mock-frowned. "I resent that."

Merikh's laugh was soft and sweet. "Come here," he murmured, pulling me up to give me a kiss. What was probably supposed to be chaste and short turned heated and long. I groaned into his mouth, startled at the sound of a throat clearing.

Merikh's smirk was devastating when he pulled away. "Maybe I'm going to have trouble falling back asleep," I said innocently. "Perhaps we should christen the floor-bed."

Caelan grinned wickedly, his blue-gray eyes darkening at the prospect. "Am I to assume this would be a group effort?"

I scoffed. "As if I'd expect anything less."

Later that night, when we were all piled together in a heap, panting and sweating and smiling profusely, I patted myself on the back for that excellent idea.

I slept through the whole rest of the night.

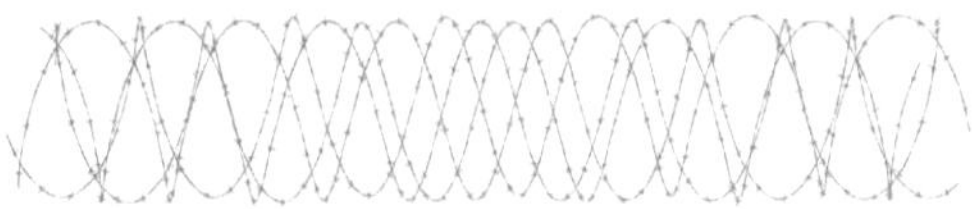

Days passed with no further incidents. The community pulled together to fortify the walls, and I felt much more confident about helping now that I knew I was sticking around. There were no more whispers behind my back or dirty looks. All the unrest from weeks ago was absent from the people that were working alongside me.

There was one conversation that had given me a moment of pause, and I still had no idea who the people talking were.

The sound of a murmured discussion from on the other side of the tent caught my attention while I was waiting in line to grab food.

"I can't believe you didn't hear," someone whispered.

"Of course they're keeping it quiet," the person responded. "I bet you don't even know that last month, we did an inventory of our supply and found a good portion of meat and dried goods missing."

I leaned closer, trying to hear better without looking conspicuous. The people in line around me were deep in conversation and had no idea what was being discussed just a foot away.

"You know it has to be someone from inside the camp taking it all," the first person said. "No way that stuff just up and disappeared so fast, and it's not like someone is sneaking in just to grab food and running off."

"Maybe raccoons? Rats?"

"You think rats could eat all of that? There's no way. And we can't even rely on fresh food from the garden, bec..."

Their voices faded out mid-sentence as they walked away from the tent, leaving me way too curious for my own good as to what exactly had happened to the supplies. Maybe–

"River!" Naia rolled her eyes, dusting her hands off. "I've never seen you so distracted."

"Am not," I declared, pulling up another dead plant root. It was mushy and purple in color, and I grimaced as it left a dark stain on my hands. "Besides, tasks like these don't require a lot of brain power."

Nerese laughed. "Only you could kill zombies and think nothing of the gore but frown at plant waste."

I shrugged, granting her a smile. She wasn't wrong, although, that wasn't to say I loved the feel of unidentifiable fluids all over my skin, it was just part and parcel of surviving. Halli sighed nearby, the corners of her mouth pulling down into a frown as she stroked a withered leaf of spinach.

"We need a break," I insisted. I knew Halli would push herself until she collapsed from exhaustion, but she'd spent the entire day working and already looked flushed and tired. She was so desperate to try to salvage the last of the crops, but it was like they'd sensed that their neighbors were a lost cause and decided to follow in their footsteps. Food production was at an all-time low, apparently. If we were going to find more seeds or viable plants to propagate from, it would have to be soon, before the height of the planting season passed.

Halli usually had more helpers, but many people were being temporarily diverted from their jobs to keep an eye on the perimeter. No one wanted a repeat of what happened weeks ago. Nerese and Naia were only able to help because the families who cared for the children were keeping them close during the day, temporarily suspending group daycare. With tensions running high and everyone on edge waiting for another attack, we wanted everyone accounted for at all times, and having the children watched individually and not cloistered in one space was better for everyone's peace of mind.

My sigh was long as I stretched my arms behind my head and winced when my back and hip cracked. I laughed softly to myself as I remembered Merikh's reaction the other day, wondering what he might say if he saw me do it again.

A sharp gasp had me jerking my head down to look at Nerese, though instead of finding her hurt or upset, she was wearing a broad grin and staring right at me.

"What?"

Her expression turned smug as she rested her hand on her hip. "Don't you 'what' me. I saw that sappy face!"

I groaned, rolling my eyes and turning away so no one would see my blush. Surely it wasn't so obvious that I was thinking of them. If someone had told me a year ago that I'd be walking around with a sappy look on my face because of not one, not two, but four men... I probably would've thrown them in with the zombies.

"She's right," Naia teased. "Your face went all soft and–"

I made a fake gagging noise and held my hand up for her to stop. "Absolutely not. You saw nothing."

The girls dissolved in laughter, gathering their things as they wiped the tears from their eyes.

"It wasn't that funny," I grumbled, hiding my grin behind my hand.

Halli shot me a droll look, clearly not fooled.

"You're one to talk, Naia," I retorted. "I saw you staring at Shiori the other day while we were all eating."

It was Naia's turn for her face to flush pink, her freckles almost swallowed by the infusion of color in her cheeks.

Nerese turned on her, happy to claim another victim to sheer embarrassment. "She talked to her the other day."

Halli's jaw dropped. "Who? Not Naia?"

Naia was notoriously shy, and we'd all pretty much accepted nothing would come of her crush so long as she was too nervous to even speak to her.

Nerese nodded. "We were late to dinner since we had to prepare the building to be out of use for a bit, and Shiori was one of the last few there. I think"—she drew the words out teasingly—"she noticed Naia hadn't come in yet and stayed to make sure she ate."

Naia's smile was incandescent as she shrugged, brushing her hands off on her long pink skirt. "She was so nice, we made plans to hang out at the bonfire whenever they start back up again." She tried to play it off as no big deal, but her shining eyes gave her away.

I was unaccustomed to the soft feeling in my chest, ridiculously happy for my friend. Maybe I was more of a sap than I thought.

"Dessert to celebrate," I declared. "I found an old recipe book tucked away in the shared materials storage and I think I can make something that tastes passable with what we have on hand."

"I can probably mix a fruity drink to go along with it," Nerese offered.

Halli brushed her curls over her shoulder as she spun around to face us. She was walking backward now, earrings swinging as she moved. "I don't know how you can drink that stuff. I swear Lincoln mixes it in an old toilet."

I pushed that image out of my mind, content to not worry about where it went before it ended up in my cup. Naia and Nerese's voices raised as they chastised Halli for trying to ruin their one good luxury while I turned my face up into the sun and smiled as it warmed my skin.

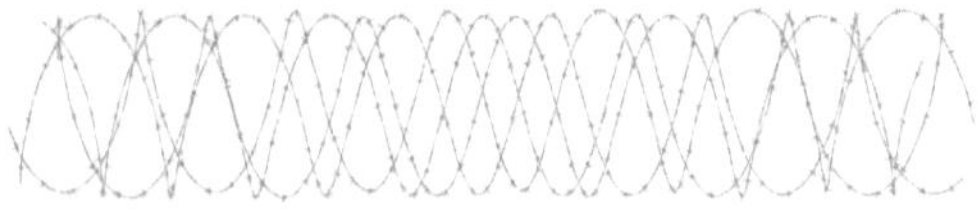

I walked into the cabin, grunts, and groans echoing from the couch where Grey had Caelan in a headlock. "I'm home," I called out as I kicked off my shoes next to Caelan's large pair of dirty boots.

Grey raised his head with a wide grin. "Did you have a good time, sweetheart?"

I shrugged off my light sweater and nodded, wiggling my toes happily when I felt the cool texture of the hardwood beneath my feet. It was scratched and scuffed, but I was so used to wearing shoes 24/7 that I'd probably go barefoot even if their floor was gravel.

Nix walked into the room wearing a small, secretive smile and leaned against the wall, content to just watch.

"Well?" I demanded, fighting back a smile of my own. His grin spread, and he walked into my arms, giving me a sweet kiss hello. Caelan and Grey went back to wrestling after giving satisfied grunts that I'd been welcomed properly.

"What has you so happy?" I asked Nix once we finally parted. Kissing him was as easy as breathing, practically addictive. There was no such thing as a short, chaste kiss with him.

"You called this place your home," he said softly, hand raising to brush my cheekbone gently.

"So I did," I remarked, a little bewildered. I hadn't even noticed, but at some point, I must have started to consider this my home. It felt good, right, that it wasn't a conscious decision but rather a natural shift. Even if I had made the comment in jest, something my dad used to say whenever he got back from an outing, it felt right.

"You were out later than we thought you'd be." He changed the subject, likely aware that I needed some time to process it. It was ridiculous how well he knew me already. "We brought food back not too long ago. It should still be warm."

Warmth spread all throughout my chest. "You waited to eat with me?"

Grey threw Caelan off him, tuning in to our conversation. "Of course we did. Besides, we had plans to eat together anyway."

I sighed quietly, flooded with a deep sense of contentment. "What about Merikh?"

"He's just washing up. Come on." He led me over to the table, pulling out my chair for me and pushing me in once I sat down. I tried to stop my jaw from dropping at the action. My dad told me he used to do that for my mom, that it had been considered chivalrous and gentlemanly. I'd loved hearing stories about them, though I'd been certain I would never get to experience anything like it.

I blinked rapidly, switching my thoughts to happier topics and hoping no one noticed the brief surge in emotion. It was amazing how far they were going to prove their insistence that I was welcome here. That I was wanted, desired, appreciated. I cleared my throat, welcoming Merikh when he strode in.

I ran my eyes hungrily over his body, admiring the way his pants hung low on his hips, how his shirt clung to his muscles and stretched tight over his golden skin. I made my way up to his face, appreciating that mess of dark waves and his intense blue eyes, my cheeks flushing when I finally landed on his knowing smirk. It was nice to be able to look him over at my leisure instead of pretending I didn't find him attractive.

"Whatever," I grumbled. "You know you're hot."

His grin spread, a small laugh rumbling from his chest as he took his seat. "Doesn't hurt to hear it." He winked. The others looked stunned at his display, and I quickly coughed before they could make him feel self-conscious or uncomfortable with their gaping mouths. I guess it must've been unusual to see him in such good spirits. I knew I was surprised, although I wasn't going to make a big deal of it. If this was him trying, then I wasn't going to discourage it.

I started to wonder if it would be like this all the time, warm and soft and *home*. I pushed back the insidious thoughts that it was too good to last, that they were just putting on an act for me, and that all good things came to an end. The greatest gift I could give myself would be to give this a real chance, no trying to dissuade myself with negativity.

A warm hand covering mine snapped me out of my spiraling thoughts. I looked over at Caelan–loud, brash, always joking Caelan–and found a soft smile on his lips. "You okay?" he whispered softly, just for me. His voice was drowned out by the others talking at full volume around us, but I heard him just fine.

I felt a burst of affection at the way he was thoughtfully checking in on me and flipped our hands so that I could thread my fingers through his. "I'm perfect," I whispered back, unable to fight my smile.

He squeezed my hand once, keeping it intertwined with mine for the rest of the meal.

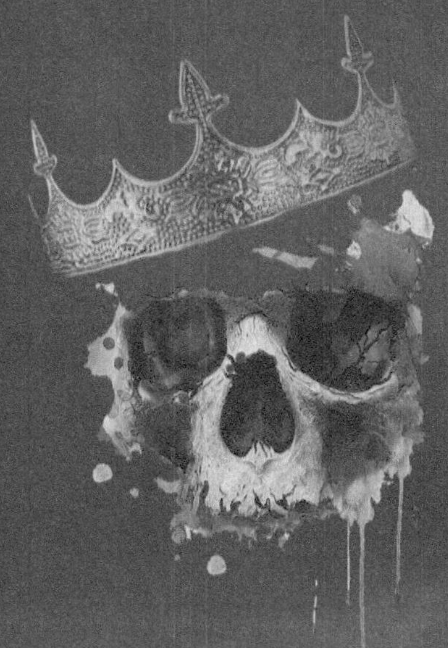

CHAPTER 22

"I want to go," I declared, trying my absolute best not to sound petulant.

Merikh's voice was firm. "Absolutely not. The more people who go, the more dangerous the mission."

"I don't see why I can't go and just be quiet. I was living out there just the other month!"

"You're not going, and that's final," he stated, softening the blow by brushing a stray piece of hair behind my ear. "I know you were just out there, and I trust that you can hold your own, but I can't–I just–" He sighed, hanging his head. When he lifted it, his voice was just a raspy echo of the solid tone he'd used previously. "I can't risk it. I can't risk *you*. Please don't make me."

I felt myself melting, no matter how hard I tried to keep my approach unwavering. How could I keep pushing the issue when it was clearly so important to them?

Caelan chimed in then, uncharacteristically serious for once. "All we want is for you to be tucked away behind the walls, safe and sound. We just got you, River. It's not even gonna be a big trip or anything. Just a few nights to check the perimeter, look for any signs of our dad, and see if the raiders have left the area."

Not sure how safe and sound it was if people were gossiping about the reason for the missing supplies being an inside job. I still hadn't managed to ask the guys what that was all about.

"Fine," I reluctantly conceded. "But you better be so damn careful," I warned, shaking a finger at them both. Their resulting smirks were devious.

"You know we will, baby." Caelan gripped my waist and lifted me up against him, giving me a moment to wrap my legs around his hips before he spun me.

"Stop!" I shrieked between laughs. "You're gonna make me sick!"

His grin was mischievous as he passed me off to Merikh like I was just a human-sized koala bear. I supposed I didn't help the resemblance because I went easily, wrapping my legs around his waist to support myself and winding my arms around his neck.

"Thank you," he said softly, our eyes on the same level for once. I leaned in to give him a kiss, moving my hips just the slightest when his tongue slipped into my mouth.

"I didn't know we were playing pass the potato with River," Grey remarked when he stepped onto the porch and shut the door behind him. "I want in."

Merikh broke our kiss to squint up at Grey. "Tell me you're not talking about hot potato."

"Oh, fuck you! Pass the potato is totally a thing," he argued.

They both turned their glares onto Caelan, who held his hands up innocently. "Don't look at me, I don't have a clue."

I buried my face against Merikh's shoulder when he huffed, attempting to hide my laughter but not succeeding.

"Ahh, princess," he whispered close to my ear, just for me. "I think your laughter's my new favorite sound."

My heart squeezed in my chest, and I nestled closer, shivering gently when his voice went even lower, breath hot against the shell of my ear. "Actually, it's a tie with the noises you make while I fuck you."

His face was smug when I pushed my upper half away from him, cheeks on fire. Who said things like that in front of other people and before they had to leave!

Caelan and Grey caught on pretty fast. I'm sure it was obvious from the way my skin was absolutely flaming pink.

"Whatever," I grumbled, squirming to be let down. "That's enough of that." I turned and gave Merikh a few pats on the chest, lingering just a little in disbelief at how strong he felt. God, he was so beautiful, stubble covering his sharp jaw and an aroused flush on his cheeks.

He laughed, exposing a crooked tooth that I absolutely refused to think of as endearing, and kissed me again.

"And you'll be back in a few days?"

They both nodded, though Caelan just had to lay it on thick. "Especially when we have you to come home to."

I made a quiet noise in the back of my throat, both choked up and embarrassed in equal measure. Yeah, he was probably exaggerating, but it felt good to hear it. To be someone's home, to be important enough to be a beacon for someone, even if all the emotion and sappiness behind it make my stomach hurt. They'd been trying so hard, each day another attempt to make up for the way we started, for all the bad blood between us. Just because I felt icky about the influx of emotions that swamped me every time they said something sweet or even better, followed it up with an action, didn't mean that I wanted to shy away from finally reciprocating it. The world outside these walls was dangerous, and I suddenly wanted–no, *needed*–them to know what they meant to me.

I took a deep breath, letting it out in a rush of words. "You know I love you, right?"

Jaws dropped. I was equally surprised, to be honest. I couldn't believe the words had just left my mouth. Merikh's stormy blue eyes darkened, and Caelan used one tattooed, scarred hand to push his hair back from his face as he stared at me. I could see Grey smiling out of the corner of my eye, and it gave me the confidence to keep going.

"I know… I know I said some things… about you. In the beginning. And there were misconceptions. And I'm not saying that I didn't deserve to be angry or that I all of a sudden don't care about any of it. Because I do–did–care. But I love you in spite of it all, and I think I forgave you days–*weeks*–ago, and I just needed you to know…" I blushed, shifting from foot to foot, feeling thoroughly scrutinized. "That I love you," I finished. It was exhilarating, gifting those words to the first people besides my father, but I was finding that it wasn't quite as hard as I always thought it would be. Grey, Nix, Merikh, Caelan, Halli, Nerese, Naia, my heart was bursting with more feeling than it had in my entire life.

Caelan was the first to snap out of it, charging forward until he was in front of me and clutching me close for a heated kiss. "I love you too, baby. So goddamn lucky to have you, so *grateful*." He spun me again, his grin dazzling. Only this time, I didn't protest.

"You really don't care about sharing?" I whispered, expecting the answer I usually got, but still nervous I'd hear something else instead.

"Aw, baby." He wrapped his arms around me. "This wouldn't be possible if you didn't love us all equally like you do. There's trust there, and loyalty. No room for jealousy or envy. I'm grateful that not only have I found the girl of my dreams, but my brothers did too. I worried about them sometimes, y'know? No anchor, no touchstone. I worried that they'd give everything they had to their anger or the camp. Then you came and changed everything. You tie us all together."

I squinted hard to keep the tears at bay, but one broke free anyway, leaving a salty path down my cheek that he swiped with his thumb.

"Ah, don't cry, River. I can't stand it."

My laugh was wet and watery.

When he finally put me down, Merikh was waiting. It broke my heart to see him so hesitant and unsure of himself. He was the last one to come around, the one who'd shouldered all of the blame and the vitriol and barbed comments. "You mean it?" he asked softly. The breeze blew a dark, wavy strand of hair into his face, and he shook it away. All I could think about were the little things, like that he had let his hair grow out to his nape, and that soon I would probably ask to cut it for him, and that it was so domestic and *normal* it made my stomach hurt.

"Yes, really. Maybe I don't agree with how I got here, but I wouldn't take it back if I could, and I'm not going anywhere now."

His sigh was shaky, and I was glad that I had tied my hair back into a high ponytail so that when I stepped into his embrace, I was able to take his weight without him getting all tangled up in my hair. I stroked the back of his neck gently, my turn to whisper in his ear and make him squirm. "Thank you," I whispered, trying to convey everything I was feeling without overwhelming him. Complete acceptance, forgiveness, and gratitude. I didn't want him to continue secretly thinking himself the villain that stole me away, and that it was only by my good graces that I was nice to him. He'd *proven* himself time and time again.

Merikh shuddered softly in my arms, turning to kiss the side of my neck before holding me for a few long moments.

"Okay," he said, clearing his throat as he stepped back. "So we'll be back..." he trailed off as I raised my eyebrow at him. "Fine," he said gruffly. "I... love you too." His cheeks were lit with a dull blush, and he averted his eyes awkwardly. God, I loved that man.

All I had to do was turn to everyone else and Merikh's sentiments were echoed. I felt like I was going to burst from how happy I was. The only things that would have made it better were if Nix wasn't off doing work and they weren't leaving today. The pit of my stomach was an anxious mess, terrified to have someone to love again, scared to get attached, only to have them ripped away. I was familiar with loss, and for the millionth time, I wished that the world was normal. No zombies, no murderers, and no virus. I knew damn well that even if I didn't say the words or acknowledge them that I would still feel the same way. It would have been selfish to hold back saying them just because it was a big step or felt too scary. An accident could happen at any second, and I would hate myself if they weren't aware of how I felt.

Grey wrapped his arm around me as we watched them leave, whispering his own words of affection into my ear as I leaned against him.

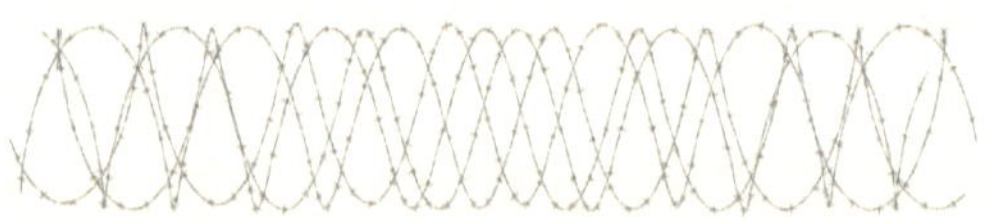

"Couldn't sleep?" Nix asked, dropping a kiss on the top of my head before rounding the couch. It was still the early hours of the morning, the air brisk from the window we'd left cracked open all night and the sun hiding just below the trees.

Grey, Nix, and I had piled into Grey's bed with me in the middle. It had been cozy and warm, but no matter how badly I tried to stay asleep, it didn't work. I woke up every hour, mind racing, body coated in sweat, and thinking about everything that could go wrong for Caelan and Merikh. It was a horrible feeling, being snuggled up in bed when two of the men I'd grown to love were outside the walls of the camp, facing off against who knew what, just to make sure we could continue being safe. It made my stomach hurt to think about and eventually I'd gotten up to sit in the living room and stoke the fire.

"Yeah," I finally replied, my voice quiet. It felt wrong to disturb the stillness surrounding us with any harsh noise. The fire was roaring in the hearth and the birds were chirping, but there was still a kind of tranquil hush in the cabin.

I tucked my feet under me when a cool rush of air made goosebumps rise on my bare legs. I was only wearing a large t-shirt of Caelan's that came up to just above my knees, and a new pair of panties that he'd presented to me with a smile. I'd looked at him oddly, wondering why he even had them, and didn't he know what a hot commodity clean underwear was? But he just smiled wickedly and told me he liked to see me in purple.

Nix stretched his arms over his head with a quiet groan, shirt rising to expose a thin strip of pale skin. His flannel pants were sitting low on his hips, and if I focused... *yup*, there were those lines I liked so much. I looked away before I embarrassed myself, busying myself by picking at the nail I'd broken yesterday when I accidentally jammed it into the counter.

"Any plans for today?" he rumbled. His voice was still thick with sleep, hair ruffled from the pillow and curlier than usual. The word edible came to mind.

I shook my head. "Nerese invited me to come meet some of her friends while they hold a sewing and mending session, but I told her maybe next time."

He lowered himself onto the couch next to me, green eyes turning an amber-like hazel as the sun coasted above the tops of the trees. It was amazing how many shades of green he had in a day. I tucked myself under his extended arm, smiling to myself when he pulled me in and held me close.

"Too worried about them," he guessed accurately.

"Aren't you? How can you just go about your day knowing they're alone out there?"

His sigh was heavy. "Same way you did when you lived with your dad and he had to run an errand without you, I suppose. It's the way of life. They know what they're doing, and we have to trust that they know how to keep themselves safe."

Not for the first time, I squashed a burst of frustration that I had not been able to accompany them. Anything would be better than this, making myself sick with worry, sitting around and doing nothing with my stomach tied up in knots.

He caught my chin, stroking my jaw with his thumb. "They will be just fine, you'll see."

The unique, familiar scent that seemed to cling to him just after he woke up was comforting, as was the dimple on the left side of his smile hiding underneath his stubble.

"I won't make you promise, because it wouldn't be fair to you." I sighed, searching his eyes. "But I'm going to worry, regardless."

"I know you wish you were out there, but I'm selfishly glad that you're safe behind these walls."

"I won't be forever, you know. I can't just go from surviving day in and day out to kicking my feet up and letting others do all the work. I'd argue I have more experience killing those things than half the people living in this camp, so why shouldn't I be the one to run scouting missions or scavenging runs?"

His full lips turned down into a disapproving frown. "Maybe one day," he acquiesced. "Not if I have anything to say about it, but... maybe we can revisit it someday in the future."

I huffed, reluctantly smiling when he brought me in for a quick kiss. I'd wear him down, eventually.

A banging noise sounded from Grey's bedroom at the back of the cabin, drawing Nix's attention.

I took advantage of his distraction, digging around in the breast pocket of Caelan's shirt to pull out Nix's bracelet and exhaled the nerves that were plaguing my stomach, hoping that he wouldn't think I'd overstepped.

"Here," I said quietly, feeling somewhat shy when he turned back to face me and found me holding his prized possession. "Halli taught me how to clean it properly and I fixed the clasp with some tools I found lying around."

He didn't say a word. His eyes were locked onto the delicate bracelet in my hand, face eerily blank, and seconds ticked by until he gingerly took it from my outstretched palm and examined it.

"I thought I'd lost it," he whispered. "It never even occurred to me to try to clean it." He rubbed his thumb over the bright, polished silver chain, mouth pressed in a firm line.

I only grew more nervous when he didn't confirm or deny that I had crossed a line. I was babbling now, worried I'd offended him. "I'm sorry, it's just–well, it broke, and you play with it so often I thought you'd appreciate having it cleaned, and since I already needed to fix the clasp... I didn't mean to–"

He shushed me gently, turning me on his lap in one smooth motion. I slung my arms around his neck, smiling shyly when he rested his forehead against mine.

"I can't thank you enough," he murmured, "for finding it for me, and taking care of it. I love it, and I love *you.*"

"I love you too," I whispered. *Gah*, I felt icky from the praise. "It's no big deal." I tried to play it off. "I noticed it in the grass after–well, the other day. I wanted to do something nice for you, like you've done for me."

He laughed, pulling my face to his and kissing me deeply. "It is a big deal," he insisted against my lips. "It was a kind thing to do. Incredibly thoughtful of you, sunshine. Did I ever tell you how I got it?"

I shook my head.

"Merikh found it in my mom's things when he was about eight. We had a small bag of her stuff my dad would bring everywhere we went. One day he just threw it out; he said we didn't have space for it anymore."

My heart ached for those three boys, stuck with just their shitty dad and then being told they couldn't keep what little of their mother they had left.

"Merikh snuck off that night to go digging through it. It took him an hour to get there and back, and we'd begged him not to go alone, but we couldn't all leave or our father would get suspicious. He brought back a little pin for Caelan, and he gave me her bracelet. He said he'd noticed how I stuffed my pockets with little trinkets to keep my hands busy and he liked to think she would have wanted me to have it." His voice grew unsteady on the last few words.

If Nix had told me this a month ago, I would have scoffed in disbelief, but it was no longer far-fetched to me that Merikh would do something so thoughtful for his brothers. He had such a soft heart, bigger than he let on, even if it was buried under all his bluster and attitude.

"I'm glad he was able to give you back that little piece of her."

Nix's laugh was rough and deprecating. "For a long while, I didn't think I deserved it. Merikh had to talk some sense into me to get me to stop feeling so guilty."

I huffed. "I'm glad your dad isn't around. I'm not sure I could see that asshole every day and keep quiet about the way he's treated you."

Grey's voice filled the room before he did, startling me, although Nix seemed unsurprised. "Good riddance. I can't stand him."

His hair was getting long, the dirty blonde strands falling to his shoulders and into his face, hiding his scar from view. His hooded eyes were darker than usual, warmer.

Nix laughed sharply. "That seems to be the consensus, yes."

Grey sauntered over, giving me a quick kiss that immediately turned heated.

Nix made a put-out noise, and my resulting laughter ended up breaking the sultry greeting. I hopped off of Nix's lap, stretching my legs and cracking my knees.

"Are you going for a swim?"

"Yeah, I haven't gone the last few days because of the weather. You wanna come?" His brown eyes looked so hopeful that I couldn't deny him, even if I wanted to.

"Sure. Nix?"

He adjusted himself on the couch, shooting Grey a mock glare. "Yeah, why not? I haven't been in a while. Too busy working around camp."

Grey nodded, pulling the blue hairband from his wrist and holding it between his teeth as he tied his hair into a topknot. I tried–and failed–not to gawk at how it showed off the angles of his face, somehow intensifying his high cheekbones and his chiseled jaw. It was rare for him to wear his hair up, but my god was it a treat.

Nix saw my reaction and laughed as he stood. "Careful, man. You're gonna break hearts if you start wearing your hair up all the time."

Grey scoffed, elbowing Nix and trading quips back and forth the entire time they got ready to leave.

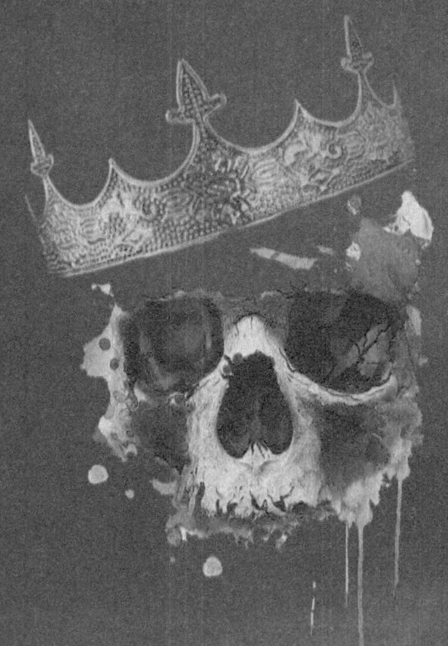

CHAPTER 23

One time, when my father was still alive, we stumbled upon a house with a cellar. It was in the back, covered with ivy and weeds and dirt. I'd only found it because I'd stumbled over the handle, buried as it was, and scraped my knees on the metal peeking through.

My dad had been so excited. We spent an hour looking over our shoulders and clearing the opening as quickly and quietly as possible. The backyard was fenced in, but we didn't want to take any chances. I held my breath when we finally managed to lift the opening up, but eventually, I had to breathe in the burst of stale air that escaped the small underground space and was racked with choked coughs.

My dad insisted on going first, like always, ready to take the brunt of whatever we found. When he reached the bottom and called me to join him, I could scarcely believe my eyes.

Shelves lined the entire left-side of the bunker, filled with cans, bags, sacks, and bottles. All food, all as non-perishable as you could get. I was younger then, and had half a mind to just live there forever. There were several cots lined against the far wall and an armchair in the corner, all designed for functionality and not so much comfort. It was clear whoever had ordered it built and stocked had never gotten a chance to use it.

My dad was ecstatic. We stayed there for months, venturing up to the surface for sunlight and exercise once a day and sleeping on the cots at night. We closed the top during the day whenever it wasn't in use, propping it open during the night for fresh air and dragging a blanket we'd covered in leaves and debris over the entrance to conceal it using a stick.

It was small and stifling, but the safety and abundance of food out-weighed all the negatives. We spent days doing an inventory of all the supplies and setting aside rations so that they could last as long as possible. Canned food and grains and bottled water and packets of seeds and dried fruits and jerky, more variety than we'd had in years. It was heaven.

We lived there for months until the food reserves were visibly dwindling and all that was left were big, heavy sacks of grain along with a few other odds and ends.

And then I got hurt.

I'd been trying to reach an item on one of the top shelves. There had been no stool, nothing to drag over so that I could reach, so I hopped onto the first metal shelf, thinking that it was no big deal because they were nailed to the wall. What was I supposed to do, wake up my dad just to get a can of peaches?

I stretched to my full height, climbing up one more shelf and silently cheering when my finger hooked around the top of the can. I pulled it toward me with a small sweeping motion, recoiling with shock when it went toppling over along with those under it and came crashing down on top of me. I lost my grip on the shelf I'd been clutching, my feet slipped off the edge, and the momentum sent me flying to the ground with a loud thud, immediately waking my father. The cans continued to roll off the structure and onto me, where I was rocking back and forth on the floor as I clutched my knee, my breath knocked loose by the impact.

The noise woke my dad and he flew off his cot and jumped into action, stopping anything else from rolling and picking me up from the mess. When I finally caught my breath, I was bawling not from the pain but from the fear that the cans had broken and I'd wasted good food. Sometimes when we opened a can and found the contents blackened and moldy, we had the luxury of making the choice not to eat it, unlike before when we had to take what we could get. That luxury went away if I ruined half our supply.

My dad was more concerned about the gash just below my knee, the scent of blood dominating the small space.

But that wasn't the worst part, not to me.

The worst part was that my dad was beyond worried, chastising himself for not bringing down a supply of first aid items, cursing the owners for not thinking to stock their bunker with them. I hated it when he was upset, and I hadn't seen him so concerned over my safety in a good while. He dried my tears and insisted that he needed to go above ground to grab supplies, bandages and disinfectant, and ointment. I begged him not to go, promising that I'd be fine, that we could just use one of my shirts, and couldn't I go with him? He told me to stay put, reassuring me that it would be a quick trip. Apparently, the risk of infection was too great to leave the cut unsterilized.

I was overwhelmed by the fact that we'd never been apart for more than an hour or two—I was only nine at that point—and given that he had no idea if the house that the bunker had been built behind had already been looted for first aid supplies, it could take him any amount of time to find some. I cried, begging him to stay, swearing that I'd be fine, but he insisted on going.

He was gone for over four hours.

When he finally came back, he told me that he'd run into a horde when he went a street over to check those houses and needed to wait it out before he could circle around back to the bunker. I was a wreck the entire time, terrified that he wasn't going to come back, that something terrible would happen, and I'd have no idea.

I felt that same crushing fear now. Merikh and Caelan had been gone for an entire week, and while it might not seem long to anyone else–people who were used to them coming and going as needed–it was dominating all of my thoughts.

It was almost like a curse to love them. The world was ruined, and though I was loath to admit it, a horrifying place. You could be the biggest, scariest motherfucker around, and with just one slip-up, become zombie food. I had to stop myself multiple times a day from hanging around the guard shack at the entrance to watch for any sign of them. I wanted them safe. I wanted them *home*.

"Please," Grey said softly. "I can't watch you do that anymore."

I quit pacing and whirled on the ball of my foot, ready to give him hell, but my ire deflated when I saw the anguish in his eyes.

He was just as worried as me, just as desperate to have them home safe. It wouldn't be right of me to get angry with him just for not liking the fact that I was hurting.

"Come here."

I huffed like I was put out, but one glance at the knowing look in his eyes and I was secretly grateful that he recognized that I needed this and didn't know how to ask. I stepped into the shelter of his arms, sighing heavily as I gave him my weight.

The sound of a muffled shout from outside the cabin had me wriggling out of Grey's embrace and running out the door. Grey must have caught it before it slammed because there was no loud bang as I'd anticipated.

One of the men who worked in shifts to watch the perimeter was covered in sweat and beaming as he jogged the last few steps to meet me halfway in the short distance left between us.

"You asked me to send word immediately as soon as we heard some-thing," he said with a nod to Grey as he came up from behind me to stand at my side. "They arrived just minutes ago, perfectly fine."

I laughed, grabbing Grey's hand and taking off at a run, kicking up dirt and a few curses from Grey, when I stopped abruptly and turned.

"Would you mind finding Nix and telling him?" I asked the man still standing behind us on the path. "He might know already since he wasn't with us at home, but I just want to be sure."

The enthusiasm with which he nodded, like it was a matter of life or death, reassured me that Nix would get the news somehow.

"Come on," I urged Grey, pulling him back into a steady jog through the forest.

His laugh was soft. "They're not going anywhere, sweetheart."

"I know." I rolled my eyes. "But it feels like it's been months." All the tension and anxiety I had been steadily collecting day after day slowly leached out of me as I got closer to the front of the camp.

I caught a glimpse of Merikh through a small crowd of people who were taking bags from his hands, and once I passed a different group that was examining the contents of one of the bags off to the side, I saw Caelan.

His face was dirty and scratched, but he looked to be okay. I must've made a noise because he looked up, his pensive frown transforming into a wide grin.

I let go of Grey's hand and launched myself at him, not caring about how embarrassing it might've looked or how on display I was.

He caught me easily, gathering me up in his arms and patting my legs where they were anchored around his torso. He buried his head in the spot between my neck and shoulder and exhaled heavily.

I was so relieved that I could hardly speak. I brushed his hair back behind his ears, smiling as he made a soft sound and kissed the spot of skin that his breath had moistened on my neck.

"I missed you," he rasped, giving me a strong hug before leaning back and kissing me soundly on the lips.

"I think that's my line," I joked, looking him over again just to make sure that he was okay and in one piece.

He put me down but kept me close by his side, gathering up my hand and tucking me slightly behind him.

"I was worried," I murmured, low enough that I wouldn't be overheard.

"I'm sorry," he said, serious for once. "We... We found something. We're gonna get everyone together and tell you all at once."

I nodded, biting my lip when Grey approached him and gave him a long back-slapping hug. They murmured to one another in low voices as Merikh joined us.

His eyes went straight to me, cataloging my entire body before snapping up to my eyes. He looked tired, dark circles smudged under his eyes and lines bracketing the corners of his mouth. He seemed almost unsure of his reception, which was absolutely not acceptable. I slipped my hand out of Caelan's and walk forward into Merikh's body, sliding my arms around his torso and holding him close. After a few seconds, he sighed softly and closed his arms around me, one hand between my shoulder blades and the other pressing my head against his chest.

"Missed you," I said, voice muffled by his shirt.

"I missed you too," he admitted gruffly.

I turned my head a little, hiding my smile, and sighed contentedly.

"Caelan said you guys had something to tell us?" I asked as I tilted my head back, still not leaving the circle of his arms.

His lips settled into a firm line, pressing together tightly. He nodded once, looking at Caelan over my head before looping a hand in my ponytail several times to tilt my head back and dipping down to kiss me.

It was sweet and hot at the same time. His lips were slightly chapped from the elements, and he smelled like smoke and ashes, but his tongue was soft and the way he nipped my bottom lip before pulling away was maddening.

I narrowed my eyes at the tiny smirk he wore and I swayed toward him slightly once he pulled away.

"Nice to know I haven't lost my touch," he whispered just for me.

I just laughed softly, elated that he was here in front of me—safe and sound.

"I'm going to gather everyone up and we'll talk?" Grey asked, having discussed it with Caelan while I was talking to Merikh.

I frowned. "Don't you guys want to shower and change and everything?"

They looked at each other, then shook their heads in unison. "It's probably for the best that we brief everyone as soon as possible," Caelan explained. "Dirty clothing and all."

My smile was wobbly, but I nodded anyway. As the adrenaline wore off, I started to register the people around us, but to my eternal gratitude, no one was looking at us weirdly or giving us any stares. It was an odd thing to be thankful for, but apparently, people started giving less of a fuck once the world has gone to shit. I hadn't once received any scrutiny or odd comments from being seen with each of the guys.

Caelan took my hand, laughing at something Grey said when Merikh grabbed my other one and tucked me into his side.

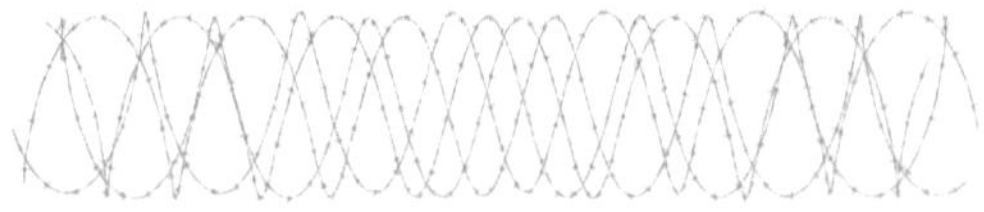

It took a surprisingly short amount of time to get everyone gathered for the briefing. I had to assume that this group of individuals gathered often to discuss the safety issues regarding the camp, but this was my first time attending, and I couldn't help feeling a little out of place. The room was filled with people that I had seen here and there but never quite introduced myself to and so I stuck close to Nix, who had shown up only minutes after I had, while the remaining few filtered into the building Merikh used for camp meetings.

Only now that everyone was settling down, eyes were turning my way. It couldn't be that I was a girl, since there were several other women gathered around the rickety folding table. Could it be that they still viewed me as an outsider? Or that I didn't look like I had anything to contribute?

I shoved my way past Caelan and Grey and found myself facing Merikh and a few other men from around camp where they were standing near one of the boarded-up windows.

"No," I said firmly before he could even begin to protest my presence. "I want to help. You don't get to shut me out this time."

"Feisty," one of the men commented approvingly. His hair fell to his shoulders in a mass of golden waves, and his beard was thick and well-groomed, though it didn't quite hide the deep dimples on either side of his smile. He looked to be about a few years older than Grey, though that neatly trimmed beard and those buff, crossed arms made it hard to tell for sure.

The glare Merikh turned on him could've blistered paint.

"Relax." He laughed. "I don't poach." He turned to me, offering a hand. "I'm Jake, darlin'."

I nodded stiffly. "River," I told him, shaking the hand he'd offered and making sure my grip was firm.

"Nice to officially meet the girl that's got these four so twisted up. I've seen you around camp but haven't had time to introduce myself."

Grey laughed, bringing Jake into a quick hug and slapping him on the back. "Haven't seen much of you lately, man. Missed you."

Jake might've been the cheeriest person I'd ever met, and that included Caelan. He hadn't stopped smiling throughout the entire interaction. "You're the one who stopped comin' around to guard the gates with me. I got stuck with Derek Latimer and he could talk the legs off an iron pot."

His southern drawl was so out of place compared to the way everyone else here spoke, but I found it endearing. Sometimes I forgot that people had gotten stuck far from home when the virus broke out and again when it mutated, and was only reminded when I encountered the odd accent.

Nix, who had made his way up to where we were all standing, tucked me into his side, and I wiggled until I could snake my hand out and slide it into Caelan's. It was a tight fit, but worth it from the huge smile he turned on me. He traced his thumb over my knuckles, sending a small shiver down my spine.

"So," Merikh interrupted. He glanced at Caelan and they had some sort of triplet conversation just through their eyes. Freaky.

"One day I'm gonna understand that," I muttered, the corner of my mouth tipping up when Nix kissed the side of my head.

"Alright." Caelan took over. "We saw no evidence of our dad, but we did notice that a few of the houses and buildings nearby were recently occupied."

Merikh interjected. "There was no way to tell if it was the same group that's been hanging around or just some random strangers passing through, but we assumed it would be smart for us to play it safe and assume it was them."

I frowned. "How recent were the signs you found? Could it have been from before the incident when we know they were here for sure?"

Caelan's free hand ran over his face, and he made a long groaning noise. "Recent," he admitted. "Cigarettes, zombie guts, food crumbs that hadn't yet been picked over by rats–all fairly fresh."

That... was not what I wanted to hear. I so badly wanted them to be gone, but I knew better than to think they'd just given up. Whatever we had that they wanted, be it shelter, territory or food, they weren't going to quit until they got it.

"So what do we do?" A woman with long, dark braids asked. I'd only seen her in passing around camp, but she'd always offered me a smile and wave, even when everything went down with Anna spilling my business and most people had given me dirty looks.

"*Imani*," Caelan whispered in my ear when I looked at him in silent question.

Merikh frowned, once again looking over at Caelan.

"Just spit it out," I sighed, much to Jake's amusement.

"We found their camp," Merikh declared, drawing gasps from around the room. "Since we wanted to confirm whoever had been holed up in the area was connected to the same group that sabotaged the gate, we decided to follow their tracks."

I opened my mouth to interject, but decided to let him finish.

"There was a steady trail of recently discarded cigarette butts and food wrappers. It took us longer to follow their tracks because zombies kept crossing our path and we wanted to take them out with as little noise as possible."

The woman behind me made a humming noise as Caelan pulled away from me to draw crude buildings and shapes onto the sheet of paper someone had procured. He pointed at certain spots and marked them as Merikh spoke.

"The trail led away from our camp, but we wanted to get an idea of where they were headed, so we continued to follow them. Around a day later, after a few times where we got turned around, found fresh signs at several of our stops, and waited around until they got moving again, we left the city and ended up in a more rural, industrial area."

Caelan chimed in, "Good news, fewer zombies. Bad news, less coverage, and the undead aren't the only threats out there. After a certain point, it was harder to tell what was fresh and what wasn't among all the debris, until eventually the tracks disappeared altogether, and we followed the noise."

I fought a shudder, hating to think of how exposed they'd been.

An older, balding man with the bluest eyes I'd ever seen raised his hand. "What do you mean by noise? How loud could a couple of men have been without ending up as zombie bait?"

Merikh's expression was grave. "Turns out whoever we were following went back to home base, and they're holed up in a warehouse near one of the airports. They didn't care how loud they were, even though they'd attracted a solid crowd of zombies around the outer fencing. We couldn't get a look inside from so far away, but did spot a couple of them walking out every so often for a smoke or a piss."

I felt Grey tense beside me and stepped forward so I could brush my shoulder against his arm without letting go of Nix.

"What does this mean?" I asked, a sinking feeling in my stomach.

Jake stroked his beard thoughtfully and huffed. "If they're camped out nearby and actively making the trip back to our area to keep an eye on us for some reason, then they're obviously not giving up. Worst-case scenario, they're planning somethin' else and this quiet period has been spent productively."

"What the hell could be so important?" I argued, frustrated that they wouldn't just leave us alone. I'd finally gotten everything I wanted, but I just couldn't let my guard down with this still hanging over our heads.

Grey shrugged, his voice hard. "Supplies: food, weapons, shelter, women. Who knows what. As long as there are people who contribute to a community and work hard to participate and prosper, there will always be those who want to take it so they don't have to do any of the hard work themselves, and don't mind using force to make it happen."

Caelan rested his free hand on Grey's shoulder, giving him a quick squeeze before sliding his hand back into mine.

"What can we do but wait?" said a man that after several minutes of puzzled glances and wracking my brain, I'd correctly identified as Hasan Akbari, Sakhira's father.

"All we can do is keep watching the perimeter and assign a few more people, restrict who comes and goes. We don't have the numbers or skills to mount any kind of offensive effort."

I worried my bottom lip, only realizing that I was squeezing Caelan's hand too tightly when he flexed his fingers in my grip. If all trips out were restricted even further, how would Halli keep the garden going? And how would we replenish the food that had gone missing? When I spoke, my voice was quiet but resolute. "I actually recently remembered this house my dad and I visited years ago…" I trailed off as I met Merikh's eyes, that somehow already seemed to be broadcasting the word *no*.

You know what? No. They didn't have a monopoly on making decisions for the good of the group, and it was time that I actually advocated for what I thought was right rather than handing over the reins and trusting them to do whatever they thought best. I rolled my shoulders back and started again, firmer this time. "We found a house years and years ago that had an underground bunker filled with supplies in the back. We ate or traded most of the cans and dried food, and drank all the water, but there were still bags of grains and seeds that we left behind that were too heavy and bulky for us to bring with us."

The older man snorted incredulously. "You expect us to believe that it's all still there?"

I stood taller as I responded. "Why wouldn't it be? It was a tiny entrance in a fenced-in backyard of an already picked clean house. Even if someone did find it, what good would they have with what was left unless they had a permanent shelter where they could cook or use it all? And it's the perfect environment to have kept those seeds unspoiled over the years. Cool, dark, and dry."

"She has a point," Imani added, lifting an eyebrow in approval.

"It's not safe," Merikh stated flatly. "Even if you gave someone detailed instructions down to the street name, there would be no way for you to remember *how* to get there unless you were in the city itself, and since you wouldn't be going, it would be a fool's errand."

"And why wouldn't I be going?"

He just stared at me. When Caelan chimed in, he sounded cautious. "I agree with him, baby. It's too dangerous."

"When will it ever not be? Are you going to keep me locked up here forever? You're telling me I can never go outside these walls again?"

Several people shifted on their feet, and one person coughed awkwardly.

Grey hummed. "We're not saying never. Just... not now."

I looked at Nix, hoping he of all people would understand that I *needed* to do this. That it was the ultimate way to contribute. Who cared if it was a little dangerous when so many people could benefit?

He shook his head sadly, eyes beseeching me not to be angry.

So that was that. I wasn't about to throw a tantrum and make a fool out of myself in front of everyone. It would get me nowhere. I nodded stoically, and to everyone else, I was sure it looked as if I had just received my marching orders, but I saw the suspicion lurking in my guys' eyes. They knew better than to believe I had just quietly accepted their rules. Already my mind was racing with different possibilities, from ways to convince them to even more drastic measures, like sneaking out. I'd sleep on it; maybe the answer would come to me after a few nights of brainstorming.

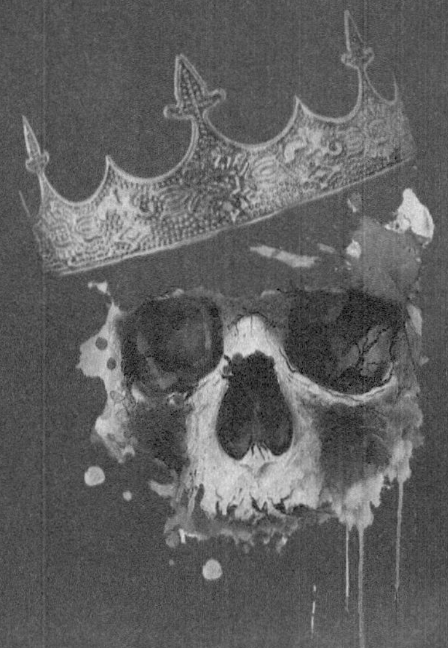

CHAPTER 24

Dinner was oddly quiet. It should've been loud, even with just the sound of forks scraping plates and murmured comments here and there, but it was like someone had put a dampener over the whole thing. Even Caelan didn't try to lighten the mood, uncharacteristically silent for once.

I still had to think about it, but I needed to play things as normal as possible if I didn't want to draw suspicion. Just in case I decided to go rogue despite their protests. Did it make me a bad person? Possibly. Okay yeah, probably. But who were they to go on a weeklong trip in the interests of the camp and then turn around and tell me I couldn't do the same? We'd gotten past all the circumstances that brought me here, worked through all the tension and the anger and the underlying issues. I was free to leave if I wanted, so why were they so insistent that

I not go anywhere when I had a good lead on resources for everyone? Resources that we desperately needed?

I cleared my throat, humming softly once I swallowed my last bite and setting my fork down with a clang. "So," I said brightly. "I don't suppose you guys ever have anything sweet after dinner?"

Merikh eyed me suspiciously. *Shit, play it cool!* No way after an argument like that would I sound remotely happy.

"No," Grey said slowly. "Sometimes we make modified chocolate chip cookies when we have eggs to spare. Before the trouble started a few months ago, we used to trade with a farmer up north for milk and butter. He's the one who gave us the chickens in the first place."

I scratched at the purple nail polish Nix had given me the other day. It had been so sweet; he'd thrust it at me with a light blush on his cheeks and I had to read the label to even figure out what it was. Lots of messy attempts to apply it later and with my nail beds covered in a deep purple, I'd gone to Naia for help.

"Y'know, it's weird. I guess it makes sense that you have chickens because I know we had scrambled eggs for breakfast a few days ago, but since I haven't seen them, yet I didn't give it much thought." I leaned back in my chair, patting my full stomach softly. "It's not like I'm used to fresh food, so you'd think I would be suspicious of where we suddenly got eggs, but I wasn't."

Merikh's smile was softer than usual. I had to pull my eyes from the way his broad shoulders stretched his thin black shirt when he started to speak. "You get used to it. Enough time here and you're not second guessing every single meal, wondering where it came from, and trying to store little pieces away in case something bad happens or we suddenly run out."

I felt my cheeks flush, and I turned my head slightly so my embarrassment didn't show on my face. Was it that obvious? Had they found the little stash I'd hidden in the back of one of Grey's unused drawers?

A chair creaked behind me as someone stood, and I realized with a rush of self-consciousness that it was because of *me*. Grey crouched beside my chair, his calloused hand reaching out to grip my chin and turn my face gently to face him.

I had a stray urge to smooth the furrow between his brows, and focused on watching his dimple as he spoke instead. "It's nothing to be ashamed of, River. We all know what it's like to go from starving for days on end, living on expired cans and tasteless concoctions to eating well every day, and several meals at that. Everyone who comes through here goes through an adjustment period, and you can bet your ass that they squirreled food away from their plates too, just in case, just because it felt safer to do so."

He moved his hands to mine, holding them tightly. "I promise you it will get better."

One glance at his warm brown eyes and I just knew he was speaking from experience. I darted my gaze around, but no one was laughing or judging me. They looked compassionate and understanding. I guess I hadn't thought much about it. It wasn't like I took food off of other people's plates or I took extra so I could hide some away. I would just eat a little less when the meal was something that I could easily store; it was no hardship. It was nice to know I had support to deal with it though.

"Okay," I whispered, squeezing his hands softly for strength. His mouth tipped up at the corner as he squeezed them back, then stood. His knee cracked loudly, and Merikh winced at the sound.

Caelan laughed. "Getting up there in age, old man? Maybe we need to spar some more."

"Oh, fuck you," Grey scoffed. "I'm only two goddamn years older."

Merikh chimed in, shooting me a wink. "Two years makes all the difference, buddy. Maybe it's time we put you out to pasture."

I relaxed at the familiar sounds of their bickering, smiling absently at Nix when he checked to make sure I was okay. Maybe it wasn't the end of the world that they wouldn't let me go scavenging right away. Surely they'd listen to reason sometime, right?

"Get your goddamn ass out of my face."

"Get your face out of my ass!"

I groaned, rolling onto my stomach and jabbing Caelan with my elbow. "Quit antagonizing Grey," I hissed.

I could barely make out his pout in the dark shadows of the living room. Merikh and Nix were silent on my other side. I couldn't quite tell if they were sleeping or just pretending to sleep and hoping everyone would follow suit. I must've only slept for a few hours before I woke up to Caelan being a bed hog per usual, except this time he had sprawled lengthwise across the bed and encroached on Grey's space.

We needed a bigger bed. On a good night, everything worked out fine. On an off night, one of us slipped into the cracks between the mattresses and woke up freezing with a sore shoulder. I had no idea if before the world as we knew it ended, they had manufactured mattresses big enough for four grown men and one of me. If so, I didn't think we'd find one near us, *and* in good condition. Once again, I found myself lamenting the fact that we couldn't just go out and pick up whatever we needed, like everyone said they used to before the literal fucking apocalypse.

I wouldn't have it any other way, though. I'd never felt as safe or comfortable as I did surrounded by my guys, cold floor and all. I was sure as time passed, we would all start circulating into the bedrooms for a night alone, but for now, it was perfect.

"Fine," Caelan grumbled. He hauled his big body upright and flopped down beside me, pulling me into his embrace as the little spoon. "Much better," he murmured, burying his nose in my hair.

I made a small noise, seconds away from telling him he was way too hot to be clinging onto me like this, when his small, content sigh convinced me to hold off. I pushed the blanket down to my waist and closed my eyes to the sound of Grey tossing and turning as he tried to get comfortable once again.

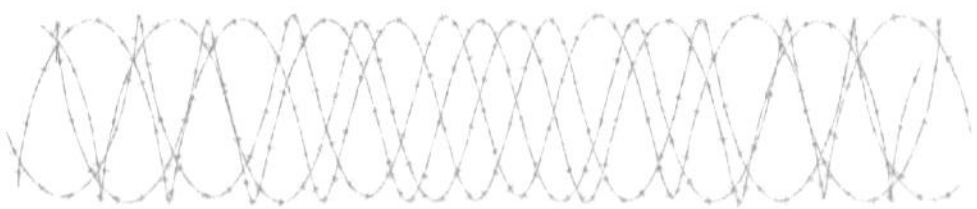

I held my tongue when Merikh came home rubbing his temples like he had a headache blooming.

That lasted a good thirty seconds before I landed on *fuck that* and spoke up anyway. "What's wrong?"

His pained glance told me all I needed to know. It was about the food supply, and he didn't want to talk about it. Well, that was just too damn bad. "I don't care if it's uncomfortable, you can't just keep me in the dark."

Merikh sighed, dropping onto the couch a cushion away from me and settling into a lazy-looking sprawl. "We found mold on some of the cured meat."

My stomach dropped in fear. I clamped down on the panic that rose to the surface and kept my breathing even. "Are you saying that we're going to go hungry?"

He shook his head, brows furrowed, and reached out to grasp my hand in his. "That's not what I'm saying. Things are just going to be tight for a bit. It's too risky to hunt and takes too many resources to cure and dry whatever we do catch, which is why we trade with the farm I told you about. It's off-season for us to be negotiating for more, but they're pretty well-off and I think we can make it work."

The sick feeling in my stomach hadn't completely dissipated, but it was definitely better than before. I used my free hand to worry at the scab on the back of my knee, then redirected my fidgeting to the bracelet Halli had gifted me. "No offense, but... what could you offer in trade that a farm couldn't do themselves?"

He smiled reassuringly, resting his hand atop the one I was using to fidget anxiously with the bracelet, then gathered up both my hands in a tight clasp. "I promise you don't have to worry," he said gently. His eyes were so incredibly blue I could hardly look away. "We scavenge and mend clothing to trade. Not only that but ammo, weapons, first aid supplies, and anything else they might need since they're too busy working the farm to look for supplies themselves and they can't afford to lose a worker that's knowledgeable in what needs to be done. They put a lot of work in during the first year after the virus outbreak to create a compound of sorts, which served them well after the mutation. They hardly ever leave, we always go to them, and it's probably even safer than this place."

I was loath to ruin this quiet, safe bubble we had created, sitting inches apart with our hands intertwined, but I had to say it. "But they don't trade dried goods or fresh foods, like vegetables or rice."

His face darkened, and he glanced away, his jaw working. "No," he eventually gritted out. "Sometimes they have vegetables to spare, but we'd have to visit at just the right time of year to receive their surplus."

I nodded, my mind already made up. "So you get how important it is that if I can help ensure we have enough seeds and grain for the next year, that I should," I insisted.

Merikh's face telegraphed his frustration, although to his credit he didn't start lecturing me again. "Not this again," he sighed. "I thought we'd agreed?"

"You agreed!" I pulled my hands from his and jumped to my feet. "I didn't get a choice."

Just then Grey walked in, clearly confused at what the hell was going on, until he looked at Merikh's face and rolled his eyes. "You told her."

"What the hell, Grey?! You don't get to keep secrets about shit just because it benefits you or it sticks me into a nice little box where I don't make any trouble."

He raised his hand to rub his chest in small circles. "That's not what we were trying to do," he rumbled. He ran his hand through his hair, leaving it a rumpled mess, and turned imploring eyes onto me. "We just… didn't want to make things harder on you. Didn't want you to worry that we were going to run out of food."

I gentled my voice, trying not to lose my conviction in the face of his thoughtfulness. "I get it, Grey, but you can't *promise* that we won't. It would be worse if we started rationing even further, and I had no idea why."

Merikh stood, crossing his arms in front of his chest in a way that made his veins stand out. *Quit looking at his muscles, for fuck's sake, you have advocating to do,* I chastised.

"She's trying to make her argument again," he informed Grey *oh so helpfully.*

I rolled my eyes when Grey made a frustrated noise, kicking myself for not just sticking with the original plan to keep quiet. Clearly, it wasn't in my nature to just not speak my mind.

"It's not safe," he insisted. "Maybe you're fine with risking your life over it, but I'm not!"

I blinked rapidly. I'd never heard him speak so loudly before.

"You know what," he huffed. "I can't do this right now."

With that, he turned on his heel and walked right back out the door, leaving me and Merikh alone in that uncomfortable silence that typically followed an argument.

Fuck that. I would show him. I'd show *all* of them. I'd been scavenging my whole life, surviving and hiding and *living* with those things. If anyone had a chance of finding the supplies we needed to keep thriving, it would be me.

"I'm sleeping in Caelan's room tonight," I muttered, leaving Merikh behind as I stormed off.

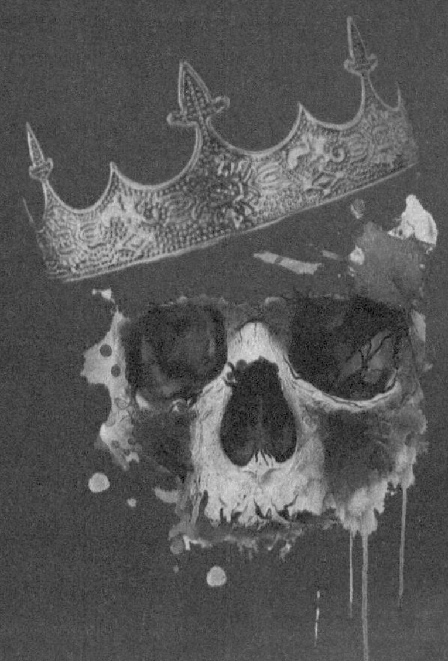

CHAPTER 25

"I don't think capybaras are real," Caelan declared out of the blue during our walk to the gate.

I panned over to him slowly, watching as his shit-eating grin grew wider. God, he looked delicious in the morning light. All rough stubble and tattoos, deep rumbling voice and messy hair.

"I don't! I saw them in a book once, but I don't understand how those creepy little fuckers could exist. I think it was a prank."

"A prank," I said flatly.

"Sure, why not? Hey, everyone, looks like the zombies are taking over, let's publish a picture book to confuse all the uneducated strangers that come after us into believing that some weird-looking cross between a pig and a rat supposedly lives halfway around the world. Maybe it's an ongoing social experiment and they're sitting up in their ivory tower looking down on the masses who were gullible enough to believe them."

I fought the urge to rub my temples to stave off the impending headache. It was way too early for this shit. The worst part was I honestly couldn't tell if he was being serious or not, because I wouldn't put this past him.

"Surely you don't believe all the stories from before. Like that we sent people into space or walked on the moon."

"You can't think every odd-looking animal that you'd previously never heard of is a conspiracy, and just because it seems impossible to you–" I started, interrupted by his waving hand.

"Yeah, yeah, I know. It's just..." He shook his head, laughing softly. "We came so far just to end up... well, here."

I caught his hand where it swung beside mine, lacing our fingers together. "Maybe someday it'll be that way again."

He squeezed my hand gently. "Yeah. Besides, I think I've got it pretty good for now."

"Oh, you do, do you?"

His laughter was laced through his words as he swung me up into his arms, ignoring my squeal. "Absolutely."

One of his strengths was the ability to cut right through tension. Last night, he'd walked into the cabin, found me lying angrily in his bed, handed me a sandwich with a kiss, then hung out in the living room to coax the others out of their sour moods. He was exactly what we needed when we all got to be too serious and in our heads.

His voice softened, and he adjusted me so that my arms were wrapped around his neck so that I could plant kisses across his jaw. "You know I love you, yeah?"

Was it possible for a heart to explode from too much feeling? Because if so, I should probably have been concerned.

"I know," I whispered.

"I mean it. You're everything I never knew I needed. Strong, brave, beautiful, fierce. I'll spend the rest of my life trying to be the kind of person who deserves you."

I tucked my face into his neck and made a helpless noise. He laughed and rubbed my back in small circles.

"I just burst your little grinch heart, huh?"

I popped my head up, wearing a frown. "What the hell is a grinch?"

He threw his head back on a groan. "For a reader, you're awfully bad at knowing popular books. Next trip we make, I'm picking up a copy, just for you."

I rolled my eyes. I was fortunate that my dad had taught me to read when many others didn't have that privilege. I spent hour after hour reading anything I could get my hands on when I was younger. Romance, science fiction, fantasy... My tastes changed as I aged, finding things with more and more explicit scenes, until I was so focused on surviving that I didn't read much at all. One thing I didn't read much of was children's books, excluding a few of my absolute favorites that I'd read until my copies fell apart. "If you find it, I'll read it," I informed him. "And maybe I would be so kind as to scavenge for a copy of the Laird's Forbidden Mistress that I just so happened to find in an older woman's home when we stayed for the night."

His laugh filled the space around us, and the people who turned to look were already wearing smiles. His joy was just that infectious, and lucky for us, he shone with it.

Soon enough we were back into the busier areas of camp, and I squirmed for him to put me down, growing self-conscious as we approached the front where more people were gathered, then made our way to the guard shack at the entrance.

An irritated huff drew my attention, and while Caelan ignored Anna with ease. I couldn't.

"Put me down," I mumbled into his shoulder, unapologetically inhaling the clean, earthy scent saturating his shirt and skin as he slid me back down his front.

I scoffed when Anna shot me a look. Even with her presence, it was better than being back at the cabin. I couldn't imagine hanging around the others all day in that small space and slowly suffocating in the tense atmosphere until we inevitably argued again.

Caelan and I settled into our spots and made light conversation, mainly using the time to decompress. Hours passed, giving me more than enough time to work through everything that had been bothering me. I knew I could do it–find that bunker again–I just needed a chance to sneak off. I'd have to grab my bag back at the cabin and make sure I had enough supplies in case I ran into anything, plus a weapon. It was unfortunate for me that the gate had been fixed and reinforced where we'd had that confrontation with the zombies because I knew for sure there were no traps set in that section, and while I'd entered the camp from this direction, it was so long ago that I didn't quite remember the exact steps I needed to take and how precise they were.

It was midday when a voice rang out, calling Caelan's name from the direction of the food tent. Anna shifted restlessly, her platinum braid falling over her shoulder as she leaned against the side of the shack. Surprisingly enough, after her initial nasty look, she hadn't spared us so much as a glance. Caelan looked from me to her, seemingly deciding we wouldn't kill each other if he left us alone before nodding to himself. "You think you can handle keeping watch without me for a bit?"

I shrugged, rolling my shoulder where it was a bit sore from catching on a rough piece of wood the previous day and nodding.

Anna just ignored us, content to watch the wide swath of land outside the bounds of the camp.

Caelan sauntered off, disappearing behind the fence as he went to go take care of whatever they'd called him for. Time ran slow just sitting around, but it had to have been at least twenty minutes after he'd been gone before the idea hit me. Why didn't I just leave now? It was serendipitous. No zombies hanging around the perimeter, no one around who could stop me or force me to come back, and the sun shining brightly overhead. It was the ultimate opportunity.

I breathed slowly and deeply, calming the restlessness that was making me jittery. I could do this. So what if I didn't have any supplies? I was resourceful; I'd find them. Worst case, I didn't find fresh water, but everyone made it a point to know that you could go several days without it before it would kill you. I could be back before then, right? At the very least, maybe there was a stray bottle somewhere in the bunker that we'd missed last time. I was shaking with nerves. I couldn't let myself think of the guys or I'd lose my courage. I wasn't ignorant. I knew they were afraid to lose me, and they weren't keeping me here out of malice, but I *had* to do this. I couldn't help that they didn't understand that.

I cast a longing look at one of the knives hanging on the wall of the shack, but I had nowhere to store it. The last thing I needed was for it to slip out from wherever I stashed it and cut me on the way down. Instead, I grabbed the bat from where it sat in the corner and took a deep breath.

Anna turned around at the sound, brushing a stray hair from her face and looking at me quizzically. "Did you see something?"

"I'm going." I gestured out past the cars with the bat. "There's a bunker I found once with my dad that should still have an unspoiled supply of grains and gardening supplies the camp could use."

"Are you fucking serious?" she hissed, stretching to her full height and still coming up to at least a head shorter than me. "You can't go out there alone, they'll eat you alive. And what will Caelan say when he comes back and finds you gone?"

I shook my head, trying not to think of the look that would be on his face once he realized I was missing. "I have to, Anna. They haven't been able to scavenge in a while since the threat level was raised and even when they did, they've picked clean everything in this area. We *need* this."

To her credit, she didn't immediately shout for Caelan. She just stood there, worrying her bottom lip and looking surprisingly docile for once.

"I'm going," I repeated. "Before he gets back." I tied my hair into a tight ponytail with the band on my wrist and prepared myself to go back out into that hellhole.

"Supplies?" she asked frantically. "You'll starve out there."

"I did it before, I can do it again. Remember, I've lived out there my whole life. I know how to find scraps to keep me going. Besides, why do you even care? I thought you hated me."

She scowled. That was more like it. "It's a suicide mission," she huffed. "Excuse me for not wanting to lose a valuable member of camp."

My grin was lopsided, and it felt wrong on my face. "Valuable, huh? That's high praise coming from you." My mind was racing, already thinking of how I'd come back with proof that the bunker existed and had what we needed, that it would solve all our immediate problems and the guys would realize that I knew what I was doing and stop underestimating me. It wasn't like I needed to cart back hundreds of pounds of food by myself. I only needed to document the exact path there so that we could mount a group effort when we had the time, preferably with a wheelbarrow or something.

I listened for a quick moment to make sure Caelan wasn't heading back, and ignoring the sharp stab of pain in my chest, left the shack to start undoing the chains on the gate.

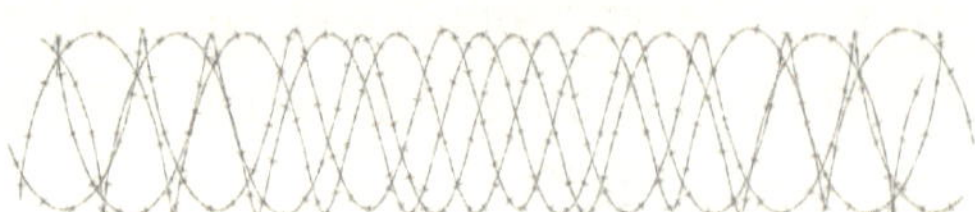

Anna made a small huffing noise as we tiptoed around the carcass of a car. She'd ended up coming with me, followed by a bunch of grumbling and bitching about how reckless an idea this was and how she should've just let me go off and die alone. She continued griping up until we got to an area where we could no longer speak without attracting unwanted attention.

I wasn't sure that I trusted her at my back, but she did lead us through all the traps that were set up without getting me killed, so that was something.

Anna's body froze at the sound of rustling nearby, and we relaxed in unison after we saw a small rat dart out from a nearby drain after stopping to scan our surroundings.

I wasn't completely ignorant. I'd left signs that we came this way, just in case anything did happen to us. I was confident, but not foolish, and I'd never forgive myself if I got eaten by zombies and the guys never found any evidence of it because they didn't know where to look.

So far we hadn't run into anyone, dead or alive (rat excluded), but I was doubtful that our good luck would last. Things seemed too quiet. Too... empty. Was I fortunate that we hadn't yet run into a zombie? Yes. Was it eerily and unnaturally silent for the area we were in? Also, yes. We were on the very outskirts of the city, still not too far from the camp, and while before the virus this area had not been heavily congested with people, there would still have been a fair number of zombies lingering about. It wouldn't be just as empty as the barren stretch of land we'd just left.

It was strange, we might not have seen anyone, but the hair on the back of my neck stood on end with the odd sensation that we were being watched. Which wasn't impossible, given that we were surrounded by worn-down and crumbling suburban homes with lots of areas to hide, but if someone was out there, they were clearly sticking to the shadows.

Anna sighed and ambled over to a flipped car, leaning back against it and resting her hands on her knees. Much as I hated to admit it, I needed a break as well. Despite the work that I'd put in around camp and the effort I put into exercising each day, those controlled sessions were a great deal different from spending all day on the move and on alert. I was already tiring, and we'd only been walking for less than an hour if I had to guess.

I noticed Anna's hair had fallen out of its hastily tied knot and was sticking to the sweat covering her face, which couldn't have been comfortable. "Here," I murmured, looking longingly at the emergency hair tie I had sitting on my wrist before pulling it off and handing it to her.

She eyed my outstretched hand suspiciously, plucking the lavender band like it was a piece of dirt. "You don't have to be nice to me, you know." Her voice was low, and she cast a quick glance around as she continued. "Just because I came with you to make sure you didn't get yourself killed doesn't mean I like you."

It was hard to suppress my smile, and something on my face must have given away my amusement because she rolled her eyes and looked away, but not before I saw the corner of her mouth twitch.

"So how far is this place anyway?"

I fought the urge to slap my skin where I thought I felt an insect land and instead squirmed uncomfortably. Sue me, I'd gone twenty-two years sleeping in the dirt and I still had a strong dislike for bugs of all kinds. Except for maybe ladybugs. They weren't all that bad, I supposed. "I can't say for sure. I have a general idea of where the house was located in the city, but it's going to take a bit of circling to find the exact area. There are also certain routes we should be taking that might slow us down a little, but are safer in the long run."

The light tan faded from her face as she grew pale. "Are you okay?" I whispered, trying to keep our noise to a minimum.

She just nodded, blinking a few times before straightening. "It's been a while since I've left the camp. I haven't been placed on any jobs that needed it for years, and I guess I forgot…" she trailed off with a sigh. "It's easy to forget the world went to shit when you're living with everyone you care about behind the safety of the walls, eating fresh food every day and waking up without fear. Even if you're distantly aware of the circumstances that lead to why you're there in the first place, if you spent every day thinking about it, you wouldn't be able to function. It's easier to forget, and to be grateful for what you do have."

I understood what she was saying. Even in the short amount of time that I'd spent back at camp, it was easier to forget what lived outside those walls and to spend each day making the best of the safe haven they'd built. If Anna had gone years peacefully living like nothing was wrong (well, as much as she could without the recent incidents), to be thrust out into the real world with no warning would be upsetting, and scary. Damn it, she'd totally managed to hit my empathy button. How was I going to keep disliking her for being such a bitch when she was making herself vulnerable?

"Thank you for coming with me. I know you didn't have to, but it's nice to have company. I've been on my own for too long and I was dreading going back to it, even if just for a couple of days."

She gave me a small smile, adjusting the handle of her knife where it was sticking out of the holster that was slung across her waist, and shuddered. "Enough sappy shit, it's making me sick. Let's get a move on."

I held back my laugh, surprised to find that she was more like me than I'd thought.

We walked for maybe ten more minutes toward the edge of the city, growing increasingly wary and watchful as the silence persisted, and keeping a vigilant eye on our surroundings.

In the end, it was a metallic clang that broke the silence, the suddenness of it sending Anna nearly a foot into the air. I found myself desperately wishing it was another rat, but knowing that would be too damn unlikely.

We subconsciously moved toward one another as quietly as possible, the hair on my arms rising as we waited. She didn't yet withdraw her knife, but she did rest her fingers on the handle in case she needed to pull it quickly.

A shadow moved along the side of one of the houses and I spun to face it fully, lifting my bat. My heart pounded loudly, almost drowning out the sounds of what was clearly a person moving, and not an animal. I took a deep breath in, willing my limbs to stop vibrating with apprehension so I could focus.

Only when the person walked out into the sunlight where we could get a clear look at them did we stand down, not out of relief but from confusion.

"Colby?"

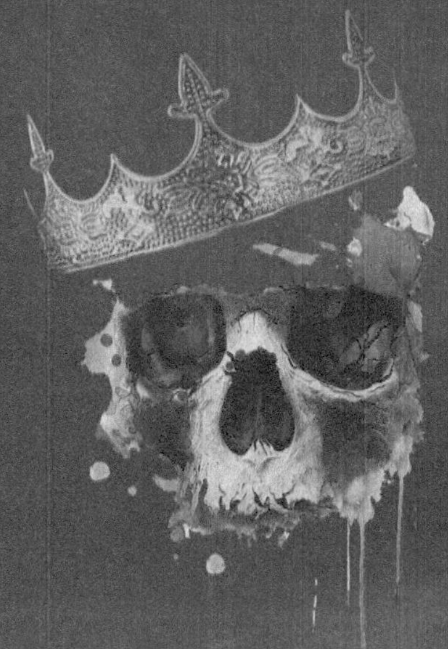

CHAPTER 26

Anna's jaw dropped as she shifted restlessly from foot to foot, hand still hovering over her knife. "What the hell are you doing here?"

Colby sneered, crossing his arms in some kind of attempt to look menacing. It didn't work. "What did you think happens to people who get banished? They get immediately eaten the second they leave? I'm too smart for that shit." Maybe he was smart enough to still be alive, but he looked terrible. His face was a shade of tan only achieved from spending the entire day in the sun, way different from the sallow paleness he'd been sporting before. Clearly, he spent a lot of time outside now. In addition to his scruffy beard, dark circles stood out underneath his wild eyes, adding to the unstable factor. His hair was greasy and tangled, hanging in messy, matted chunks down to his shoulders.

I was vibrating with nerves as I watched him. Something was off. It was too quiet here, too coincidental that he was so close by and still alive. The man Merikh kicked out of camp wouldn't have lasted a day on his own, let alone weeks. Just what the hell was going on?

I had a sick feeling in my stomach that he wasn't just going to let us wish him well and head on our way.

"I can see it on your faces that you're confused. What, did you think I'd just throw myself at the nearest zombie and hope for a quick death? Who else would I go to but the men with weapons hanging around right on our doorstep?"

My heart pounded sluggishly as I put the pieces together. "You," I said accusingly. "You're the one who gave them all the information on the camp, that's how they knew the back gate was vulnerable." So it wasn't the remaining members of the group that had attacked them years previously, using their previous knowledge to enact their revenge. That filled me with a small amount of relief.

He sneered, looking oddly pleased. "I'm flattered that you think that was all me." He stopped, refusing to elaborate, and I fought the urge to yell at him to explain. Finally, he grew too impatient to continue drawing out the suspense. "Aren't you tired of all the rules? The way they tell everyone what to do and control everything?"

Anna scoffed. "And what, would you be a better choice? Is that what you're getting at?"

His grin was downright evil. He shuffled anxiously and spat on the cracked concrete beneath him. Fucking gross. "Nah, sweetheart. Why have all the rules and all the soft people when we could just come in and change it all up? What good would it be for someone like me to run things when there's no one with enough vision to enforce it? Nah, that's what Gunner's for. And for keepin' an eye on the camp like he asked, I'm gonna be right by his side," he boasted proudly.

I was so dizzy with anger I could hardly think straight. This lazy fuck was mad about the rules? And he'd told the raiders all our weaknesses just for petty revenge? "Surely you're not that dense," I said flatly. "You were a source of information. That's all. Not nearly important enough to reap the benefits with them. No one wants a lazy right-hand man. Besides, you're just their errand boy."

There, I thought smugly as his smile dropped. Colby's eyes narrowed as he scowled. "They're gonna love you as a prize. Both of you. Besides, what better way to get revenge on those fuckers than to take two of their women? You're in high demand around these parts. Can't be too picky."

Anna recoiled in horror, finally pulling her weapon from its holster and holding it in front of her.

His laugh was loud, too loud. After spending so long whispering with Anna, our voices cut through the silence like a knife, and I suddenly realized why it had been so empty.

If the raiders were staying nearby, then they would have cleared the immediate area. But zombies were like roaches, they never quite left a territory and they were pretty damn resilient. It didn't matter how many of them the men had killed, they could come back.

"Just quiet down at least," I hissed, eyes darting to our left and right. It was empty now, but for how long?

"There you go again." He laughed. "Thinking you can tell me what to do and how to do it."

That was enough of that. I rushed him, swinging the bat toward his face and trying to catch him off guard. He stumbled backward fast enough to miss the blow, not expecting me to come charging at him.

Without saying a word, Anna tried to cut a wide circle to end up behind him. His eyes were wild as he watched us both, confidence draining by the second. He might've been a little rougher from his time spent surviving outside the camp, but inside he was still the same weak man as before. Slightly leaner from all the walking, but no calluses and only a hint of muscle. Put that up against two women who regularly trained in self-defense, frequently handled weapons, and killed zombies? Bad odds for him.

"You're gonna regret this," he snapped, pulling a gun from the satchel hanging at his side. Immediately, I dropped the arm holding the bat and froze. Was he unstable enough to use the gun? Maybe it didn't have bullets, maybe after all these years the mechanisms had stopped working and it wouldn't fire, but... it wasn't worth the risk. Anna must've had the same thought, because she quickly stopped inching toward him and lowered her hand.

"That's right," he hissed. "Now you be good and follow me down the block to meet up with the others. I'm sure you'll both be a hit."

I bit back an irritated outburst, everything in me screaming not to go with him. If we could just take care of him, we'd be able to get out of the area and take a different route, or even head back to the camp. I wasn't so stubborn that I'd insist on going to the bunker after exhausting myself. It killed me to admit it, but maybe the guys had made a good point. I was so foolishly convinced that I could handle anything outside the safety of the camp because I'd done it so long that I forgot that sometimes the most dangerous things of all were unpredictability and man and their greed.

While I was racing over my options, he was growing more impatient by the second, body periodically twitching. "Well? Get a fucking move on!" He gestured sideways with the gun, urging us to get going.

It was incredible how fast everything happened. One second, we were in some weird triangular face-off, and in the next, Anna was darting forward and slashing at him with her knife.

He jerked backward to try to avoid it but didn't quite succeed, as she caught the edge of his shoulder. He raised the hand holding the gun and pulled the trigger as she lunged again, determination written all over her face.

I watched in horror as she cried out, the bullet clipping her shoulder when she darted to the side. Colby's grin was triumphant, and he was momentarily pleased until we heard the first groan.

I ran through a list of curses in my head, angrier than I could've ever remembered being at his sheer recklessness. Who the hell fired a gun out in the open like that? It was like the time I got stuck in the supermarket all over again. I turned my attention to the zombie that came stumbling around the corner, faster than I'd ever seen one move. Then again, every time I saw one, people made as little noise as possible in order to not draw their attention. Meanwhile, Colby may as well have just rung the dinner bell.

His face grew ashen with fear, and he fired off a couple of shots as even more followed that first zombie to the area where we were standing. "Fucking reckless piece of shit," I muttered. I turned and grabbed Anna's uninjured arm, figuring that Colby was too occupied by the zombies to bother us at the moment. "You okay?"

She shook her head yes, rolling her shoulder back. "Stung like hell, but I'll be alright. It only clipped me. For someone so eager to use a gun, he sure has a shit aim."

The sound of Colby's panicked grunt drew my attention, as did the frenzied clicks of the trigger. Nothing happened. Either he was out of bullets, or it had jammed up somehow. Only three zombies lay sprawled out on the ground before us, though it felt like he'd fired way more than that. The gun fell to the ground with a clang, and he began to take slow steps backward.

Panic was the number one cause of fatal mistakes, so I frantically tried to filter out all my fear and terror to leave just determination. Sure, there was a bigger crowd than I'd dealt with before, but I could do this. I'd done it before, and I'd do it again.

The first zombie put on a burst of speed, grasping at the strap of Colby's bag when he tried to run in the other direction. I let him handle it himself, more concerned about the others that were congregating only feet away. I decided to go on the offensive, lunging forward and bashing at the head of one wearing a shirt that was mostly just strings at this point. Anna followed suit, slashing at one that was gnashing its teeth at her.

They. Just. Kept. Coming. There must've been at least fifteen, and the fear came creeping back in when I heard Anna cry out. One had managed to snag her arm, but she threw it off her with a huff and kicked it as hard as possible. Meanwhile, Colby was beating anything near him with a pipe he'd found nearby, probably because he knew there was no chance he'd be able to run away and not get chased. I was under no illusion that he was still here just to make sure we lived so he could bring us back with him.

I darted around one that was groaning at me, grimacing when I got up close and personal to its decaying, grayish face. It was too close to swing my bat, so I kneed it, cheering internally when it stumbled backward and then smacking it as hard as I could. I cringed as it rolled onto its side to grab my ankle, ripping at the dirtied hem of my pants, and smashed my foot into its skull, trying not to gag at the squelching noise as I pulled it back out. We were down to around five zombies now, practically swimming in gore up to our ankles, and the odds weren't looking so insurmountable anymore.

A whistle heralded the arrival of a few men, and I cursed myself for not getting us away from here sooner.

Colby turned to see who it was, and once he was distracted, one of the zombies closest to him took him down in a clumsy tackle, riding him down to the ground. It snapped its teeth in a frenzy, catching the exposed skin near his wrist and leaving behind a mess when it pulled back.

Anna gasped when she noticed, slowly backing away from him without taking her eye off the few left. His arm was clearly sporting a bite, and if we didn't take care of him soon, we'd have to deal with him next. I was loath to take my attention from the approaching men, but I needed to make sure the immediate threats were disposed of so that we didn't end up like Colby.

"Fancy seein' you here," a burly man commented casually, talking over the growling, sucking noises from the zombie as it ate Colby while he strode up in the lead. "Might've gotten here sooner but… well, we had to kill a few on the way here, and let's be honest, who wants to defend him when he's going around firing guns? Now if we'd known he had company…" He gestured at where Colby was beginning to froth at the mouth, one of the men behind him killing a zombie with one fell swoop of his ax. Was that an ax? I thought axes were bigger. Maybe it was a hatchet. Or were those the same thing? I should probably learn more about weapons before I made a fool out of myself.

Focus, I snapped at myself, tired and hungry, covered in dirt and gore. It was like I'd gone back in time to a couple months ago. I had to keep myself sharp, but it was easy for my mind to wander after a stressful event. Although the last zombies were being dispatched, I had to remember that these men were not my friends. I hadn't suddenly become safe. I was in the exact boat I'd found myself in before the carnage had started.

I let out a deep breath, trying desperately not to gag when the third man walked over to where Colby was writhing on the ground and slit his throat, then took off the head of the zombie munching on him. Who the hell can take a zombie head clean off like that? No sawing, chopping movements while it tries to bite you? Sure, it was mostly decayed but still... I shuddered.

"So," the man said, eyeing me appraisingly, his red hair and bushy beard practically a beacon in the sunlight. "I guess Colby found himself a little prize."

I held myself stiffly, looking around as discreetly as possible.

Anna was gone.

I ground my teeth, turning back to the men and planting my feet. Could she have left to get help? Possibly. Chances were she was just saving herself, though, because there was no way I'd still be in the same place whenever she got back. A tiny voice inside my head argued that she wasn't as evil as I was making her seem, but I ignored it. She'd been a bitch to me since day one, so why would I expect anything different now? Though as upset as I was to have been abandoned, I was still rooting for her to get somewhere safe.

The second man cleared his throat, probably because I still hadn't said a word. "Suppose Colby explained things before, well..." He inclined his head to Colby's rapidly cooling body. My eyes watered and I fought the urge to squeeze them closed and wash them out with water. The smell was unbearable, far from the scents of fresh food and grass back at camp.

"Sure," I said drily. "Poor little man got kicked out for being an ass, ran to you with information, even bigger asses, and wants to use me for currency. I got that right?"

The guy with unruly dark hair, so greasy that I don't even think he could get a comb through it, eyed the redhead.

It was a long second before anyone spoke.

"That's right, sweetheart. Not much of a loss that he's dead. We got all the information we were ever going to, and he was sure as hell whinier than any bitch I've ever met. Just good for doing chores and watching you lot." The men behind him laughed.

I felt a sharp ache for Grey upon hearing the pet name he was so fond of. "What makes you think I'll go easily?"

His eyes darkened. "Not much of a choice, is there? Either you come with us quietly, or we tie you up and let the zombies get you. Maybe carve a few designs in you to get 'em really rabid. I think you'd agree that it would be a real waste of a pretty girl like yourself."

The parallels between what happened with Merikh, Caelan, and Nix and these men right here struck me like lightning. There had been vague threats of me getting eaten if I ran, but none of the disturbing joy at the thought of causing me harm like there was radiating from these men. There had been no sexual references, no creepy leering; it had been all business. Completely different from what I was facing right now, and I was a fool to have ever thought they were the same.

"Alright," I said slowly. Without thinking twice, I raised the bat and swung wildly, my entire body twisting with the motion. For all that he was built like a rock, the man moved like liquid. He darted back, chuckling softly before wrenching the bat from my hands. My callouses scraped painfully against the handle as it left my grip, and my muscles protested the strain I felt while trying to cling to the very end.

I lost my footing when he jerked it backward, crying out when the thud of something wooden crashed into my head and sent me sprawling. My vision went black and then...

Nothing.

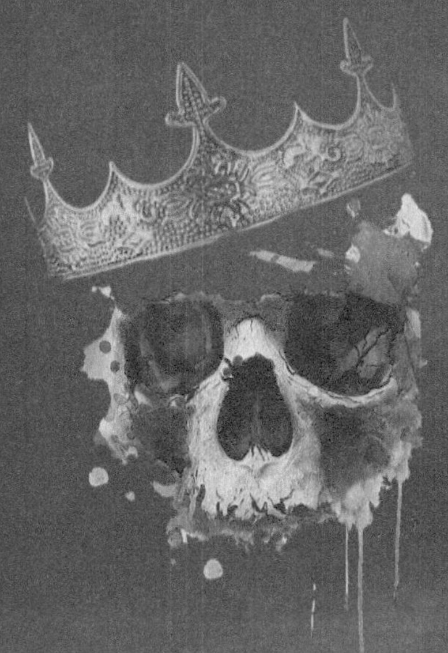

CHAPTER 27

I woke in stages. My mouth was painfully dry and the sunlight creeping in behind my closed eyelids made my head spin. My body felt heavy and tired, and I was lying across what felt like concrete, as if I were a discarded sack of grain.

Murmured voices had me squinting my eyes open as little as possible, trying to get a good look at my surroundings without signaling that I was awake. I let out a slow breath when I realized no one's eyes were on me and allowed myself to look a little more freely. My memories came back to me in droves, accompanied by the constant throb of what felt like my brain shoving up against the confines of my skull in protest. Something stung on my arms, and a quick inventory of my body had me realizing that my wrists were bound together with some kind of thick and frayed rope.

The three men from earlier were standing around and talking quietly, halfway across the room and almost around the corner. I wasn't even sure they could see me from where they were standing. We were in a dilapidated building, graffiti and dirt covering almost every surface. There was a hallway across from me, and the ceilings were tall and vaulted, but other than that, the room was empty. Sunlight shone in from some crumbling holes in the ceiling, one particularly strong beam hitting me right in the face when I moved. I groaned quietly, turning my head as slowly as possible to escape the brightness.

Although what I found next to me had me seconds away from shrieking and breaking my silence. "What the hell, Anna?" I whispered urgently, surprised to find her lying on her back beside me.

"So nice of you to join us, sleeping beauty," she hissed.

"I got hit in the goddamn head, of course I was going to be knocked out," I argued with a roll of my eyes. Same old Anna. I didn't know why I'd expected anything different.

She huffed quietly, eyes moving to where the men had left the intersection between the two rooms to occupy the second. "I know," she said finally. "I'm just..."

She didn't say scared, but she didn't have to. There was a large bruise on her cheekbone, and her long blonde hair was tangled and greasy from dirt and sweat. I felt an acute pang of disappointment that she hadn't managed to make it to safety after all.

"Where are we?" I whispered.

She shrugged as best she could with her good shoulder. "We walked for a good couple of hours. We weren't tied up until they found this place and decided to rest for a bit. Before that, they took turns carrying you in pairs and sometimes dragging you on some kind of tarp whenever we were in a field or something. There were a surprisingly small number of zombies, but that tall lumberjack-looking motherfucker killed 'em whenever they got too close."

Lovely. No wonder my body felt like one big bruise. Another glance at the ceiling revealed the sunlight overhead to be a burnt orange, signaling the sunset that had been hours away when we'd first left camp. "I thought you'd gotten away," I admitted, wincing when I rolled more fully onto my side.

She was quiet for a long moment, worrying her bottom lip with her teeth. "I was watching, trying to think of a way to help, but there was no way I could've taken them all on, not after they hit you. Then I thought if I was able to make it back to camp..."

"I understand." And I did. It was hypocritical of me to have expected her to put her own life at risk to save me when the odds were better that she grab help elsewhere. It's not as if she'd planned to abandon me and go back pretending I got eaten by zombies or something. Maybe there was a heart deep down in there somewhere.

"I tripped on a broken piece of concrete and fell onto a discarded lawnmower," she huffed. Sure enough, a quick glance at her knees revealed a variety of scrapes and bruises. "So I scraped out a quick SOS in the dirt and tossed your hair tie on top of it–sorry–and then ran in a different direction so they wouldn't find it, because at that point they were practically right behind me."

"That was smart thinking. If they find that, along with the X's we carved on the way there, maybe we're not doomed after all. Assuming that they know we got snatched up by the very same group whose base they found on this past trip."

We sat in uncomfortable silence for a long chunk of time before I spoke again. "Do you know what they want with us?"

She shook her head, eyes growing dark when a voice rang out across the hollow space. "Glad to see you're finally awake," the man with red hair commented as he nodded at me. "Now we don't have to carry your heavy ass all the way back to our base."

Ex-fucking-scuse me? The man was at least three times my size, surprisingly built for someone living in what was supposedly a huge metal and concrete box in the middle of a zombie apocalypse, and he was complaining about *my* deadweight? He was the reason I was unconscious to begin with!

"I'm so sorry to have inconvenienced you," I said sarcastically. Feeling oddly vulnerable lying on the floor like I was, I ignored my blossoming headache and worked myself into a sitting position against the wall at my back, using my elbows. Anna maneuvered with me so we didn't yank on each other's arms where they were tied together.

His eyes narrowed. "Don't get smart with me, lass." I heard a murmur around the corner and muffled laughter. "We'll be there in an hour or so. No bitching unless you wanna be gagged. We leave in ten." With that, he left.

"Could be worse," she muttered weakly.

I rolled my head to the side to eye her incredulously. "If you say so."

So much for my fucking "heroic" plan.

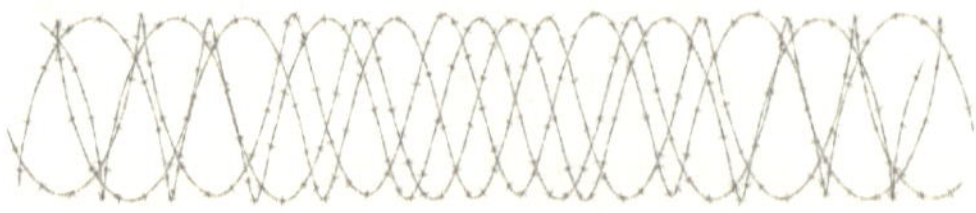

We reached their base just as the sun set for the night. It was exactly as Merikh and Caelan had described, except for the zombies they'd spotted around the fence line. We were facing a couple of large warehouses, and behind us were nothing but empty fields. A few torn-up parking lots sat to our right. Now that I knew we were in the same place the guys had spotted, the only question was if they would know we were here and how long it would take them to figure it out.

"Come on, then," the dark-haired man urged, pulling me by my elbow and tsking when I stumbled. Anna followed behind me, no longer tied to me by the wrist. We made our way down the gradual incline and navigated through all the fencing to end up right at their front door. This was just perfect, the exact thing that the guys had been worried about and I'd delivered myself on a silver platter, and not only that, I'd dragged Anna down with me.

One of them knocked an odd rhythm on the set of heavy doors until we heard the sound of a bolt unlocking before they were yanked open, and we were ushered into the large space.

I took advantage of the fact that we were momentarily standing still and looked my fill of the place. It was much darker than outside, due to the lack of windows. The only light came from the narrow windows near the ceilings and the candles decorating the shelving units against the walls of the warehouse. There were multiple doors to the right and at the back was a door that must've led to a room or hallway. It was just as messy as I'd predicted on the way here, huge boxes filled with paper and trash that I suspected they didn't care enough to haul outside or into another building.

Multiple men were ambling around the space, some were even playing cards in the corner. They had fewer numbers than we'd assumed, clearly having experienced the joys of natural selection, or maybe they were just so shitty that everyone steered clear and they were never able to replenish the few they lost.

Anna made a small noise, and I stopped short when I followed her line of sight and realized what was sitting in the center of the room.

Women.

They weren't gagged, sobbing, or bleeding like I would've expected. They were largely silent, watching us with surprise and maybe a little suspicion.

The girl in the middle caught my eye first. She was wearing a long lilac-colored dress, and her dark, unruly curls were tied back in a tight ponytail. She somehow seemed different from the others, more self-assured and confident. The other three were in a sloppy huddle, making quiet conversation as they kept a wary eye on us. What the actual fuck was going on here? To see up close, the worst-case scenario that had been preached to me day in and day out by my father... It was like diving into icy water and having my senses shocked.

"Come on," a new man said gruffly, shoving a hand into the middle of my back to get me moving. I hadn't even noticed him coming up behind me. Anna grumbled a curse, clearly displeased with all the shoving.

The smell was unbearable. Clearly, they didn't have access to enough water to shower with and it showed. It was throwing me back into my past, when I'd go weeks without finding a safe enough area to bathe, falling asleep every night trying not to cry about how dirty I felt and the sheer gratitude when my dad had found a tucked away stream or a home with a working well.

God, I was so privileged to have been so angry about being at their camp. Naïve, selfish, childish. I rubbed my hands over my face. I hadn't understood how good they had it. Sure, I'd heard stories about these kinds of groups and how they operated, but it was one thing to hear whispers and another to see it up close in all its glory.

"Take 'em to Gunner," the new man commanded. He was older than the others, skinny as a rail with a beard down to his chest. I ignored his ogling and marched along after the red-haired man we'd come with. The other two broke away, greeting their friends and casting the odd glance in our direction and they filled them in while we were marched to one of the doors along the right wall, right in the middle. He knocked several times, waiting patiently until someone grunted for us to come in, then swung the door open.

The room was fairly small. A medium-sized window lay against the wall opposite us, and a desk took up nearly the entire room. The floor was covered in trash, and an odd smell filled the space. My eyes landed on the man sitting in the office chair. Large, grizzled, intimidating. His long, scraggly beard hit his stomach, and when he smiled, his teeth were yellowed, missing, and chipped from what looked like years of poor dental hygiene. Even when I'd had only a cupful of water left, I used a minuscule amount to brush the toothpaste off my teeth after leaving it overnight. This man looked like he hadn't touched a toothbrush in twenty years.

"Fresh meat?" he asked with a leer, eyes scanning their way down my body.

I resisted the urge to shudder, clenching my fists tight so that my nails dug sharp divots into my palms. Anna made an indignant noise and received a pinch to the arm from the man behind us.

The man—Gunner, I supposed, if the guy outside was to be believed—crossed his arms over his large belly and leaned back in his chair, content to watch us. Back at camp, everyone was filled out, the result of years' worth of steady meals and having enough for seconds. But out here in the wild, it was uncommon to find anyone eating well. To see this man comfortably fed when his men and the girls outside were underweight and hollowed out was a good indicator of what kind of leader he was. Selfish, greedy, self-serving.

"Nah. Found these two with Colby. Guess he knew 'em from the camp. Whiny fuck fired his gun and drew a horde. He's dead."

"Good riddance. We had no more use for him anymore anyway. Got all the information we need." I kept my mouth shut as he watched us. "He wanted revenge, y'know," he said casually. "It only took two seconds for him to throw your entire camp under the bus just for a taste of it."

That didn't surprise me one bit.

"They'll come for us," Anna threatened. I had the simultaneous urge to both cry and scream. Didn't she know not to antagonize them? Why engage them in conversation and give them more ammo against us?

Gunner narrowed his eyes. "And who would that be? Don't see how they'll know where to find you, even if they did want to waste their time rescuing you."

Anna rolled her eyes, popping a hip. Damn, she was nothing if not bold even in the worst of times. I wished I had half her defiance because I was maybe, slightly spiraling just a little. I had to cut myself some slack, all my worst nightmares were coming true. Well, some of them, at least, since I'd yet to be gnawed on by a zombie... so that was something.

"The guys who run the camp. If not for me, then for her." She gestured a hand in my direction, wrist looking chafed and reddened by the rope they'd had on her hours ago. For once, she sounded oddly unbothered about the fact that I'd gotten involved with the guys. I supposed she very well couldn't be if it was currently working in her favor.

I ground my teeth, close to telling her to shut the hell up before she told them something important. The man who was hovering at our sides glanced at Gunner, a look passing between them that I had no idea how to decipher.

"So," Gunner grumbled, almost to himself. "Finally got a girl, huh? Bagged all of 'em too. Must have one hell of a pussy," he commented, looking my way.

I recoiled in disgust, bile rising in the back of my throat at what he was implying.

"Calm yourself," he snapped. "Got no energy for disrespectful whores like yourself."

That was something, at least. Although it didn't escape my notice that he'd said nothing regarding his men. Anna turned a sickly pale color, seeming to realize that she'd slipped up in her attempt to get us set free. Something about that fact had interested them, and I wasn't so sure that was a good thing.

"Put her in the spare room," he ordered the redhead, nodding in my direction.

"And the blonde?"

"Put her out with the rest. She'll make a nice addition to their group."

Anna started cursing under her breath as the men grabbed her, escorting her out and expecting me to follow.

Gunner warned my back as I left the room. "I'll see you soon, girl."

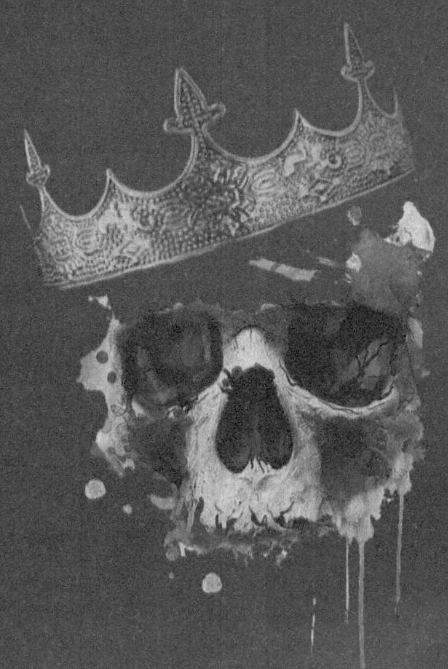

CHAPTER 28

I'd been in this small room for what felt like forever, although it was only the next day. It was an average room, in surprisingly better shape than half the places I'd stayed, probably due to the industrial aspects. It was just me, the concrete walls, dirty floors, and an off-putting musty smell. Fortunately, it was absent of the clutter and trash covering the floor in the main room. I could hear voices coming from outside, girlish tones that rose and fell accompanied by what sounded like giggling, and non-stop shouting or raucous laughter from the men.

I'd had to pee in a bucket, and much to my mortification, I'd made eye contact with the woman who was sent to collect it. Fortunately, I'd had nothing to eat or drink since before Anna and I left camp, so although I was starving, I had no sudden urge to go again.

The bright midday sun shining through the tiny window told me it was around noon. I'd spent the night curled up on the cold floor and berating myself for being so foolish. I missed the comfort of the cabin, missed Caelan tossing and turning in his sleep, trying to take up as much space as possible and everyone else grumbling at him for it. There was a keen ache in my heart when I thought of my guys, and if I made it out of this alive, I'd have no problem admitting that they were right.

I bolted upright when the door opened with no warning, hastily composing my facial expression. I'd never make it out of here if I wore my despair and regret on my sleeve. I needed to bottle it up to get through this. I could always sort through my emotions when I was back somewhere safe.

The man who entered was the opposite of whatever I'd been expecting. He must've been in another room when I was paraded through last night; I would have noticed him otherwise. Tall, dark, and expressionless, he was handsomer than he had any right to be. Goddamnit, why do the murderous assholes get all the good looks?

He looked to be around Caelan's age, maybe a little older, and I was surprised this group had any younger blood. His dark brown hair was overgrown and clinging to his neck where it curled slightly and his eyes were just as dark, a rich brown so deep they looked black. If I'd thought they would show some measure of disgust or disapproval at opening the door to find a starving person sitting on the floor, I would've been wrong.

I watched as he reached into his pocket, salivating when he pulled out a battered protein bar and tossed it in my direction. Seconds later, he pulled a clear plastic bottle from his other pocket. The water inside was a cloudy color, and I stared at it with suspicion.

"It's from a communal supply, boiled rainwater." Sounded plausible enough, and to be honest, I was too thirsty to care. I was banking on the fact that it would make no sense to drug me. I chugged it in seconds, sighing deeply at the full feeling in my belly and the way my throat instantly felt less parched. "We try to scrounge up warm meals now and then," he informed me, his voice deeper than I'd predicted. "If we do one tonight, I'll be sure to bring you a bowl."

"Why?" The question left my lips before I could stop myself. Why the hell would I ask him that? What if he rescinded the offer, and I was stuck eating a bug or something equally horrid just to avoid starving?

His mouth tipped up on one side like he could read my thoughts, but he didn't answer. Instead, he took a few more steps into the room and slid both hands into the pockets of his pants. "You have something they want," he drawled, looking out the window at the miles of concrete and wasteland.

They? Not we? I filed that away for future reference, setting my back to the wall and crossing my arms over my chest as I watched him, worried over his potential response. "And what would that be?"

He sighed as he turned to face me. "Leverage."

Leverage?

"I'm going to tell you a story, and I'm hoping that in doing so, you'll have a better understanding of why you are here."

I took a steady breath of the stale, musty air and let it out slowly. "Alright." A loud laugh from outside the door drew my attention until he began speaking.

"We've been nomadic for years. We scout for safe buildings that meet our needs, clear them out, and stay as long as possible."

I was following so far, but what did this have to do with me?

When he continued, his voice was surprisingly monotone. "We lost a good chunk of members last winter after an incident with an unsecured building. A few months later is when we heard about your camp." It slowly dawned on me where he was going with this. "We had no way of knowing how many people inside were armed, or what kinds of resources you had. But the scavengers we spotted looked well-fed and happy enough." His expression grew troubled, and it appeared like he almost had to force his next words out. "My... father. He was tired of starting over, never really *living*. He got greedy, and selfish." He huffed a bitter laugh. "He's always been greedy and selfish. But all that loss... I suppose it does something to a person. He's not the same man he was years ago. Anyway, he wanted it for his own. The camp. His men were starting to act out, everyone was starving, and he was steadily losing control. So he told his men to watch from afar, seeing who came and went, how often, and where."

It clicked that he was referring to Gunner. I really hoped the adage like father like son didn't apply here. I could use any semblance of an ally, and if this guy was willing to spill so much information *and* had pull within the group, he would be a good one. I didn't dare interrupt for fear he'd stop talking altogether, but I wanted to ask just what the point of letting the zombies into our camp was if they wanted to take it over so badly.

"Eventually, your leader left. Mark." My stomach soured. "Gunner was getting tired of watching and waiting. We were ordered to ambush him at one of the nearby homes, and he was presented with an ultimatum. Provide us with food, resources, and weapons, and we would keep our distance. We were in no position to mount any kind of takeover, not once we learned how many you all have behind those walls, but he didn't know that. Trained or not, we would have been massacred, and our numbers were already low. He got us whatever he could, smuggled it out whenever he got a chance, and left it at a drop point. It worked fine for several months until Gunner started demanding more. More resources, more meat, more, more, more."

His voice grew raspy, like he wasn't accustomed to speaking for so long. He cleared his throat, taking a few moments to just breathe.

"We've been running low on certain things," I murmured.

He nodded. "I'm not surprised. We—they—increased the demand until Mark just couldn't meet it anymore. He came to us over a month ago, confessing that the camp was starting to run suspiciously low in certain things, that we needed to lay off or we'd get nothing. He stayed with us while we negotiated but, unfortunately for him, we met Colby a few days later. My—Gunner—thought it was divine intervention. Mark is giving us trouble, he was growing impatient and irrational, and here comes this angry fount of information who's all too eager to share every bit he can about the camp and its residents and the best part is that the only thing he wanted in return was revenge. With actual information on the inner workings of the camp, maybe taking over wasn't so far-fetched after all."

It finally hit me what he was saying. "You killed Mark. You no longer needed him." Yeah, by all accounts, the guy was a complete bastard, and the triplets probably wouldn't care, but a loss was still a loss. I supposed it was good that they'd have a definitive answer instead of wondering what had happened to him forever.

"Yes," he said quietly. "They killed him. With all this new information from Colby, there was no need to stay in the shadows, waiting for scraps. We had a list of weak spots, guard changes, weapons supply, a rough headcount; everything we could need to go on the offensive. They started by weakening you slowly, driving up paranoia and mounting small attacks, like what happened with the zombies."

I wanted to be furious. I wanted to be so mind-numbingly angry with their entitlement, and their greed, but I felt surprisingly empty. Despite the fact that this man kept switching between *we* and *they*, I got the sense that he wasn't completely aligned with their motives at all. There was a faint note of disgust when he spoke of his father and his men's actions, and I had no energy to hate someone who was just as much of a pawn as I was. "That was quite a plan," I said tonelessly.

His flinch was subtle, but there. "I hope... there were minimal casualties."

I could've refused to tell him. I could've lied and said there were many deaths or told him about how little Khira had gotten stuck outside and was most definitely traumatized, but I didn't. "No one was seriously hurt."

He let out an almost inaudible breath of relief.

"What does this have to do with me and why I'm in here while my friend is out there?"

He rubbed the furrow between his brows, cold mask slipping incrementally. Regret, frustration, exhaustion, and sadness all flashed across his face before he straightened and his face was blank once more.

"Gunner knows all about Mark's sons. He knows that they would run the camp in his absence. So upon hearing that you're their girl?"

Horror filled me when I understood what he was alluding to. "You don't need to take it over by force anymore if you have a bargaining chip."

"Exactly. Why waste time and possibly lives when he has the next best thing in his possession? Given the way Mark spoke about them, we knew they might not care if we used him as leverage, but you? Well..."

"I don't understand what the hell he plans on doing with everyone already in the camp. They're the ones who know how to run things smoothly, who perfected the meals and the garden and the upkeep. Surely Gunner knows they wouldn't just sit back and allow you all to trample over everything after what you've done?"

He tapped his fingers against his thigh in a repeating pattern that I could see from the outside of his pocket. "No. He would keep the women and children, because he's so *magnanimous*, and the men would either be forced out or allowed to stay on a trial basis, given that they listen well and do as they're told."

I thought of Caelan, Nix, Merikh, and Grey. Jake, Hasan, Harry, and Thomas. Dozens more, being evicted from *their* home, what was sure to be a death sentence. My anger returned.

"Just what gives you the right?" I hissed.

He met my eyes, his own cold and dead, leached of any emotion; and didn't respond.

"Of course." I laughed bitterly. "Daddy dearest commands it and you just go along, right?"

A muscle jumped in his jaw. "It's not that simple," he muttered, looking at the door.

I decided to de-escalate, hoping I didn't scare him off. "I don't even know your name."

"Ryder."

"River."

He nodded. "River. Okay. I'll be back later with more water and something to eat. In the meantime, don't make any noise or draw attention to yourself."

Before he opened the door to leave, I called out his name. "The girl I was brought in with, Anna, is she okay?"

Ryder hesitated for a short moment, then nodded. The second he slipped out the door, and it shut behind him, I sank to the floor and rested my head in my hands, resisting the urge to wallow in my self-loathing and pity. *What the hell have I gotten myself into?*

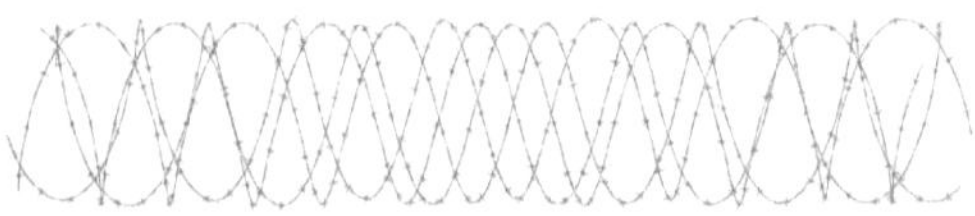

I spent the entire afternoon plotting and scheming, frantically trying to think of a way to keep my guys safe when they came for me. Because they would. I knew they would.

I hadn't made any progress.

I didn't know who they would send, and I wasn't thinking clearly enough to draft a situation for each pairing. I didn't dare think all four of them would come. If they did, who would watch the camp? Who would lead if something went wrong?

The sound of voices right outside my door had me jumping to my feet. My stomach rumbled, anticipating Ryder's visit. I drew backward when a man that was clearly not Ryder but who I faintly recognized entered the room.

"A little birdie told me that we had a guest," he said with a leer.

I scoffed, feeling oddly vulnerable in my dirty, torn clothes. Miles away from the girl who'd argued with Merikh over every little thing, prancing around in her new outfits.

"Aw, don't be like that. We could have a lot of fun if you just tried."

He looked the exact same as he had when I'd spotted him beneath the tree where I was hiding with Sakhira, though up close there were a few more teeth missing than I'd remembered.

"Get out." I was out of patience: tired, hungry, stressed, and angry, and this waste of space was what... propositioning me?

His grin was lopsided. "I don't think I will." He took a step forward for every step I took back until he was close enough that I could smell the sweat coating his body. I was startled when his hand shot forward and grabbed my jaw, hard enough to leave bruises. "Now, I don't know where you get off telling me to get out, but we're gonna have a good time together, you and me."

I pursed my lips as best I could in his crushing grip, and spit on him.

He stood still for a short moment, chuckling quietly and then pulling his hand back to slap me across the face. Hard. The shock of it pulled a cry from me and I stumbled back a step, clutching my cheek and mouth where the blow had landed.

"That wasn't very nice. Maybe I should teach you some manners while I'm at it?"

My face scrunched up in disgust as he backed me up against the wall, grabbing my wrist and twisting.

"Get the hell off me," I hissed through gritted teeth.

When he twisted harder, I brought my knee up and jammed it right into his crotch. He immediately grabbed himself, howling loudly as he spat curse after curse. The door flew open and Ryder entered, his face stormy as he took in the situation.

"What the hell were you told about bothering her?" he asked coldly, his voice somehow more intimidating covered in ice than it would've been if he'd yelled.

The man sputtered apologies, even as Ryder grabbed him by his collar and practically tossed him out on his ass.

Voices rose when he landed outside, mostly laughter and taunts.

Ryder looked me over for a moment. "I'm going to be right back," he said, stone-faced, and left.

It was several long minutes later before he returned, this time with someone in tow. It was the same woman I'd seen when I first arrived, wearing the lilac dress. She inhaled sharply when she saw me. "Oh, dear. It looks like you're bleeding a little." Her voice was low, and soothing. She took a few hesitant steps my way, bringing her hand up slowly enough that I had time to view the dampened rag she was clutching. She brought it to my lip, dabbing lightly. Up close I could see her eyes clearly, light gray with flecks of blue closer to her pupil, and it was easier to see that she was around my age.

"There," she murmured, dabbing once more, but this time with a dry corner. "It's probably going to bruise," she informed me with a sympathetic look.

Ryder's eyes had softened as he watched her tend to me, but they grew hard when he realized I was looking.

"I'm sorry he bothered you. I was in another room and didn't notice him enter, although Seraphim here did. He will be suitably punished."

He didn't owe me anything, so I was surprised to hear that he would punish him on my behalf. I pushed back at the burgeoning hope in my chest that I would be able to rely on his support if it came down to it. Did I trust him?

Seraphim smiled softly, like she could guess where my thoughts were taking me. "I go by Sera, by the way. He's a good man," she whispered under her breath before stepping away and speaking at a normal volume. "We're making chili tonight. Perhaps you can come out and have a bowl, meet some of the others." She looked to Ryder for confirmation, beaming when he nodded in agreement. His gaze was pained as he watched her leave. He couldn't be all that bad if he was capable of having a soft spot for her, could he?

"I'll come get you later. It's probably best if you stay here for the next few hours until everyone settles down."

I nodded, this time not waiting until he left to slide down to the dirty floor, using the wall at my back.

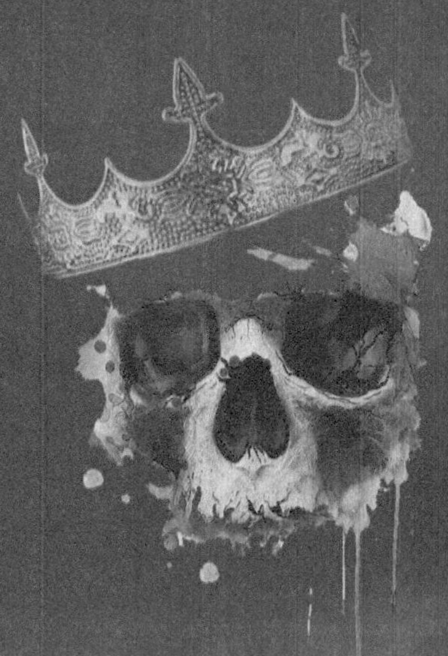

CHAPTER 29

I looked around at the room I'd only had a quick glance at before I'd been sequestered. In the moonlight shining through the windows up high, it looked a little more intimidating. Most of the men were in the far corner playing a card game on a foldable table, and no one batted an eye at me leaving my confinement. Fortunately, the man from earlier wasn't there, maybe in the back or outside.

A sharp laugh drew my attention, and I gasped quietly when my eyes landed on Anna. The side of her face was one big, colorful bruise. I veered away from Sera, who'd come to fetch me, and rushed over, dropping to my knees in front of her. "Anna, what the hell happened?" My hand hovered over the bruising on her arm, and after several seconds, I noticed the deepened rope marks on her wrists.

"Don't worry about it," she said casually. "Apparently they like their women a little less mouthy, and I had no intention of making things easier on them."

"For fuck's sake," I murmured under my breath, swamped with guilt over the fact that I'd been safe in that room all day and she'd been out here surrounded by the same men who took us.

She caught my hand, looking decidedly un-Anna-like for a moment. "I promise it's okay. Besides, it took the attention off them for a little." Only when she cocked her head toward the other women did I realize that they were staring at us.

"Hi," I said weakly, receiving a few nods in return. Sera sat back down, bringing their count up to four, not including Anna or me.

"Heidi's been with them for a couple of years," Anna whispered. The oldest woman here, maybe in her early thirties, raised her hand shyly. It was hard to gauge a person's age just from their appearance since everyone matured deceptively fast in times like these, but I was pretty certain I'd guessed correctly. "The rest, maybe a few months to a year."

"Anna's been telling us about your camp," a young woman with dark brown skin informed me with a wistful smile. "It sounds too good to be true, if you don't mind me saying."

"It's all true," I murmured, heart aching. "I wouldn't have believed it either. It took weeks for me to adjust."

The girl with tangled, curly red hair eyed me skeptically. "Nadira's right. I bet they eat people or something equally horrible. If it's so safe, how did you all end in someplace like this? You get sent here as payment or something?"

Anna snorted, and I sighed sheepishly, explaining all the rash decisions that had led us here. When I was finished, they all looked at me like I was dreaming. Which, yeah, fair.

"Soo, you left... your safe camp... for a bunker?" she asked, frowning in confusion. Her question wasn't malicious; she looked genuinely stunned.

I shrugged off my defensiveness and answered honestly. "I've been living outside the safety of their walls my entire life, either by myself or with my dad. And they were desperately low on food. I thought... of anyone there, I had the skills and the experience to contribute. Plus, I'm the only one who knows where I last saw the bunker...." I sighed. "It sounds foolish looking back on it, but I really thought I was helping, not just making more work for everyone."

Heidi smiled softly, only twitching a little when one of the men cursed loudly from across the room at what must've been a losing hand. "I don't think it's all on you. Your men could have set you up for success, made sure you had all the resources you needed and their support instead of just warning you off going. Seems like they must not know you very well if they thought that would work," she said with a teasing glint in her eye.

Anna cackled at that, drawing the attention of one of the men who had just entered the space from the door at the back. He grinned as he approached us, stinking of cigarettes. "Suppose I should pick myself a lovely lady for tonight," he announced.

My eyes widened, and Anna spat on his feet when he reached us.

He kicked her without warning, sending her sprawling into my lap. Sera jumped up when he drew back to do it again, laying a calming hand on his arm. "Now, now, Charlie," she soothed. "What good is she if you mess her all up? Don't waste your time on her."

Anna made an angry noise, and I fought to get her upright so that I could stand. The man grinned, his bloodshot eyes looking Sera over with renewed interest. "Don't mind if I do."

He grabbed her wrist, and I was seconds away from intervening, consequences or not. There was no way she was going to sleep with that creep while I was here.

I took a step forward when a deep voice filled the room, sending us into an icy silence. "Get your fucking hands off her," Ryder warned from where he'd just exited the same door that the man had come from.

Charlie dropped her wrist, chuckling nervously. "Come on now, I know she's your favorite, but..."

He didn't finish his sentence, but it was clear what he was alluding to. Sera stepped back to stand beside me while Ryder crossed the room to confront Charlie.

He slid his hands into his pockets, calm as can be. It was telling. No sane person trapped their hands when they might need to use them to defend themselves. "I don't believe I asked your opinion," he said calmly, the complete opposite of before. All his anger has turned into a frosty, bored tone. "She's off limits. Always has been. So whatever the fuck you thought you were doing here? I'd think twice before you get sent out as bait."

Charlie gulped nervously, not daring to look back in our direction before he scurried over to the card table where the men were all watching the spectacle.

Ryder's eyes met Sera's for a long moment before he scanned her to make sure she was okay and turned on his heel to head to his dad's office.

"Holy shit," I whispered as I crouched next to Anna. "What the hell was that?"

Heidi giggled. "We think he's soft on her. He claimed her almost as soon as she showed up."

Sera scoffed, covering her smile with her hand. "He's just possessive. He doesn't... feel things. Like that."

I'd beg to differ. If anything, I'd bet he was like Merikh, desperate to feel in control, to keep his composure.

"So they just... pick you here? And you... they..."

Nadira pursed her lips thoughtfully. "I know this isn't going to make sense to you, fancy camp and all, but it's better than starving and dying. We get meals, albeit irregularly, and we get a safe place to sleep."

I swallowed down the bile that rose thinking about how easily this could've been me. Would I have turned to a place like this if I had been unable to find food or shelter? I had no way to know, and it would be unfair of me to insist I wouldn't; I had never been in their place. Even when I was starving, I still had rations here and there. I knew the area;

I was good at avoiding the undead. Some people don't have that luxury. "I thought…" I trailed off, unsure of how to word it. I certainly hadn't thought they were willing participants.

"It's not all that bad," the redhead insisted. "Really. I know what you're thinking, but… they don't treat us poorly. We're not here against our will."

I worried my bottom lip. "Come with us," I blurted. Rushing to clear the skepticism on their faces, I elaborated. "I promise there's room, and you'd be welcomed with open arms. Simple chores, nothing to do with… well. You wouldn't be obligated to sleep with anyone if you wanted to stay."

Heidi's face lit up, and the others looked pensive. "Come on, Jamie." Heidi elbowed the girl next to her gently. "You always say that we're gonna find something better. This is our big chance."

Jamie frowned, tucking an errant red curl behind her ear and sighing when it sprung free seconds later. "You're sure? They don't… fry people up when they get desperate? Or tie people to stakes or anything?"

Anna laughed quietly. "I promise you, they don't." She looked at me awkwardly. "Maybe sometimes people can be a bit… bitchy," she rushed to say, "and maybe those people were worried that without someone strong or powerful looking after them that if worse came to worst, they'd be fucked… and it's possible they realized that you're not so bad after all and they're capable of more than they thought."

I hid my smile. I was pretty sure everyone caught on to what she was saying. "It takes a brave person to follow a stranger into the middle of nowhere. Pretty sure you're forgiven. Besides, it gave me character. My first bully? Bring it on."

Jamie broke out into giggles, laughing quietly until everyone quietly joined in.

"Honestly," Anna continued. "I've lived there for years, and everyone has been nothing but nice and helpful. It's a real community, and every-one works to keep things safe and prosperous."

"I'll go," Nadira declared, punctuating her words with a firm nod.

Jamie nodded in agreement, but Sera... She looked torn. If Ryder was as sweet on her as I suspected, then she'd have a hell of a time leaving him behind. It was clear he looked out for her.

"About that," I whispered. "I just might have a plan."

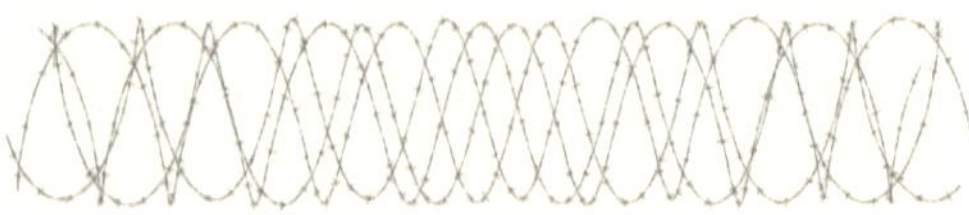

I tossed and turned, cursing the cold concrete floor. It was freezing in here and my bones were aching. I'd given up on trying to sleep after several hours of trying, instead lying awake to focus on the plan.

I'd thought over it the entire past three days, and decided I couldn't just wait for the guys to come to our rescue. Besides, if I was capable enough to strike out for the bunker on my own, I was capable enough to break out of here alone too. Except I wasn't really alone anymore, was I? I had Anna, and now the other women too. There was a slight possibility I could count on Ryder as an ally, but I wasn't sure where he stood yet. If he cared about Sera so much, why were they still here, separated under his asshole father? Why did he spend day in and day out planning shit to do with our camp and talking with those bastards outside like they weren't terrible people? No, I'd reserve my judgment for later. Assumptions might just get us all killed.

I held my breath, listening intently for any noise outside the door. If everything had gone according to plan, the men would be knocked out right now. It was all up to chance, and that was what worried me. If the prescription sleeping pills that Jamie's mother had given her before she passed still retained their potency, the men would be fast asleep by now. That was assuming she'd even gotten a chance to put them in the water. It was frustrating that I had no idea what was going on outside this concrete box, but at least Jamie had quickly turned my haphazard plan into something viable with the medicine she'd tucked away in the hidden pocket on the inside of her shirt. I shuddered to think of her needing to use it for the reason her mother intended when she first gifted it to her. Hopefully, once she was safely behind the walls of the camp, she wouldn't have to think about how long she'd lived with that ever-present possibility so close to her chest.

A soft tapping noise drew my attention, and I pushed myself to my feet, swearing I'd have a good few days of straight sleep and relaxation once I was home.

Home.

When had it become home to me? When I made my first real friends? Had consistent warm meals? Fell in love? I wasn't sure, but it felt good. The feeling flowed through me like a warm tonic, healing all the parts of me that had gotten bruised growing up with only my father to rely on and the barest hint of living another day.

A sharp scraping noise on the door drew me out of my thoughts. "Got it!" Heidi hissed triumphantly as she pulled the door open, the padlock dangling loosely from her fingers.

"How the hell did you manage that?" I asked, mouth gaping. "I thought we were going to have to break it?"

"I managed to get the keys off Joey. He's so knocked out, he didn't feel a thing."

I pressed my lips together, shaking off my nerves. We could do this. Everything was going to be fine. I slipped out of the room, following Heidi, and met the other girls in the far corner. The sound of snores filled the room, all at varying volumes. Most of the men slept in the back, what was apparently some kind of conference room, but a good few remained in here.

"We're not sure if Gunner had any of the water," Nadira told me, twisting her hands nervously. Her dark brown eyes were wide with concern. "He filled up his mug and took it back to his office, but we haven't heard a sound in hours."

I spent a long moment rushing over different possibilities and outcomes, thinking about how this could affect the plan and trying to account for it. "Okay," I whispered urgently. "We proceed as planned.

You guys go first. I'll grab the chain I saw near the entrance and tie it as best I can to jam the main doors and then follow."

Everyone's eyes glowed wildly in the flickering candlelight, looking more energetic than they had in days. We were all jittery from adrenaline and fatigued by the pitiful rations of food, and it made for a bizarre combination.

"Sera...." I hesitated. "Is—ah, Ryder joining us?"

Her face was set like stone, impassive and cool. "No," she said quietly, and that was that.

I nodded once, turning to face everyone. "Remember, quietly, so we don't draw any of the undead. We can meet at the outpost down the road."

I received several determined nods in return and a bit of hesitancy from Anna. She worried her lower lip, leaning in close to whisper, "Are you sure I shouldn't stay and help?"

"I'm sure. Even if the others might be able to leave, there's no way you or I are getting out of here *and* taking their women when they're all awake without a fight. Someone has to lead, and someone has to make sure they can't easily follow. Who better than the same person who followed me out into a wasteland and walked this whole distance while I was half-unconscious just days ago?"

Her smile was tremulous, and I watched as she stood a little taller. "We'll meet you there, then."

She ushered the women into a small group, each carrying the little belongings that they traveled with plus a small amount of clean water, and headed to the door. Jamie had assured me that the men who were set to patrol tonight were fast asleep in the back and wouldn't pose an issue.

I flinched when the doors made a creaking noise as Anna propped them open, and kept an eye on the room to make sure no one stirred at the sound. The silence after everyone slipped out, punctuated by the odd snore, made the hair on the back of my neck raise.

I waited at least five minutes, giving them a chance to get far enough away before making the necessary noise involved in my plan to stall the rest. Nadira had insisted that if they were knocked out, there would be no point in implementing any emergency measures, but I didn't trust it. What if the medicine had lost its potency so many years after its expiration date? It would take seconds for a noise to wake someone up and get everyone else awake enough to chase after us before we reached the camp.

The thought made my stomach churn. They would know where we went, of course they would. What was to stop them from taking it by force? Fueled by anger that we'd slipped out right from under their noses, what was to stop them from launching a full-out assault? Should I... Was there any way I could take care of the problem at its source? I couldn't do that... Could I? It felt like I was standing at the edge of a precipice, and one stumble could change everything. Gunner was just desperate enough to unleash zombies on the very camp he was trying to claim just to thin out its numbers, so the possibilities of what else he would do made me break out in a cold sweat. The kids, the elderly, the injured, they didn't deserve to spend every night in fear that it would all come crashing down because of a group of entitled assholes.

The real question was if I had it in me to kill defenseless people. Assholes or not, could I really murder them all while they were in a drugged stupor? I would do anything to survive, to protect the people I loved, but it felt... wrong. Dishonorable.

I took a slow breath in and out, focusing on the dancing flame of a nearby candle. No. The answer was no, I just wasn't cold enough to kill them all where they slept. We'd find some other way, together.

With that out of the way, I tiptoed my way over to the corner to pick up the heavy chain I'd seen the other day. It was in one large, rusty coil, and I dreaded the noise it would make as I picked it up. All I had to do was haul it outside and spend a few minutes winding it through the door handles and locking them together as best I could. There was no other exit in this place unless they kicked out the boarded-up back door Heidi had mentioned. By the time they did that, we'd be long gone.

I worked quickly, untangling the chain and winding it into a loose circle. I breathed a sigh of relief when I was able to verify it wouldn't fall apart at first touch. The metallic scent of iron and dirt assaulted my nose as I made each loop, coating my hands in a flaky mess. When the heavy weight was finally draped over my arm, I stood, my knees aching from crouching for so long.

Except, in that one moment of peace before I took it outside… I felt the back of my neck tingle in warning. It was silent. Unnaturally silent. Where had the sounds of snoring gone?

I spun around to face the room, blood draining from my extremities, when my eyes landed on Gunner. My hands felt tingly and numb with nerves, and I quickly grew light-headed as I watched him smirk.

"Up an at 'em," he shouted, voice echoing off the walls. One by one, his men began to filter out from the back. Ryder was last, moving through the ranks to stand beside his dad. The ones behind him simply stood, like they weren't tired at all, as if it were no trouble to wake from a dead, drugged sleep by command.

Unless they had never been asleep in the first place.

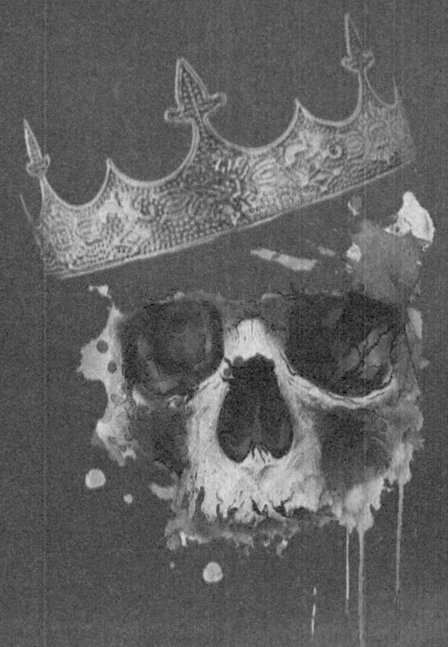

CHAPTER 30

My heart was pounding so loudly, it felt like I was listening to him speak through a closed door. Everything was muffled and distorted. "I thought we'd have a little fun, let you slip out, and have ourselves a proper hunt. Maybe feed the blonde to the zombies to teach you a lesson about respect. But here you are," he clicked his tongue, "served up on a fancy platter just for me. We can always find new pussy, but we can't pull a bargaining chip out of thin air. And look, you tired yourself out so nicely. Wasn't it kind of me to let you finish winding up that long as hell chain?"

My surprise and disbelief quickly shifted to a defeated bitterness, clearing away any of the lingering fuzziness in my hearing. "You were never drugged," I stated woodenly, eyes darting around as I tried to plan my escape. It was now or never. I couldn't wait for the guys to get here, because there was no way they would trade my life for their camp, nor did I want them to, and what if something happened to them while they tried to get me out? It was too risky.

He tsked. "Surely you weren't ignorant enough to think we didn't notice your little puppet slipping shit into the water?" His laugh was snide. Ryder stood stock-still beside him, face impassive. Though a glimpse of movement caught my eye, and I looked down to notice his fingers tapping against one another at his side.

I tried to stall as I frantically thought of a plan. "There are only, what, fourteen of you? Not so big and bad after all, huh?"

Gunner's face grew dark, all traces of the derisive laughter from before gone. "Listen here, *cunt*," he spat, his voice a low growl. "No more fancy separate room for you. You get to stay in the corner from now on, eat, live, and sleep in your own shit and filth until those goddamn men of yours come back here with the guy I sent to negotiate. Then maybe, just maybe, I'll let you all go to live in some dirty fucking house while we move into your nice little camp."

My hands curled into tight fists, nails drawing blood from my palms as I finalized my plan. I would head for the door, throw the chains at the nearest person, and run for my life. It was a shitty strategy, but at least it was something.

"Besides," he added with a sly smirk, his anger gone like he hadn't just been foaming at the mouth with it. "Whatever you filled those women's heads with, it won't matter one bit once we get a whole camp full of 'em to pick and choose from."

I. Saw. Red.

Over my dead fucking body would these bastards get access to the women I'd worked alongside for weeks. I threw the chains at the face of the man nearest to me on my right, and instead of falling backward and causing a commotion as I'd anticipated, he spun wildly while screaming and clutching his face right into the nearest row of candles, sending them flying. We all watched in what felt like slow motion as they ricocheted off a few others, sending those rolling as well. The stacked cardboard boxes on the lower shelves ignited, dry and brittle from years of disuse.

Shouts rang out as the fire spread to the old newspapers and trash scattered across the floor. Several men rushed over, attempting to stomp it out. One man whipped the shirt off his back and began fanning the growing flames, and several others followed his lead. For fuck's sake, don't they know anything about fire safety? They were only making it worse.

I met Gunner's eyes through the surrounding chaos, a stare that was only broken by the sound of shouts outside. I took advantage of his wandering attention and tried to cough as discreetly as possible, not wanting to telegraph any weaknesses. The smoke was spreading and quickly filling the area surrounding us. For some reason, they were still trying to put it out and salvage their temporary base rather than leaving, even though the embers just sent one of those trash filled boxes up in flames. I had no such misguided attempts planned. Any second now, I was going to run out those doors for freedom.

They'd had the good sense to keep a somewhat clean area near the doors, leaving it largely free of flammable materials. Unfortunately, the dirty and gore-stained clothes that had been tossed haphazardly several feet from the door whenever someone would get back from scouting lit up like a bonfire from the embers of a box filled with aged paper as it went up in flames, blocking my exit.

My hesitation deepened as the faint sounds of shouting grew closer. Zombies couldn't make noises like that, and the men with me were all accounted for... so who the hell was outside those doors? And which would I rather risk, running through the fire and out into the unknown, or waiting for Gunner to snap out of his inaction and focus his attention on me?

The doors bursting open took the choice right out of my hands. I recoiled as several people filed into the already crowded space. A line of fire zig-zagged across half the room at this point, and everyone's faces were lit eerily by the flames. Half of them were covered by makeshift masks, using any article of clothing to try to filter out the smoke.

I blinked my eyes rapidly, trying to clear them of tears, and stumbled back when Grey materialized in the smoke behind the fire separating us. My eyes were watering for a whole different reason now. Merikh came next, followed by Nix, Caelan, and Jake.

The men behind me were yelling at each other now, beginning to catch on that this was the equivalent of a sinking ship. The fire might not have compromised the concrete surrounding us, but there were still plenty of flammables that would turn us into slow-roasted zombie dinner if we didn't get the hell out. Only as they tried to round the growing line of fire circling the perimeter and half the room did they realize there were strangers in their midst.

I struggled to keep my composure, wanting to throw myself into Caelan's arms while he shouted at me over the ruckus. I was due a breakdown. "What the hell did you get yourself into, baby?" His words were teasing, but his expression was very much not. Each of my guy's faces were filled with fear, anger, surprise, and a dash of relief. Emotions I didn't even think they were *capable* of flashed across their faces as they eyed the fire separating us.

Merikh wrangled his expression back into something calmer, but I could just barely see his hands fisted tightly at his sides, a machete in one. "Couldn't just wait for us to rescue you, huh, princess?"

"No damsel in distress here," I joked, my voice trembling slightly and giving away my fear. I saw more than heard the growling noise Nix made when he heard me speak.

The fire was growing louder, as were the men, and our impasse was almost at its end. It was either burn while trying to escape the flames, or die. Gunner was shouting orders now, sending the majority of his men to the back to try to break down the door.

My jaw dropped as I noticed several of his guys lying on the floor behind Gunner, Ryder standing innocently behind them. He winked at me when I met his eyes. *What the actual fuck is going on?*

Fuck it. No way was I condemning us to a fiery death. I took a running start toward Nix, whose mouth opened wide with shock and brows furrowed deeply in concern as he watched me approach the burning piles of clothes, but a sudden bellow had me jerking to a stop and tripping over a discarded shoe. The momentum sent me careening into a flaming pile of boxes to my right, and I held back a scream as I jeered to the left in order to just clip it and not collide head-on. "Be fucking careful," Merikh yelled, jogging back and forth frantically as he searched for something he could use to smother the flames. I begged them inside my head not to try to go through them. The smell of burning hair was acrid in my nose, growing stronger with each minute. Embers and sparks were flying through the air all around us, singing my skin wherever they landed. The flames were a dull roar at this point, crackling and snapping as they consumed the flammable material around us, yet not loud enough to cover Gunner's voice. His arm was wrapped around Ryder's throat. Clearly this was the source of the bellow I'd heard. Ryder was slowly turning red, trying to maneuver out from under his hold, but his father was relentless. "Traitor," Gunner screamed. "Lying filth." Around them were a few more bodies than when I had last looked. Already being consumed by the fire, but clearly not having been killed that way. It seemed someone had been busy.

"Come on!" Grey shouted, coated in sweat as he started to move toward me, fire be damned, hand outstretched. "Let's get the hell out of here!"

Under Gunner's arm, Ryder made a choking noise as he tried to speak. "Fuck y-you," he gasped while he struggled, and while I couldn't hear the words, I read them on his lips.

"Let's go!" Nix screamed. Grey was beside him, clutching his hair in fistfuls and pacing wildly. Jake just barely held Caelan back from jumping over the flames, using his entire body to block his progress.

"I love you," I yelled. "Focus on finding a way to get us out of here."

And with that, I turned and ran toward Gunner.

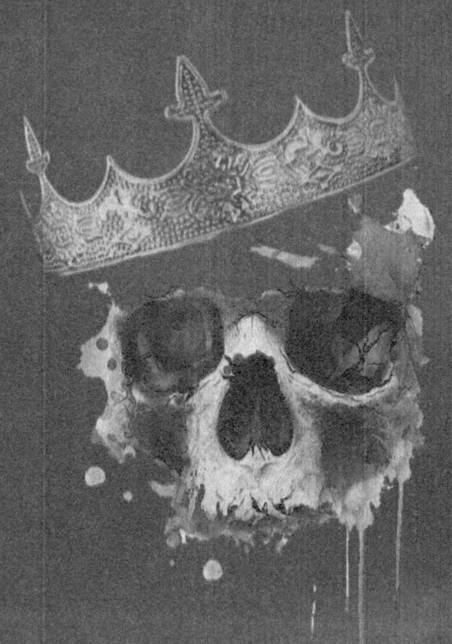

CHAPTER 31

It was hard to ignore the pain in their voices as they screamed at me to turn around. I had a feeling it would haunt me for years to come, if I even got to live them. Dodging a flaming pile of boxes and dashing through where the fire was lowest to the ground, I darted around several burning bodies to reach Gunner.

He was too busy to notice my approach, preoccupied with Ryder as he desperately pounded and scratched at the arm over his throat. I glimpsed a discarded piece of metal tubing nearby, nearly crying out when the heat of it seared my palms. "Shit," I muttered to myself, angry I hadn't thought to realize it would be near scorching from the heat of the fire. Rather than drop it to try to case the pain, I took a small breath in, trying to inhale as little smoke as possible, and blinked the stinging tears from my eyes. I crept up behind Gunner, pulling my arms back and bringing the pole downwards with a hard thud against his skull. He dropped like a sack of potatoes, freeing Ryder in the process. I winced as the heated metal pulled at my callouses when I dropped it, trying not to look at the blistered skin on my palms, and made my way over to where Ryder was gasping for breath.

"Here," I rasped, pulling my shirt over my head and ripping it in two. It meant less protection from the flames and embers, but it was past time that I needed a face covering. I handed him the other half, watching diligently as he took my lead in tying it around his face.

"Damn bastard is built like an ox," he croaked.

"You killed them," I confirmed, nodding toward the men at our feet.

He nodded. "About time," was all he said.

There were an increasing number of loud bangs from the back as the couple of the men that had been hovering around Gunner joined to help break through the boards over the door. With my guys at the main doors and the fire between us and them, there were way smaller chances of them making it out alive going that route, so I could understand the appeal of throwing yourself at a blocked door rather than risk going the hard way.

"Come on," I shouted hoarsely, yanking on his arm to pull him back the way we came. I cursed the building for not having any normal windows, stumbling slightly over the disfigured body of a man and nodding gratefully when Ryder caught my elbow to steady me.

Caelan was occupied by poking at anything on fire with a pole he'd found, trying to push it out of our path from a safe distance away, while Jake was arguing with Nix over something. Meanwhile, Grey and Merikh were staring right at me and yelling something incomprehensible. Hopefully, the open doors behind them were helping a little when it came to smoke inhalation. Between the screams of the men behind me, the roar of the flames, the ringing noise in my ears, and the sounds of all their voices overlapping at once, I had no chance in hell of hearing what they were trying to say. Ha, hell.

A sharp pain in my neck stopped me from moving a single step farther. Grey's eyes grew wide as his voice rose above all the others, screaming obscenities at the man who held the knife to my throat, tears from the smoke streaming down his face as he watched helplessly.

A low grumble reverberated from Ryder's throat as he stared at his father. I could use his help, but I knew he was still weak from the smoke and being choked, so it was on me to get us out of this.

It hit me with all the subtlety of a knife to the chest that I was going to die. There was no way I was making it out of this mess alive. Maybe I'd had a small chance earlier, but now? With the blade at my neck and the fire growing larger with every second? I was fucked.

The tears I'd been desperately trying to hold back spilled over to run down my stinging cheeks. I wasn't even sure if the guys could see my face through the smoke, but I had to try anyway. *I love you*, I mouthed, wishing I could tell them one more time.

"Not so smart now, huh, whore?" Gunner barked in my ear. "I'm going to kill you just for the pleasure of it, let the flames eat you up until there's nothing left for your little friends to mourn but a pile of ashes. Then I'll take care of them next, take the whole damn camp on my own, without my coward of a son."

He had to have been delirious with pain. His hand was trembling wildly as it gripped the blade and scraped against my skin. The smoke and the blow to the head had surely done a number on him, he just needed one last push. I fought to push back the fogginess threatening to consume my thoughts, not yet ready to succumb to death. I turned in increments, just enough to watch Ryder from the corner of my eye as I tried to formulate one last plan. His attention was elsewhere, and I followed his gaze just in time to catch the movement ahead of us.

Without warning, Grey threw himself through the flames, ignoring everyone around him as they shouted. I felt my stomach drop, my heart cracking wide open as he didn't even stop to smack at the flames licking at his clothes before running up to me. He shook with the need to touch me, to save me, and it was killing me. The thought that he was reliving his worst nightmares all over again was going to break me. If I died, I would never forgive myself for hurting him–all of them–in such a permanent way.

"Sweetheart," he uttered hoarsely, voice cracking.

"Grey," I breathed, careful not to exhale too heavily. The blade cut into my throat anyway, sending a drop of hot blood running down my chest. The arm wrapped around my waist tightened as Gunner grew antsy. The embers stung my bare torso where they landed like snowflakes, leaving behind angry welts.

Grey made a small broken noise, leaning forward with his hand outstretched like he was going to pull me away.

"Hands off," Gunner growled, yanking me back a step. Grey lowered his hand, eyes darkening as he stared at Gunner over my head.

"I'm going to fucking *kill you*," he hissed between bared teeth.

"I'd like to see you try, pretty boy," Gunner replied, his words slurring as he spoke. "One small swipe, and that's it. Don't think I'm above taking this bitch down with me if it comes to that."

Grey stared at me, desperately trying to tell me something with his eyes, but I had no idea what. He ground his teeth when I stared back at him like a lost puppy, eyes darting to Ryder, where he stood a good few inches away from me. After what felt like a lifetime but was probably just a few seconds, they both sprang into action simultaneously. Ryder kneed his father in the gut, while Grey took advantage of Gunner's stumble and wrenched his wrist away from me. Finally understanding what it was Grey had wanted, I dropped out from under his arm, throwing my head back to crack against his face and rolling away from his body so he couldn't grab me again.

"Fuck!" Gunner screamed from where he was lying on the floor, blood streaming from his face where he held his broken nose.

"That's for taking my girl," Grey grunted as he kicked Gunner right in the stomach. "That's for terrorizing my camp"—he kicked him once more, this time in the knee—"and for trying to kill the love of my life," he shouted furiously, landing one more on his ribs.

"Enough," Ryder ordered. Grey turned on him like he was next. "He's mine."

"Grey," I rasped, pushing myself into a standing position. All the tension left his body as he completely forgot about Ryder and turned to face me. I threw myself into his arms, seconds away from sobbing uncontrollably when they surrounded me, holding me tightly. I could barely hold it together, but I needed to. Just for a little longer. Then I could cry all day long, surrounded by the people I loved. I buried my face in his neck, tasting the acerbic bite of smoke caught in his hair, and pulled back. That small moment of comfort had to be enough. It just had to. He pulled me in for a quick kiss, grabbing my hand tightly.

"Me and you, sweetheart." His voice was guttural and torn to shreds from the smoke.

"Let's go," Ryder declared gruffly, stepping forward to join us and freeing up the view of his father's body just seconds away from being consumed by the flames, knife impaled in his chest. *Good riddance.*

Jake had disappeared, but Merikh, Caelan, and Nix were right there, ignoring the open doors behind them and pressed right up against the fire as they shouted at us.

"We're going to have to jump," I croaked, threading my fingers through with Grey's.

The fire was reaching a crescendo behind us, consuming the fallen bodies like fuel. I didn't look back. There were some things I didn't need to see.

Grey counted to three under his breath, yanking me along after him as he reached three and using his body to shield me from the flames as he powered through them. To my surprise, Ryder was right at his side, making sure to block me as best he could. I pressed tightly against Grey's back, unable to hold back my screams as the fire licked at my ankles and legs. The pain had me close to passing out, it was unlike anything I'd ever felt.

"Let's go!" Merikh roared, grabbing onto Grey's arm while Caelan grabbed Ryder's and pulled them over that last threshold. They were yanked outside and thrown immediately onto the ground, as was I. I used the last vestiges of my strength to roll wildly over the small patch of grass, my body shrieking in pain as my skin came into contact with the asphalt beside it. Nix and Merikh dropped to my side, while Caelan helped Grey roll until he lay still beside me. We were all coughing loudly, hacking up our lungs. Ryder was a few feet away, staring up at the night sky and laughing to himself like his mind had finally cracked under the pressure.

"You're okay," Nix asserted hoarsely, hands hovering over me as he stared in horror at my injuries.

"How scary do I look?" I tried to tease, my attempt at humor falling short as his eyes filled with tears.

"Never again," he said shakily, taking a deep breath of clean air.

Caelan leaned in for a deep, claiming kiss between coughs, leaning his forehead against mine for several long breaths. "Love you, baby. Knew you could do anything you put your mind to."

My laugh sounded like I had gargled with glass.

"But if you ever leave the camp without one of us again, I'm going to tie you to the bed and spank you until you can't walk," he growled, blue eyes blazing.

"Don't make me tingle, you big bastard, my nerves are shot."

He laughed gruffly, lifting my hand gently using the unblistered part and pressing a kiss to the back of it, then placing it in Grey's with my palm face up.

I turned to face a silent Merikh, expecting to find his composed mask once more, but instead found him simmering with emotion. Agony, torment, anguish, he looked like he was unraveling at the seams.

"Come here," I whispered, holding out my arms.

"I don't want to hurt you," he whispered back, throat wrecked.

It would hurt. There was no way it wouldn't. Every single inch of my body had gone through hell tonight, but it would hurt more to not be able to hold him in my arms, to soothe him with my touch and let him know that I was *there*.

He weighed his decision, ultimately caving, and collapsed into my arms. He buried his face against my neck, body shaking wildly from the residual fear and adrenaline. "I couldn't do anything," he whispered, tortured. Something hot and wet hit my skin where he was tucked away.

I brought my hand up to caress his hair, biting my tongue when my raw skin came into contact with his head. "What could you have done? It would have been reckless to go through the fire with Grey. Too risky. The camp needs you, I need you. I need you to go on living even when there's a possibility I couldn't." It was a lot of words, and my throat was screaming at me to shut up already so it could take a break. Even my breaths hurt.

"*Don't*," he cursed with a gravelly voice, pulling his face back so I could see his bloodshot eyes. "Don't talk like that. Nothing matters–*nothing*–as much as you do. Not the camp, not any of our luxuries, and not us. I don't care if it's unhealthy, I can't imagine living in a world without you in it."

"I love you," I rasped, reaching up to caress his cheek and pulling my hand back at the sting. "All of you. I would do anything to make sure I made my way back to you so that together we could live the life you promised me."

Grey, Caelan, and Nix chimed their assent, all making sure they were touching me in some way.

"Fuck's sake, you lot are going to give me a toothache from all this sappiness," Ryder muttered, his laughter having stopped a minute ago, and I fought the laugh that bubbled up.

Despite all the pain racking my body, I felt a sudden, freeing sense of peace. For the first time in days, I was *safe*. I had my people back. Everyone was alive, and the threat to the camp was no longer an issue.

Everything was going to be okay.

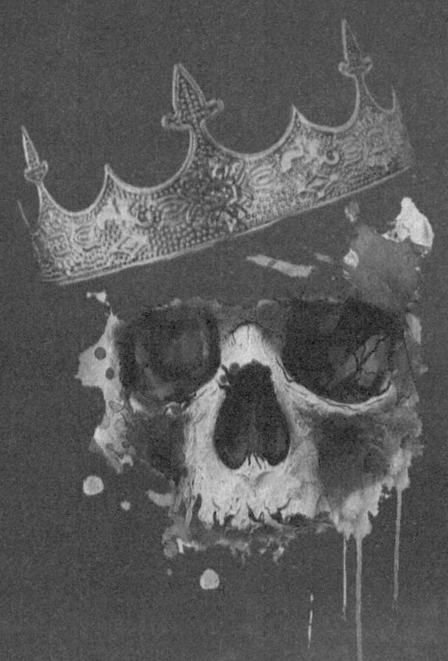

EPILOGUE

Everyone gathered around to watch Halli plant the last seed. She made a big production of packing it in tightly and then drizzling water on top. We all clapped when she stood and took a bow, backing up to look at the finished product. Row upon row of freshly planted seeds graced almost every plot in the garden, ready for the new growing season. We had a good feeling about their viability. When Caelan, Merikh, Jake, and Harry ventured into the city with me last week to hunt for the bunker—with supplies, comfortable sleeping bags, and weapons galore—we were surprised to find it tucked away on a side street near where they'd first found me.

We'd been thrilled to find that it hadn't been opened since my dad and I last sealed it, and to my disbelief—maybe I'd been too young to care or note the significance the first time around—there were a great deal more seed packets, gardening supplies, and fertilizer than I'd remembered.

Bags of rice, corn, barley, oats, and more still lined the shelves. It was the perfect amount to supplement us until we were able to trade for more meat and dairy products. The best part, for me at least, had been when Merikh found a pocketknife under one of the cots in the corner, engraved with my dad's initials. I'd had nothing of his to carry with me but his knife, so it was like having a little piece of him back. I'd felt a little guilty being so happy over it given that we'd discovered their dad had died, but they all reassured me that it was the best scenario. There was definitely no love lost there.

"Gonna miss me, darlin'?" Jake asked Sera, lips sporting a smug smile. He was all set to make a trip up to the farm to trade whenever the weather warmed up just a little more. He twirled a lock of her dark hair around his finger and smirked at Ryder over her head when she gave him a smile in return.

Ryder shot him a disdainful glare, and I had to hold back a laugh at the barely suppressed irritation radiating off his person. I wasn't sure if Sera had any clue that Jake liked to use her to needle Ryder, and if she did, I wondered if she didn't put a stop to it because of the note of truth behind each and every one of Jake's flirtatious gestures. When we'd arrived back with Ryder in tow, I'd fully anticipated something to come of all the longing glances and possessive scowls, but he'd yet to do a thing about it. Even so, he couldn't stand Jake's favorite pastime of getting in her space and making her laugh.

Caelan and Merikh were wary about having Ryder stay, but after weeks of him conveniently ending up wherever Sera was, contributing whenever possible, and keeping to himself–in exactly that order–they realized he had no greater designs on the camp like his father. Apparently, our chaos had been just the excuse he was looking for to get rid of Gunner and his crew all at once, especially when we found that the door at the back of the building had never broken open, despite their best efforts.

Nadira walked up with Thomas in tow, Heidi's arm threaded through her elbow, and walked over to join Jamie, Naia, and Shiori. Nadira and

Thomas hit it off immediately upon meeting, and she'd moved into his cabin with him after several weeks of non-stop talking. She said something under her breath and Heidi threw her head back and laughed, rubbing the baby bump that had just started to show. She had an idea of who the father was out of Gunner's men but didn't care to look back on that time in her life, even though she didn't regret it because it had led her to this point. Either way, she was excited beyond all belief to become a mother, and everyone here was thrilled for another baby to spoil. Apparently, Naia and Nerese had run out of things to knit with the yarn we'd brought back and were already getting started on baby blankets and socks.

I looked over at Nix, slipping my hand into his and receiving a warm smile in return.

"I love you," I whispered, overwhelmed with happy feelings from being surrounded by new friends and new beginnings.

His smile was practically lit from within as he raised my hand to kiss the back of it softly. "Love you more," he whispered back.

I only startled a little when Caelan pressed his front to my back and slid his arms around me where I stood beside Nix, leaning in to nuzzle my hair. It wasn't distracting at first, and I was easily able to continue looking around at all my friends as they chatted excitedly over all the new developments of the past month from off to the side like I was, but it grew harder and harder to focus when his thumbs slid brushed back and forth in small sweeping movements across my hips. I was surrounded by people, wearing a slightly thicker top than usual now that the weather had cooled a bit, and yet the circles his thumbs were making gave me chills. I wriggled a little in his grip so that he'd move his hands, and heard a low chuckle from above my head where he was resting his chin. He drew his hands back to rest on my hips, and if I was expecting that to put an end to the low heat stirring in my belly, I was sorely mistaken.

Nix choked on his laugh when he caught a glimpse of my face, sobering up when my expression turned into a glower. It wasn't funny, damn it! They'd been treating me like glass for the past month while all of my injuries healed, which meant they'd allowed me to accompany them on trips outside for some reason but drew the line at anything sexual.

That didn't exclude sensual touches, soft kisses, or teasing, but maybe it should've. What kind of masochists got people all fired up and then denied any sort of release!

Two could play at that game. I leaned back into his embrace, and I saw Nix and Caelan exchange puzzled glances.

"What are you up to, baby?" Caelan murmured into my hair, sounding highly entertained.

I shrugged, tilting my hips back, so that they were in direct contact with his pelvis, and smiled cheekily when he sucked a breath in.

"It's time for us to go," he told whoever was listening, his voice slightly hoarse, and grabbed my elbow to usher me away. I snorted, drinking in the sound of Nix's quiet laughter from behind us as he followed along.

"Oh, so you can dish it, but you can't take it, huh?" I teased.

"Damn right," he muttered, stopping behind a small group of trees to adjust himself, much to my amusement.

I shrugged, backing away down the path to the cabin at a brisk pace and calling back over my shoulder, "I suppose you'll just have to take a cold shower, then."

He let me get halfway there before swinging me into his arms and carrying me the rest of the way. "I don't think so," he mock-growled, hissing a breath in through his teeth when I leaned forward to bite his nipple through his shirt.

"Fuck!" he shuddered, passing me off to Nix once he carried me over the threshold so he could strip off his shirt.

"You're not very good at abstaining," I said primly, trying not to burst out laughing when his face contorted.

"Maybe I can concede that you have a point. We wanted to be extra careful with you! You know it would kill us if you were in pain at any point."

I heaved a conciliatory sigh, patting Nix softly on the shoulder so he'd set me down and giving him a grateful kiss in return.

"About time you guys got back here," Merikh grumbled, walking out from the hallway to prop his hip against the doorway.

"What's going on?"

Grey followed behind him, wearing a pleased smirk. "What's going on is that you're completely healed and there's no reason to keep waiting." He raised his eyebrows, and my excitement grew when I realized what he was saying. Nix placed his hands on my waist from behind and bent down to brush my hair aside so that he could kiss my neck. I moaned softly, reaching back to palm his head and leaning into his touch.

"No way Nix gets to have all the fun," Caelan complained, rubbing his hands together. "Let's go already."

They led me by the hand back to Grey's room. My jaw dropped as I examined the space. What looked to be three double beds and one twin were lined up side by side, pretty much wall to wall, with only a sliver of space large enough to walk through on the side with the doorway, where we were standing. In the corner of the room was an armchair with a side table beside it that had a little candlelit wax warmer on top. My hands flew to cover my mouth, and I turned to whoever was closest in excitement.

"You guys did this just today? For us?"

"For *you*," Grey gently corrected. "Although technically for all of us. We wanted to be able to actually use the main room again for relaxing, and we thought what better way than to turn the largest bedroom into a sleeping area that would fit all of us? No more falling between the mattresses at night or waking up to Caelan on top of you"—he talked over Caelan's protests—"if you don't like it, we-"

"No!" I interrupted, much more loudly than I'd intended. I cleared my throat and walked to the edge of the mattress closest to us and sat down with a thump. "No. I love this idea, truly. An entire room of beds. What more could I ask for?"

"I can think of something," Merikh said with a smirk, walking over to stand in between my legs.

I spread them a little to accommodate him, leaning back on my hands and glancing up at him coyly through my eyelashes. "Is that so?"

"It is," he rumbled.

Caelan took a seat on the other side of the bed, as did Grey, and Nix went to sit in the armchair. It was scary how in sync they were.

I pulled my hands out from underneath me, letting myself drop fully back against the mattress and frowning when I heard a crinkling noise. I peeked down to find myself laying on some kind of stiff white fabric and looked at Merikh for an answer.

"Mattress protector, princess. We might be messy, but we're not heathens."

I laughed breathlessly, trailing my fingers up the center of my dress until I reached my collarbone.

Merikh brought his knee up and placed it firmly between my legs. I moved my feet in closer from where they sat on the floor for leverage, lifting my hips to get more of that delicious pressure where I needed it. Merikh's eyes widened, and his breaths came faster as he watched me squirm beneath his touch, desire rampant in his gaze. "Fuck, River. Are you wet for us?"

I inhaled sharply, nodding once. I clenched my thighs together for the friction I so desperately craved, practically riding his knee. A low groan had me tilting my head back so that I was watching the others from upside down. A quick glance was all I needed to get a glimpse of the hunger written all over their faces.

"Fuck yourself with your fingers. I want to watch," Merikh commanded.

I moaned, sliding my hand down my body to pull the dress up and over my hips to expose my soaking pussy.

Merikh drew in a sharp breath, eyes riveted to the spot he'd asked me to touch. "Seems you already had plans for how today was going to go, princess. Such a naughty girl."

My smirk was wicked, thinking about how I hadn't even needed to use that weapon in my arsenal. I slid my hand down my stomach until I reached my wet entrance, and dipped a finger in before sliding it up to my clit and rubbing in small, teasing circles.

"That's it," Merikh coaxed, eyes firmly on my hand. He started to rub himself through his pants, shifting uncomfortably. I heard the swoosh of fabric behind me, as someone else most likely did the same. A peek behind me revealed heavy-lidded eyes and sprawled limbs as they watched me touch myself, just out of their view.

"Now suck him," he commanded, inclining his chin toward Grey, who was casually palming himself.

I hesitated, considering making myself come real quick to tide me over before he drew it out any longer.

He bent down slightly, gripping my jaw and rubbing his thumb across my lips, and dipping it into my mouth. "Suck. Him," he whispered lethally. Despite the irritation I felt at receiving commands, I was filled with a rush of explicit pleasure. Something about all that heated intensity directed toward me made butterflies explode in my stomach.

I tilted my head back to look at Grey. "Come here, sweetheart," he said with a flirty wink.

I turned my head toward him when Merikh tightened his grip on my jaw, using a light pressure to turn my body and direct me to climb up onto the bed on all fours.

"Crawl," he rasped.

I shuddered, head dropping down for a moment. I felt wild: uninhibited, and slightly apprehensive, but just curious enough to try. My ass swayed behind me as I crawled seductively as best I could over the soft surface until I reached him, where he was sprawled across the bed. He greeted me with a heated kiss, guiding me off the bed to stand between his legs and grabbing my dress by the hem to help me slip it over my head.

I palmed Grey's thighs once I was completely undressed, bending over where I stood and setting my mouth close to his exposed cock so that all he could feel were my rapid breaths. Then I watched in fascination as it twitched, as the strong, calloused hand that had already begun stroking in anticipation minutes earlier returned as he grunted impatiently.

I took a moment to admire the potent scent of citrus and sandalwood he always seemed to be covered in before I darted my tongue out to lick the head, just a teasing flick to start with. His free hand found the back of my head, just resting as I continued my exploration.

Taking just the tip in my mouth, I weighed it on my tongue. Grey moaned, turning his hand to grip a section of my hair in his fist. After several minutes of sloppy teasing, I took his length more fully into my mouth and increased in increments until he reached the back of my throat. I choked slightly, and when he made a gentle easing motion to get me to pull back, I disregarded it, coughing once then diving back in.

"Unghh," he groaned, flexing his thigh muscles under my hands. I felt a bolt of satisfaction, proud that he was feeling such pleasure under my touch.

A finger ran down my spine, not stopping until it reached my throbbing clit.

"You didn't think I was done, princess, did you?"

I huffed, unable to resist arching my back as his finger traced me lightly. "No, no, no," he tsked, laughing wickedly. "I have plans for you."

I remained still for him, adding my hands to the length my mouth couldn't reach on Grey's cock.

"Good fuckin' girl," Merikh groaned. His fingers gathered the dripping wetness from my pussy and massaged my entrance. "This isn't enough. I want to taste you."

I whimpered impatiently, grinding my hips downwards to get more pressure.

Merikh clucked at me, stopping his torturously slow movements. I debated telling him to fuck off, but I was dripping in anticipation. Just from the strong muscular thighs beneath my hands, the thickness and heat of his cock in my mouth, the quiet groans and stuttered breaths from Caelan beside me as he watched. I was beyond ready, aching, and needy. Only with them could I let myself go like this, would I allow him to hand down orders that I would follow whenever he was feeling particularly bossy.

I relaxed my body, hoping he would take it for the surrender it was.

"That's it, sunshine," Nix murmured from behind us, observing our whole interaction.

Merikh must have found that satisfactory, because he hummed and drove a finger deep inside me, dropping down to his knees and planting soft kisses along my thighs.

"Shit," I exclaimed, fingernails digging into Grey's skin. He moaned, and I tucked that little piece of information away for later.

I stiffened slightly but relaxed under the sharp smack of Merikh's palm. He soothed the sore spot with a sweeping motion, kissing my thigh softly. It was so contradictory, his gentleness and his roughness, and I loved every second of it.

He spread me open with his thumbs and finally put his mouth where I needed it, teasing me with long, flat strokes of his tongue. I whimpered, twisting my hips as he added another finger and picked up the pace on Grey's neglected cock, causing fresh groans to leave his lips. The soft sounds of moving fabric beside me let me know that Caelan was enjoying the show so far.

Merikh hit a spot inside me that had me seeing stars and I resisted the urge to throw myself back on his fingers and instead used my words. "Right there, fuck, Merikh, right there. Don't stop."

"I wanna see you come," he groaned, going back in to continue licking and sucking in alternating motions. I was close. His thumb caressed my clit amongst the skilled motions of his two fingers and tongue, and I could feel myself winding tighter and tighter. I pulled off of Grey to pant heavily, bracing myself for the pleasure I was sure to come.

"Just... not until I'm in you," Merikh added slyly, withdrawing his hand.

"What the fuck, Merikh!"

He just smacked my ass, getting to his feet and pulling me back by my hips into the cradle of his. I made an angry mumbling noise while sucking Grey and doubled down on my efforts out of spite. Sure, he wasn't the one depriving me, but he was the only one I could take it out on at the moment. He grunted loudly, throwing his head back and clutching my hair tighter as he came with a shout. I stayed there until his thighs twitched from the sensations and pulled off feeling drunk with pleasure, probably looking debauched as hell, and I hadn't even come yet.

Nix made a pained noise in the back of his throat. "You'd better finish sometime soon, Merikh. Not all of us are as patient as you."

Merikh laughed roughly, grabbing my hips and entering me in one smooth motion. I moaned, clutching Grey's thighs where he was now lying back on the bed and panting heavily as he watched me. His blonde hair was darkened with sweat and clinging to his flushed face.

Merikh's hands came around to grab my breasts and maneuver me up so that my back was plastered to his front. I had a front-row seat to Caelan as he watched us, stroking his glistening cock with a tattooed hand and biting his lip.

"Look at her take you so well," Nix groaned.

"Mouth or pussy?" Merikh asked. The irritation of being talked about as if I weren't there was overshadowed by my surprise at him offering someone else a choice while he was in this mood.

Caelan answered instantly. "I need in that mouth." He moved from his spot on the bed to stand in front of me, putting his cock right up against my lips as Merikh bent me back over with a firm hand. Caelan hesitated for a moment, but once I glanced up to give him a pleading, begging look, he slid the head into my mouth. He grabbed my chin, tilting my head back so I could meet his darkened eyes.

"No teasing," he chided. Need flared in his eyes and sweat beaded on his forehead. He was desperate for it, for me. I honored his request, taking his full length until it hit the back of my throat and choking slightly. Tears filled my eyes as I gave it all my effort, working up a good rhythm. As I pulled back, Merikh gave a particularly hard thrust, the first of many.

"Yes!" I screamed.

He withdrew slowly, ignoring my begging whimpers, and once again powered forward.

"This tight little hole loves me, doesn't it, princess? So fucking warm and snug, so needy. Fuck, Caelan, if you could feel how tightly she holds my dick."

Caelan rasped out a groan. "I'm close."

I was too. The sheer eroticism of being taken by two men was overwhelming. I smirked as I inadvertently clenched around Merikh, tightening my inner muscles and receiving a moan in response. I loved it when I made him make noise.

I hollowed my cheeks, sucking with as much force as I could, just as Merikh increased his pace to a punishing level.

"Touch yourself," he ordered. "Come for me. I wanna feel you come all around me."

I moaned helplessly, reaching a hand down to rub my clit furiously. Caelan grunted loudly, palming my head as I swallowed every drop of his come. I licked my lips, throwing my head back as my rubbing and Merikh's thrusting pushed me over the edge, then came with a scream, shuddering wildly as I had my first orgasm in weeks. The pleasure was indescribable, flooding through every inch of my body and leaving me wrung out. Merikh loosened his grip on my hips and when he pulled out with a soft grunt, something wet hit my lower back and I realized he'd finally succumbed to the pleasure. The room smelled of sex and debauchery, and I was coated in a fine layer of sweat.

After using his shirt to clean me off, he collapsed onto the bed beside Caelan, and Grey, who was already growing hard once more, and I turned my attention to Nix.

He watched me with hooded eyes, having pulled just his cock out of his shorts and stroked it slowly. He looked painfully hard, but he offered me an out anyway. "You don't have to," he rasped. "If you need to rest. If you're too tired."

"You've been so patient," I crooned. "I think that deserves a reward."

His eyes slid shut for a moment, the sheer pleasure on his face increasing mine tenfold. I swung my hips as I sauntered over, climbing into his lap so that I was straddling him. He lined up perfectly with me, and I dropped my weight down so that I could slide back and forth on his length.

"No teasing," he murmured, green eyes the color of the trees outside the window.

I leaned forward to kiss his neck, using my knees to lift up slightly and grabbing his cock to position it just right before sliding down with a satisfied groan.

"You feel so good," he whispered hoarsely, squeezing his eyes shut.

I slid my arms around his neck, leaning in to brush a kiss against his cheek and then lifted up and sunk down on his cock in smooth movements. The room was filled with whimpers and panting, moans and grunting, and I was already so close from all the prior stimulation that I was thrilled when after several minutes Nix grunted, "I'm–I–*unghh*."

He steadied my hips, rocking his own upwards and slamming into me once, twice, three times before coming with a groan. I rode him faster, grinding down with each movement so that I was stimulated in every possible area before throwing my head back and making sure I joined him in his release.

We sat like that for a long moment, steadying our breathing, until my muscles could no longer hold me upright and I collapsed against his chest. He laughed softly, cradling my head and standing so that I was secured in his arms and setting me down on the bed beside the others.

"Aren't you glad we didn't put sheets over the mattress protectors?" Caelan asked, a brow raised in question.

Even my laugh was exhausted. I curled into Merikh since he was closest and shut my eyes contentedly when he pulled me tighter against him and began to stroke my hair.

"We'll run you a bath whenever you want to get up, okay?"

It was such a sweet gesture, something I never thought I'd get to have, that I found myself speechless for a moment.

"Aw, sweetheart," Grey said, as he shifted onto his side. "Can't you picture it? Days filled just like this one, safe and comfortable and *loved*. Warm fires, fresh food, and hot baths..." his voice trailed off, and I reached over to grab his hand at the image. I had the kind of love I thought I'd never get to experience, the kind my dad used to tell me he had with my mom. I was finally home, had finally put down roots, and they were there to stay.

AUTHOR'S NOTE

I'm so grateful to everyone who made this journey possible, I couldn't have gotten this far without you! Thank you to my family, for your endless support even though refuse to tell you what exactly I'm writing. I'm especially thankful to all the readers who took a chance on one of my books! It's because of you that I continue to write. Thank you to Ky for being so incredibly helpful throughout this entire process, and to Mackenzie for being such an amazing editor.

I hope you all loved this book as much as I did, and if so, please consider leaving a review!

www.ingramcontent.com/pod-product-compliance
Lightning Source LLC
Chambersburg PA
CBHW021407310726
48971CB00005B/1231